THE SECRET FIRE

... major news organization for twenty years. His bests...
first novel, *The Malice Box*, is available as a Penguin paper...

The Secret Fire

MARTIN LANGFIELD

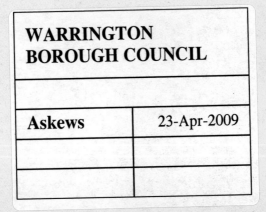

WARRINGTON BOROUGH COUNCIL	
Askews	23-Apr-2009

PENGUIN BOOKS

PENGUIN BOOKS

Published by the Penguin Group
Penguin Books Ltd, 80 Strand, London WC2R ORL, England
Penguin Group (USA) Inc., 375 Hudson Street, New York, New York 10014, USA
Penguin Group (Canada), 90 Eglinton Avenue East, Suite 700, Toronto, Ontario, Canada M4P 2Y3
(a division of Pearson Penguin Canada Inc.)
Penguin Ireland, 25 St Stephen's Green, Dublin 2, Ireland (a division of Penguin Books Ltd)
Penguin Group (Australia), 250 Camberwell Road, Camberwell, Victoria 3124, Australia
(a division of Pearson Australia Group Pty Ltd)
Penguin Books India Pvt Ltd, 11 Community Centre,
Panchsheel Park, New Delhi – 110 017, India
Penguin Group (NZ), 67 Apollo Drive, Rosedale, North Shore 0632, New Zealand
(a division of Pearson New Zealand Ltd)
Penguin Books (South Africa) (Pty) Ltd, 24 Sturdee Avenue, Rosebank, Johannesburg 2196, South Africa

Penguin Books Ltd, Registered Offices: 80 Strand, London WC2R ORL, England

www.penguin.com

First published 2009

1

Extract from *Requiem for a Nun* by William Faulkner, published by Chatto & Windus in the UK
and Vintage in the US. Reprinted by permission of The Random House Group Ltd.

Typeset by Rowland Phototypesetting Ltd, Bury St Edmunds, Suffolk
Printed in England by Clays Ltd, St Ives plc

ISBN: 978-0-141-02507-0

www.greenpenguin.co.uk

For Noor Inayat Khan, Pearl Cornioley,
Arthur Staggs and Betty Ozanich.

For all the unsung heroes.

Contents

Day Five   1

Day Four   25

Day Three   145

Day Two   241

Day One   309

Day Zero   397

Epilogue   457

A Note on Sources   459

Acknowledgements   462

On 30 June 1944, in an attempt to alter the course of World War Two in favour of Nazi Germany, an agent from the Occult Bureau of Heinrich Himmler's SS tried to detonate a weapon of mass destruction in central London.

Sixty-three years later, he is about to succeed.

Day Five

New York

25 June 2007

The hidden drawer opened at Robert's first touch.

For a split second the room seemed to twist and roar about him, buckling and cracking, as if the walls of the world were caving in. Robert raised his arms over his head, pushing his chair violently back from the desk, knocking it over onto the wooden floor. He stood staring at the drawer, breathing hard.

Voices rustled at the edge of his mind: *go no further,* they whispered. *Stop now.*

Hatred echoed around him. For an instant, he had seen a bloodless face, stark-eyed and vengeful, floating in the darkness that had descended on him. A familiar face.

'You're dead!' Robert hissed in anger.

Outside the window was a fifty-foot drop to the street below. There couldn't be anyone there, and he was alone in the apartment. No one could be whispering to him.

Robert slowly lowered his arms, peering into the darkness outside. Wraiths of mist swirled and eddied in random patterns. No apparition there now. He stood still, listening intently, blood rushing in his ears.

The face was that of a man Robert had fought to the death, two and a half years earlier, a servant and soldier of the Enemy. The memory still haunted him, nightly, in terrifying flashes: trapped underground, a stark sense of loathing rumbling around him like slow thunder . . . For a moment Robert was back there, and he tensed again, ready to defend himself, fists clenched, feet firmly planted, hyper-alert to his surroundings.

Nothing. Silence.

He'd seen pale skin, a halo of white hair, piercing eyes . . . it was a face he knew, yes, and yet it was different. There was something else to it that he couldn't name.

Robert brought his breathing under control, allowing himself to relax slightly.

He let his eyes roam over the desk he had been working at, the abandoned workspace of dear, crazy, loving Adam, his friend, whom the Enemy had destroyed.

His eyes returned to the hidden drawer, now open. Was this what Adam had wanted him to find?

Robert and Adam had been friends at Cambridge University twenty-five years before, rivals in love through the years since, co-conspirators in existential games, mostly of Adam's devising, colleagues and competitors in the international news business. They'd been two halves, perhaps, of a single man. Air and fire were Adam: spontaneous, daring, ungraspable; earth and water were Robert: grounded, reliable, unstoppable.

Each in turn had sought and won the hand of Katherine, the blue-eyed, raven-haired penitent spy who was now Robert's wife.

There had been darkness over the decades. Adam had tipped over into madness in the 1990s, clawing his way back to the light with Katherine's and Robert's help. And throughout, they had been watched over by their mentor, a man charged with guiding them even when they rejected him: Horace Hencott, an Anglophile American and some-time academic, a wartime colleague of Adam's grandfather. He was an octogenarian mage, the overseer of their individual psychic gifts, which each of them had denied, espoused, fought with, lost and regained over the years.

It was Horace who had brought them to their darkest game nearly three years earlier, a contest with real risks and real victims, the one that had claimed Adam's life. The Enemy had tried to detonate a doomsday device in Manhattan. Millions of lives had hung by a thread, millions more had faced unbearable suffering. Robert had succeeded by the skin of his teeth in stopping it, at terrible cost to others, and to himself.

But, as Horace had said, the snake was never killed, only scotched. The Enemy had been angered, and would be back, working through new avenues, through new souls, aiming at new targets. It would have to be fought again.

Robert, still agitated, stepped forward again to Adam's desk. On either side were stacked the last of the files Horace had instructed Robert to go through after the events in Manhattan, seeking to understand just what Adam had been focusing on in the final months before his death.

Robert was sure Adam had left a message, a series of clues. With Adam, there had always been one more game to play, one more riddle to dragoon his friends into solving, one more chance to organize a party, a scavenger hunt, or another shot at self-discovery.

Robert stood, hands on his hips, staring down at the most recent batch of papers and photographs he had been examining. It had been his *obsessive project*, as Kat had called it, part of the recovery process Horace had devised for him after 2004: track down and gather together all the research papers and writings Adam had accumulated over his years in London, Miami, Havana and elsewhere, as well as in New York. See what he had learned about himself, and about the Enemy. It was a way of making peace with Adam's memory, and with the things Robert had done.

Robert raised his eyes and peered into the hidden drawer

that he had not noticed until this evening, until a glimmer of light, like a sunbeam reflected on water, had fallen on it repeatedly as he'd worked. A shard of ghost light, from God only knew where.

Snatches of words formed in his mind: *Mar . . . regret . . .* Robert shook his head, dismissing them, banishing the last echoes of the vision. Focus.

He reached inside the drawer.

It contained a sealed envelope. As he took it out, the air grew colder around his neck and shoulders. Robert felt eyes upon him, and he shivered.

The letter was addressed to him in Adam's handwriting. Robert took a paper knife and slit it open.

Dear Robert

I cannot be saved. Forget me.

But if you are reading this, it is because you have survived, which means that you were able to defeat the Enemy.

Know this: If you defeated it, it will be back. It will try other ways to achieve its aims. It is patient, but it will never rest. And it will want revenge – personal, ad hominem, brutal revenge – against those who stopped it. It will come for each of you, to destroy you.

Who is the Enemy? It is a single force, with countless names – a force of unspeakable evil, in this world and the next. It is other-worldly, but it works through beings in this life. There is one servant of the Enemy in particular, named Isambard, who is the most powerful of all. Expect him to come for you now. Creatures like Isambard are the instruments of hell in this world. They are drawn to suffering, seek to create more, feed and grow stronger on it, induce us to cause more of it under their tutelage.

One force, many names.

In your old neck of the woods, where you grew up, the Enemy's servants are called the Lantern Men, the dark spirits with their mesmerizing lights who lure men to their deaths in the lonely, shallow waters of the Fens.

In other times, in other places, its servants have been called the Clouded Mirror, the Shadow Brotherhood, the Fraternity of IWNW. This last – IWNW – is the name under which we met its soldiers in Manhattan. It refers to one of the places where the Enemy first won servants to its side: a priestly Egyptian city, later called Heliopolis by the Greeks, where spiritual masters first turned from the light, choosing instead the Enemy's path to power: the infliction of suffering on others.

The Enemy is all around us. It is alive to our every thought, yearning in every instant to dwell in the physical world, to incarnate in this life. It constantly seeks servants and victims, and it can reach us everywhere. It lives on our fear, our hatred, our cowardice, and feeds it all back into us, in a never-ending cycle. In one sense, it is ourselves. We can never hide from it, not in the end. Even death may provide no sanctuary from it. It must be fought, again and again.

Robert, you don't know yet what you are. You have started down a road that must lead you back to your own people, to the gifts and nameless arts you were brought up to despise, to the powerful Fenland witches, to the cunning men and wise women from whom you spring, and from whose world you were always shielded.

Go back, to go forward.

I've set aside some historical records, some potential discoveries and troubling anomalies for you to peruse. In part they concern my own family: my grandfather Harry Hale, whose rooms I occupied at Trinity College; and his brother, Peter Hale. The good people of the Club of St George, off Fleet Street, will provide my papers to you, on receipt of a note from me (enclosed) and a suitable code word. The word you must give them is the name of your favourite weather event.

There is a date to be mindful of – June 30, 2007. A full moon, and a 'blue' moon in London, the second in the month. I don't know why, but I have seen it.

My love to Katherine, always,

Adam

The letter, finally, was what Robert had been looking for. He smiled tightly at the choice of password. *Georges.* That was typical of Adam. *Georges* was the name of the hurricane that had been raging near Miami on the night when Katherine had chosen Robert to be her second husband. In succession to Adam.

He put the letter back in its envelope and stowed it in his jacket pocket. *June 30, 2007.* Five days away.

Katherine would be driving over to Adam's old apartment building shortly to pick Robert up. He stared out into the darkness, defying the mist to form again into the face of a dead man. Nothing. He turned out the lights and went downstairs.

She didn't come.

Puzzled, Robert wondered if she could have forgotten. It would be uncharacteristic. He called her cellphone, but it kicked over to the answering service. Could she have parked instead in the building's underground garage? She'd done so before, though not since winter ... After standing in the street for 10 minutes, he went back inside and took the elevator down, to see if she was there.

~

An unnatural, bone-numbing chill exuded from the concrete floor and pillars of the parking garage, and Robert's breath formed a cloud in the air before him. The smell of motor oil pricked at his nostrils. Water dripped from a leaking pipe. Again, he felt himself watched. He scoured the shadows of the cavernous underground chamber, hairs raised on the back of his neck, nervous and wired, looking for his wife. The car was there, but she was not. It was one o'clock in the morning.

Overhead, a neon light began to buzz and flicker, then went out.

He heard a footfall behind him. His eyes strained to pierce the blackness.

'Kat?'

Just beyond his field of vision, at the very edge of perception, Robert could feel someone drawing closer, the air thickening behind him. He felt heat at his neck, by his ear, in his face, like breath, soft and warm.

Robert, he heard. *Come to me.* An image formed in his mind of a childhood scene, parents and cousins and grandparents, in black and white . . . he realized it was a photograph, one he had glimpsed as a boy. The family he had never known, the ones he had been kept away from. *Margaret* . . .

Instinctively he ducked. He felt air displaced above his head, something heavy, right to left. A body crashed into his, and Robert lashed out with his elbow. He heard a cry as boots scuffed the concrete floor behind him with a metallic echo. Then his kidneys exploded with pain, and Robert dropped to his knees.

There were two or three of them. No words spoken. He heard the click of a flick knife opening. Robert rolled to his right, ducking his head, his heart hammering. In the darkness, he collided with a pillar, hitting it hard with his shoulder. He used it to lever himself upright, hands up above his face, fists formed, his back to the concrete column. He couldn't see his attackers. But he was too angry to be afraid.

A steel-capped boot slammed into the pillar beside him, and Robert stooped instinctively in the blackness, grabbing the ankle and twisting it hard to his right. A shriek of pain rang out and a body hit the floor.

Robert felt a hand grab his hair, and a fist drove into his solar plexus. He fell to the ground, his chest in spasm, straining to breathe. He was thrown onto his back.

Then the darkness thickened, and he knew nothing more.

New York

Later that day

Robert forced himself to move. Gritting his teeth, he made one more effort and drove himself upright in the hospital bed.

A jagged, jarring musical phrase shrieked in his mind, over and over again, as his head swam and waves of pain consumed his body. Electric guitar. Words he couldn't grasp. Something about a helter-skelter ride.

Katherine. Where was Katherine?

His left arm gave way at the elbow. Tubes and sticking plasters tugged at Robert's skin as he wrestled to right himself. His chest was burning, and through pain-clouded eyes he saw that blood had seeped through his dressings, making a pattern on his flesh. Barbed lines.

Blackness rimmed his vision, and a shrill, piercing note grew louder and louder in his head until it threatened to split his skull. Robert saw nurses descending upon him, forcing him back down. *John*, he heard. *John Doe. John Doe's awake* . . .

'My wife! I must see my wife!' he shouted, struggling.

Out of the corner of an eye, he saw a syringe being readied, adjustments being made to a drip-feed.

'Don't sedate me!' he roared at the top of his voice, oblivious to how it sounded to those around him. A shriek? A croak?

One of the nurses leaned closer, her lips forming words: 'Where is she?'

'I need to get out of here.'

'There's no way . . .'

The room swam. When it came back into focus, a doctor in her forties was leaning over him, and Robert realized he was flat on his back again.

'Sir? Sir. We need to know your name. What is your name?'

'Where's Katherine!'

'Katherine?'

'Where's my wife?'

'What is your name, sir? We don't know who you are. We don't know about your wife. No one was with you when you were brought in. You had no ID. You were found in the street. Do you understand? Your name. Tell me your name.'

Robert fought a sudden, narcotic rush, as whatever drugs they were giving him kicked in.

'Robert . . . I have to get out of here.'

Her words were fading, the room receding.

'You're not going anywhere, Robert. You're lucky to be alive.'

Hate, he heard, in whispers around him. *Hate crime . . .*

Minutes or hours later, he came to. A deep ache filled his body. He was made of lead, sinking into the bedsheets, incapable of moving.

The jangling, shrieking guitar began again. Something about an endless spiral, going round and round. What was the song? What did it mean?

He saw himself running endlessly up spiralling steps, reaching the top of a fairground slide, sliding down, reaching the bottom, climbing again to the top, spiralling down on a kind of rough, thick hessian mat . . . It was a visit to the fair in Peterborough: towering pink candyfloss and sticky, sweet toffee apples . . . a gypsy fortune-teller who frightened and fascinated him, her dark long hair falling in a thick coil over one shoulder . . . He was maybe six years old. Other worlds, suspended rules, out past bedtime . . . sharp electric and neon lights in the dark night, and across from the fairground, over the river, the silent white towers of the cathedral, unmoved, unmoving.

The song faded.

He had to get up. Christ, Katherine. Where was she?

He braced himself, then lifted a leg. His stomach and chest screamed at him. Despite new dressings, he could see whatever had been cut into his torso had bled again.

'Nurse!'

He shouted at the top of his lungs.

'Help me!'

A woman with kindly eyes in a floral topcoat came to check on him.

'I'm checking myself out,' he said. 'Now.'

'I don't know if you . . .'

'I can do it, and I am. Please unhook me, or I'm taking all this gear with me.'

~

Katherine was not at home when he got there. He'd hoped against hope that she would be. Her cellphone was still off, or out of range.

Now, head swimming, staring at himself in the mirror of the bathroom, Robert saw what had been done to him, and understood the whispers: *Hate crime. Hate.*

His attackers, the ones he feared were now holding Katherine, had carved a symbol onto his chest.

It was a Nazi swastika.

13

Anger and revulsion rose in his throat. Then he let out a defiant roar.

'I know who you are!' he shouted. 'You can't have her!'

His vision blacked over. Holding onto the bathroom sink to keep his balance, Robert struggled to stay conscious.

Police. But . . .

He'd learned from Horace that the authorities could often make things worse. That some things were simply not understood . . .

He was too weak to try reaching out to Katherine mentally. The skills he had developed, since learning of his true nature in the summer of 2004, were beyond his reach right now.

It had been a shattering thing to learn.

Robert was heir to a powerful tradition he had been brought up to shun, that of the East Anglian *nameless art*. There were aunts and uncles who possessed the power. But seeking a better life for him, one free of superstitions and dangers from another age, Robert's parents had brought him up to disbelieve in all such things, to unwittingly bury his own nature. He was to be no witch. An unknowing psychic of immense potential, he'd grown up a rationalist, a deep sceptic, a practical, earthbound soul.

In 2004, Horace had lifted the scales from his eyes, forcing him to undergo an awakening of his gifts so strenuous that Horace himself, the old man had said, could not have survived it. Without Robert's forcibly ignited powers – through seven ordeals in as many days – they would have been unable to defeat the Enemy.

Then afterwards, the great array of powers – bursts of great physical strength, the ability to bend fragments of time and matter to his intention, a capacity to see into the very stuff that he and the world were made of – had abandoned him as quickly as they had come, and had since only returned in fleeting and mercurial snatches.

He chose to call Horace. But before he could do so, his cellphone buzzed. It was Katherine's number.

Robert snatched the phone up.

'Kat?'

There was no one there. He looked at the phone again. It was a text message, all in capital letters.

STOP WHAT YOU ARE DOING OR SHE IS DEAD.

Below the letters was a hyperlink. It opened up a video clip, which loaded quickly to reveal the old converted brick warehouse in the Red Hook neighbourhood where Adam had stored his papers, a few hundred yards from Robert and Katherine's own Brooklyn apartment. The camera zoomed shakily to the top of the building, just as two figures in black, their faces masked, threw a figure off the roof into the street below. The figure wore a red summer dress, the one Katherine had been wearing the previous day. The figure had long black curly hair, like Katherine's. The clip ended before it hit the ground.

'No!'

It had to be a mannequin, someone else in her dress. Anything.

Robert frantically called Katherine's number. Answering machine.

'If you hurt her, I will hunt you to the end of this world and any other stinking hell that you crawled out of,' he shouted. 'Do not hurt her!'

A wave of pain broke over him. Robert poured all his will-power into staying upright, remaining conscious, fighting.

He made his way into the living room and looked out

across Brooklyn towards the warehouse. He could see nothing on the roof now. He and Kat had binoculars in the house, but in his current state he couldn't reach the shelf where they were stored.

His thoughts came in jagged spurts. Could he drive over there? He had no car, it had to be still at Adam's place. Unless the kidnappers had taken it. Run? He could barely walk.

He forced himself to focus. They wanted leverage over him. It would make no sense to kill her, or their leverage would be gone. It was all in the threat.

Robert pulled his clothes back together as well as he could and strode to the elevator, mind filled with purpose, painkillers in one pocket, unused as yet. He didn't want to numb his mind. He marched through the lobby and out to the car park, past their empty parking space, into the street.

It was a humid, overcast day. The Manhattan skyline was almost invisible in the haze. Robert pounded along the stone-flagged streets of Red Hook, past derelict, weed-choked lots and nineteenth-century warehouses given over to garden centres and art studios, theatrical stores and community groups.

Sweating and cursing, he came to the building he had seen in the video clip. The camera had been pointing at the south face. If there were anything . . . He looked up at the roof. They had to be long gone, the video had to have been shot while he was still in hospital . . . Robert scoured the grounds where she would have fallen. Nothing. He found nothing. No witnesses, no one to ask. Katherine was nowhere.

As he walked back, his mind racing, he called Horace. He had to, though the old man had almost entirely shunned him for the last year. Robert didn't understand why, or what he had done to merit the sudden frost. But he remained Robert's only mentor, the only one he could turn to. A retired academic and sometime businessman, Horace had been in the OSS, the predecessor of the CIA, during the Second World War. There couldn't be a more hard-nosed mystic in existence, yet a mystic he was.

London

Horace Hencott stepped away from the noise of the black-tie cocktail reception at Australia House and slipped out onto a quiet balcony where he could talk.

Gazing down at the great curving thoroughfare of Aldwych in the cool evening air, Horace drew in a deep breath and slowly expelled it through his lips, clearing and calming his mind. The final days of a cycle begun decades earlier were finally at hand.

'Tell me what happened, Robert.'

Horace listened carefully to his protégé's account.

'You must get to London.'

'No. I have to find Katherine.'

'You will not help Katherine by looking for her in New York. You'll help her by getting on a plane to London, going to the Club of St George, and finding the material Adam described to you. They will only give it to you.'

'Katherine . . .'

'All roads lead to England in this matter. She is a tough girl, she can look after herself. I'll try to track her, but you have to follow the trail that Adam has left for us.'

Robert was angry now.

'Horace, I need to find her.'

'There are flights tonight. Get moving. Immediately.'

'Where are you?'

Horace ended the call.

'Trust me, Robert,' he whispered to himself.

Horace put away the cellphone in the inner pocket of his

dinner jacket, made for him at Poole's on Savile Row in the early 1950s, and looked out bleakly into the London night.

If Robert realized Horace was in London, not in New York, he would in all likelihood refuse to get on the plane, and go on looking for Katherine in America. They couldn't afford that.

At last, soon, there would be resolution. Down below, on the site of a holy well at the very heart of London, past and present would braid and unbraid, and redemption would be possible. But redemption for whom?

Already Horace could feel the gathering storm. His adversary was out there, yearning to complete the game, dying to live again. Horace turned the name over in his mind, pronouncing it in the French fashion, as he had heard it from the creature's own mouth, in Paris in 1944. Isambard. *Eezahmbar* . . . The cold green eyes. The colourless accent. The close-cropped white hair.

Horace could see, and he could not see.

He knew that Isambard was coming back. He knew that a knot in time, one that Horace himself had helped to tie sixty-three years ago, was starting to unravel. He knew that the consequences were terrifying if the knot tore apart, and he knew he didn't know how to stop it.

He knew, too, that things he bore in private shame – decisions he had taken as a younger man, in desperate times, with little experience – were at long last forcing their way to the surface, like splinters ejected from deep under the skin. The past was no longer to be buried or denied.

There was a man called Peter Hale. There was a woman called Rose. Ghosts, both, of his service in World War Two. A time of fear, of betrayal, of lost love. A time of victory so costly as almost to kill the victor.

Snatches of piano music and cocktail chatter wafted from the reception out into the night air. Horace looked down at Aldwych, and into history.

The Thames had lapped closer in Saxon times, when the Strand was the shore, and west of the River Fleet a dozen streams and rivulets had run across the marshy land below him, where traders and their families had made their homes, outside the walls of the crumbling Roman city that had been Londinium.

Lundenwic, the Saxon settlement had been called, more than a thousand years earlier.

Saxon . . . a glimmer of hope flashed across the dark, and faded before Horace could grasp it. He screwed up his eyes in frustration. There were dead zones in the landscape of what was to come, places he couldn't see, powerfully shielded and camouflaged. They were to do with Robert's past, and with his own, and for all his power and skill, accumulated over many decades, Horace couldn't penetrate them. *Saxon* . . . he marked the sensation, noted it, let it go.

Looking closer in time, Horace saw the medieval bridges over the Aldwych streams, in the area then sometimes called London Fen, leading up from the Thames to the meadows of Holborn. One creek ran into the Thames at the bottom of what was now Essex Street, a stone bridge over it built by the Knights Templar in the time of Edward III; another stream joined the Thames between Catherine Street and Wellington Street; a third, called Ulebrig, later the Ivy, joined the great river at Cecil Street.

He saw the streets stretch and grow as time flowed, the streams and springs covered over and forgotten except in names: Holywell Street, a narrow road of bookstores and inns; the wooden houses of Wych Street, slums around Clare Market in the time of Dickens, torn down in their turn at the start of the last century to make way for the elegant crescent of Aldwych as it now stood.

Though the streams were gone, two islands remained, surrounded not by rushing water but by torrents of motor traffic, each graced with a church: St Clement Danes, resting just east of Australia House, also built above the sacred spring; and St Mary-le-Strand, where a maypole had stood, an echo of London's pagan past, until as recently as the eighteenth century.

Horace scanned backwards and forwards again, looking for the crack in time, the point when time slipped.

It was a faculty that had come with painstaking progress, achieved over more than fifty years since leaving the OSS, towards the ultimate goal of all those of his kind: Horace sought the prize known as the Great Work.

To achieve the Great Work was, simply, to attain a fabled state of consciousness, a perspective both in time and outside it, both individual and universal, that gave transfiguring powers to whoever achieved it. It was the most powerful, most dangerous, most transformational state a human being could achieve. It was to be sought for only one reason: to benefit one's fellow man. Although Isambard had taken another route . . .

Horace was close to achieving the Work. He also knew that he would never attain it without a final ordeal; and he saw that the ordeal was about to begin.

He looked away from his inner world out again onto Aldwych.

Then he saw the crack in time, and the world shattered. Horace saw what might have been, what might still be.

All was black, covered in cinders.

London a smoking ruin. South-east England a grey, ash-strewn wasteland, as far as the eye could see.

Two emaciated men, twitching and shrieking like hyenas, clothes ragged and torn, their feet unshod, ran up a slope of blackened bricks where St Catherine's House had once stood. They were pitiful, insane. Fleeing something. One turned and hurled a brick in defiance at unseen pursuers, shouting incomprehensibly.

Horace looked for the source of their fear. Then he saw it, edging slowly past the ruins where St Clement Danes had stood, creeping from the remains of Fleet Street onto the devastated Aldwych. A platoon of soldiers in black uniforms, pointing their rifles edgily at the piles of rubble, advanced slowly towards the men, nervously scanning the pestilential, boiling horizon.

The two fleeing men hurled more bricks, taunting them, perhaps trying to draw them towards their location. Perhaps just mindless with hunger, or pain. Horace heard a northern English accent, perhaps Tyneside.

There was a burst of sub-machine-gun fire. One of the men hollered hoarsely and fell dead, blood spurting from chest and throat wounds. The other screamed as his legs shattered beneath him.

The troops stopped firing. The platoon leader surveyed the scene through binoculars, then signalled instructions, and they moved on in the direction of a blackened, devastated Trafalgar Square.

The wounded man's cries grew shriller, then slowly weaker. He was calling for his mother.

The soldiers' armbands and helmets bore the mark of the swastika.

A hand fell on Horace's shoulder, jolting him from the appalling vision.

'There you are! Ready to go down to the basement?'

Horace's companion, who had joined him on the balcony, was a high-ranking diplomat at the Australian High Commission. Horace's purpose in attending the reception had been to visit the waters of the holy well below Australia House, which were never shown to the public.

Horace breathed hard, trying to compose himself.

'The basement?' He tried to banish from his mind what he had just seen. 'Yes, yes, of course.'

Horace stepped back into the reception, shaken and afraid.

New York

Back at the apartment, Robert's body went into spasms. Vomiting, then dry heaves.

How could he get on a plane? He could barely drag himself to the next room.

In his distress, he tried reaching out mentally again to Katherine.

Nothing.

Then, through sheer effort of will, he hauled himself into the shower, protecting his chest wounds as best he could, and rinsed the sweat of fear from his body.

When he had finished, doubting Horace even as he trusted him, Robert dressed and called a car to JFK.

Day Four

London

26 June 2007

The Club of St George lay in the warren of lanes south of Fleet Street once known as Alsatia, home to the Whitefriars monastery in the Middle Ages, a place of sanctuary for those fleeing persecution, then later a lawless, violent den of criminals where seventeenth-century officers of the law had feared to set foot.

More recently, in Robert's time, it had been a centre of the newspaper industry, the place where he had cut his teeth as a reporter at the international news service GBN; though that, too, was now all gone, removed to the Dock-lands.

There was no plaque on the door of the modest, under-stated house on Whitefriars Cut, and Robert, who'd headed there by train and taxi straight from the airport, took several minutes to find it, just as he had on his first visit, nearly seventeen years before. On that occasion, he'd been attending the private premiere of a play put on by Adam, and he'd sat next to Katherine in the audience. She had been married to Adam for barely a year at the time, working at the Foreign Office in London after some stints abroad, and she'd been nursing her husband through a period of penury and depression, his work as a freelance foreign correspon-dent drying up after a disastrous tour in Central America. She'd helped him complete the play, which they'd first worked on together in university days.

The play had been Adam's way of presenting to a limited, learned audience some research he and Kat had done, benevolently watched over by Horace, on Sir Isaac Newton's secret alchemical work. But in true reckless form, Adam had incorporated into the production a real Newton document he had been entrusted with, of such secret contents that as soon as he began to read from it, scuffles had broken out. There had been fist fights, and unidentified members of the audience had tried to steal the document. Items of scenery had caught fire, and an actress had been badly burned. It had tipped Adam into a breakdown, eventually ruining his marriage to Katherine, and leading him to break with Horace for several years.

Now Robert hoped for a happier outcome, and a quick one.

A towering Sikh attendant let Robert into the marble-flagged foyer of the Club of St George and, after hearing the nature of his business, led him into a comfortably appointed library to wait while further enquiries were made.

'Would you care for coffee, sir?' the doorman asked.

'I regret I have very little time,' Robert said.

'You'll be seen shortly, sir.'

Robert set his mind on Katherine. Thinking dulled the pain. He'd get whatever information Adam had left, walk ten minutes to the Waldorf Hotel, get a room, go through it . . . it would lead to Katherine, one way or another. To the people who had her.

'Mr Reckless?'

An older man who reminded him of Horace appeared at the library entrance. Kindly eyes, stocky build, a vigorous man in his seventies.

'Reckliss. With an I.' It was a correction Robert had spent his entire life making. *No, I'm not reckless. Not me.* He wondered if Adam had left instructions to mispronounce his name, just to taunt him one last time.

'I apologize. Mr Reck*liss*, would you be so kind as to come with me?'

'Where to?'

'To the safety deposit vault. Thank you for the letter from Mr Hale. He says I am to ask you for a certain *word . . .*'

At the hotel, Robert opened the file and began to remove its contents, sitting on the bed and placing the items before him in a semicircular array. He examined them one by one. He felt sure they would make a pattern. He couldn't see it yet, but he had to. Katherine needed him to.

There was a black-and-white photograph, taken somewhere in France to judge by the shop signs, and dated on the back *1943*, showing a man in civilian clothes identified as Harry Hale-Devereaux, next to another man, also in civvies, whose face was scratched out. On the rough paper where the features should have been, someone had drawn a swastika in blood-red ink.

Robert placed a hand on his chest, tracing the wound in the same hateful shape, willing the raw pulsing to stop. Blackness fringed his field of vision.

There was an undated note, in Adam's hand, titled *Anomalies and fragments.*

There was a Frank Zappa CD, with the name of a song circled in black on the track list.

There were eyewitness accounts, official reports and photographs of a particular incident in World War Two – the explosion of a V-1 flying bomb on Aldwych in 1944, just a few yards from Robert's hotel, near where Fleet Street joined the Strand.

There was a Sotheby's catalogue from 1936 for an auction of papers belonging to Sir Isaac Newton.

There was a DVD, its label identifying it only as a transfer from a reel of old Super-8 movie film, which was also included, packed in a yellow-and-red cardboard box marked *Steeplejack*.

Robert picked up Adam's *Anomalies* note and read it.

> — *there will be a defector, one who for decades has been preparing to cross from one side to the other.*
> — *there is a shadow over London.*
> — *these locations make no sense: Temple. St Martin in the Fields. St Nicholas in the Fields. St James. St Julian. Abbotsword.*
> — *the key lies in a children's song. I can hear its cadences but cannot grasp it.*
> — *best to keep the window closed, or you can catch your death.*
> — *the past can be healed. But it can also be poisoned.*
> — *London Fen. Time and place elide.*

Robert picked up the CD. *Guitar* was the name of the album, with the third track on disc two, entitled 'But who was Fulcanelli?', ringed in black ink. He listened to it with impatience – a meandering Frank Zappa live guitar solo, quite dreadful to his ears, less than three minutes long, with no lyrics. He played it again, several times over, hitting *back* each time it ended. He let his mind wander, treating the music as a kind of white noise.

The guilt never left him. To be a killer. To have failed his friends. He owed Adam, and Adam's lover Terri, debts he could never repay. Could he have saved them?

In the final fight in Manhattan with the servants of the Enemy, it had come down to this: a sacrifice was necessary. Robert had been prepared to give himself, to die to save others. But it had not worked out that way. Terri had saved Robert's life, giving her own to do so. And Adam . . .

destroyed from within by the Enemy's corrosive poison, riddled through with its hatred, holding out till the very end but unable to break free of the grip it had established on him, Adam had *asked* Robert to kill him . . .

And in order to defeat the Enemy, to help Adam take it down, Robert had done so. Asking to die instead, Robert had killed, and been allowed to kill.

How to atone? How to even think about what he had done?

Was it enough, as Horace had told him, to become all that Adam could have been, to become fully himself, to follow his gift to wherever it led him? It didn't feel like enough. It could never be . . .

Stop. Robert shook his head, trying to clear his thoughts. He forced himself to focus on the task at hand.

He popped the CD out of his laptop and inserted the DVD.

Scratches on the old film writhed across the screen, like hair-thin snakes trapped in the projector lens. Countdown numbers appeared, and then, captured in the lurid colours of 1960s film stock, a tough-looking man in his late forties or early fifties appeared, grey-haired with a military moustache, and the assured vowels of the pre-war British landed gentry, sitting in an armchair. A caption said the film was of Harry Hale-Devereaux, Adam's grandfather.

He was speaking with an interviewer, someone off camera.

'Who was Peter Hale, you ask? Well . . . He was my brother. A troubled soul. Someone I thought I could trust, though he turned out to be a monster. A devil . . .'

Paris

1919

It was a world of dresses and shoes and trousers, chairs and tablecloths: a garden in Paris, adults in their summer finery, Peter Hale a small boy flitting among them, rapt in his own private games.

But suddenly he was plucked up to adult face-height in his mother's arms, the crucifix around her neck glinting, and he was introduced – no: shown, demonstrated – to a moustachioed man with piercing eyes who called him *jeune homme*, or was it *young man*, or *junger Mann*, and he was told the man was a great – something wondrous and slightly unreal, something exciting and forbidden, made frightening by the cold depths of his eyes – a great *sorcerer? Sorcier? Zauberer?*

A name was pronounced, of that he was sure: *Isambard*. And at the moment of its utterance, Peter grabbed the crucifix and pulled it from his mother's neck, breaking the delicate chain, and then suddenly burst into tears.

~

Everyone said his mother was a beauty, even those who spat at her name.

Maman had been a country girl, the story ran, a country girl who'd run away to the city. She'd been an actress and dancer in Paris, in venues high and low, worked in cabarets, lived the Bohemian life.

She'd made the mistake, they said, of going home to visit

32

her ailing father at his farm on the Marne in 1914. When the invasion had come, she'd been raped by a German soldier, and an *enfant du barbare* had been born. A barbarian's child, a thing of horror, born in 1915.

Welcome to the world.

How could he forgive her? How could he not?

After the war, as Peter was brought up in Paris, a kind of cocoon formed among his mother's old acquaintances, within which she found more social acceptance than elsewhere, at least to her face. Despite the names he was sometimes called on the street, he was doted on within this small circle of his mother's literary and artistic friends. There were parties, *salons*, a social whirl, half-glimpsed ceremonies of a kind he didn't understand. There was sometimes happiness.

But there were also anomalies in the story.

In return for a generous but mysterious stipend, for example, he was made to attend German-speaking schools. Yet he learned never to speak the language in his mother's presence. She could not bear to hear it.

His nameless father, Peter came to feel, was watching always, from afar. He was a sinister presence, yet one he deeply longed to know. The rapist. His creator.

In the early 1920s, a new man began to appear with regularity at his mother's side – never quite with full predictability, but with greater assiduity as her health worsened.

He was a wealthy Englishman, an aristocrat, a dabbler in business affairs, a man of the world. The little boy understood things perfectly: *le bon milord* Hale-Devereaux was married, but not to *maman*; he had a family to which he owed his primary duty, with his own son, Harry; nevertheless there was tenderness towards this second family, that of the mistress, the ailing *artiste* and her lonely son, whom other children mocked and who would very soon be an orphan.

When *maman* died, a seemingly simple transaction took place. Young Pierre, already known as Peter at the German schools, became in 1924 young Peter Hale-Devereaux, charity case, adoptive brother to Harry, and adoptive son to the grand *milord* Hale-Devereaux of Poldhu, and there was an end to it. He was henceforth an Englishman, to be raised in the great Hale-Devereaux household, tutored in the language, and damn lucky too. Right thing done all round. No fuss required.

Troubled young Peter, who could do dark things with his mind, who never forgot the German and the French languages and always felt like a cuckoo's egg in an alien nest, grew himself a carapace of Englishness that in time formed a perfect veneer on the outside, and a plausible story to tell himself on the inside: you belong. You are from this land. You are an Englishman, all stains wiped away.

Yet always, and still, he was an outsider, an alien to his own family, an inconvenience, an embarrassment. He was a charity case. There were shameful words for what he was, words whispered behind his back, looks exchanged in his presence that spoke always of a dreadful secret in his very origins, that said: don't let him come any closer, remember his stain.

To be a bastard was one thing. To be what he was, was unspeakably worse.

And so it began as a kind of revenge.

Peter had known from an early age that he could see further, or deeper, than other children. If he concentrated really hard, or got very angry, he had found, he could make accidents happen to others. One child who had tormented him because of his origins, Peter had caused to be scalded with boiling water. Another he had made fall from an open window and break his arm. He had only ever told his mother what he could do, and she had made him promise never to tell another living soul, and never to abuse what he had discovered.

'You have been given a very special way of seeing, because God loves you very much,' she had said one sunny afternoon in the Luxembourg gardens, after taking him to see a marionette show. 'God will be angry unless you use it for the good, and *maman* will be angry too.'

'What happens if I don't use it for the good, *maman*?'

'The hurt we do to other people rebounds upon us, *mon petit chou*. And the more we think we get away with things in this life, the more we must pay in the next.'

'Do you believe in hell, *maman*?'

'Oh yes. And in those who serve it.'

'And what is the good?'

'Well . . .'

He heard her think, as clear as a bell, her gaze settled on him with a look of love so intense it hurt: '*To survive . . .*'

But she said nothing for several moments, her eyes clouding with emotion.

'The good is to treat others as you would like to be treated yourself . . . even when you are not treated that way.'

'Why, *maman*?'

'Don't torment your mother, Pierre. Those are enough questions for one day.'

She had never answered the question to his satisfaction. No one had.

Pulling the crucifix from his mother's neck was Peter's earliest memory. For some reason, he'd felt he was saving her, though in later years he was sure his action had caused her death. He'd blamed himself for it ever since.

Cornwall

1928

The decayed wooden cover over the shaft was hidden by autumn leaves, and when thirteen-year-old Peter Hale put his foot down, it cracked like balsa wood, opening a sudden void beneath him. Peter fell, banging his nose and wrist on the edge of the shaft. Then down he went into the darkness, a fall that lasted for endless terrifying minutes in his mind, the world above narrowing to a small circle of light. Semi-stunned, he landed like a sack of potatoes in a flooded tunnel at the bottom. The wind shot out of him, and for a few moments he panicked as his lungs gasped for air, his heart hammering, blood roaring in his ears.

'Peter!'

His brother Harry's voice sounded far away, in a distant world. The water was freezing, and it was up to Peter's neck. In agitation he gulped in a huge lungful of air, then another, and tried to stand, but his right leg wouldn't move properly. He felt cold and numb at once, and very frightened.

A face appeared at the top of the shaft, blotting out the light.

'Can you hear me, Peter?'

For the strangest moment, Peter had the impression that Harry was laughing. Then he realized he must be crying.

'I'm so sorry, Peter!' the boy shouted down the shaft. 'I made you go that way.'

They had been playing tag, a long way from the house, in the part of the grounds called the No Man's Land. They were not supposed to be there.

Peter tried to call out that he was all right. He wanted to produce a stentorian bellow with his scratchy, breaking voice, but it came out as a shrill howl.

'I'm all right, Harry.' He tried again. 'I've hurt my leg, though.'

'I'll go and get help!'

'No! We'll get into trouble!'

He got breathless again. He took two deep breaths to calm himself. 'Get me out! Find a rope!'

Harry hesitated, alternately blocking and unblocking the light as his head bobbed back and forth at the top of the shaft.

'I'll look for one.'

Peter felt a dull, deep throb begin in his right ankle and left wrist, and on one side of his nose. One nostril had bled, the other not. Funny, he thought.

Harry came back.

'I can't find one. I can't find anything!' Harry sounded scared, his voice strange and liquid. 'I'll say it was my fault,' he shouted down the shaft. 'I'll take the blame!'

'Don't leave me!' Peter shouted. It was miles back to the house. It would take him for ever. But Harry was gone.

The stuff of Peter's nightmares began then. The water seemed to be rising, forcing him to strain harder and harder to lever himself up, the throb in his ankle slowly growing into an excruciating, stabbing pain he could feel in his teeth and behind his eyes.

They told stories of the old smugglers' tunnels that led to caves on the beaches, and the secret entrances and shafts that led down to them, some of them hundreds of years old. Great blind fish lived in the tunnels, they said. Ghosts of drowned smugglers, or hanged ones, lived under the ground, and came out on full-moon nights to hunt for children and drag them away.

He tried to get his eyes used to the darkness, looking away from the circle of light. Eventually he saw a kind of ladder, metal hoops hammered into the sides of the shaft, rusted and bent. The nearest was more than a foot above his head, if he could reach it ... Six times he tried, and on the last he hurt his ankle so badly he made himself sick, and in abject misery and fear Peter slumped back down into the freezing water and began to cry, vomit on his jumper and in the water.

Then something brushed against his legs. Peter screamed and jumped upright in adrenal response, the pure instinct of fear taking over his body. The rusted lowest rung appeared before his eyes, and he grabbed it with his good hand, holding on for grim life. Had it been an eel? A fish?

Peter breathed hard, feeling dizzy, his ears ringing.

He didn't know how long he could maintain his grip.

Terrified, he began to count.

When Harry returned with their father and some men, Peter had nearly reached three thousand.

True to his word, Harry tried to take all the blame upon himself, and for his pains was beaten heavily with a cane by their father. Harry didn't utter a sound. In sheer rage at Peter's protests about the punishment, their father threatened the same treatment to his adoptive son as soon as Peter was well enough to get up off his sickbed. Neither boy had ever seen him in such a thunder, and never did again.

The nightmares began immediately. For almost a month after his fall, Peter relived the loneliness of his slow, deliberate count in defiance of fear, and of the mounting agony of his one-handed grip on the metal stanchion that ultimately had saved his life.

Whenever he shouted out in the night, Harry came to his room and sat by the bed, staring at the strange creature who had become his younger brother. And Harry sang half-forgotten songs in Cornish he had learned from his nanny to soothe Peter back to sleep: songs of loss and tenderness that for Peter were, in a way, magical.

Paris

1932

France eventually drew Peter back.

Returning to his source, returning to his mother's city, he studied in Paris as soon as he was allowed, without supervision from the age of sixteen onwards, *le bon milord* Hale-Devereaux keen to be done with his obligation, happy to fund Peter's departure. He had been a sporadically kind but distant man, for whom the second son, and adopted at that, should find his own way in the world as soon as possible, inheritance of title or fortune being out of the question, quite naturally unthinkable, but a small income being perhaps manageable, in exchange for a certain distance, for a certain not darkening of the door.

In Paris, Peter found, he was remembered in his mother's circles, and they soon proved to be very interesting circles indeed. He found himself quickly passed from individuals who had known his mother socially to others who had known her in more discreet, esoteric settings.

And things began to get dark.

In early 1932, young Peter Hale was introduced, by an acquaintance of his mother, to a ring calling itself *Les frères d'Héliopolis,* one of an array of loosely interlinked esoteric study groups in the Paris of the day.

From there, he was put in touch with other, similar groups. And he found that certain groups did more than just study, and that the aims of their members were not limited to endless poring over dusty alchemical manuscripts.

There was work to be done, some of them told Peter, and it was necessary to work with the best adepts in the field. A reordering of the world was coming, they said, and it would be important to be on the right side when the chips were down.

But the best French adepts, they said, were dead or dying, or didn't have the stomach for the coming fight. The best work, they told him, was now being done in Germany. Introductions could be made, especially for someone of his language skills, his *background* . . .

Seeking guidance, Peter went to see a dying man in the late summer of 1932 who was said to be a founder of *Les frères d'Héliopolis*. In a stinking sixth-floor garret on the top floor of 59 *bis*, Rue de Rochechouart, in the 9th arrondissement of Paris, he met Jean-Julien Champagne, the illustrator – some said more than just the illustrator – of a legendary book called *Le Mystère des Cathédrales*, published six years earlier, in a print run of just 300 copies, that was said to reveal, for those who read it with the right eyes, the art of transmutation. The author's name was given on the title page simply as *Fulcanelli*. Some said Fulcanelli didn't exist, that the book was a hoax, and that he was just an invention of Champagne's – the artist was a notorious prankster – to draw attention to himself and his group.

Champagne did not rise from his sickbed for Peter's visit. The stench in the cramped room was almost unbearable. Gangrene was rotting the man's left leg, and where his bandages had come loose Peter could see that his flesh had turned black.

'Who are you, and what do you want, young man?' Champagne asked, with a dreadful rasp.

Peter handed over a photograph of his mother, by way of introduction.

'How old are you, boy?'

'Eighteen,' Peter lied. Champagne eyed the photograph and sighed.

'*La belle Sophie*,' the moustachioed, long-haired figure said wistfully, prompting some surprise in her son, for whom her name had been Hélène. 'A muse for many of us.' He handed back the photograph. 'I painted her, you know, before the war. Scandal! An allegorical painting, in which she represented the beauty of the Great Work ... she was naked, naturally. *Pardon!* She was exquisite, her death a great tragedy.' His eyes softened. 'You were small, no older than four or five, perhaps, when we knew you.'

He observed Peter's efforts not to look at his rotting leg.

'You see before you the results of protecting that which does not always wish to be known,' Champagne said. 'I tire quickly, young man. How may I assist you? Speak up, be brief.'

'After my mother died, I was adopted by her lover, an English lord,' Peter told him matter-of-factly. 'I was raised in England, in Cornwall. A kind of prize monkey, a living example of his generosity. I did not see much of Lady Hale, who rarely spoke to me. For me it was a man's house. There was the *milord*, there was a kind step-brother, Harry. There were servant girls below stairs, but ... I've returned to Paris as soon as I could to learn more about my mother.'

Champagne shifted his weight on the rancid bed, grimacing.

'And what have you found?'

'Confusion. Some people say she moved in circles involving devil worship, black magic, bestial practices.' Champagne

43

snorted, whether in disbelief or pain Peter couldn't tell. 'Others that she was vilely used, unfairly maligned and cast aside, a woman of great gifts and goodness who fell in with the wrong crowd.'

'What do you know of such gifts? Did she ever speak to you of such things?'

'My mind, sometimes . . . allows me to do things. Dark things, when I'm angry. I try to control it. She warned me about it.' Peter paused, half afraid to meet Champagne's piercing stare. 'I want to know what it is.'

'These people you have spoken to . . .'

'They talk of Germany. They say those in France with the requisite knowledge are no longer capable or willing to do the necessary work. I don't understand. They want to draw me in, to welcome me. But they scare me.'

Champagne looked past Peter for several seconds when he had finished, sweat beading his brow, his eyes far away and haunted. Then he spoke.

'You must take great care, *jeune homme*. The closed world that you are being invited to enter, that your mother once frequented, is in the throes of a terrible conflict, one that may determine – I am not exaggerating – the future of us all. The conflict is about power, nothing new there. Man is man. But the kind of power I am talking about has not been seen before on this earth. Are you familiar with the name Marie Curie?'

'Yes, of course.'

'She and her late husband, and now her daughter and son-in-law, the Joliot-Curies, have all tinkered around the edges of this power, with their work in this very city, on what they have chosen to call radioactivity, with their discoveries of polonium, of radium. We hear now of particles smaller than atoms, of other discoveries made by probing the very heart of matter. These scientific enquiries are playing with fire.'

'How so, sir?'

'Great physical energies may be unleashed. No bomb or explosive yet imagined can compare to them. And they are probing only the physical world, paying no heed to the mental, the spiritual. There are others who work in all these domains at once, as they should. I have been one of them. I am a brother of Heliopolis. Admire the result.'

A hacking cough convulsed him for several seconds. Peter fought nausea as Champagne's convulsions loosened more of the filthy bandages on his blackened leg.

'What happened to you, Monsieur Champagne?'

'You should be more concerned about what may happen to you. Among my supposed brothers in the Great Work, there are two divergent views. One, simply put, holds that there are superior and inferior races, just as there are men fit to rule and men fit to serve. These are the people who have been talking to you, who are keen to connect you to their friends in Germany. They are the people who speak ill of the Jewish race, in particular. Of the Slavs and gypsies, too, and of others. Until about ten years ago, here in Paris, a group of them even wore a uniform, in protest against what they saw as the frivolities of fashion. They wore dark shirts, boots, riding trousers. They wanted to work simultaneously in the esoteric and political spheres. They have gone underground here. They may simply have disbanded. Or . . . we now see similar costumes, I am told, on certain political thugs in Germany.'

'You oppose this group?'

'They were led by an individual called Isambard, whom no one has seen in Paris now for several years. A striking man, tall, long white hair, from Alsace, impossible to determine his age. They wanted – they demanded to be given – the knowledge of *Les frères d'Héliopolis*. This was blasphemous. You must understand, for us, that the city of Heliopolis signifies the enlightened state, the mental and spiritual abode one enters upon achieving illumination. One enters the city of sunlight, we say.'

'Is this what is meant by the Great Work?'

Champagne's eyes met Peter's, and burned with exhausted intensity.

'That is one term for it. It is the greatest jewel of mankind,' he whispered. 'It is our greatest gift, our greatest capacity, our greatest challenge.'

Now Champagne's eyes misted over with pain. 'Those who master the Work can perform miracles. Transmutations . . . that is the danger. The knowledge must be guarded constantly, against efforts to abuse it.'

'I still don't understand.'

'The prime responsibility of those who attain Heliopolis, who achieve the Great Work, is to ensure its flame is never extinguished. They must keep knowledge of it alive until mankind is ready to make proper use of it. Do not think we are ready. We are not. The experiments of the atomic physicists show only a part of what a true master may achieve. To disturb the physical world, without an equal mastery of the inner world . . . however brilliant their manipulation of matter, along that path lies madness. Destruction. The gates of Heliopolis must only open to the worthy.'

'But Heliopolis was an ancient Egyptian city, was it not?'

'It was. The Greeks renamed it Heliopolis when they invaded, after Helios, their god of the sun. It was originally called Iwnw. In the Bible, it is called On. But the true Heliopolis is not a geographical location. It is a metaphor. It stands for a perspective, a way of seeing, a sunlit abode.'

46

'To which Isambard sought access?'

Champagne's hands began to shake. Peter felt waves of pain emanating from his rotting body.

'I greatly upset him and his followers. I barred them from *Les frères d'Héliopolis,* denied them our knowledge, which must be kept sacred. You see, the view I espouse – the one he detests – honours all mystical traditions. The Jewish, the Christian, the Hermetic, the Sufi, all. It sees no distinction between races, discriminating only against men driven by the lust for personal power – or, heaven forbid, racial power. Of those latter men, of course, there are more, in all walks of life, than would openly admit it.'

Peter sighed. He didn't want a lecture about politics. *Milord* Hale-Devereaux had thoroughly drilled Peter in what he should think: that the world was going to have to choose between Communism and Fascism, and that Hitler was the greater evil, and that he would have to be defeated, whatever the cost to Britain. He saw no help coming from America. Peter had come to agree with him almost entirely, except on the identity of the greater evil . . . Defying his adoptive father, he had come to think the Bolsheviks were the worst of the bunch. *Milord* Hale-Devereaux had coloured his view of the world, to that extent. But in the end, Peter didn't really care. They were all equally corrupt. He had other concerns.

'What happened to you, Monsieur Champagne?'

'I swore an oath to keep something secret. I shared it – not the secret itself, just the fact that I kept it – with only one person, my most trusted friend in the Work, my *soror mistica.* Your mother.'

Champagne's eyes glistened. He pointed with a wooden walking stick to a stack of books and papers in one corner of the tiny mansard room. 'Since you are her son . . . pass me that folder. Gently.'

Peter leaned across the room – he barely needed to get up from his chair – and took a yellowing cardboard file from among the papers. It was held closed by dark green ribbons tied in a bow.

'Give it to me,' Champagne said, pushing back his sweat-soaked pillow as he tried to sit up.

He undid the bows and, with great delicacy, removed a small booklet made of stiff drawing paper, folded and roughly cut, covered in minute handwriting in dark brown ink. It was stained with dots of oil and wrapped in a folded cover sheet that bore just a scribbled signature and the numeral 2. The cover sheet was made of paper of a different, lighter manufacture.

'Before the Great War, I worked for the Chacornac brothers, booksellers, who kept a stall on the Seine. It was my job to assess private libraries, usually from the provinces, that came up for sale, and to pick out unusual volumes. I was an artist, you understand, I lived from hand to mouth, I sought patrons where I could, but I did all kinds of work. Technical drawings, frontispieces for books, whatever came up. This bookshop work was appealing to me. Occasionally a tome of genuine value in the pursuit of the Great Work would pass through my hands. One day, I found this.'

He held it up for Peter to see, carefully turning the pages.

'I found this in a very rare volume of manuscript writings by Sir Isaac Newton. His alchemical writings. It was bound into the inside back cover. It describes experiments to make the reds and blues of the extraordinary stained glass at Chartres cathedral, of which the manufacturing secret has long been lost. The colours at Chartres completely permeate the glass – they were created alchemically, as part of one route to achieving the Great Work. Priceless. You must understand, at around this time, my associates and I were spending a great deal of time in the libraries of Paris, studying alchemical manuscripts. And we were finding that pages were vanishing from them. Key pages were being cut out, with razorblades or scalpels, and taken heaven knows where. Some suspected the Jesuits were taking them, to ensure only they had the knowledge. Others suspected my group, a vile slander. I, naturally, blamed Isambard. In such circumstances, to find this volume of Newton, and then within it this manuscript, was astonishing. So I stole it.'

His eyes lit up with glee as he confessed to the theft. Then another fit of coughing and retching shook his body. Champagne took a metal can from the side of his bed and held it to his nose, inhaling its contents deeply. Peter caught a whiff of a strange, unpleasant musk.

'Galbanum,' the ailing man said, holding the can toward his guest. 'A resin, with restorative and vision-inducing properties. Want a sniff?'

Peter demurred.

'Was the manuscript you showed me by Newton too? The little booklet?'

'It was unsigned. I initially thought it was from the nineteenth century. But I took advice, and came to believe it was his, yes. Especially when, nineteen years later – nineteen years! – I was finally able to perform the experiment it described.'

His eyes shone with pride.

'You made the glass? The red and blue glass?'

'I did.' He hissed with excitement at the memory. 'In 1930, I did.'

'And then?'

'I had sworn to tell no one. Your mother was dead by then, of course. A great tragedy. She is the only one I would have told. But someone heard of my achievement, the devil only knows how – Isambard. He tried to force it from me. I refused to tell him anything.'

'And?'

'Look at me. He struck me down with this . . . palsy. For weeks, I was unable even to speak. And I fear he has worse in store for me yet. He wants to torture it out of me. Slowly. He wants me to suffer as much as possible. Be careful what you swear, young man. Be sure you can fulfil your obligations.'

'Where is the glass you made? What will you do with it?'

'Its sole purpose, apart from simply being admired for its beauty, is to help attain the next stage of the Work. And the next stage will allow me to cure myself. Somewhere, this document says how.'

'You have the glass here? You'll use it to defy Isambard?'

'If I can, yes. I do nothing else. I read, I reread, I try to understand.'

Champagne was silent for a long time, his gaze elsewhere, his agony palpable. Eventually Peter dared to speak again.

'Who is Fulcanelli? Can he help you?'

'Isambard and Fulcanelli are like mirror images of one another. That is all I may say. I spoke earlier of a city of sunlight. St Augustine wrote of the same place, in a different way. He called it the City of God, imagining it all around us, co-existent and co-located within the mundane city we inhabit, accessible to all, if only we can learn how to love. But there is another invisible city, besides the City of God. It is the City of Fear. Both are real, the thinnest veil away from the everyday city we all inhabit . . . the City of Fear is where Isambard and his ilk wish to take us. The sun is black, there.'

'Where is he?'

'In Germany, I am sure, with his Nazi thug friends. And

yet, when he chooses . . . he is right here. In this room. Please, I have little time . . .'

'How can I pursue the Great Work?'

Champagne gave a bitter laugh. Then he made to speak, but no sound emerged from his mouth. Another convulsion set in, and it was all the stricken man could do to raise his walking stick again and point to the door. Peter saw fear and panic in his eyes, and tried to lean forward to help him. Then Champagne's paralysed vocal cords were freed up, just long enough for him to rasp a single instruction.

'*Casse-toi! Casse-toi!* Get out! Get out!'

Jean-Julien Champagne, rotted with gangrene, died in his Montmartre garret on 26 August 1932, a few days after Peter's visit. No coloured glass or Newton papers were found among his effects. Word spread in Parisian esoteric circles that Fulcanelli himself had recovered them, and hidden them away somewhere in the city, until a worthy keeper could be found for them.

Two years later, Peter Hale-Devereaux went to Germany, telling his adoptive parents, and himself, that he intended to study Nordic culture in Berlin.

His family, without saying anything, understood perfectly: he was going to look for his true father.

In his luggage, known only to him, Peter took an anonymous letter that he had found pushed under the door of his modest Paris hotel room one morning in the summer of 1934. *Your mother was not raped, do not believe all you have been told*, it said. *It was a love match, and more. Your father is a man of wisdom, and more. Seek him in Berlin.*

New York

26 June 2007

Katherine put together what she knew, and kept her mind on the positive.

She was alive, unmolested, unhurt but for the bruises on her arms and legs where they'd grabbed her. Her hands were bound in front of her, wrapped tightly at the wrists with duct tape.

If the purpose had been to kill her, she'd be dead already. Therefore, she concluded, she was of value to them. Had they killed Robert? Kidnapped him too? She didn't know. She put uncertainty from her mind. She'd think about Robert later, when she was less scared. Yet the idea of him being hurt . . .

What did they want?

All the things she'd learned over her years at the darker end of the Foreign Office, and later at one of its American counterparts, were out of date – it wouldn't make sense for them to be after intelligence information, unless they were simply idiots. And to judge by the room in which she was being held, they had at least some idea of what they were doing.

Her cell was just a stone box of breezeblocks cemented together, a door with a peephole in it, a hatch in the wall next to it, and a narrow gap right at the top, to let in some light. Too high to jump to, too small to get through. There was no electricity, nothing she could use as a weapon.

Katherine, mostly raised in Britain, born of an American mother and an Argentine father, had worked for MI6, in the field and at home, for a decade. She'd got out of the game after losing an agent, and as a consequence losing her faith in the value of the work, in the mid-nineties. Leaving the spying game, leaving a world of lies and unhappiness, she'd also left her husband, Adam, and in beginning a new life had re-found Robert, her rock, her anchor. As he'd risen in the news bureaucracy at GBN she'd moved around with him, Miami to London to New York. Then after 9/11 she'd got back into the game, secretly and for all the wrong reasons, even while kidding herself that it was noble. She'd betrayed a basic human trust, luring a man and handing him over to shadowy authorities for torture, and she'd been unable to forgive herself. Katherine had ended up almost helping the Enemy kill her husband, along with millions of others. Katherine had seen deep into herself and been appalled at what she'd seen. She'd been able to help stop the Enemy in the end, and took solace from that. But it had cost her, as it had cost them all.

Was this kidnapping to do with the Enemy? Had Robert found something in Adam's files that had sparked this?

She'd been trained to face kidnapping situations. She concentrated, surveying herself and her surroundings.

She was wearing ill-fitting sweatpants with no drawstring, a sweatshirt, no bra. She'd been undressed, then: her summer dress was gone, and her bra taken, presumably because of the wire it contained. Her flesh crept at the idea that they had stripped her, seen her naked. Her rings were gone – the engagement ring, and the heirloom wedding band that had been in Robert's family for more than a century.

Oddly, her feet were unbound. They might come to regret that. Already, she was pretty sure she'd broken the teeth of at least one of them when they'd grabbed her in the parking garage. Maybe cracked a few ribs on another.

They only seemed to want one thing: to make her think about her grandmother.

The only item in the room, apart from a coarse woollen blanket, was a sheet of paper on which was typed the name of Rose Arden. The rest she only half understood. It was in German, and it bore wartime dates and official stamps. *Geheime Staatspolizei*. Gestapo.

Rose Arden was Katherine's maternal grandmother, and the person she most admired in the world, even though she had never met her.

A tiny Californian of hurricane-force personality and iron convictions, by all accounts, Rose had been studying in Paris when war broke out. She had spied on the Nazi occupiers for as long as she could, made her way to England, and then flown back into Nazi-occupied France in 1943, working clandestinely for the British Special Operations Executive, her US nationality no impediment, her command of French and enterprising fearlessness most welcome.

The SOE was the secret organization that Churchill had ordered to 'set Europe ablaze' through unconventional warfare, resistance and sabotage during the darkest days of the Second World War.

'The question was not whether Rose met SOE's exacting standards,' her recruiting officer, according to Katherine's later research, had once said, 'but rather whether we met hers. I didn't interview her; she interviewed me.'

Family bare-bones accounts had been enough to inspire Katherine to seek a career in intelligence work in her own turn, one that had subsequently almost destroyed her.

But Rose had had it worse. Katherine's grandmother had not returned from the war. All that was known of her ultimate fate ended in a single, chilling word: Dachau.

Katherine had wanted to write her grandmother's biography for many years. With the recent release of SOE personnel files by the British government, industrious searching in US and German archives and several visits to France, she had been able to start work on telling Rose's story in 2005, while Robert worked away on his own obsessive project with Adam's voluminous papers, the task Horace had set him, in part, to help him recover from his shattering experiences in Manhattan.

But she had never seen anything like this document.

The hatch in the wall opened, unexpectedly. A shotgun pointed at her.

'Step back against the wall, opposite the door.'

The voice, its accent unplaceable, came over a good-quality speaker set somewhere up above her.

She stepped back, her bound hands half-raised and ready in case an opportunity arose to attack.

Then the door opened, and a tall man came in, his face masked, powerfully built, his trousers and shirt black. He carried a chair, upon which he quickly sat. He gestured at the sheet of paper on the floor between them.

'Do you understand what is said here?' It was an educated American accent, perhaps from the north-east.

Katherine didn't answer.

'Things will go more easily if we speak to each other.'

She stared blankly back at him. Resist, or engage? She tried to read his eyes. Then she chose.

'I don't speak German.'

'Allow me. Rose Arden. Your grandmother. An interrogation report from Gestapo headquarters in Paris. There are, I regret, some ugly confessions here. Against herself, and against the network she worked with in Paris. Do you know what Steeplejack was?'

Katherine stared at him with revulsion.

'Do you know, Katherine?'

'Why don't you tell me what it was?'

'Come, now. Part of SOE's F Section operations – F for France. But not a regular sabotage network, like the others. Nor yet a regular spying and intelligence network, like those of MI6.'

'Go on.'

'As I say, what we have here is one of her interrogation reports. After her capture, she spoke quite willingly. After a while, at least.' He let that last phrase eat into her mind for a few seconds. 'Do you know what happened to her in the end, at Dachau?'

'No.'

'Would you like to?'

'No.'

She stared defiantly at him, her face a mask. Her heart was hammering, and deep in the depths of her gut she felt fear. But she'd be damned if she'd show it.

He changed tack. His remit was to confuse her, at first. Confusion, and then suffering. Those were Isambard's orders.

'What's Shadowbox, Katherine?'

Christ.

'Never heard of it.'

She shrank slightly from him, couldn't help it. No one knew about Shadowbox.

'Well, you've heard of the Increment, have you not? One of those off-the-books sections of British Intelligence that doesn't exist? Not even really a section, more of a facility. An option? It's a bit like that, isn't it? Only spookier?'

She played for time.

'That was in the newspapers. They said the Increment covers things like SAS troops loaned to MI6 to carry out paramilitary operations that never officially happen. I've no idea if it was true. How would I know? The papers get things wrong, you know. Never let the facts get in the way of a good story.'

'But they got some parts right. There are other off-the-books oddities, too, you know as well as I do. And one is called Shadowbox.'

'I don't know.'

'I think you do. It's been around, in one form or another, at least since the time of Queen Elizabeth I and John Dee, if you follow me.'

'You want me to believe that British Intelligence employ psychics?'

'Not exactly. Not in the *Dial-a-Psychic* way that that sounds to most people. But yes, in a way, they do. You know they do.'

She was good, he thought. Well-prepared. Good masking, good reaction control. Her eyes were cold blue, impenetrable. Except when he'd mentioned her grandmother and Dachau.

'The newspapers also say the Soviets and the Americans did something similar during the Cold War,' Katherine spat. 'Is that what you have in mind? We could save time and you could just bring the *Daily Mail* in and read it to me.'

'Shadowbox doesn't make hard predictions. It can't. But it can do a few things, can't it? One is to forecast the *weather*, so to speak. Not the real weather, but the threat climate. Bad things coming, attacks being planned, imminence of something awful. Sometimes they get hits on individuals, but mostly it's a sense of gathering storm-clouds, lightning on the way. Did you ever work in Shadowbox, specifically?'

'I was at the Foreign Office. The only weird stuff I ever dealt with was the office politics.'

'Katherine, please. They called you recently. What did they want? When they called?'

He didn't miss a trick, did he? She hadn't even told Robert yet about the call. So these people could bug phones. What else? She was learning more about them all the time.

'They asked if you could help in any way to understand a weird message they had received. For purely historical reasons. Whether you might know why anyone would have an interest in bringing your grandmother Rose's name forward now, or even in faking a message about her. Were there any keepsakes you might hold? Had anyone been in touch with you or had access to anything your grandmother might have given you?'

Katherine tried again to play for time. They'd heard the whole conversation. Jesus. Between the lines, in slang and code talk, the caller, a former colleague named Desmond, had said they'd also been picking something up about the end of this month, something in London. Had her captors understood that too?

'Now we know, Katherine, that they can't usually give anything firm, but it can be useful if they mesh their material with hard intelligence, it can bolster a suspicion here, suggest a line of enquiry there . . .'

'And /. . ?'

'What kind of message were they talking about?'

'This is just nonsense. If you want to talk about something, let's talk about you. Who are you? What's with the natty black outfit? Is it a neo-Nazi thing? Aching for another go at it?'

'Katherine, please. There's a kind of Defence of the Realm side to what they do at Shadowbox. They are not quite as nonsensical as you suggest.'

An image stirred in Katherine's memory, of the stories

she had heard about Robert's family, and dreadful events during the war, and what had become of his late Great Aunt Margaret, as everyone knew her.

'Defence of the Realm?'

'The Spanish Armada. The Nazis. How the witches of England can raise what they call a *cone of power* to deter invaders . . .'

'Old wives' tales.'

'Really? What do you really make of it, though? You who know so much about such things. Or are you being brave and loyal? Ah, but I forget. You, too, have problems with betrayal, don't you? With letting people down, with lying to them, with using them for your own ends . . . Your grandmother did too, you know.'

She let it get to her, though she knew she shouldn't. She felt her eyes start to well up, and opted for anger and attack to disguise it.

'Fuck you. What are you? Let's hear it. The fourth Reich?'

'We serve a very great man named Isambard. And you are required to suffer for him. Now step back against the wall, please.'

The hatch in the wall opened, and the shotgun pointed directly at her again. She did as she was asked, and when she was at the furthest point from the door, it opened to let her questioner out. Katherine paid close attention. There was no opportunity for her, no chance to break out.

Katherine was sure they were watching her response now that she was alone, so she took care to exhibit no emotion whatsoever. She ignored the sheet of paper on the floor and, after a suitable pause, slowly moved to another wall.

So was that it. Rose, and Shadowbox. They wanted to know what Shadowbox was picking up about an upcoming threat. They wanted to know what they made of a mysterious message Shadowbox had received, ostensibly from her own long-dead grandmother. Who was Isambard? Why suffer for him? Was he a servant of the Enemy?

It made no sense.

A few evenings earlier, she and Robert had stood on the roof deck of the apartment where they had begun a new life together, in their converted old coffee and cotton warehouse in Brooklyn, and watched a spectacular fireworks display, launched from a barge at the foot of the Statue of Liberty, that was perhaps a rehearsal for the Fourth of July. At the end, after the final climactic explosions, all the ships and ferries off the tip of Manhattan had sounded their horns. It had been a spellbinding moment, and they had held one another as they had in their early days together. She had felt only love for him.

She allowed herself to think of Robert now, and of that evening. Just for a moment, to draw strength from the memory of his arms around her. She tried, tentatively, to reach out towards him, but ran into a mental wall. That was interesting. Wherever they were holding her was blocked off, psychically shielded. Her captors were getting more frightening by the minute.

During Robert's work on Adam's papers, he had begun to transform himself. It had been maddening, but Kat had kept faith. She'd known – not quite knowing how, but with intense conviction – that he would emerge a better, fuller man on the other side of the experience he was going through. In her mind's eye she had seen him in a kind of chrysalis state, halfway between one person and another. She had known, too, that she wanted to be there when he came through it. What she had been less sure of was whether she could bear the period in between, not knowing how long it would last.

His behaviour had been, by stages, compulsive, obsessive, almost autistic in its self-absorption, even when focused on the good of others. Not only had he been going through Adam's papers and books for eight hours a day, but he'd also begun putting himself through hard physical training – running, yoga, martial arts. And then he'd started volunteering at a Brooklyn hospital, where – to his own initial surprise – with the touch of his hands he'd been able to reduce patients' pain after surgery, and shorten their recovery times. It was the one aspect of his gift that had returned to him with any reliability after the climactic fight in Manhattan in 2004. And during all this time, he had also been reaching out to his own people in eastern England, trying to trace some of the bearers of the secret knowledge held by the estranged side of his family. Most had summarily shut him out. Only his cousin Jack Reckliss had shown any inclination to meet him, though he had delayed and stalled whenever Robert tried to suggest a firm date.

Horace had tried to help them both during the months of counselling he had given Robert, before inexplicably breaking off the relationship.

Horace had come into Katherine's life in March 1981, when an evening of undergraduate horseplay with an occult flavour, involving her, Robert and Adam, had gone badly awry, unspoken jealousies and desires mingling with buried psychic gifts in each of them. A fire had started in Adam's college room that had almost killed him and Katherine before Robert had raised the alarm and dragged them out. She'd spent several days in hospital, and upon her release Adam had introduced her to Horace as someone who could mentor her, as he had Adam. She'd drifted away from Horace at different times in her life, made mistakes, returned to his orbit, wished she'd stayed closer. A stocky octogenarian who looked to be in his fifties, mild and shy in his manner until angered, he was the person, after Robert, whom she would most trust with her life.

For months on end, Robert's behaviour had almost driven her mad. Today she felt he had been preparing, consciously or not, to face the ordeal that was now upon them.

She tried to keep track of time. By her reckoning, two hours passed before the sounds began. Deafening and nauseating, pumped into her room, echoing off the concrete. The sounds of pigs being led to slaughter. Of fingernails dragged down a blackboard. Of a scratchy recording of a young woman's voice, an American, saying over and over: 'I, Rose Arden, confess to the crime of murder. I have sacrificed others so that I might live. I am a war criminal . . .'

Berlin

1934

In October 1934, just weeks after his arrival in Berlin, Peter received a telegram at his lodgings. Congratulating him on his choice of academic subject – he had chosen to specialize in the study of the runic alphabet, or *futhark*, and its links to magical belief systems – the telegram offered him a special educational stipend and invited him to report to a certain address on Prinz-Albrecht Strasse the following week.

Peter already knew the address. It was the most feared building in the country: the headquarters of the SS. The appointment was in the *Persönlicher Stab Reichsführer-SS* – the personal staff office of SS chief Heinrich Himmler.

Peter presented himself at the required time and was ushered to the waiting area outside the office of one *Sturmbannführer* Schneider, or Major Taylor, as Peter called him inwardly, trying to calm his nerves while waiting to be received.

Barely a month after the Nazi declaration of a thousand-year Reich at Nuremberg, Peter's abiding impression of the SS headquarters was one of prim bureaucratic efficiency, leavened with an almost maniacal energy directed into appearances, punctuality and detail. Amid the red, white and black swastika flags and armbands, the beautifully tailored black uniforms, the riding boots and leather gloves, the precise, energetic clacking of hundreds of typewriters and the constant ringing of telephones, suppressed murmurs of conversation and sudden barks of *Heil Hitler* from distant desks, Peter thought everyone he saw was living in a state of narcotic, heightened excitement, heavily ritualized in its objects and settings, that allowed nothing to be mundane, everything to have meaning and purpose, the individual to have a role far greater than himself, in return for a willing sacrifice of the will. It was a sexualized, bureaucratized cult, built on fear and hatred, underpinned by brutal violence, and it was a drug.

'So, you're studying the runes of our great ancestors, I see?'

Schneider briskly reviewed a batch of tightly typed, stamped memos and slim brown document folders on his desk, looking up just for a moment as he read, to gauge Peter's surprise at the thoroughness of their information on him. 'Born 1915 in Paris, adopted in 1924 by Lord Hale-Devereaux of Poldhu after mother Hélène died of an undiagnosed illness of the heart, a reader of Houston Chamberlain and Guido von List . . . your adoptive father is a noted enemy of our Reich, I see, whereas you . . . seem more at ease with us?'

What else did they have in there about him, he wondered. Clearly they had gone through his lodgings, perused his bookshelf. Did they know who his real father was, what he was?

'*Jawohl, Herr Sturmbannführer.*'

Best to say as little as possible.

'We, too, take great pride in our history,' Schneider went on, reaching for a framed photograph and passing it to Peter to examine. It showed an array of symbolic shapes, including a swastika and the sharp lightning runes that made up the collar flashes of the SS, carved into a weathered rock face. 'Iceland, many thousands of years old. The last golden age of our people.'

Peter said nothing, aware already that people around Himmler were twisting and falsifying science in all manner of disciplines in an effort to bolster the Nazi view of history and race. It had become dangerous to voice opposition to them, even in the confines of the university. This was not his concern.

'So, let us come to the point. You are perhaps wondering, Herr Hale-Devereaux, why you were asked to come here today?'

'I would be grateful if you could tell me, yes.'

'We have people who have taken an interest in you.' A pause, an icy stare, enjoying the knowledge that such words, uttered in slightly different circumstances, could constitute a death sentence when spoken in this place. 'Not anything to worry about, I am sure, but it is a sad fact that we have to follow these things up, tie up loose ends, and make sure nothing is left unclear. I am sure you understand.'

Peter cleared his throat, frowning slightly, preferring not to say anything.

'You are an adopted Englishman, raised in the culture, thoroughly at home in it, though I would venture to say, not entirely accepted by it, in some significant way? They are like us in many ways, in many ways our natural allies, yet always with a stubbornness, a pig-headedness, a snobbish exclusivity . . . Does this ring a bell, as I believe they say?'

Peter nodded.

'Yet here we find you in Berlin, at a time when many of your compatriots – your adoptive compatriots – turn up their noses at us. In search of something deeper, perhaps, in your identity, in search of your roots, could we say?'

'My mother . . .'

'We know what was said about your mother. The vile insults, the whispered lies, the stigma. That must have been awful for you, no matter how much she tried to shield you from it.'

Peter found himself staring into the past, looking again at the strands of disparate facts that he could never weave into a coherent story.

'I don't believe she was raped. She never said she was. Only others said that. My mother only ever spoke of tragedy, of tragic events.'

'And your father?'

'She said he was a remarkable man who had died before she really knew him. But I was never to speak of him.'

'Why not?'

'I think because he walked out on her. Because, clearly, he was a coward, or a philanderer, however much she loved him. From my looks as I grew, from the timing of my birth, I was clearly of Germanic stock. I think in some ways she preferred the rape story because, after the war, it was better than having it thought that she had consented.'

'Do you know what really happened?'

'Do you?'

Schneider stared at Peter for a moment, as though taken aback by the impertinence of the question. He squared the papers on his desk. 'Alas, no. Even we, I confess, cannot find out everything.' A slight smile indicated that in actual fact, they could, but in this case, they were holding something back. 'We simply note for now that, as the son of a German national, clearly of a good, pure line, the National Socialist state is happy to offer you special support with your studies. A quite generous stipendium, but also access to certain of our experts here, attached to the personal staff of *Reichsführer SS* Himmler himself.'

'Experts?'

'In certain of the traditions you have begun to study. Runic lore, and associated matters. Esoteric matters. You will be attached to this office. You are German, and you should take this chance to draw closer to your true identity. Shall we say commencing Monday? Please report here at nine a.m.'

'And if I decline?'

Schneider let a few moments pass before replying.

'We might be able to find out who your father is, Herr Hale-Devereaux. Work with us, and it may be possible to arrange a meeting. He is most certainly not dead, whatever your mother may have told you.'

Nationality papers followed within weeks. There was a special arrangement, it was put to him, whereby he could be issued a secret German passport, without affecting his existing status as an Englishman. Just in case he should ever need it. His people looked after their own, and really, despite all the current rhetoric, such brother nations shouldn't even really need separate passports, they were all citizens of a single race . . .

From the fledgling group of academics and mystics around Himmler that would later become the many-tentacled *Ahnenerbe*, the Ancestral Heritage office also known as the Occult Bureau, Peter within months found himself being asked, in order to ease the payment of his stipendium, to nominally join the *Schutzstaffel*. Purely a bureaucratic thing, Schneider said, God knows it's enough to drive us all insane, these unbending fools can't see beyond the inkpots on their desks. Even nominal entrants, of course, had to undergo a little basic training, little more than a summer camp, a discussion group with hiking and PT . . .

And then he was sent to study at the fledgling inner SS school at Wewelsburg, in the mountains of Westphalia.

~

'Peter Hale-Devereaux,' Isambard said with a cold smile. 'Welcome to Wewelsburg.' He rose slowly from his desk as Peter stood in the doorway awaiting an invitation to enter. 'Or should I call you Pierre?'

A tall, well-built man with white hair, stark green eyes and an ageless demeanour, Isambard looked like a precision watchmaker, or perhaps a dentist to the very wealthy. A jeweller's loupe hung on a cord around his neck, and in his left hand he held a small bronze lozenge, which he turned over and over in his fingers. He wore the black SS uniform, without the jacket, which was hanging on the back of his desk chair.

Isambard was, still, as Peter saw him in his childhood memory: striking, compelling even, but with a wintery, haunted depth to his eyes, a cold indifference in his manner. Should Peter say he remembered meeting him? Caught between fear and the desire to understand, between guilt and lust for knowledge, Peter decided to say nothing.

Isambard walked towards Peter, inspecting him as he progressed, a barely contained vigour in his movements. The older man wanted to be moving; his surroundings – all surroundings – were a constraint upon him.

Peter, still framed in the doorway, clicked his heels, lowering his head momentarily, and stammered a respectful greeting.

Isambard came and stood before him, staring searchingly into his eyes, a wrinkle of amusement lightening his expression. Then the older man raised his right arm at the elbow, almost sardonically, palm open and facing forward.

'Heil Hitler,' he said dryly, undemonstratively. His eyes

never left Peter's. A quizzical note entered his demeanour as Peter hesitated, unwilling to respond in kind, unsure of what to do.

'Ah. Forgive me. You do not fully . . . commune with our work, as yet. Unfamiliarity, I expect, or the effects of enemy propaganda. You have been told we are monsters.'

'I bear no preconceptions . . .' Peter began, fumbling still for a form of address. He had been given no rank or title to use in talking to the man. Just the single name.

'Good. I am not doctrinaire. I am interested only in what works. Come in.'

Isambard turned on his heel and marched back to his desk, the bronze artefact still held in his hand. Once back at his seat, he gestured for Peter to sit opposite him, and opened a heavy metal cigarette case on his desk, next to a bank of four telephones.

'Do you partake of this foul habit? No? Better.'

He lit one for himself, then reached into a desk drawer and drew out a file, which he placed heavily on his blotter. He had spoken in neutral, colourless English so far, but now he switched to German, which he spoke with a faint French accent.

'So. I am to instruct you . . . By the way, out of interest . . . If I told you most of these pages were empty, but we stack the files with blank sheets in order to give people in your chair the impression we know everything about them, would you believe me?'

He riffled the pages. Peter imagined that in fact they were all closely typed, a sea of dense record-keeping and assessment of his every move since accepting the invitation to SS headquarters.

'Some of the idiots we must work with, even in this organization, measure their worth and others' purely in such things. Height of stacked paper. Number of reports generated. Kilometres of typewriter ribbon exhausted.' He smiled. 'I imagine you are not one of those . . . bureaucrats.'

'No, sir.'

'Good. I feel, reviewing your reports, that we perhaps are getting to know more about you than even you do. You have done well, so far, in your studies. You have made a good decision, I feel. We have been observing carefully.'

'Thank you.'

'You will want to know a little of what I am working on here.'

Peter tried to maintain a correct, formal manner. He had been told it was a high privilege to be asked to work with Isambard himself. And yet . . .

Isambard reached into a different drawer, and took out a black, leather-bound case. Opening it, he revealed an array of thin metal instruments. He screwed the loupe into one eye and held up the bronze lozenge for inspection.

'A simple device, one would say.' Holding each end between his fingers tips, he pulled it apart to reveal coloured wiring and tiny electrical components. In mid-conversation, he switched to flawless Parisian French, Peter noted. He didn't sound like a German in any language.

'Difficult to . . . calibrate.'

Isambard put down one part of the device, a kind of cowling, and selected a long, slender screwdriver. He carefully applied it to part of the interior working of the instrument, probing it with controlled precision. Peter now saw, as the older man turned the mechanism, that it also had a kind of stubby, retractable needle. 'The dosage needs to be . . . commensurate.'

'May I ask, sir, what that is?'

Isambard did not answer, but continued to adjust settings inside the device. When one of his telephones rang, he put down the screwdriver in mild irritation and answered briefly, giving only a number. In response to a few scratchy, indistinguishable words on the other end of the phone, he grunted, then asked: 'And units seven and eight?' He raised an eyebrow in response, then hung up.

Isambard stubbed out his cigarette, which he had allowed to burn down almost to the end in his ashtray.

He eyed Peter again. 'This is a prototype of a device I am working on, a weapon called the *geheime Feuer*. The Secret Fire. We still lack certain information that would enable us to perfect it . . . Through the door behind me, and in all our work here, we are exploring the nature of human resistance. We are also studying the nature of nature, if you will forgive the redundancy. The nature of what is real, in terms of the human brain, and in terms of our relations with the earth, with our planet. We are exploring what forces may be orchestrated, and how, to concerted effect. We are exploring the limits of the human being.' He grunted in annoyance. 'Some specimens are more *resilient* than others. Tell me, have you ever had a dog?'

Peter nodded.

'You have? Good. Now, what, would you say, is the prime thing that a dog needs to know, if he is to live happily with his master?'

Peter's mind wandered.

'Where to eat, where to sleep?'

'No.'

'I'm sorry.'

'Don't apologize, learn. It is quite clear: the dog needs to know who his master is. He needs to feel the sensation, at an early stage, of surrendering to a superior being, one that can make him feel weak. That is how a dog becomes happy – he learns he is not the master. In the wild, too, hierarchy must be established. The strongest wolf, shall we say, makes the others submit. It makes the others feel that shame of weakness, perhaps only once, but as often as necessary. Then they all know their place.'

'Until the strongest wolf grows weak. Then the process begins again.'

'Quite. Nature is red in tooth and claw. The strongest wolf is eventually overthrown, perhaps banished. Left to die, in effect. But we can improve on this. One of the things that interests us here – that interests me, in particular – is the change in the brain activity, and in the psyche, when this relationship is established. The sensation of being bested, of inadequacy. A small experiment?'

He stood, indicating that Peter should do so too. Isambard took the two parts of the instrument he had been adjusting, and slotted them back together. From a drawer, he then took a canvas armband with a pocket sewn into it, into which he placed the device.

'Your arm, please. Just a small test . . .'

Peter removed his jacket and rolled up his shirt sleeve. Isambard tied the band around Peter's upper arm, then stepped back.

He spoke almost casually.

'Curse your mother's name.'

Peter's eyes met Isambard's. He saw a neutral, disinterested gaze. Yet there was force behind them that he did not want to test.

'I'm sorry?'

'You heard me.'

'I am not sure, perhaps, if I am a suitable subject . . .'

Isambard barked an order. 'Curse your mother's name.'

Anger flared behind Peter's eyes.

'I will not! No!'

Isambard raised a hand, as though performing again his

perfunctory Hitler salute. But then he pointed, casually, at the device strapped to Peter's arm.

The effect was stunning. Peter felt the needle press his flesh, not even piercing the skin, and he went straight down on one knee, his head lowered, tears in his eyes. A conviction, an intense inner sensation of humiliation, filled him with shame. It was as though he were a schoolboy again, and he had been chased in the street, the chants of *filthy Kraut* and *sale Bosch* ringing in his ears, his puny fists not strong enough to defend himself against the mob of taunting children. He felt unmanned. A bullied boy, weak and vulnerable. Helpless.

Isambard stepped forward, a smile playing on his lips.

'Come, come, let me help you up, these devices . . .'

He felt Isambard's hands heaving him up and into his chair.

'Damn it, Peter, you must forgive me. So hard to calibrate. A brandy, perhaps. Yes, a brandy.'

Slumped in the chair, Peter lost consciousness.

~

When he came to, Peter was in a different location, stretched out on a military camp bed in a small wooden room which also contained a table, two chairs and a single cupboard. His first sensation was one of utter dread.

He climbed groggily to his feet and lurched to the door, pulling it open. He felt frozen to the core, though the room was uncomfortably warm.

Peter was in a long hut of corrugated metal and wood, filled from one end to the other with metal cages. The sound was deafening. The cages were occupied by howling animals, most of them monkeys, though he also heard the plaintive, fearful baying of dogs – or were they wolves?

Stacked one on top of another, the cages reached up into the rafters, perhaps 400 in all, on either side of a central walkway. Wooden stairs led up to gantries used for feeding the animals in the higher cages. The stench of excrement was overpowering.

He stepped outside the room, fear corroding his ability to think. There were perhaps twenty rooms like his own at one end of the hut. At the other end, he saw a sealed-off area, marked with its own sign: Section Four. *Eintritt Verboten.*

Isambard appeared at his shoulder, and Peter felt himself cringe. He fought the sensation, though.

'This is a key part of this first stage of the Wewelsburg complex,' Isambard said. 'It is the laboratory I told you about earlier. We spoke earlier in my office in Section Four, at the far end.'

His tone was dry, almost dead. Isambard's English was so neutral in its vowel sounds that he could not be placed in any niche of the social grid Peter and all native Englishmen carried in their psyches, nor yet could he be categorized as a foreigner. The effect was profoundly unsettling. Peter felt completely unmoored around the man.

'Now, describe your feelings.'

Part of Peter wanted to flee more intensely than he had ever wanted anything. His mind fled back to the cold, dark shaft in Cornwall, the circle of light at the top just a distant white sun, the searing pain of hanging on to the rusty metal rung and praying for rescue. Then he slid further back again, to the street taunts and fist fights of his earliest Parisian years. And yet ... This man had knowledge, and Peter wanted to find the strength to acquire it.

'What did you say that device was again, sir?'

'One that hundreds of millions may one day know.'

'What does it do?'

'It connects the controlled will of the operator with that of the subject and his environment. It's all a question of the calibration. Set lower, it triggers a submissive response in the subject. Set far higher, it may one day be able to tear matter itself apart. Now, your sensations?'

'I feel . . .'

Isambard punched him on the chest, and Peter felt himself shrink in physical humiliation. He couldn't help himself.

'Obey me in all things,' Isambard said. 'You will find it leads to knowledge, and to security. From there, you will acquire happiness.'

Peter hesitated. His entire body was trembling with fear. Yet the knowledge he sought was here. He wanted to know everything, and this man could tell him.

'Yes,' he said, raising his head and meeting Isambard's ice-green eyes. 'I accept.'

A drawn-out cry of agonizing pain, different in tone to all the others, echoed the length of the hut, from somewhere within Section Four.

'That was a human being,' Peter whispered. 'That was a man.'

'Not a man,' Isambard said. 'A sub-human. You are not required to worry about such matters for now. Put it from your mind.'

'But . . .'

Isambard gently slapped Peter's face, twice.

'You are young. Put it from your mind. We will not study this. We will study the runes, the ley-lines and geomancy. We will study the force known as *vril*. You will focus on this. Now go back to your room.'

'I . . .'

'Go.'

Peter did not – would not – defy him. Not yet.

London

26 June 2007

Robert would take the painkillers if he absolutely had to. But he needed a clear mind. He chose instead to treat his wounds himself, if he could. After carefully putting away the items from Adam's file, he stretched out on the bed and placed his hands over his chest, palms down. After a moment, a bubble of heat formed between his palms and his wounds, and he let the intensity slowly build.

He didn't know where it came from. He'd read widely and found references to similar phenomena in *qi gong* and other eastern practices, in Mediterranean traditions of healers with 'hot hands', even in his own family's East Anglian lore, where the life force was known as *spirament*, though others called it *qi, ruach* or *prana*. He only cared that it worked.

Robert closed his eyes and moved his hands over his chest, tracing the evil form cut into his body, filling it with heat. Then he moved to his head, his stomach, the different sites where he'd taken blows while trying to fight off his attackers. A deep, pulsing throb filled his wounds.

The jagged, shrill grating of the electric guitar came to him again, intruding, forcing its way into his consciousness. Words about running up, sliding down, going round. Then a phrase, a new one: *This is a song Charles Manson stole from the Beatles. We're stealing it back . . .*

What was it that he couldn't see yet?

Helter Skelter. It was the legendary Beatles White Album song – distorted guitar, Ringo Starr's blistered hands on the drums – that Charles Manson had defiled with his murderous *Family* in 1969. The Sharon Tate killings. Then at some point in the 1980s Robert had seen a U2 concert movie, *Rattle and Hum*, with God-struck Paul Hewson reclaiming the song from hell with those words. *This is a song Charles Manson stole from the Beatles. We're stealing it back.*

Robert lowered his hands again, filling his scars with intense heat. It was serving to dull the pain, and he let his mind roam. He thought of Katherine.

There was an aspect of Horace's advice he had always struggled with, and he wrestled with it now, too – that to prevail, it was necessary to fight without anger. Robert couldn't see it, especially right now. If he could get hold of whoever had taken Katherine, he'd kill them.

She was everything to him. Without her, he would have no life worth living. No life at all, even. Through betrayal, through lies white and black, through loss and hurt, estrangement and rediscovery, over nearly a quarter of a century, from their first kiss in college to their last before he'd headed out to Adam's apartment, she had been his guardian, his sidekick, his blue-eyed, black-haired, tough-as-nails guiding angel.

They protected each other, and she needed him now. He had to find her. Had he done the wrong thing in following Horace's advice to come to London?

There was a knock at the door.

Breathing in deeply, then exhaling till his lungs seemed to creak, expelling as much pain and toxicity as he could, Robert lay still and gathered himself for a moment. Then he got up carefully, grabbing a shirt from his bag, and moved to the door.

'Who's there?'

'Open up, Robert.'

Horace?

'What the hell are you doing here?'

'Open the door. We don't have much time.'

Robert ripped the door open.

'You're supposed to be looking for Katherine.'

Horace pushed his way in.

'I am.'

'She's here? In London?'

'Robert, it is a pleasure to see you too,' Horace intoned. He was wearing a very dark blue business suit and a sober dark red, almost crimson tie. He shook hands, but there was no warmth in the gesture, and the frost in Horace's eyes did not melt. 'I'm so sorry about the formality, but I've been settling some business here involving Hencott subsidiaries around the world. One wears the costume one must.'

Horace's vigour was extraordinary for a man of his age. White hair cropped close around the bald dome of his head, the skin of his face and neck lined with age but firm and supple, he was strongly built, with a judoka's air of balance, a transparent yet piercing gaze, and the demeanour of a kindly college professor, a mask he could drop in an instant when crossed.

Horace, among other responsibilities, had been involved for some time in running down the family mining concern, and liquidating – or hiding – its assets. 'Now shut up and listen. Did you get the Adam material from the Club of St George?'

'Yes.'

'What do you make of it?'

'What the hell is going on?'

There had been too much left unsaid between the old

78

man and himself. But Robert had to overcome it. However angry he was with his mentor, Robert needed him.

'Show me the documents you got from the Club, please.'

Robert took them from the table.

'These are . . .'

'An assemblage of items whose pattern you have been unable to fathom, yes. That's understandable.'

Horace opened the grey box file and removed the items, one by one. He held the photograph of Harry Hale-Devereaux in his hand and gazed at it for a long time. Robert pointed to the scratched-out face.

'Do you know who that is next to Mr Hale?'

'A man I sent to hell.' He held Robert's eye for a moment. 'In Paris. The photograph was taken in Paris.'

'Who was he?'

'One thing at a time. What else?'

Horace inspected the items one by one, sinking deep into his own thoughts, looking up at Robert once or twice in what might have been amusement or, implausibly, fear.

Eventually he spoke.

'I'll wait for you outside while you dress.'

Robert joined him in the corridor a few moments later, and they walked the hotel's long corridors towards the elevator.

'Shall we have coffee? Tea?'

'Are you insane? No. There's no time.'

'You will have been suffering some pain,' Horace said, his eyes crinkling with sympathy.

'I have. I thought you were in New York when I talked to you.'

'Never assume. Any recompense for your pain?'

'Not much, I have to say. Little enhanced wisdom or insight, scant up-tick in holiness or sanctity, in fact quite the opposite. I'm ready to tear someone's head off. Possibly yours.'

The elevator came, and they rode down to the lobby. Robert stared at the mentor and guide he had come more and more to see as a disappointment. Horace looked, if it were possible, slightly younger than the man he remembered. More vigorous, but also harder. A tough old bird, not one to overdo the sentimental aspects of things.

'It is not always my role to be available to you. It is sometimes my role not to be. Tell me one thing. Of your gift, what has remained? Is there anything at all? Apart from the capacity to piss me off?'

Robert couldn't help but be shocked. He didn't think he'd ever heard Horace curse, even mildly, before.

'Horace, you're not the man I knew.'

'Speaking strictly, I am not the man you needed in the past. That man is dead, as are your past needs. For a while, too, you needed me to be absent.'

'And what are you now?'

'I am someone who may be useful to you again. Once more, what has remained of your gift?'

Robert hesitated.

'The heat in the hands. Apart from that, almost nothing. I occasionally experience . . .'

'What?'

'The intense sense that people are trying to reach me. Dreams. A feeling of presence. Nothing else. Just that.'

Horace gazed at the elevator's floor counter for several seconds as it counted down. Three . . . two . . . one.

'Foster it,' he said eventually. 'Control it. It is meaningful, though dangerous.'

They reached the ground floor.

*

Walking through the lobby, they headed out into the overcast London morning. Horace took his elbow and guided him east, towards Fleet Street.

'We are dealing with one event in two times,' the old man said, as they walked vigorously to Kingsway and crossed the street. 'It is an action split between different times. And the second time is coming, the one that runs backwards to 1944 and completes the action, all our actions, the one that completes the handshake between past and future.'

'What do you mean?' Robert asked in frustration.

'A cycle is completing, Robert. One that we are all part of. A great arc of time is closing, and we are all being called to action.'

'What kind of cycle?'

'There are things I cannot see yet. But you must look to your past, Robert. As I must to mine. Katherine too. You both must look to your families.'

Robert shivered, despite himself. 'What's happening? Where is Katherine?'

'I don't know yet. She is alive, she is so far unharmed, this much I have been able to see. But she is behind a barrier of some kind, a powerful one.'

'Who has her? How do we get her?'

'The people holding her possess the fatal flaw of considering themselves better at their work than they truly are. They are no fools. But this will give her an opening, an unintentional one, at the right moment.'

'Is she here?'

'She may be. She may be still in America. They don't want her here, unless they can turn her to their view of things. Then she would be a very powerful ally, of course. As would you, or I. But she won't turn.'

'What are they doing to her, Horace?'

'Trying to persuade her.'

'Who?'

'The Enemy. They want revenge.'

Horace stopped opposite the east wing of Bush House and fixed Robert with a piercing stare.

'Put her out of your mind for just a moment. You need to understand. You will have heard of Heinrich Himmler, head of Hitler's SS.'

'Of course. But . . .'

'Various special units worked for him. In industry, in weapons design, in other areas. Sealed-off areas of the Nazi state, answerable only to him, hidden away behind multiple rings of security. The longer the war went on, the greater his power.'

'Go on.'

'When the D-Day landings took place in early June 1944, it is one of the most closely guarded secrets of the war that a member of one of Himmler's special units tried to turn the tide of the war with a single action.'

'What? One of the Hitler assassination attempts? Weren't there dozens?'

'There were, but no. This individual tried to detonate a weapon of mass destruction in London. Right here, actually, on Aldwych, just a few yards from where we are standing. His name was . . .'

Robert guessed. 'Isambard. Adam described him as . . .'

'The worst. The most powerful of his kind. Yes.'

Horace pointed into the middle of Aldwych.

'There is still a slight depression in the road, you can see, where it happened.' Then he gestured up at the facade of Bush House. 'You can still see the shrapnel marks, too, actually.'

'But you're saying it went off?'

'Partly.'

'How was it delivered?'

'In the nosecone of a V-1. A flying bomb. A doodlebug, as they were also known.'

'But you said a weapon of mass destruction. They didn't have the atom bomb. They weren't even close. Do you mean nerve gas, or something like that? A biological weapon?'

'The SS were working on all kinds of weapons. Some have passed into popular mythology, been misunderstood, joked about. Some never got off the ground. Their efforts at novel flying machines, for example, were unstable and kept crashing, like our own after the war. Much nonsense has been written about this. Flying saucers and the like. But at the core, there was something, and it was out of this world. *Das geheime Feuer*, it was called.'.

'What?'

'The Secret Fire. It was – it is – a component of what the alchemists call the Great Work. It is described, always, in paradoxical terms. The water which does not wet the hands. The fire which burns without flames. It is sometimes called the universal solvent, because it can dissolve all matter. It can be used to transmute – or to destroy. In the hands of one who knows how to use it, it can turn lead into gold, but also gold into lead, and into worse things.'

'What is it?'

'From your own experience in Manhattan, you know that we all bear within us a form of power. We are all endowed with, if I may use the phrase, a form of lightning trapped in a bottle, or in a body. Call it *qi*, life force, *prana* . . . Whether we are aware of it or not, it is there, coiled within us. It is our own Secret Fire. The weapon developed by the Nazis was an instrument that served as an interface, and an amplifier, for this power. It allowed the operator – only a very particular kind of operator – to marry up his own inner state, his own lightning, if you will, with that of the earth itself, with the immense power that runs along the lines people call dragon lines, or ley lines. This is the earth's Secret Fire. It too, has other names. The Celts call it *druis lanach* – druid's lightning. Certain Nazis around Himmler called it *vril*, both in its earth-bound and human forms. And here's the Nazi twist: it can be poisoned. Both in individuals and in the earth. It can be yoked to an evil purpose.'

'What could it do?'

'Wrong question, in a sense. Wrong tense. The question is what *can* it do? The *geheime Feuer* weapon is a kind of time-bomb.'

'With a clock that's been ticking for sixty-three years?'

'Walk with me.'

They crossed the street at the east end of Aldwych, onto an island in the stream of traffic, and entered the church of St Clement Danes.

Horace led Robert to a wooden pew near the altar, and they sat. Above them rose a magnificent vaulted ceiling of white and gold. Ranged around the church, display cases protected elegantly lettered books of remembrance listing the names of all Royal Air Force men and women killed on active service. Horace prayed for a few moments, Robert itching with impatience at his side.

'What happened in 1944?' Robert eventually barked.

'It went off,' Horace whispered. 'Isambard actually succeeded, to a degree. But it was contained. Frozen in time. In a sense, it is still exploding now, right around us, but in a different time. I don't know exactly how it was contained, even though I was partly, unwittingly, involved in it. But if we are going to help Katherine, we have to find out. Because the effect is running out.'

'It's unravelling?'

A name flashed across Robert's mind. *Margaret.*

'Very fast. And when it unwinds completely . . .'

'It explodes. Now, in the present day.'

'The effect in the present day will be as if an unimaginably powerful bomb went off. It will destroy London and southeast England. Everything built in the affected area since 30 June 1944 – *everyone born in the affected area since 30 June 1944, and all their descendants* – will cease to exist, right up to the present. *You* cease to exist. *Katherine.* Genocide, right down the generations. But there's more.'

Robert stared at Horace in disbelief. 'What more could there be?'

'In actual fact, it will explode in 1944. It will halt D-Day in its tracks, kill all the major Allied leaders and commanders in England. The Normandy invasion grinds to a halt. Southeast England is left a smoking ruin, the rest a starving, defeated nation. The Nazis are able to turn their attention to the Eastern Front, in 1944. Perhaps they prevail, perhaps a bloody stalemate is reached. The Nazis survive. Perhaps they even prosper. America withdraws into itself, outgunned, not yet able to build the atom bomb, and Europe is left a totalitarian hell.'

'A time-bomb.'

'Now you see. The *geheime Feuer* device is a variation on the weapon we saw in Manhattan. Only more susceptible to . . . temporal disruption.'

'And it goes off on 30 June? Can it be stopped?'

'We have four days. I must stay in London to find out more about the materials Adam left. You must go to the Fens to find out more about your family's past. I can't see far into this, but the answer lies there. There's a man you should talk to, today if you can, an old friend of Harry's named Romanek.'

'Horace,' Robert insisted, anger in his voice. 'Can this unravelling be stopped?'

'I don't know.'

'You're forgetting about Katherine.'

'I'm not. The quickest way to help her is to defeat those who want this to happen. Defeat Isambard.'

Wewelsburg

1936

In the second year of his star pupil's instruction, directly before sending Peter back to England, Isambard began to focus on London's key artery of power. It was a ley line, the strongest of several in the British capital, linking places of geomantic power, often holy wells or sacred mounds, on which churches had been built in later years – Christian shrines atop places of pagan worship.

The course of this artery, even in the modern age, was marked by churches built along its course, or just to either side of it, even though they were often dwarfed or obscured now by taller buildings around them.

Isambard also taught that folk knowledge and old secrets, often garbled and no longer understood, could still be found, by those who knew how to look, in such apparently innocent repositories as fairy tales and children's songs. And so he had shown Peter how the song 'Oranges and Lemons', its true meaning long forgotten, encoded for posterity the course of the line of power, when correctly understood.

Peter, like many English-raised people, had gleefully played a version of the sinister game when young, chanting the names of London churches while forming an arch with another child, hands raised above heads, as the rest of the children passed under the arch in a circle, till the final lines came:

> Here comes a candle to light you to bed
> Here comes a chopper to chop off your head

Chip, chop, chip, chop, the
Last
Man's
Dead

Chopping down with their arms on each of the closing syllables, trapping and releasing a child each time, until the last one – on *Dead* – was claimed by the hangman, and had to leave the game.

Beyond the short version of the song used in the party game, Isambard taught that there was also a longer, older version, listing more churches, that contained the secret, hiding it in plain sight through the ages, as long as the right churches were understood, which were at times not the traditional ones.

Gay go up and gay go down, to ring the bells of London Town.
Oranges and lemons, say the bells of St Clement's
Bullseyes and targets, say the bells of St Margaret's
Brickbats and tiles, say the bells of St Giles
Ha'pence and farthin's, say the bells of St Martin's
Pancakes and fritters, say the bells of St Peter's
Two sticks and an apple, say the bells of Whitechapel
Maids in white aprons, say the bells of St Katherine's
Pokers and tongs, say the bells of St John's
Kettles and pans, say the bells of St Anne's
Old father baldpate, say the slow bells of Aldgate
You owe me ten shillin's, say the bells of St Helen's
When will you pay me, say the bells of Old Bailey
When I grow rich, say the bells of Fleetditch
Pray when will that be, say the bells of Stepney
I do not know, says the great bell of Bow

'*Gay go up and gay go down, to ring the bells of London Town.* This is simply the preamble, and might be held to have no secret meaning,' Isambard said. 'Except that *ringing the bell* of a sacred location is an expression we use to signify tapping into its power.'

He pointed to a map of London on the wooden table between them. 'Now let's study how to ring the bells of London in our own way, and for our own purposes.'

Peter leaned forward.

'The first key is to note the inclusion of the phrase *St Giles*. This is a reference to St Giles's Greek, a term for thieves' cant or slang. It tells us that a special language is being used in this song, one where the ostensible term does not necessarily represent the real meaning. It is like reading the words and illustrations of an alchemical book. Having noticed the presence of the phrase, we can discard it. It does not refer to any of the St Giles churches in London, it is merely a marker. For the uninstructed, of course, it serves simply to confuse the pattern. *Oranges and lemons, say the bells of St Clement's.* This is commonly held to refer to a St Clement's church in Eastcheap, near wharves where fruit was loaded from the ships in past times. But in our reading, its reference is to the church of St Clement Danes, a central point on London's artery of power. It sits at the eastern end of the modern, crescent-shaped street known as Aldwych, which was built in the early twentieth century over the torn-down Holywell Street and Wych Street. We will return to this site.'

Isambard drew a square around St Clement Danes on the map.

'*Bullseyes and targets, say the bells of St Margaret's.* This refers to the church of St Margaret Lothbury, just north of the site of the Bank of England on Cornhill. Just to the north of our line. *Ha'pence and farthin's, say the bells of St Martin's.* In our reading, this is St Martin-without-Ludgate on Ludgate Hill, again just above our line, setting its northern limit. The font here is engraved with a fascinating palindrome in Greek, did you know? *Niyon anomhma mh monan oyin.* Cleanse my sin and not just my face. I would say for your upcoming mission, rather: Disguise my sin, and not just my face, yes?'

Isambard gave a tight, bloodless smile, sustaining it until Peter reluctantly joined him. The younger man felt a combination of dread and pride. Isambard, in recognition of Peter's prodigious progress in his studies, had chosen him above all others, despite his young years, for this special mission, for which his background uniquely suited him. It would take Peter back to the England that had never accepted him, the land where he had always, even in his happiest moments, been an outcast. It would also take him away from Isambard, a thought he did not dare admit even to himself, lest it somehow be intercepted.

The mission would be – simply put – to poison London's soul. He was to trace its dragon lines and holy sites, and imbue them with psychic toxins, the better to prepare the way for the inevitable invading armies of the Nazi state, and within it, Himmler and Isambard's SS. He was to foster submission in the populace by seeding the psychic environment for defeat. Was it good to do so? Was it evil? Peter knew only that removing himself from Isambard's immediate presence – his compelling, mesmerizing influence – was the only way he could even hope to ask himself the question of what he was becoming.

'More. *Pancakes and fritters, say the bells of St Peter's,*' Isambard continued. 'This is St Peter upon Cornhill, which claims to be the earliest Christianized site in Britain, just below our line, framing it to the south. *Two sticks and an apple, say the bells of Whitechapel.* This refers not to a particular church, but to the famed bell foundry of Whitechapel in general, and so to the principle of bells, of harmonic resonance, and so to our unnamed art. It does not appear on our map.'

Isambard drew squares around the churches he had named since St Clement Danes and continued.

'*Maids in white aprons, say the bells of St Katherine's.* St Katherine Cree in Bishopsgate, just south of our line. *Pokers and tongs, say the bells of St John's.* St John the Evangelist, formerly on Friday Street, destroyed in the Great Fire of 1666. Just south of our line. *Kettles and pans, say the bells of St Anne's.* This marks the continuation of our line to the west, and refers to St Anne's in Soho. It sits squarely on our line. *Old father baldpate, say the slow bells of Aldgate.* St Botolph-without-Aldgate, just south of our line in the east, a kind of junction point, as you will see as your full mission unfolds. *You owe me ten shillin's, say the bells of St Helen's.* St Helen's Bishopsgate, directly on our line in the east. *When will you pay me, say the bells of Old Bailey.* The reference here is to the death knell rung at the church of St Sepulchre, and later at the Old Bailey itself on its own bell, on days of public execution. Apparently an outlying marker, north of our line. For this reason, we consider it in the symbolic sense. The wages of sin is death, is perhaps the best summary, where sin is understood to be the misuse of the power of the sleeping dragon.'

'What would constitute misuse, sir?'

Isambard frowned.

'Failing to yoke its power to noble ends, such as our own. Yes?' His eyes bored into Peter's again, demanding acquiescence. Peter gave it, choosing to do so. 'Now pay attention. *When I grow rich, say the bells of Fleetditch.* This was later altered to *Shoreditch*, but in the earlier versions the song said Fleetditch, referring to St Bride's church, on the banks of the River Fleet before it was culverted. St Bride's is directly on our line. *Pray when will that be, say the bells of Stepney.* St Dunstan's, in Stepney, directly on the continuation of our line to the east, and mirroring St Dunstan-in-the-west on Fleet Street, situated just north of our line. *I do not know, says the great bell of Bow.* St Mary-le-Bow on Cheapside, the church all true Cockneys are said to identify themselves by. Directly on our path.'

Isambard drew boxes around the remaining churches he had named, and drew a straight line across London, east to west, framed by the marks.

'In Sir Christopher Wren's plan to rebuild London after the Great Fire of 1666, the eastern part of this line I have drawn, from St Helen's to Temple, was a single, straight boulevard, a grand avenue along the great London line of power,' Isambard said. 'They should have listened to him.'

Peter stared at the map in fascination, thinking . . .

'I have no doubt about your success on this mission, nor about your loyalty, though some have questioned whether it is wise to send you,' Isambard said.

Peter's heart stopped. How deeply could Isambard see into his mind, and read his secret intentions?

'It is natural, perhaps, that after such an intense period of apprenticeship, you might foolishly look forward to removing yourself, albeit slightly, from my influence. Perhaps even operate in an independent manner. This is what will happen if you try.'

Isambard reached into the air, his green eyes drilling into Peter's, and formed his fingers into a fist. Peter felt a blow like an axe handle on his back and fell to his knees, every nerve in his body on fire. He screamed.

'There is no escape from my oversight. Now . . .' He released Peter from his grip. 'For this mission, you will have a special name. *Falke*. Falcon. You will be Falke. You are to spy on the English. You are to administer certain poisons in London. And you are to hunt down for me one half of a very particular document written by Sir Isaac Newton.'

London

1936

Falke paid the hefty sum of seven shillings and sixpence for an illustrated catalogue and walked into the Sotheby's auction room, where perhaps three dozen men were waiting for the afternoon's proceedings to begin. It was still a few minutes before one o'clock, and some of the assembled booksellers and professional collectors were conversing in restrained tones with their neighbours, while others pored over newspapers or marked with careful pencil strokes the lots they would be bidding for.

For an auction of such importance, it was hard to credit how thinly attended it was, and how little public attention it had excited. All the better for Falke and his mission. He sat down towards the back of the room and perused *The Times*.

Three more British battalions being sent to Palestine. Disturbances in Valencia. Tensions between Nazi Germany and Austria. Well, yes. Inevitable. Necessary. The world was changing, and it would be for the better. He turned to the cricket pages to see what the touring Indians were up to, half-amused at his own instinctive Englishness.

Was there no sense of greatness left in this wretched country? All of London was talking about the rival auction at Christie's of the Henry Oppenheimer art collection, while virtually no one was paying attention to Sotheby's and their offering today: the papers of no less a genius than Sir Isaac Newton. Even a death mask of the great man was going under the hammer. The Oppenheimer auction, admittedly, included sketches by several Old Masters. But here, for those who could see it, was treasure beyond all compare.

A few more men came in, among them one of powerful presence, a good six and a half feet tall, in his early fifties, accompanied by a younger, shorter man. Falke recognized the taller figure at once, from his briefings and from newspaper photographs, as the great economist John Maynard Keynes, and had to stifle an urge to immediately stand and introduce himself as an admirer.

But it was not the purpose of Falke to draw attention to himself, nor even to take part in the auction. Of the 174 lots on offer on the first day, only one interested him, for his instructions were specific, and the prize he sought was not to be acquired publicly.

Among those classified as 'alchemical', it was listed as Lot 78, a three-page manuscript of about 1,200 words entitled *The Three Mysterious Fires*. There was even a photograph of it, he noted, in the excellently prepared catalogue, which described in detail the trove of documents left by Newton upon his death. Newton had left no will, causing them to pass into the hands of his niece Catherine Barton, and thence by marriage into the hands of the Portsmouth family who were now selling them. The photograph, Falke was pleased to see, did not show the key page that he had been sent to recover: an addendum, not described in the catalogue, of incalculable value for anyone who recognized it for what it was.

Falke riffled through his newspaper. The All India team had at least managed to beat Ireland at cricket, he saw. Hardly something to write home about. England were a far stiffer proposition, and had already won the first Test at Lord's, but the colonials had some talent, he had to allow, and it wouldn't do to give them an inch. Had their man

Jahangir Khan not just killed a sparrow with a cricket ball when bowling for Cambridge University? The sparrow was to be stuffed for posterity, he had heard. The English – his own people, and yet not – were such sentimentalists.

Falke brought his attention back to the auction room. What could Keynes' interest in the auction be? He was a Cambridge man, to be sure, but of King's College, not the Trinity of Newton. The great economist's languid gaze suggested less interest in the proceedings than that shown by his companion.

The Newton paper Falke sought had survived many threats to its existence. There had been a fire in Newton's laboratory in the winter of 1677–8; the cull of his own papers by Newton himself in 1727 at Leicester Fields in London, with many pages again committed to the flames; then the terrible fire of January 1891 at the Hurstbourne Park home of the Portsmouths in Hampshire, which had destroyed the great house but barely touched the Newton documents residing there. One would think the things blessed, or damned. Or at least one of them.

'Good afternoon, gentlemen.'

The auctioneer's introductory remarks broke Falke's reverie. It was one o'clock precisely, and the auction was beginning.

'We'll move straight to Lot 1, *Alchemical Propositions*, in Latin, three pages . . .'

At mid-afternoon they came to Lot 78. Bidding opened at £15, and was immediately taken up by a balding, mildly corpulent man in a grey suit sitting on a bench to the right of the room. A slim, hawkish character just behind him, with brilliantined hair and sallow complexion, began immediately to compete. Both had bid earlier on other manuscripts with about equal success.

'Fifteen pounds . . . and ten . . . sixteen pounds . . . and ten . . .'

The auctioneer ran smoothly from one man to the other as the slim man waved his catalogue with a dismissive flick each time his tubby, sweating rival raised his hand to make a new offer.

'Seventeen . . .'

There was a pause as the thin man seemed to hesitate.

'Seventeen pounds . . .'

A third man on the bench opposite waved his hand, prompting a murmur of curiosity among the onlookers.

'Seventeen pounds and ten shillings, new face, thank you sir, seventeen and ten . . .'

The tubby man punched his hand in the air again, prompting the immediate response from his new rival of another wave of the hand.

'Eighteen pounds . . . eighteen and ten . . .'

The auctioneer eyed the thin man, who almost imperceptibly shook his head.

'No sir? Selling at eighteen pounds and ten shillings . . .'

Once again the tubby man's hand shot up.

'Nineteen pounds . . . selling for nineteen pounds . . . can sell, will sell . . .'

Again all eyes in the room focused on the slim man and his lowered catalogue.

'Selling for nineteen pounds . . . fair warning . . .'

The auctioneer's hammer hovered in the air, about to descend. Then the light green catalogue whipped up one more time, prompting muffled cries from those watching.

'Nineteen and ten! Nineteen pounds and ten shillings . . .'

The tubby man slumped slightly.

'Can sell, will sell for nineteen and ten . . . selling for nineteen pounds and ten shillings . . .'

The auctioneer cast his eyes one more time around the room, then cracked his hammer down. 'Sold to the gentleman from Francis Edwards . . .'

Falke jotted down the sale price and thereafter took careful note of the movements of the buyer.

Keynes, he saw meanwhile, was paying scant attention to the alchemical section of the auction. The great man perked up when fifty-three lots of letters to and from Newton came under the hammer, and placed winning bids on several. Then, once they were sold, the first day's proceedings concluded. The auction would continue the following day, 14 July, with a collection of biographical material, theological and chronological writings, Newton's Royal Mint papers, portraits and that death mask.

But Falke's work was done.

He observed from a discreet distance as the representative of Francis Edwards, the booksellers, settled accounts and took with him the twelve lots he had purchased, including *The Three Mysterious Fires*, in a voluminous brown leather briefcase.

Falke discreetly followed him out of Sotheby's front door onto New Bond Street and then onto Maddox Street, past the unusual twin obelisks outside St George's church. He tracked him north along Regent Street all the way to Oxford Circus Underground station, staying well back, and when his quarry boarded the eastbound train on the Central London Line, he got into the same carriage at the opposite end, confident he was not observed. The man's mind was elsewhere, Falke felt. He could have sat right next to the bookseller's agent and not have sparked any fear.

As they rode the two stops to Holborn, Falke concentrated his mind, twisting inside his leather glove the gold signet ring he had received as a token of his initiation, of the trust placed in him by some of the highest men in the land. The other land. Its motif was innocent, and simple: a cross, and four dots. It stood for another symbol, one easily made by connecting the dots in a certain way, that spoke to his secret life.

He had been well trained. To spy, to lead the clandestine life, had been a thrill, a pleasure, a duty. To operate at so many levels at once, as an Englishman, as a stateless architect of the new world, as an initiate of a new military order, to deceive the flabby, weak minds of his adoptive countrymen, this was all a heady pleasure for a young man of twenty-one, flushed with pride at his own capabilities.

Yet this would be new.

When they reached Holborn, the rail-thin man left the carriage and changed lines, walking to the platform that would allow him to take the shuttle to Aldwych station. Falke followed, drawing closer now, confident in his invisibility to the distracted target. He was going to the theatre, Falke thought with some surprise, then corrected himself: it was Monday, most theatres would be dark. Perhaps he was meeting someone at the Waldorf Hotel to hand over the Newton manuscripts? Best to act immediately.

Three people rode in the car with them, two young women of secretarial demeanour and an older man in cap and scarf. Too many witnesses. Falke saw his chance when the train drew in to Aldwych station. The bookseller's agent, lost in his thoughts, exited well behind the other passengers, and as the train pulled out again the two of them were alone on the platform.

Falke feigned interest in an advertisement to allow his man time to reach the steps that led to the lift, then followed him, a few steps behind. He called out to his target when they had both reached the top of the stairway.

'I say, excuse me, you dropped this.'

The man turned in surprise to see Falke smiling at him and holding out a silver object of some kind, perhaps a cigarette lighter.

'No, I don't think so.'

'Are you sure? I distinctly saw it drop from your pocket.'

Falke drew closer, concern etched on his face. He was, he knew, a compelling figure. Young, six feet tall, blond.

'Look here, I haven't got a lighter like that,' the man said, uneasiness creeping into his voice.

But then Falke's face was just inches from his, and a gaze of startling depth and intensity was boring into his consciousness.

'I mean . . .' the man stuttered.

Falke worked quickly, taking the briefcase from the man's hand and pushing him gently back into a darkened passageway at the top of the stairs. At the end was a padlocked metal door. Falke pushed him against it, his eyes locked on his victim's. It was a test of mental power, a domination trick akin to hypnosis, that he had been taught alongside other dark arts at the inner SS instructional camp.

'You felt dizzy in the Underground,' he whispered to the man. 'You felt indisposed for a few seconds, then pulled yourself together and went about your business. You saw no one. Do you understand?'

His victim nodded almost imperceptibly, staring blankly ahead.

No one was coming. Falke opened the briefcase and flicked quickly through its contents. No one should realize the document was missing, he had been told. No one should know of its existence. He found Lot 78 and carefully withdrew it from its stiff cardboard folder. Three pages, as described in the catalogue, covered in Newton's handwriting. His fingers trembled. Was it here? A cover sheet of paper, bearing just a scribbled signature and the numeral 1, was folded around the three pages to keep them together. He had been told to look for an addendum, a half page, part of a full page torn in two, placed with the *Three Mysterious Fires* manuscript. But there was none.

'Listen to me,' he hissed. 'Have you taken anything from the folders? Did you touch Lot 78 in any way? Tell me the truth. Tell me it now.'

The hypnotized bookseller's eyes stared back through Falke as if he were not there. He murmured: 'More than my job's worth . . . never interfere . . .'

Falke looked closely at the edges of the cover sheet, noting one of them had been torn unevenly.

He heard voices. The lift was bringing more passengers down from street level. He had to act quickly. Falke took the torn half-sheet and placed it as gently as he could into the pocket of his jacket, then replaced the three pages of Lot 78 in the folder and slid it back into the briefcase, which he dropped at the man's feet.

'You felt dizzy but now you feel fine,' he whispered. 'You saw no one. Count to five in your mind and on five, wake up.'

But then it went wrong.

'Thief!' the man started to shriek, his voice quavering. Falke clapped a gloved hand over his mouth.

'Be quiet, or I'll kill you,' he hissed.

The bookseller's agent lunged for Falke's throat with wiry hands, and Falke had to head-butt him, hard, to regain control, one hand still over his mouth. Then he slammed him backwards into the wall. The man's legs went limp and his arms flapped down by his sides.

It was getting messy. Why had his hypnosis not worked

properly? He heard the voices of passengers coming and froze, holding his position as a group of people walked past the mouth of the passageway on their way down to the platform. No one saw them, but it was only a matter of time before they were spotted.

Falke kneeled and quickly examined the padlock on the metal door, keeping one eye on the unconscious figure beside him. If he could open it, he could get his victim out of sight and win some time to think. He would not abandon his mission, but already this scrawny creature had ruined the script Falke had written in his mind, and it was time to think coldly and calmly. Falke took a leather pouch from his pocket and selected a skeleton key. The padlock opened easily. When the next train pulled into the station, Falke forced the door open, its metallic shriek masked by the sounds below, and dragged his victim through. When the train pulled out again he closed the door, plunging them into darkness.

It was his first offensive operation, the first involving physical contact with a target, and he was in danger of botching it. The man had seen his face, and would be able to identify him. But he could still make it right.

Falke waited for his eyes to grow accustomed to the blackness. He realized they were on a bridge crossing the train line, of the kind that usually led to another platform on the other side. Walking carefully to the far end, he ascertained that a flight of steps led down, mirroring those leading to the platform where he and his victim had alighted. A disused platform. Falke went back and grabbed his man by the armpits, dragging him to the steps.

'You had to resist,' he said to the unconscious figure. 'That was very silly. Now you pose me a problem.'

Falke ran through his options. Should he kill the man? A

dead body left on the platform below, better yet on the disused tracks, fodder for rats, might take weeks to find, if the stench did not give it away. But his instructions had been to acquire the document without leaving any sign that it had been removed. Could he leave the briefcase somewhere it would be found? Could he try again to hypnotize this bloody fool, and send him on his way with no recollection of what had happened? Threaten him? A body would be messy; a missing bookseller would attract a lot of attention, even if his purchases were recovered intact.

Falke reached down to the supine form at the top of the stairs and slapped his face to wake him. There was no response. He felt for a pulse. Then he realized his decision had been taken for him. Falke, on his first offensive job, had made an error. The man was no longer breathing.

Cornwall

July 1936

Harry Hale grunted in annoyance at the shiftiness the butler was exhibiting. With his dead father still warm in the master bedroom upstairs, Harry — now, as of thirty-five minutes ago, Lord Hale-Devereaux of Poldhu, meaning it was actually *his* butler who was acting shiftily — felt scarcely in the mood for guessing games or shilly-shallying, and let the man know it in no uncertain terms.

'Heck's the matter with you, Seeton?'

'Matter, sir?'

Then Harry realized that Seeton, the very exemplar of unflappability in Harry's twenty-three years' experience thus far of the world, was not behaving evasively or duplicitously, but rather was simply embarrassed. The man didn't know what to say.

'Spit it out, man. Whoever that was crunching up to the house along the gravel just now — in a taxi, I shouldn't wonder, since it beat a retreat as soon as it had dropped them off — can hardly bring me more unwelcome news than I've already had today. Or has somebody else died too?'

By 'unwelcome news', Harry didn't mean the fact that he was inheriting little beyond a crumbling stately pile on Lizard Peninsula and a promontory of debt, but simply that his beloved father, a font of kindness and vigorous instruction, for all his eccentricities, was dead. Just that: father was dead, and he didn't know quite what to do.

'It's your brother, sir.'

'My brother has died?'

'Oh no, sir. He's downstairs. He does look a little peeky, but . . .'

'Devil's he doing here?'

'His father has died, sir.'

'His too?'

'No, sir. His adopted father. Your father. Lord Hale-Devereaux.'

'Ah. Quite.'

'Shall I send him away, sir?'

'What?'

'Those were your father's standing instructions. Politely to refuse him entry. Send him on his way. With a flea in his ear, sir, if I may say so.'

'Since when?'

'Since he was sixteen. A good few years, now. Since he went to Paris, I believe, sir.'

'I didn't know.'

'No, sir.'

'Well, I'll have no more of that. Send him up.'

'At once.'

Seeton withdrew, a certain disconformity emanating from his retreating back.

Within two minutes, Harry's younger sibling – adopted, but for all that the tow-headed urchin of his childhood memories, keeper of shared experiences – stepped into the library. Harry heard him, but continued to inspect the gardens, his back to the door. For reasons not entirely clear to him, to do perhaps with hierarchy and legitimacy, Harry decided not to turn round until he was spoken to.

'Harry.'

Not a question. Certainly not an imploration, nor a supplication.

He turned, and for the first time in five years laid eyes

upon his younger brother, who stood just inside the entrance to the library, a look of chilly arrogance on his face, one hand clutched to the other, twisting a gaudy little ring he bore on his finger.

Wondering how on earth Peter could have known so quickly that father had died – for events had moved so quickly that no one had thought to contact Peter to let him know the old man was in his final throes – Harry prepared to tell his adoptive brother that, according to their father's will, there would be no inheritance of title, land or property for him whatsoever, and that the modest income on which Peter lived would end upon his twenty-second birthday, in 1937.

London

July 1936

Falke liked to hum to himself as he walked London, slowly laying bare the city from Bishopsgate to Mayfair, east to west like the sun, then back again. He liked to pause along his route and enjoy the special flavour of each site, taking the time to close his eyes and imagine how they would have looked a thousand years earlier, two thousand, longer . . . before the cathedrals, before the abbeys and churches, when all had been green, and when the same holy places had been venerated by other priests, serving different gods.

Oranges and lemons . . .

He liked to pause for a moment, early on his route, on the forecourt of St Helen's Bishopsgate, a site of gentle, calming power. There was a stone tomb there carved with a skull that often drew him to meditate, to weigh his task and measure himself against it, as he sat in the shade of the ancient church and the great Baltic Exchange directly to its east.

The English were ill, and it was well known that a small dose of poison could cure ills, where a larger dose could kill.

You owe me ten shillin's, said the bells of St Helen's . . .

It was his job to heal, not to kill – to prepare the patient, so to speak, to lay the groundwork, here and elsewhere, by walking the city, so that when the day came, there would be diminished resistance to the cure, the one brought by the Nazi armies.

So far Falke's work had been different. He had successfully performed his secret function of surveillance on targets of interest to his regular spymasters. Most notably, he had successfully worked in disguise as one of a family of match-sellers, each taking his turn at a tiny stall outside St James's Park Underground station, secretly photographing the comings and goings at the Minimax Fire Extinguisher Company at number 54, Broadway. In doing so they had captured the faces of many of the staff of MI6, whose secret head-quarters it was – the organization did not even officially exist – and sent them to the Gestapo for future reference, should war come. As it would.

But then there was his doubly secret work, for the particular office of the SS called Occult Bureau Section Four, unknown to the uninstructed thugs who handled his regular material.

He poisoned.

Not with witchbane and deadly nightshade, not with mercury or cyanide.

He poisoned by contaminating holy wells, places of power, sacred mounds, in ways that involved fear, that would spawn paralysis and dread when the time was right. He had been trained to do this by his mentor, the same man to whom now he would have to explain the death of the bookseller's agent. Peter felt Isambard's potential wrath only a hair's breadth away, in the thickness of the air, in the stare of every person he passed on the London streets.

He spoke his secret phrase, known only to him: his poisoning chant.

Lucem in tenebris occulto . . . I hide the light in the darkness.

Falke moved on to his next site, ruminating on his mission. There was no direct route to the next point – though there would have been, if Wren's plan for the city had been adopted – but walking south along Bishopsgate and right on Threadneedle Street to the old Cornhill, the highest point in London, now home to the Bank of England and the Royal Exchange, then along Poultry, brought him within view of it, the golden dragon atop its spire marking his destination: the church of St Mary-le-Bow.

Turn again, Whittington . . . The bells of St Mary-le-Bow had called Dick Whittington back from despair, the story ran. Would there be a chance for Falke to turn now? He entered the church and took a pew, preparing himself to meditate, to deliver his draught of spiritual poison. Would he turn now, if given the chance? He didn't think so. Not yet. He was too angry at England. He was still learning how to use his power. And he didn't think he'd be allowed to.

After a while, Falke rose from his pew at St Mary-le-Bow and left the church, walking south on Bow Street, then west on Watling Street. Now the great dome of St Paul's cathedral, his next destination, filled the sky at the end of the lane, dominating the city from atop Ludgate Hill, one of the key centres of the city's hidden power. He passed the site of the destroyed church of St John the Evangelist at the corner of the old Friday Street, burned down in the Great Fire of 1666 and never replaced.

It was time for Peter to meet his mentor, who had taken the enormous security risk of travelling to London immediately after receiving the radio message saying what Peter had acquired from the bookseller's agent.

They'd had an initial contact a few days earlier in Regent's Park, at which Peter had handed over the ostensibly blank piece of paper. Now they were to meet again at Aldwych. Peter tried to control his fear.

Isambard and Peter walked in silence down to the river, past the Savoy, to Victoria Embankment and Cleopatra's Needle.

'This monument is mislocated,' the solid, white-haired figure said as they stood by the obelisk's base, gazing into the timeless grey flow of the river. 'When the moment comes, it will be placed directly on the line of power, where it should reside. In my own view, which I have had put to the *Führer* himself, St Clement Danes should be demolished, and the obelisk placed directly on the island in the Strand, the one occupied by the church.'

'Can one get a proposal so easily to him?'

'Not easily. And he is a man who decides suddenly, without warning, when strategic visions come to him. I have been informed of no decision, but suddenly, out of the blue, one can be summoned. I am ready to make my case. He does not entirely trust those of us who work on the inner side of things. So, for obvious reasons of affinity, I deal primarily with Himmler, a true believer.'

He pointed at the London skyline.

'Church spires and obelisks, these are all the same thing: points of focus and concentration for the power of the earth. St Clement Danes sits by London's key holy well at Aldwych, just as St Paul's sits on its key sacred hill.'

They walked along the embankment toward the Houses of Parliament, talking in subdued tones as they went. Peter had failed and succeeded, his mentor told him. He had failed in killing the man. This was untidy, it attracted attention, it caused questions to be asked.

'I had thought I was ready to kill,' Peter said as they walked. 'For the greater good, for a higher cause. But it troubles me to have killed unnecessarily. Out of clumsiness.'

'What thoughts come to you in the night, when you try to sleep? Do you see his face?'

'Yes.'

'This will fade. In time, they become just one blurred face. It is the mind's way of making it more bearable, for we all find it a burden, believe me. The tempering of the true warrior takes time, and involves hardening our heart to ordinary human feelings. We are soon to be at war, remember. Extraordinary feats are required, and we must go beyond ourselves to achieve them. You are blooded now, and it will bind you to us more strongly. There is no way back.'

'There's more. I see his face, but I also see something else. I see myself through his eyes.'

'This is natural. A way of asking yourself who you are. Who you have become.'

'When I see myself through his eyes, as I kill him, the thing that troubles me is this: I am smiling.'

They walked on in silence for a while. Isambard did not directly address Peter's confidence, then or ever, but eventually, with an air of ending the conversation, he spoke a few lapidary words.

'You are the new man striving to be born. It *is* a pleasure to kill, one on one, hand to hand. To say otherwise is hypocrisy. The new man does not fear his own enjoyment in killing, for he is not weak. You'll do well to remember this, Falke.'

Peter began to protest.

'Be quiet. I have more to tell you.'

'I need . . .'

Isambard barked at him suddenly. 'What are you, some kind of ninny? Some kind of girl? We will speak of this again only if I say so, and not before. Be a man.'

Peter dared not push further. They trudged on in silence.

'Good. Now I want to tell you about the document you recovered. You have performed a great service. Now that I have confirmed its true nature, I am authorized to congratulate you on behalf of *Reichsführer SS* Himmler himself.'

Peter's heart soared. He had been expecting severe punishment, pain, perhaps a recall to Germany.

'How were you able to do that? With no laboratory, no resources here?'

'It is written in a relatively simple invisible ink, long known in the circles in which I move, which were also Newton's. I was able to read it within 24 hours of your giving it to me.'

Isambard stopped and turned towards the river. It occurred to Peter that his mentor was too elated to look at him without betraying his emotion. Isambard's voice cracked as he continued.

'What you have found here – as I predicted – is one half of a secret that will win the coming war for Germany, for us. It will establish the Third Reich as the world's dominant power for generations.' Isambard clenched his fist. 'And – you must by now be aware of this – the other half has also been shown to us. To you.'

He still didn't understand everything Isambard was saying.

'Shown to me? How?'

'In Paris, you met a man called Champagne, did you not? You have seen the other half of this legendary paper with your own eyes. A summary of Newton's alchemical work on the phenomenon we call *das geheime Feuer*. A document so dangerous it was split into two, hundreds of years ago, perhaps even by the author himself. Its two halves lost, dispersed by time. Now your mission in London is over. Someone else will complete the pattern you have been building here. Go to Paris. Do the same work there. And find the other half.'

Wewelsburg

1938

Peter failed in Paris, for no reason he could understand. Despite his own assiduous research, and occasional tips, born of psychic glimpses, from his mentor, the missing half of the Newton document was simply not to be found. After two fruitless years, in the autumn of 1938 he was selected for 'advanced special training'.

Isambard ordered Peter to leave the French capital for three months to return to Wewelsburg Castle in eastern Westphalia, the site earmarked by Himmler as a planned future SS Vatican, and home to the inner SS school where they had first met.

~

Peter walked with Isambard in the fog-shrouded grounds below the three-sided castle, staring up at the great circular North Tower at its apex.

'Your lack of progress in Paris suggests you are still too soft,' Isambard said. 'Hundreds of witches, perhaps thousands, were tortured and executed here in the seventeenth century.' Isambard pointed at the castle with his walking-stick. 'They were people like us, persecuted by the Christians. Burned in the name of their weakling Christian faith.' He spat. 'The emaciated spirituality of the Christians will be replaced, along with the blood-sucking parasitism of the Jews. Yes?'

Peter walked on in silence, daring not to answer. At

twenty-three years old he had already killed once, accidentally, in London. He had been blooded, as Isambard was wont to put it, and was hence not only initiated, but also vulnerable to blackmail, or betrayal. It was difficult to think about ever going back. And yet . . .

'You will recall we spoke of the need for a new morality,' Isambard said. 'For men of strength who embrace not only the virtues of loyalty, honour and strength, but also those of ferocity, coldness and imperturbability.'

They were walking towards a clearing in the woods where previously Peter had undergone shooting and unarmed combat training. From the sounds up ahead, it seemed there was another group undergoing instruction there.

'Where we are now walking will, when the victory comes, become the centre of the new world,' Isambard said. 'Great plans are afoot for this place. A great complex will be built, centred on the North Tower, which will be a kind of Grail Castle for us. It will require workmen, but the labour camps will provide us with what we need. There will be sufficient sub-humans to do the work, as long as they are capably led.'

They entered the clearing. Peter saw a circle of black-clad SS students such as himself, about ten of them, and in the centre of the circle, shackled hand and foot, dressed in rags, another young man of his own age.

'Heil Hitler!' Isambard shouted, making the Nazi salute in his almost mocking, half-hearted way. The SS men snapped to attention and responded as one. Peter joined the circle, afraid of what he was about to witness. Yet he was avid for power now, and for knowledge.

'This man,' Isambard said to the group, his voice low but piercingly clear, 'is an enemy. He is worthless, the opposite of everything we stand for. Worthless but for two things.'

He stared into the eyes of each man in the ring, walking

from one to the next, his walking-stick brandished like a club. 'He knows something we want to know. He knows the whereabouts of an assassin who is planning to carry out an attack on the *Führer* himself in the next 24 hours. He is a member of the ring that has been planning this assassination attempt for several months. The Führer's security, of course, cannot be breached by anyone who expects to survive the attempt. But desperate men may be prepared to sacrifice their own lives to get within striking range of our leader. The assassin I speak of is one such, and he must be found.'

With a casual gesture, Isambard swung his walking stick and hit the prisoner hard in the lower back. The man winced, trying hard not to cry out. Peter saw defiance in his eyes, but also raw fear. A wave of nausea flooded over Peter. Yet he did not dare look away.

'The second thing is that here, at Wewelsburg, we stand at a centre of earth power, of the dragon power that may be tapped and directed for our purposes. And so the suffering of this wretch – and he will undoubtedly suffer – will feed the power of this land, just as the suffering of our forebears did, at the hands of the Christian inquisitors.'

Isambard turned to Peter.

'Falke, take your knife and ask him the first question.'

~

Peter weighed whether to simply refuse, to throw down the knife and take the wrath of the group, and of Isambard, onto himself. He felt Isambard's eyes on him, and knew he was trying to read his thoughts. The prisoner stared up at him in defiance. Should he feign excessive zeal, killing the man quickly and cleanly, claiming incompetence as an interrogator? The life of the *Führer* was in jeopardy, to whom all these men, if not Peter, were fanatically committed. They would view killing this wretch before he talked as tantamount to complicity in the plot. And Isambard? Were the Nazis anything more than just a vehicle to him, a means, as they perhaps were to Peter, to attain his own ambitions? What was Isambard's real commitment to Hitler, or even to Himmler?

Peter had to act. He could not afford to hesitate. Yet killing a man was one thing; torturing one was another.

Kill or be killed. Torture or face torture himself? All eyes were on him.

Peter decided.

He grabbed the man's head and hissed urgently into his ear, holding the knife against his throat as he did so.

'Say something. Say anything. Lie if you want. Make it credible. When you finish speaking, I'll kill you cleanly. It's your only chance.'

Peter broke away, kicking the man as he moved back, cursing him as loudly as he could.

The prisoner looked up at the circle of shaven-headed thugs, anger and fear stitched on his face. And then he broke down. Weeping, he began to give details of a plot, spilling out names, addresses, locations and dates in a tumble of mangled sounds.

'Where is the assassin?' Peter roared at him.

The man gave an address in Berlin. Spat it out, three times. Peter heard Isambard repeat it. Then Peter stepped forward and stabbed the man in the heart.

~

That night, Peter expected to die.

Arrested on Isambard's orders immediately after stabbing

the prisoner, Peter was thrown into a cell in the castle and left to languish for hours. When they came for him, it was with rifle butts and boots to the fore, kicking and beating him until he could barely walk.

Half dragged, half-carried across the castle's internal courtyard, he was then taken to the North Tower by his SS guards, past special security troops whose insignia he did not recognize, under rounded arches that ringed the circular chamber on the ground floor, and thrown at the feet of a black-clad figure in the centre of the room.

Peter looked up in fear, expecting to see the icy green gaze of Isambard. Instead, he saw a plump, short man with thick eyeglasses and a weak chin, clad in the regalia of the *Reichsführer SS* himself. Peter stared into the eyes of Heinrich Himmler.

'I observed you this afternoon. Why should you not be killed like a dog?'

Peter was speechless.

'You are worthless, and yet very valuable, I am told. Otherwise you would be handed over to your fellow students, whose view is that you should suffer the same fate that the wretch you killed was to have faced. You deprived them of a toughening experience, of a chance to harden themselves.'

Peter dared to look around. Romanesque arches ringed the chamber, tall windows behind each one. Niches were set into the walls. The floor was grey marble, with a jagged pattern that he could not discern set into the floor, where Himmler stood.

'Isambard speaks for you, so you will not be executed. You will instead be dedicated to a special task.'

He raised his arms and indicated the round space above them.

'Where I stand – this very spot, beneath my feet – will be the centre of the world, when our victory is complete. A new German empire, centred on this place, will extend in all directions, across all continents. A gold disk will be inlaid at the very centre of the design, which we call the *Sonnenrad*. The sun-wheel.'

Himmler stepped back.

'Observe it. Twelve *sig* runes, the symbol of the SS, flaring from a central dark sun.'

The inlaid pattern was in dark green marble, almost black in the twilit room. The design also seemed to incorporate swastikas into the rune shapes.

'The inner order of the SS is the creation of myself and Isambard, the man who has saved your life, my closest adviser in these matters. You should be duly grateful to him. What you see here, laid into the floor, is the true meaning of the SS initials. Only sworn initiates may know the true name. Are you worthy?'

Peter stammered, shaking with cold, wanting only to live.

'Yes, sir.'

'Isambard, what do you say?'

Isambard walked towards them from beneath one of the rounded arches.

'I say he can be told. He will, after all, be a key instrument of the new order.'

'*Die Schwarze Sonne*,' Himmler whispered. 'That is the true meaning of the SS name, for its core initiate warriors. The Black Sun.'

Peter babbled to himself, still delirious from his beating. 'The enemies of Heliopolis. The black sun perverting the Great Work . . . that's what Champagne said.'

Isambard strode forward and kicked Peter in the gut.

'Do not speak of that man again. The *Reichsführer SS* has

allowed you to live tonight, at my request. Show some respect.'

Peter mumbled some garbled phrases of thanks, his stomach churning.

'Very well,' Himmler said. 'I understand you have things to discuss. I will bid you a good night. I am needed in Berlin. Heil Hitler.'

Isambard returned the salute with none of his usual languor. Then, after Himmler had left, he stood at the centre of the dark sunwheel.

'So, heredity is strong in you.'

'I don't understand,' Peter groaned, trying to sit up.

'You are an interesting case, a unique experiment. You have your mother's charming blue eyes, of course, but also her other qualities. Her humanity. Her softness.'

'What do you mean?'

'There was no assassination plot, by the way. That prisoner had no knowledge to give us. The plot was an invention, to test you all. He was a demonstration piece, to see how far you would all go. Especially you.'

'What do you mean about my mother?'

'Pierre, have you still not worked it out? Are you still so obtuse? I am your father.'

Paris

Autumn 1940

Choosing her moment carefully to avoid detection by German soldiers or French police, Rose Arden took the anti-Jewish proclamation down from the inner glass pane of the telephone booth and folded it so it would fit into a pocket of her overcoat. It wasn't resistance, exactly, or even a thought-out action, but it was something.

'You can kiss my Okie ass, Mr Hitler,' she whispered to herself, shivering with equal measures of cold and anger. The announcement detailed, with fine legalistic precision, the categories of employment that would henceforth be denied to Jews in France. Government jobs, the armed forces, radio and cinema, newspapers, teaching . . .

A woman answered the number she had dialled.

'*Allô?* Berthe?'

'Mademoiselle Rose?'

'Can I visit you this afternoon?'

'Yes, of course, though . . . I must tell you that I have received no news from madame since we last spoke.'

There would be no money, then. Rose felt almost relieved at not being further beholden to someone who had already done so much to help her. Berthe would feed her, though – she and her husband had a small farm outside Paris that provided supplies already unobtainable in the city – and she would be grateful for the sustenance, which would have to tide her over for several days of turnips and ersatz coffee.

'I quite understand. I will call around five o'clock. I am looking forward to seeing you again.'

Berthe was the housekeeper of her guardian angel: Natalie Clifford Barney, known in literary circles as *l'Amazone*, whose salon at 20, Rue Jacob on the left bank she had regularly attended before the Nazi occupation. Natalie had all but adopted her as her 'Californian sun-child', and had interceded with the French authorities to regularize her residency papers after the expiry of her student visa and the end of her English teaching job at the Lycée Montaigne.

L'Amazone had herself left Paris on a train to Italy just weeks before the French capitulation, but Berthe was still there, running the house with her husband and coordinating as best she could the distribution of her mistress's alms to those of her acquaintances who were now facing their first bitter Nazi winter in Paris.

Rose crossed the Seine on the Pont Notre Dame, dipping her head into the biting wind, heading south across the Île de la Cité to meet her friend, as agreed, at the little park by the Petit Pont on the left bank.

It had taken the Nazis, and their Vichy friends, little time to show their true colours. The *Statut des Juifs* – a public proclamation, a copy of which now nestled in Rose's overcoat pocket – had come into force just weeks earlier. Gangs of thugs, French ones, had taken to forming outside Jewish stores, hurling insults and threatening anyone trying to shop there. Rose had tangled with them twice already, giving one of the thugs a black eye the second time before friends had dragged her away.

Rose's mother was French-Canadian, from just outside Montreal, married at eighteen to an itinerant oilman, a proud, bitter, demanding man she'd met at a dance and who'd taken her south to his home state of California, to where the work was. And so Rose had imbibed French with her mother's milk, and she'd grown up speaking it even though there were no other kids to share it with, and it was the language in which she was most a girl, and most a woman, the one in which her mother had raised her and taught her about the world through a woman's eyes.

Never be a slave to men, her mother had said. *Never be a slave to love.*

Rose's first year in Paris, studying medieval French literature and teaching English at the Lycée, had been a dream. Tight for money but near-drowning in love with the city, she had set up home in a tiny walk-up fifth-floor apartment off Rue St Jacques, and thrown herself into the expatriate literary world.

Already, before leaving California, she had started giving out 12, Rue de l'Odéon, the address of the Shakespeare and Company bookstore, as her mailing address in Paris. It was what young writers did, and the charming, birdlike Sylvia Beach had dutifully welcomed Rose upon her arrival, just over two years previously, and provided her first introductions and invitations to readings. Henry Miller was still in town, and had made a drunken pass at Rose one evening in a café while her escort was in the john; she had seen James Joyce, ailing and almost blind, tapping his way towards the bookstore one afternoon as she left, but had been too overawed to approach him. Many of the original 1920s Lost Generation of Americans had gone, but a grittier crew in a grittier post-Depression time had arrived or hung on: *the lifers and desperadoes,* as she had called them in one of the first pieces of her work she'd dared to read publicly.

Rose, who'd learned dress-making from her mother, had also found work elsewhere: by walking straight into the Molyneux fashion house on Place Vendôme and telling them to employ her. Forest Yeo-Thomas, a stocky, tough-looking man of the world who ran the place, had been so taken by her demeanour that he'd hired her on the spot.

Peering south as she stepped onto the Petit Pont after passing Notre Dame cathedral, its stained glass all removed for safekeeping the previous year, Rose looked for her friend's red winter hat in the little park but didn't see it, though another woman she didn't recognize seemed to be waving at her. Rose, confused, made to respond but then lowered her hand as a commotion in the foreground caught her attention. Three toughs in leather coats were pushing and shoving a bearded older man, who was trying to shield a young boy from their blows. Rose could hear the taunts and curses: though they were in German, she knew what they had to be. *Parasite, yid, dirty Jew.* Though she thought she heard another word too, a puzzling one: *Vulcan? Canelli?*

She had felt the Nazi invasion of France was an event she could not flee; that it was even, without knowing it beforehand, the ordeal she had come to the City of Light to undergo.

'I'm not leaving,' Rose had said, quite simply, when the first suggestions had reached her from the Embassy that as an American she would be best advised to quit France before something dreadful happened. 'Even if Hitler himself drives down the Champs Elysées in an open-topped car, I'm staying right here.'

A woman of conscience, a woman of letters and of action as she aspired to be, could not walk away from such a challenge. By whatever means open to her, she would oppose the dreadful night now falling on France, and on Europe.

Right now she couldn't help herself, even as she saw the woman she didn't know crossing the road and starting to run towards her. Rose, who was smaller than all three of the goons, walked up to the mêlée and inserted herself right in the middle, shielding the old man and daring any of them to take a swing at her.

'Try picking on someone your own size,' she said, jutting her chin out. 'American Embassy. I am a neutral diplomat. You have no right to attack these people.'

For a moment, the thugs were paralysed with surprise. Two wore Gestapo uniforms. One, a bruiser with a crew cut and a broken nose, stood with his fist held in mid-air, breathing hard, the words *American* and *diplomat* sufficient to give him pause. The older Jewish man drew himself up beside Rose, still shielding the boy.

Out of the corner of her eye, Rose saw the mysterious woman drawing closer, fear in her demeanour. Rose tried to signal unobtrusively to her to stay out of it. Or perhaps she just thought she did.

In June, Nazi troops had indeed marched along the Champs Elysées, though Hitler himself was not with them. The *Führer*'s own visit to the conquered City of Light had been an almost furtive affair a few days after the Occupation, starting at six in the morning and taking in the Opera, a viewing of the Eiffel Tower from the Trocadero, a visit to Napoleon's tomb at the Invalides and a few other tourist sites before blowing out of town as quickly as he had come. Would he return? Rose hoped so. Given half a chance, she'd be willing to take a shot at the guy herself. It was a question of meeting the right people.

Soon there would be resistance, she was sure of it, even with the Communists abiding by the Hitler–Stalin pact and sitting on their hands as though nothing had happened.

But for now it had been a question of surviving, of accumulating information that might be useful to someone, hopefully to the British, if the British could hold on, and waiting for a moment when she could make a difference.

Rose's boss Yeo-Thomas – gone now, probably back to England, as he'd been dying to sign up to fight the Nazis – would know what to do, if only she could get a message through to him. She was trying.

Rose had stayed when others had left, and because it was important to find something positive to do, she had, for example, helped her friend Sylvia carry all the stock of Shakespeare and Company up to the fourth floor of 12, Rue de l'Odéon, volume by volume, from the bookstore shelves below, to hide them from the likes of the rapacious Nazi officer who had shown up with a motorcycle escort one day to demand that Sylvia sell him her one and only copy of *Finnegans Wake*, or face the consequences. Sylvia, bless her, had refused, and chosen instead to close the bookstore.

Rose couldn't be less brave than Sylvia, now.

The tallest of the men, speaking perfect British English, drilled his stark blue gaze into Rose's and held out a gloved hand. He wore civilian clothes.

'May I see your diplomatic papers? Some form of accreditation?'

Rose shook her head.

'I have no obligation to show you anything. I suggest we let this man go about his business, and we can talk about this like civilized human beings.'

The boy behind her was crying, and Rose could feel him clutching her skirts. She was shaking at the knees, as she always did when she got herself into a fight. She took a deep breath.

The city had virtually emptied itself ahead of the arrival of the Nazi tanks, millions of Parisians joining the miserable streams of refugees who had flowed through the city and out towards the south in May and June. US Ambassador Bullitt himself, who had strongly urged Americans to return to the United States at the start of the Phoney War, had opted to stay and serve as a neutral go-between in the handover of Paris to the Nazis as an undefended Open City. The Hotel Bristol had been taken over by the Embassy as a residence for American citizens in Paris, though Rose had spurned it. Then with autumn stretching towards winter many Parisians had begun to return, as it became clear the German forces were behaving with a degree of initial restraint and decorum, and the city was not being reduced to rubble. Their lives were there, and their homes, and they came back.

'You are no diplomat,' the tall Nazi said, reaching for the frayed label of Rose's overcoat and assaying its quality. 'A diplomat does not dress like a cheap streetwalker.'

'You have a damn nerve, sir!' Rose drew herself up to her full height, playing it out for as long as she could. 'The ambassador will hear of this. I'll have your name?'

'My name?'

The tall man smiled in amusement.

'My name is Peter . . .'

And then Rose slapped his face, throwing herself forward with the impetus of her swing to crash into the other two Gestapo men and block their path.

'*Courez!*' she shouted to the boy and his father.

But the little boy, maybe eight years old, found his way blocked. He climbed instead onto the stone balustrade of the bridge, shouting now in high-pitched fear. His father reached for him but fell beneath the blows of two of the thugs. Coshes came out. Rose kicked one of the Gestapo men as hard as she could in the groin and dealt a second slap to the tall man called Peter.

Then the boy's foot slipped, and he fell into the river, screaming.

Rose looked down at the bearded father struggling to rise to his feet, cursing his assailants. The gull-eyed man loomed suddenly before her, reaching towards her neck with gloved hands. Then Rose head-butted him in the chest and leapt over the parapet of the bridge.

It took far longer to fall than she'd expected. Her lungs were empty as she hit the water feet first, the last visual impression that of the spreading ripples from the point where the boy had gone in first, the last sound that of a voice shouting his name. *Jakob.*

Then she hit her head on something coming up from below. The impact stunned her, the cold froze her mind. Rose vaguely felt she couldn't stop going down. Her fall wasn't stopping in the water. Winded, her lungs bursting, she kicked ferociously, straining not to breathe. She couldn't tell which way was up. She wasn't floating. Casting about with her arms, she felt a solid object, and grabbed onto it for grim life. She felt skin, clothing. It was lifeless, limp, unresponsive to her grip. With her last rational thought as darkness closed in and her lungs sucked in water, Rose realized the boy was already dying or dead. Rose's body went into spasm, and fear gripped her mind.

She kicked for the surface, blackness closing in. She felt her arms weaken.

She had ruined everything.

A stranger saved her.

A Frenchman, she later learned, ran down the stone steps to the river embankment and launched himself fully clothed into the freezing river, forcing himself under, straining to reach the point where the boy and Rose had fallen.

Somehow he had found her. He'd dragged her to the surface and back to the bank, both of them already turning blue, and looking up at the bridge, in the instants before losing consciousness, Rose had seen the Gestapo thugs laughing and starting to saunter away. All but the tall one, who for a long instant had stood, silently, staring at her, before slowly walking off. He had looked almost puzzled.

When the Seine finally released little Jakob's body, washed up downriver days later, he'd become almost unrecognizable, his eyes and nose eaten by eels, she read in the papers.

Rose stayed in Paris. She returned as soon as she could to the detailed note-taking she had begun about German military units in Paris, about the effects of the Nazi occupation and the French response to it. All through the bitter winter of 1940–41, and into the following spring, she documented whatever she could, devising her own codes, disguising her work as pages in the thick manuscript of her planned novel, *No One's Story*. Berthe helped her keep body and soul together. Then, with great difficulty but iron determination, she made her way into the unoccupied zone, taking a bus to Spain, a train to Lisbon, her manuscript in her suitcase, and from there by ship to London, where she found work at the US embassy and quickly tracked down the right people to talk to about going back into France. The British SOE's F Section snapped her up almost immediately, her nationality no object.

Rose, codename Belle, flew into occupied France on an RAF Lysander out of Tangmere airfield near Chichester on the night of 16–17 June 1943, as an undocumented late addition to the passenger list. She accompanied two other women: an exotic-looking, dark-skinned radio operator, or 'pianist', like herself, and a blonde courier, older than them both, who spoke French with a marked English accent. As the latecomer, Rose was obliged to sit on the floor all the way to France, though the other radio girl, who called herself Madeleine, offered to swap with her.

Nevada

26 June 2007

Unexpected callers are not welcome when you are in Witness Protection. They are even less welcome when you are in it against your will, and when the purpose of your being there is not so much to protect you as to protect the federal government. The things Peter Hale had witnessed were absolutely never to be shared with a rapt jury in a courtroom or in any other public setting. He had been dropped down a deep dark hole in the middle of nowhere under a kind of house arrest that masqueraded as hard-earned retirement, generously underwritten by a grateful nation, but that involved the wearing of an electronic bracelet of unusual design.

A robust nonagenarian, German–French–English–American, a veteran of overt and unavowed wars through seven decades, Peter growled like a cornered animal when the shadows appeared in his mind, several minutes before they showed up on his doorstep. They were not his guards, the ones he called his *undertakers*, those whose job it was to keep him buried. Nor were they any of the regular delivery people, nor the plumber he needed to fix the leak in the bathroom, nor the vigorous widow with whom he had a standing tryst on Wednesdays after Bible study.

They were his enemies, and his masters. Three of them, always three, in his dreams, in the unguarded private corners of his mind. Instinctively, he checked the location of his nearest weapons. There was a pistol, undeclared to his keepers, hidden in a hollowed-out arm of the sofa in his living room. Framed on the wall, supposedly dulled and safe behind a glass cover but actually honed to razor sharpness and easily released for use, he kept in plain sight one of his most precious souvenirs from World War Two – a Fairbairn-Sykes fighting knife, the kind the British issued to commandos and secret agents. He opted, though, for something that might have more chance of success against these particular visitors, if needed. From a drawer in the front hall, he took his mother's crucifix.

Peter kissed the small silver cross, holding in his mind his memory, if memory it was, of his mother's face in the instant before he'd grabbed it, the perfection of her joy in him the instant before he'd ruined it, before he'd killed her by trying to save her. Then he fastened it around his neck and slipped it inside his shirt. The shadows now were at his door.

'Sit,' Peter said. 'Speak.'

Two of the white-haired men took up positions on the couch, while the third remained standing, his back to the fireplace. Peter stood too.

'You can be useful to us again,' the leader of the three visitors said.

'I'm retired.'

'You can never retire.'

'Do you see how they coop me up here? I can't go more than three miles from this house without . . . consequences. Severe ones.'

'Excuses. Such things can be overcome. Let me say again: you can be useful. Isn't that the great fear of old age? That we are no longer of any use to anyone?'

'I have my own fears of old age. Being useless is not among them.'

'You must fear all the unconfessable things you have

done. You must fear that you will be unable to escape the consequences of your actions, especially the actions you cannot admit to, the actions you cannot confess even to yourself.'

'You can be certain that if I ever feel the urge to confess, it will not be to you.'

The leader of the men stared at him without expression for several seconds, as though gazing at an unusual insect.

'Always the prodigal son. Your father will be proud.'

Peter held his gaze.

'To business,' he said. 'Please.'

'Horace Hencott, Peter. You may recall the name.'

'Hencott, yes.'

'He is vulnerable now. Through his own deeds. Through the completion of a pattern in time. And, uniquely, through you. He can be reached in a special way, in these days. Do you know what I am talking about?'

Peter shivered.

'I do.'

'Horace Hencott believes you vanished from the face of the earth in Paris, in 1944.'

'I've given him no cause to think otherwise.'

'Perhaps it is time to change that. A window may be opening. An opportunity. We require your special gift for malevolence. To help your father complete his life's work. To take revenge on Horace Hencott, and on those close to him. Robert Reckliss. Katherine Rota.'

Horace Hencott. At last Peter's chance had come. It was the opportunity he had prayed for.

Peter stared at his white-haired visitors one by one, looking each in the eyes, shielding his innermost thoughts. These men were asking him to serve his father, and the forces of hatred that worked through him, one last time. He had to say yes. Yet accepting would revive Isambard's influence over him in ways he might not be able to control.

'There's more to this than you are letting on,' Peter said.

'Certainly there is. You will have a role to play in a grander scheme. More than a walk-on part. But you are certainly not the only actor.'

'Give me a taste.'

'For now, we will just say, with William Faulkner: *The past is never dead. It's not even past.* You know this.'

'What do I know?'

The leader of the group smiled quizzically at him.

'The world is like a mind, Peter, and like a mind it has memories. Past events can occasionally be . . . reprised. Even *rectified.* There are certain events of the 1940s that we have a unique opportunity to *improve*, shall we say. Using the same instruments as those we use to bring Horace Hencott, at last, to his just desserts.'

Peter stared into his past, all the way back to the evening in London when he had stolen a torn sheet of paper that contained a mystery deeper than any he could hope to understand. *Falke* had been his identity then, his operational name.

He didn't trust these creatures. Yet as he weighed their words, he saw the opportunity to free himself at last, if he could find the strength to *come in*, to obey the secret summons that for decades had been reaching out to him across time, inviting him, begging him, to atone for his failures, for his harmful, poisonous life.

He twisted the golden signet ring on his finger.

'Tell me more.'

'You will need to go to England immediately. Time is already running out. We have arranged transportation. Cars. A private plane.'

'Where will I go?'

'We have brought an item that will help you with that. It belongs to the Reckliss family. We took it from his wife. With your gifts, it will give you . . . a trail to follow. An entrée into his mind.'

He handed over Katherine's wedding band.

'For the rest, look inward. You will know.'

The doorbell rang. His *undertakers* were here, to perform a long-scheduled check on his ankle bracelet, the one that filled his mind and body with acidic, biting pain if he moved more than three miles in any direction from the house.

Peter blinked, and the three white-haired envoys were gone.

His powers were returning, both for good and ill. It was time.

Cambridge

26 June 2007

Robert met Dr Romanek, a retired anthropology professor and former SOE colleague of Harry's, at the Eagle pub on Bene't Street, at the specific request of the latter.

A barrel-shaped man of moderate height with rheumy brown eyes and a well-trimmed grey moustache, Romanek had a slight trace still of Czech origins in his spoken English, which was grammatically flawless apart from a sporadic tendency to drop the definite and indefinite articles from his sentences. A wry smile played constantly on his lips.

'I like place where you can feel history above your head and in seat of your pants,' Romanek said. 'Makes me feel less like museum piece.'

Robert looked up and across the pub, following Romanek's eyes. During the Second World War Allied airmen had inscribed their names, messages to the future and humorous or obscene ditties with lighters and cigarette tips on the pub's legendary ceiling. It was a timeless tableau of camaraderie and defiance. The Eagle was also the pub where Francis Crick had walked in, one day in 1953, and announced the discovery of DNA, or as he termed it, the secret of life, by James Watson and himself.

Now they sat at Crick and Watson's favourite table.

'Let me tell you first what I remember Harry saying about Steeplejack,' Romanek said, when installed with a pint. 'Their team was called Steeplejack, by the way, because all SOE F Section teams were given names based on English professions. He said they were initially briefed on the operation in tawdry little house near St Giles' Circus. It was a rum mission, a lot of twaddle, he said. They were asked to hunt down an alchemist in wartime Paris who common sense would tell you didn't even exist. Bring him back or kill him. Didn't even have name, just pseudonym: Fulcanelli. Seemed like wild goose chase to him, and it all ended rather badly. The group was infiltrated.'

Romanek's face darkened, his voice thickening as he went on. Horace had explained to him that Romanek had trained with Harry in Scotland and at the SOE 'finishing school' at Beaulieu, before being infiltrated into his occupied homeland to organize anti-Nazi resistance. He was the only member of his network to have survived the war. Afterwards, settling in England, he had become an academic. 'Radio operator they were using was betrayed. Wonderful girl. She was American woman, real handful. Tough. No names, no pack-drill. He'd always remember her, he said. She was really something. Tiny scrap of a thing, but brave as lion.'

Robert, on edge and in pain, asked Romanek what else he remembered.

'Well, Steeplejack was unusual team, because they were not primarily about setting up resistance operations, arming *maquis*, preparing for D-Day and so forth, as other F Section *réseaux* were,' Romanek said. 'And they were not just about low-key intelligence gathering, as MI6 were. MI6 hated SOE, by the way. They hated everything SOE stood for, not least because SOE was created, in part, by taking MI6's own dirty tricks and sabotage section away from them. They didn't like SOE blowing things up. Attracted too much attention. Silly buggers. We were all fighting the Germans. Anyway. Steeplejack didn't blow much up. They did get lot of people killed, though. Nazi reprisals. Same thing happened in my country. That's all I know, I'm afraid.'

After a moment, Romanek raised his pint glass. 'To Harry Hale. Good man.'

Robert joined the toast. 'So I hear.'

After dinner, Robert asked Romanek about witches. Despite the happy chatter of tourists and locals in the pub yard, Robert felt chilled to the core. Something evil was stalking him, hiding in the crowd, lurking behind the smiling faces and the merry eyes. He laboured to concentrate, driving his pain away.

'Well some believe in all this, and some don't, but the fact is, many followers of what they call the *elder faith* came together during war,' Romanek said, pushing aside his plate of fish and chips. 'To fight Nazis. To stop them invading, first of all. They were called Fenland Workings. There were several. The first was on Lammas Night in 1940. Another important one was night of 23 October 1942. Does that date ring a bell for you?'

'Not specifically.'

'It lasted through to dawn of following day. A full moon night, fullest just after five in the morning.'

'What was it for? What happened then? And how do you know all this, Dr Romanek? Horace said I should talk to you, but . . .'

'Interviews. Local anthropology has always been hobby of mine.'

Robert made a wild surmise.

'You spoke to someone from my family?'

'Yes. I spoke to man called Reckliss. He would have been *old boy* at the time, as they say around here. Youngster. My records are all in storage in some college vault these days, but I keep index at home, and I checked when you called me. Kids' parents took them along to Workings. They needed everyone who knew how. Germans were across Channel in

France, ready to come. Just like Napoleon before them. And Spanish before that.'

'The Armada?' There had been tales he'd heard as a child, the lore of his people . . .

'Yes. They say there are certain things *elder faith* in this country is only allowed to do in times of national jeopardy. Across the country, each in their own tradition, they raised what they call cone of power, in 1588, to protect against Spanish invader. One of your ancestors, Old Dolly and her people in Aldwych, made *enhardening spell* – that means powerful protective action – as moon was waxing full. The July working, or Alde Wyche working, they called it. Now you can think what you like, but next night, Drake had favourable wind and sent in fire-ships against Armada at Calais, breaking up their formation, and day after that, the English, with weather in their favour still, drove Armada up towards Scotland, where gales did the rest.'

Robert looked around the pub yard. He was feeling colder and colder. He began to shiver.

'Are you all right, Robert?'

'Go on, please. About the Armada . . . do you believe that?'

'It doesn't matter what I think, Robert. The English struck commemorative medal that said *He blew with his winds, and they were scattered*. Some understand by that the Protestant God. Some around here understand their own Great God Termagant. Same thing happened in July 1804, they say. Napoleon was at Boulogne with his invasion army. The whole nation expected him to come. They sang the great protective galster again, your people included, as moon was waxing full in July. Napoleon ordered his flotilla of barges into Channel for manoeuvres, and storm devastated them. Hundreds of his men were drowned. He gave up.'

'And later? October 1942, you said?'

'Does it mean anything to you? 23 October of that year?'

'It doesn't. I know it should, but . . .'

'*The turning point of the war.* Not my words. General Montgomery's, just before they went into action. *One of the decisive battles of history,* he called it.'

'El Alamein?'

'Now you see. *Before Alamein we never had a victory,* Churchill said. *After Alamein we never had a defeat.* The battle began that night. Turned the war. Stopped Germans getting Suez Canal, stopped them getting all the Middle Eastern oil.'

'Do you believe this?'

'It's what they say.'

Though he was freezing cold, Robert was sweating, a shrill note of fear ringing in his ears, drilling behind his eyes. Someone was coming for him. He tried to envisage them. He got nothing but static, a fleeting impression of green eyes, hard like glass. A wave of pain flowed over him.

'I wasn't told much about all this,' Robert said. 'What I heard, I got from the other kids, when my parents weren't watching. Members of all our families took part in ceremonies of some kind, to stop the Nazis coming. Like for like, was a phrase I heard. And something went wrong. Someone was terribly hurt, or died. Old Dolly, they said.'

'Well, that's hereditary name that's passed from one witch to another. Back in 1588, when your people still lived in London, it was one of your forebears, as I say, who led the Working against Spanish Armada, at the site of holy well at Aldwych. You go all the way back in that area to ninth century.'

'Really? When did we move here?'

'At beginning of the 1600s, after James I came to power and passed new Witchcraft Statute. That's why village is called Oldwick Fen where you grew up. Your people brought the name with them.'

'It means Old Witch?'

Romanek laughed.

'You'd think so, but it's not true. After the Romans left London, the locals there didn't live in the walled Roman city, they preferred open lands to the west. They didn't move into walled city until Danes came raiding and burning along River Thames, start of ninth century. When they abandoned the old Anglo-Saxon settlement, it became known as Eald Wic or Alde Wyche. Old settlement.'

'Aldwych.'

'Right. When Alfred eventually forced Danes to submit, at end of ninth century, he said Danes who'd married English women could settle just west of the city, on site of the old settlement. That's where church of St Clement Danes gets its name. They took over old wooden church that was still standing from the old days, they say.'

'We're a mix of Dane and Saxon from those times . . .'

'There's a bit of everything in most people from around here, Robert. Celt and Jute, too, maybe some Romany . . . Lady's name who sang the great galster, as they say, who raised incantation against the Armada, was called Old Dolly Redcap, and the name has passed down in family since. What they say Old Dolly did that summer, after Armada was defeated, was something to ensure the incantation could be renewed any time nation was in danger. There's a bell at St Clement Danes, the Sanctus Bell. It was cast later that same year, 1588, by Robert Mot of Whitechapel. He wasn't of *elder faith*, but she used her power, one way or another, to persuade him to melt some items of iron into bell when it was being cast. Not just any items, mind you.'

'Isn't St Clement Danes the Royal Air Force church now?'

'That's right, they rebuilt it after it was gutted in Blitz. It all fits together, you see. Defence of realm, and all.'

'So what were these items?'

'Iron magic . . . they say they were iron wall anchors, in the form of double S or fylfot, ceremonially prepared, used as talismans, in the enhardening spell against Armada.'

'Fylfot? Enhardening? Bear with me, Dr Romanek, I wasn't brought up in this stuff.'

'You know what wall anchor is, at least?'

'Kind of a metal brace, to reinforce a wall.'

'Right. The end-part that shows is usually a sigil, protective rune or symbol. Out here they use the S form a lot, or double S, to ward off lightning, demonic attack, that sort of thing.'

'And fylfot?'

'Like a double S, but sometimes with straight arms. You'll have seen it in another context, I'm afraid.'

Romanek took some salt, and bled it between his fingers to make the shape on the table between them. Robert blanched. The wounds on his chest, less dulled by alcohol than he'd hoped, began to blaze, as though the older man were pouring the salt straight into them.

'A swastika?'

'That's what it's called in English these days, yes. It's been around a lot longer than those Nazi scum, though. People have used it out this way for centuries, as symbol for power of the sun, or power of Thor's mell, his hammer. It's not evil; on the contrary. The anticlockwise form is masculine power. The clockwise form is feminine power. That's the one the Nazis used.'

'Yin and yang.'

'If you say so. But around these parts, the fylfot is good, no matter which way you draw it. Always has been.'

Oldwick Fen

26 June 2007

Death was coming.

The mechanical growl, impersonal and pitiless, filled Margaret's ears. A dark sigil sped across the cloudless white London sky, tracing an arc of hatred.

Margaret gathered all the strength left in her, renewing the fight. She clung to life, twisting the bedsheets in agitation around her aged limbs.

Just a few more days. Just a few more hours, after so long.

The flying bomb was nearing the River Thames. She could see it. Soon it would begin its final dive. The sound was in the sky, all around, triggering ancestral memories of danger: a guttural rumble, echoing on the stone facades of buildings, raw and pulsing. Inescapable.

Margaret called for water. Her throat was burning.

It was a machine, blind and powerful, but it was human too: there was intention behind it. There was evil.

She cried again for water.

Then came its second sound: the silence, the non-sound of its fall, flaps depressed and engine cutting out, the fifteen seconds of paralysing fear.

They said you either heard it explode, and knew you were still alive, or didn't hear it, and were already dead.

She clawed in agitation at the sheets of her sickbed. Sixty-three years on, and it was coming still.

She knew this would be her last fight: to live these last remaining days, to be alive when it landed, when time came around again, so that the past, like the spectral Lantern Men of her native East Anglia, could be chased away back into the night.

Soothing hands brought a cool cloth for her forehead. She sipped water.

Still the bomb fell, endlessly.

The Lantern Men wanted to carry her unsuspecting descendants off to their deaths. They were gathering now, spectral Fen lights at the fringes of her dream, waiting for the moment when the window between worlds would open, so they could take off her grandchildren, and everyone else's.

She had to live, to pass on the nameless art to a successor, at the appointed hour, when her own art expired. Then the enhardening song would hold, renewed, good for another generation. Jack Reckliss, her grandson, would not do. She had looked into him, and at the last moment had seen his weakness. It would need to be his cousin, Robert. Again, always, she tried to reach him.

She saw the moons crossing the sky, cycle after cycle, the turning of the great wheel of the world. Always new, always the same.

The Lantern Men were never defeated, only ever banished for a short while, till the next time. The seal had to be constantly renewed, the galster endlessly re-sung.

For sixty-three years she had protected her people. She had to live, just a few more days, to finish the job.

Day Three

London

Early 1943

It was a dingy room at the Hotel Victoria on Northumberland Avenue, stripped almost bare, and the man sitting across the plain wooden table from Harry Hale-Devereaux had an unprepossessing look about him, despite his army major's uniform.

Harry had felt his heart sink slightly on entering room 238 and seeing just the hard wooden chair awaiting him, under a dim exposed light bulb. While it wasn't glamour he was looking for, he had hoped this mysterious interview might be his avenue to a more exciting way of taking the fight to the Nazis than his current job as a liaison to the notoriously prickly Free French headquarters staff of General de Gaulle. Harry had been evacuated from Dunkirk, and he was burning to go back and settle things.

'Now you've signed the Official Secrets Act, so I don't need to labour the point about not repeating anything you hear in this room,' the interviewer said. He had sharp eyes, Harry allowed, behind a demeanour of unexceptional dullness.

'Why don't we start by talking a little about your family? *Vous avez vécu en France . . .*'

Harry began to tell him about his childhood in France and England, first-born son and heir to the grand Lord Hale-Devereaux of Poldhu, and soon found himself in unexpected terrain, the conversation shifting, by subtle degrees, to a shared investigation of whether resentment of his father ever motivated him, whether romantic attachment had eluded or found or abandoned him, whether personal unhappiness might be a reason to seek fulfilment in this kind of work, with the precise nature of *this kind of work* tantalizingly never quite spelled out, but clearly war work of an unconventional nature, possibly highly dangerous.

As they talked further, Harry found himself warming to the nondescript older man before him, finding they shared a discerning love of France and the French, an enjoyment of crossword puzzles, a disdain for impetuous action, an admiration for a certain kind of rugged honesty and dependability in people and things.

'Now of course when you were at Dunkirk, you were dive-bombed, the Stukas gave you a pretty rough go of it, and I suppose it would be natural to want to take *revenge*, wouldn't it . . .'

The probing and simultaneous revealing and concealing went on till late in the afternoon, touching on questions of personal and national honour, the general war situation in France, the kinds of work it might be possible to do for a fluent French speaker with proper training and know-how . . .

'I suppose I'm being a little more forthcoming than I might usually be at this stage of things,' the major said. 'And of course you'll need to go away and think about all this for a day or two, and if it's not something you can see yourself doing, well, there's certainly no black mark or anything of the kind, you'll need to be as sure as any man can be that you want to do the work . . .'

'Excuse me, sir.'

'Yes?'

'About the work. Could you possibly be a little more precise?'

'Ah. Well. Not very, you see. I must be completely frank.

There is great risk, really a high risk, of being caught, and of course that means interrogation by the Gestapo, which no one in their right mind can contemplate with anything but great trepidation. Not being in uniform, of course, you wouldn't be protected at all. Probably shot, if captured. Very valuable work, but I won't need to convince you of that.'

Harry had picked up enough on the grapevine at the Free French headquarters at Duke Street to know that Frenchmen were being sent back into the country clandestinely to help arm and coordinate resistance to the Nazi occupation. He'd also heard guarded talk of something mysterious lurking behind the vague label of Inter-Services Research Bureau, of dark goings-on at Dorset Square.

'I've often thought, sir, that I could make a better contribution to the war effort if I could get myself sent back to France. The Free French only take Frenchmen, though, as far as I know . . .'

'Well, let's stick to generalities for now, but . . .'

It was the most astonishing conversation of Harry's life. By the end of it, not quite knowing when it had happened or quite how, he found himself being invited to join the Inter-Services Research Bureau, an organization he would later know as the Special Operations Executive.

Paris

1943

The man was a bloody mess. Peter couldn't look at him, yet he couldn't look away. Isambard's presence was too powerful.

The prisoner was trembling, perched on the edge of the bathtub filled with freezing water, a heavy iron chain around his neck. His arms cradled his naked, unprotected body.

'I will ask you once again,' Isambard said. 'Where did Fulcanelli hide the document? Where is Fulcanelli?'

The man began to shake uncontrollably, weeping now.

'Please. I don't know. I don't. Please.'

Isambard grunted and nodded to one of his interrogators, who yanked the chain as hard as he could, forcing the prisoner to fall back into the icy water. Beefy men in Gestapo uniforms stepped forward and held him under, punching him in the belly, forcing him to swallow water. The bathtub frothed as the man's limbs flailed and the contents of his lungs bubbled to the surface.

They dragged him out as he was about to drown and threw him on the floor at Isambard's feet. His skin was blue, his stomach swollen tight as a drum where he had swallowed the contents of the bathtub.

'Ask him again, Falke.'

The prisoner lay retching and choking on the floor, water mixed with blood flowing from his nose and mouth. Peter kneeled down to speak into his ear.

'This makes no sense. This has to stop. I'm begging you to make it stop. It defiles all of us. No one wants this. Just tell us. Where is the document hidden? Where is Fulcanelli?'

Shaking, trying to curl up into a ball, the man averted his eyes from Peter's.

Isambard's assistants stepped forward, one at his head and one at his feet, and grabbed his limbs, forcing him to stretch his arms above his head. Isambard stepped forward and placed his boot on the man's distended stomach, pressing down. Water poured from his mouth, seeped into his windpipe, sending his whole body into spasms of panic. His gurgling, weeping plea echoed around the interrogation room:

'Please. No more.'

'Make it stop,' Peter intoned. 'End this.'

'Kill me,' the prisoner whispered.

Isambard removed his boot.

'Again,' he said, nodding to his staff and indicating the bathtub. 'Another hour. Then take him back to Avenue Foch. I'll see him there later. Falke, come downstairs with me.'

They emerged onto Rue des Saussaies, outside the former French Interior Ministry building, now repurposed as a Gestapo facility. It was evening.

'Take me to your route. I will accompany you.'

To get there, Peter took him east, along Rue St Honoré to the Comédie Française at Palais Royal, then along Rue de Rivoli to the Tour St Jacques, a flamboyant Gothic tower that was the only remnant of a medieval church at the corner of Rue St Martin. A reputed alchemist called Nicholas Flamel had been buried there, under the church he helped build, legend held, with transmuted gold.

'Flamel,' said Peter. 'Was he truly privy to the Great Work? Did he achieve it?'

'No,' Isambard replied. 'He was just a wealthy butcher. His legend was created many years after his death, by others, as a way of hiding certain secrets of the Great Work in plain sight in the stories about him. This crossroads is a site for the Paris *geheime Feuer*, though. That's why it forms part of the route you have been tracing for me, north and south from here.'

They walked south together, along Rue St Martin, towards the Seine.

'That man knew nothing, of course,' Isambard said. 'I knew he knew nothing. The important thing was not to make him talk. It was his fear. His despair. His suffering. It enhances our power. It strengthens my own *geheime Feuer*.'

Peter felt sick. *The man had known nothing.* He strained to hide his shame.

'Your anguish at the torture makes you a highly effective interrogator,' Isambard said. 'Prisoners feel that you are genuinely appalled. Are you?'

'I find it . . . difficult.'

'Your mother made you weak. But you are redeemable, you've done excellent work. In London, and here. The force of our Secret Fire in this city is palpable. Look at them.'

Isambard pointed to a crowd of fashionable Parisians milling around the entrance to one of the city's theatres where a new play had just opened, a theatre formerly named after the actress Sarah Bernhardt, her Jewish name now stripped from it. 'Their will is eroded. They have accommodated us. Almost all of them, willingly or not. They have made their grudging peace. Handed us their Jews. The shape, the mark of power you and your colleagues have walked into this city has fostered – magnified – the sensation of submission, of humiliation, in the psyche of everyone in this city.'

'Thank you,' Peter said, guardedly. 'Will it have the same effect in London?'

Isambard stopped as they reached the river.

'In London, since the *Führer* does not currently plan to invade, we will use it for a different purpose. It will help us deliver a kind of killer blow, when the time is right. Which is why I must strengthen, to the maximum, my own, personal *vril*. And which is why we must find Fulcanelli and the second half of the Newton document. The part we possess tells us what materials to assemble in order to focus and magnify the *geheime Feuer* as we wish to do. We have all the materials, including some of the original stained glass from Chartres cathedral. But the missing half tells us how to assemble them: in what proportions, under what conditions.'

'They say it is a life's work.'

'Not so. If one has acquired the materials, and has prepared oneself suitably over many years, the assembly itself is said to take only a few days.'

'Will you tell me how to achieve the Great Work?'

'When I learn how, you will find out too,' Isambard replied, his crystal-green eyes clouding over.

They walked on, tracing the north–south axis of a mighty seal or stamp of power Peter had helped impress on the heart of the City of Light, pausing at different focal points of the city's invisible, constituting power and filling them with psychic poison. Again and again, Peter whispered his secret phrase: *Lucem in tenebris occulto* . . .

And as they went, Peter tested, with growing confidence, his ability to shield a small, selfless corner of his mind from his father, and thanked in his soul the woman who had given it to him.

London

Summer 1943

Five months into his SOE training, Harry Hale-Devereaux reported to an unassuming house in Primrose Hill, just north of Regent's Park, for further briefing on the specific mission he was to undertake.

The living room of the house was furnished in comfortable but unspectacular style. Harry sat on the settee, his briefing officer opposite him in an old leather armchair. He was a pale, stocky man in his fifties who wore the uniform of an RAF Wing Commander and gave his name as Smith. A younger man, in American uniform without insignia, sat in an armchair and was not introduced.

'Your specialist training is going to take a slightly unusual turn,' Smith said. 'What you are about to hear is classified Most Secret, and is additionally protected by the fact that anyone who heard you repeat it would think you were either unhinged or a blithering idiot. You will, naturally, not even think of testing that statement.'

Harry had almost coasted through the early weeks of preliminary training, which had taught him little about soldiering he didn't already know and revealed to him little about the outfit he had joined.

Things had begun to look up with the five weeks of advanced paramilitary training he and his fellow future agents had undergone in the remote highlands of Scotland, around Arisaig in Inverness-shire. Based in shooting lodges, they had hauled themselves up and down the craggy, bleak terrain till they dropped, and then some more, acquiring advanced map and compass skills, and learned fascinating things about demolition, commando tactics and, above all in Harry's book, the art of silent killing, taught by two extremely tough former Shanghai policemen called Major Fairbairn and Major Sykes. Then he had done parachute training jumps at Ringway airfield near Manchester.

Finally, at what the SOE called its 'Finishing School' at Beaulieu in Hampshire, they had been told who they worked for, what it did and what they would be doing when they were sent abroad. Much instruction had focused on how to recruit agents, how to create or expand resistance networks, maintaining operational security and working successfully in enemy-occupied territory. They learned the art of disguise, burglary and lock-picking, codes and ciphers, and how to resist interrogation for as long as possible. They were told of the 'L-pill' or suicide pill they would all be issued with, should they choose to take that option upon capture.

A further stint was scheduled at a Specialist Training School, covering skills as disparate as industrial sabotage, propaganda and microphotography, but Harry had not yet been told which one he was to attend. He expected to find out now.

Harry felt the eyes of the young American on him, but resisted the temptation to address him or ask what he was doing there. He was about Harry's age, or even younger, perhaps in his mid-twenties. Yet when Harry sneaked another sideways look, a few minutes later, he could have been ten or fifteen years older. His gaze, when it fell on Harry, had the intensity of a searchlight.

'In July 1936, an auction was held at Sotheby's of some of the personal papers of Sir Isaac Newton,' Smith said. 'The proceedings attracted relatively little attention at the time, though among these papers were items of great interest to a small community of people around the world.'

'I remember something about his Royal Mint papers being donated to the nation.'

'Quite. We are not concerned with those, but with certain other papers, one in particular. Now let me take you forward to the night of May 10, 1941. Ring any bells?'

'A hellish night. One of the worst nights of the Blitz, perhaps *the* worst. House of Commons destroyed. St Mary-le-Bow, Queen's Hall, St Clement Danes, all burned out. The East End. Elephant and Castle. Westminster Abbey. Hitler's last big go at London before getting a little bored and taking on Stalin too. I helped fight the fires at St Clement Danes.'

Smith smiled at him.

'You may be forgetting that Deputy *Führer* Rudolf Hess flew to Scotland that same night of May 10, though it was reported a few days later.'

Harry had forgotten.

'They were surely unconnected. The man is said to be barking mad, isn't he?'

'He is. Said to be, that is. However, he is not without useful information. Much of his strange babble upon landing and in interrogation has been listened to by experts. We've tried all kinds of tricks with him, some more fruitful than others. His bragging about a super-weapon that the Germans hope to use against us, for example. He called it *das geheime Feuer*. The Secret Fire. He talked about certain people in Paris holding the key to this weapon. Some of the secret is in Germany, he said, but the missing part is in Paris. On and on he went about finding the missing part to make the device. We were led to think, naturally, of the Joliot-Curie family in Paris, and their research to do with radiation, as well as Dr Heisenberg, an eminent German physicist. Expert opinion seems to be that making a weapon out of atoms is not possible for decades, if ever. We – some of our unusual friends and I – are not so sure, however. Hess, in his ramblings, spoke of another man, someone altogether more elusive. The name he gave was Fulcanelli.'

'Not a name to me.'

'He will be. You are to go to France. Find this *geheime Feuer* secret. Find this man. Bring him back, but if you can't, kill him.'

Silence fell in the room as Harry digested Smith's words, which had been delivered in the flat tone of someone running through items on a shopping list.

The young American now spoke for the first time. He had a well-educated, New England intonation that sounded almost like an Englishman of comparable social background, though more businesslike than plummy. He was about action, and he came to the point.

'It is crucial for the war effort that we ascertain from Fulcanelli the whereabouts of a certain sheet of paper. A half-sheet, to be precise.'

'We?'

'I'll be going with you. After we complete your specialist training. We'll have other help in France too, but you don't need to know about that now.'

'May I ask who you are?'

The American stood and stepped forward to shake hands. Harry rose to his feet.

'Horace Hencott. I'm with the OSS, your sister organization in the States.'

Horace settled now on the settee, perching on the arm and turning to speak to Harry in an informal, easy manner.

Bloody Yanks, Harry thought. Have to be so cool about everything.

'Fulcanelli, or whoever is concealed behind that name, is said to be a master alchemist. The real thing, living in Paris in the present day,' Horace said. 'It is feared he may know atomic and other more esoteric secrets, and be in possession of the sheet of paper I told you about – the other half of a Newton document stolen by the Nazis here in London, after the 1936 auction.'

'How did they manage that? Why didn't we get it? On our own turf, for heaven's sake?'

Smith gave an embarrassed half-look at Horace.

'We did get it, actually. The bidding was arranged, without the knowledge of Sotheby's, naturally, so that our man would win this particular lot. But he was killed on his way to hand it over to us. The Nazis got his half. This Fulcanelli, it is reported, has the other.'

'The two halves of this document must never be conjoined by the Nazis,' the American said, his eyes cold with determination. 'It must be denied to them, by whatever means necessary.'

'It tells how to make this Secret Fire? This atom weapon?'

'It can help make a weapon of unimaginable power, yes. Whoever possesses it will win the war. Of that, we have no doubt.'

London

27 June 2007

Horace rubbed his eyes in fatigue and tried to see further. He started again. The tips of his fingers just brushing the document on the desk before him, he silenced his mind and let the object speak.

A flash of emotion came to him, tied to a visual impression of glass falling, shattered glass falling down the faces of buildings like sleet, fear and horror mingled with relief . . . Then it was gone.

He looked about himself. There were perhaps a dozen people in the tiny circular reading room at the very top of the Imperial War Museum, perched inside its dome like pigeons in a rooftop loft. Some were pursuing professional research projects or college papers, others looking up family history.

Horace had arrayed before him several files of letters, diaries and unpublished memoirs from the Second World War, all of which contained some reference to V-1 attacks in London in June 1944. One by one he was reading them, as very few people could – not for their words, but for the link they provided through time to the past, to the real events their authors had witnessed.

Like all use of the outer reaches of psychic ability that Horace had attained, in decades of study and practice, the work was hugely draining. Yet the effects could be remarkable.

It was like music. Just as the emotions felt by a skilled composer – his joy, his melancholy or despair – could come alive again, hundreds of years later, upon the playing of a musical piece he had written, so all objects, to a greater or lesser degree, could be decoded, or played, and their psychic contents experienced again. Mental and emotional states – spiritual states, even – could be unconsciously encoded in objects, and shielded from the erosion of time.

For there were two kinds of time, Horace had learned. The first was the time of convention, of the reality everyone agreed upon, the clockwork succession of minutes, seconds and years that timepieces marked, subdivisions of familiar cycles – the turning of the sun, the earth, the moon. Human beings had so fully internalized it that often no other kind seemed to exist.

Then there was the second kind. It was the time of strangeness: of time linked to space, of time that can eddy and flow back like a river. It was the time of Einstein's science, time that could be distorted by mass and speed, slowed and accelerated for different observers, time freed from the shackles of clockwork.

This was also the time of inner, lived experience, the time that made being alive a symphony of recollection, of triggered associations and involuntary memories, that allowed childhood impressions to be more vividly present than tasks we had performed ten minutes ago, that could bring sensations and emotions – the taste of a slice of fruit, the softness of a kiss, the emotional pain of exclusion or heartbreak – barrelling unexpectedly out of the void, to stun us with their intensity.

And in the second kind of time a force operated that was invisible in the first. The secret – one of the many secrets Horace had learned, and one of the most powerful – was that in this second time, aspects of the physical world and the mental world were connected. An interface could be found, and exploited, so that with suitable magnification – achieved through differing means, in different cultures – mind and matter could grip each other, exert action upon each other.

This was the nature of the Great Work, and of the use of the *geheime Feuer*, as he had tried to explain to Robert. The Secret Fire was a form of force that flowed within human beings, and within the earth. Its time was not conventional time, but the time of strangeness.

And that was the time in which events were playing themselves out.

Horace cast his mind back to wartime Paris.

He shivered.

The day he dreaded, the paying of accounts for decisions and mistakes made six decades earlier, was fast approaching.

The man he had sent to hell, he could see clearly now, was coming back. The past was not dead. It was happening still, in a secret place just an atom's breadth away, and it was about to erupt again into the present day.

He had been a young man back then, untested as yet, embarking upon a path he did not understand. He had dealt with impossible issues, faced intractable dilemmas, and dealt with them the best way he knew how. Would he change any of the decisions he had taken back then, if he could, now that their consequences were finally coming home to roost?

No, however much he might wish to.

He had made a trade-off. His life, at some future time, in exchange for something precious, to himself and the world. He had made a deal with the devil, in the form of Isambard, in order to achieve a higher good. He had made promises. And now it was time to face the full consequences of his actions.

And to fight.

The battle was always fought with imperfect information, with clouds of doubt and uncertainty. Neither side, for all their prodigious abilities, could fully see what the other was doing. Each had a critical blind spot about their adversary. The Enemy – the IWNW, Himmler's Section Four, however they might frame themselves – could not see through selflessness, were blind to love.

The other side, Horace's side, could only see as much evil as they acknowledged in themselves. The higher reaches of his training had consisted of exploring his own capacity for evil, without allowing himself to be seduced by it. Fortunately, Horace knew himself capable of much.

He took up the next letter, this one including a sketch, by the author, of the devastation left by the Aldwych V-1. Horace placed one hand on the sketch, and the other on a photograph from the material that Adam had collected about the incident, showing remnants of the V-1 itself amid the damage.

He breathed deeply, closing his eyes, clearing his mind.

And then he saw.

The London air-raid sirens howled.

The V-1 tore across southern England at over 350 miles per hour, faster than almost anything the British could put in the air against it, skipping past the barrage balloons' steel cables aimed at tearing off its wings, outpacing all the efforts of the anti-aircraft gunners to traverse their guns fast enough to blow it out of the sky.

On Aldwych, at the eastern end of the Strand, dozens of people queuing outside the Post Office on the ground floor of Bush House looked skywards. Girls on their lunch break at the Air Ministry at Adastral House opposite, sunbathing on the roof, hurriedly covered up.

In the basement of Australia House, just east of the post office, a young serviceman on leave cued up a shot at the snooker table, oblivious of the looming danger overhead.

Double-decker buses let passengers on and off, lined up just east of Kingsway on the semi-circular Aldwych kerb.

A black silhouette against the brilliant blue summer sky, the V-1 began its final dive over South London, somewhere above Waterloo Station, the mechanical growl of its pulse-jet engine suddenly cutting off.

Then the dreadful silence as it fell.

In the East Court of Bush House, alarm bells rang inside the building, indicating 'enemy action imminent'.

A young man and his friends from the post room at the BBC's Foreign Service, returning to work at Bush House after spending their lunch hour fooling around by Cleopatra's Needle, saw the dark shape disappear behind the buildings in front of them. They threw themselves to the ground.

Several young women inside the Air Ministry massed at a window, trying to get a look at the 'ghastly thing'.

Some bus passengers tried to take cover. Others in the bus and post office queues trusted to luck or God, resignation and indifference in their faces, knowing that if they heard it explode, they would probably still be alive. Helplessly, they watched it fall towards them.

A young woman at the Air Ministry, chatting with a colleague in their boss's office, saw the flash of the explosion reflected in her friend's eyes, a split-second before the deafening blast hit them.

The V-1 fell in the middle of the street between Bush House and Adastral House, the home of the Air Ministry, at 2:07 p.m., making a direct hit on one of the city's main loci of power, the site of the Aldwych holy well, directly on the London ley line.

Brilliant blue skies turned to grey fog and darkness.

The device exploded some 40 yards east of the junction of Aldwych *and Kingsway, about 40 feet from the Air Ministry offices opposite the east wing of Bush House.*

As the Australian serviceman took his snooker shot, the plaster ceiling in the basement of Australia House fell in on the table in front of him.

The Air Ministry's 10-foot-tall blast walls, made of 18-inch-thick brick, disintegrated immediately, deflecting the force of the explosion up and down the street. Hundreds of panes of glass shattered, blowing razor-sharp splinters through the air. The Air Ministry women watching at the windows were sucked out of Adastral House by the vacuum and dashed to death on the street below. Men and women queuing outside the Post Office were torn to pieces. Shrapnel peppered the facades of Bush House and the Air Ministry like bullets.

A double-decker approaching Aldwych reared up like a frightened horse, settled for a brief moment, then veered over at an angle of 45 degrees, first to one side, then to the other. The roof of the bus in front peeled back, as if cut by a giant tin-opener. The other double-deckers waiting on Aldwych were shattered, their red bodywork ripped to pieces, their passengers torn apart.

Australia House's great glass dome shattered, fragments smashing down into the vestibule.

Broken panes from all the damaged buildings fell like sleet into the street.

The blast wrecked the facade of the Aldwych Theatre on the corner of Drury Lane, killing an airman at the box-office window as he was buying a ticket for that night's performance of the anti-totalitarian play There Shall Be No Night by Robert Emmet Sherwood, starring Alfred Lunt and Lynn Fontaine.

Outside Adastral House, a heavy door flew off its hinges, crushing the doorman standing outside.

The blast killed all the sunbathing women on the roof of the Air Ministry. Dust and smoke spewed everywhere.

Part of the casement of the bomb lay burning at the corner of Kingsway. The dead and dying lay scattered in the street. Groans and cries of pain filled the air, though many could not hear them, deafened by the concussion. Some of the victims were naked, their clothing blown from them by the blast.

Aldwych was covered in every direction with debris and broken glass. Banknotes blew in the breeze. A private car stood shattered near the twisted remains of an emergency surface water tank, its 11,000 gallons dispersed, the steel sheets of its walls blown apart.

People walked around dazed, blood pouring from wounds some didn't know they had, the crunch of broken glass under their feet ubiquitous. One woman walked down seventy-nine steps of an Adastral House stairwell to the street, not realizing her right foot was hanging sideways, feeling no pain, stepping over bodies.

Staff and guests from the nearby Waldorf Hotel ran to help. Ambulances and fire engines sped to the scene. Police directed the injured to a First Aid post in the basement of Bush House, casualties receiving treatment for the next three hours.

Still it was not safe.

One man stepped from a doorway after the blast and was sliced vertically in two by a sheet of falling glass.

A news editor of the Evening Standard who came upon the scene couldn't take his eyes off the trees. Their leaves had all been replaced by pieces of human flesh.

A Reuters office boy who'd been on one of the double-deckers, running to help, came across a middle-aged woman sitting on the pavement, propped up against a shop front, her face deathly white, cuts all about her face and neck, one shoe missing and her stockings torn. She had auburn hair and was still clutching her handbag. He bent down to see if he could help her. Then a voice behind him said: 'There's nothing you can do for her, chum. She's gone. Died about two or three minutes ago.'

Soon the junction of Kingsway and Aldwych was a sea of stretchers, *the occupants all dead. Experienced ambulance workers worked in quick and practised drills to remove the dead and seriously hurt.*

When the counting was done, about fifty people were killed, 400 seriously wounded, another 200 lightly injured.

The BBC boy and his friends went back to work at Bush House. Staff at the top secret Political Warfare Executive and other nearby offices did the same. After a strong cup of tea back at 85 Fleet Street, the Reuters boy wrote his first news story, with the help of some kindly sub-editors. One woman went back into Adastral House and tried to help clear up, though soon she and her colleagues were sent home for the day. She had the presence of mind to telephone her mother and say she was all right. Many phones routed through the local Temple exchange, though, stopped working.

Horace removed his fingers from the documents. Tears were in his eyes, sweat was pouring down his face. A middle-aged lady researcher across the room gave him a look of alarm.

He examined a copy Adam had made of a contemporary bomb-damage diagram, drawn hours after the blast on semi-translucent tracing paper and kept at the National Archives at Kew. It recorded the point of impact as a star, in vivid red pencil. An arrow pointed to a 'small crater' – the V-1 did not burrow deep into the ground, but propagated its deadly force at surface level.

Horace tried to understand what he had seen.

As terrible as it was, the 1944 Aldwych V-1 attack had been a failure, on its own terms.

London, and hence England, was left standing. The D-Day landings were not disrupted, their commanders not killed, the Allies not dealt a crippling blow. The intended cataclysmic explosion – the biggest conflagration yet known to man – had been contained, frozen in time, by prayer and the nameless art, by fearless souls calling on the power of the holy site where the V-1 hit, and on acts of willing self-sacrifice to save others.

Horace had helped stop it, sixty-three years ago.

He began to gather his papers.

He thought he knew how it could be stopped again.

SOE Special Training School 17

Late summer 1943

Sweat stinging his eyes, a stitch like a hot needle stabbing his gut as they pounded along the hedge-lined country lane, Harry swore at the American between rasping breaths.

Hencott was very fit, he had to admit. They'd agreed to take a five-mile run every morning together before breakfast, and now, by their fourth day of specialist training in rural Hertfordshire, it had already become an unspoken point of honour for each of the men to try to run the other into the ground.

As they approached the big old country house, where despite rationing a hearty English breakfast awaited them, Harry put on a spurt and overtook Horace on the final straight, hoping to beat him for the first time since the first morning. Horace responded immediately, though, drawing level as they approached the small gatehouse that marked their informal finishing line, and nosing ahead just as they entered the grounds, sprinting full tilt.

'Damn you!'

Harry ran through onto the gravel of the main drive and slowed until he reached one of the manor's spectacular London plane trees, then let loose a further stream of invective against his rival, his legs wobbling beneath him. Horace, for his part, stood with his hands on his knees, breathing hard and staring at the ground with his eyes closed. Friesian cows ruminated in the early morning mist, ignoring them.

*

After bathing and breakfast, the two men went to the library, where they had been told to expect a special guest, one of several invited to brief them on particular aspects of their upcoming mission. The briefings alternated with continued physical training: unarmed combat, running, pistol shooting.

When they reached the library, to their surprise there was already someone there, sitting with his back to them in a leather armchair, staring out of the window towards the gatehouse. He rose with some difficulty when they entered and turned to greet them. Clad in a generously cut tweed suit, pale, heavily built and bald, he looked like an obscene Humpty Dumpty.

'Gentlemen,' he boomed at them. 'I am told to say my name is Grey. It isn't, but it'll do.'

Harry felt the urge to shrink away from the apparition's soft-skinned handshake, but resisted. It was all rather rum. They'd already had a half-mad artist called Spare with a paralysed arm who'd been bombed in the Elephant and Castle and who'd told them all about his forays into sex magic; an elfin little Welsh lady by the name of Violet who'd briefed them on the importance of communing with the national spiritual archetypes of England and Germany in order to influence the outcome of the war; and a charming man from Holborn called Cockren who claimed to have made drinkable tinctures of gold in his alchemical laboratory that could ward off illness and prolong life by several decades. Now this ailing but somewhat fearsome individual.

'I am to brief you on some aspects of Nazi occult practices, as they have been reported to me by some associates of mine in Germany, and I am to help separate fiction from fact,' Grey said as they arranged themselves around a work table.

'I am also honoured to present you with a slim and, alas,

unbound selection of my recent poetical works on patriotic themes.' He handed each of them a sheaf of typed pages. 'We who are too old to fight may still be of service in other small ways.'

Harry eyed the man with suspicion, accepting the offering without comment. Horace thanked him effusively and with great charm, confirming Harry's conviction that Americans, for all their many virtues, could usefully acquire a little more reserve.

'The first thing you must know is that Hitler himself has little time for magic or mysticism,' Grey began, 'except when tolerating such beliefs helps him achieve his own aims. He is a utilitarian, and an opportunist. Nevertheless, there are those around him who are true believers, for whom the Nazi project is in part an undertaking of what *you* would perhaps call black magic.'

Harry tried his best not to snort.

'What would you call it?'

'I would call it dangerously misguided. In any event, the actions of this man Hitler, whether carried out consciously or not – his military adventures, his thuggish social repression, his cruelty towards opponents – have occult consequences of the most severe order. Others take his hatred, the fear and misery that he breeds, and work through it, tapping it for their own ends.'

'Who?'

'Heinrich Himmler, for one. Alfred Rosenberg. Those who would create a twisted Nazi version of the old Odin religion, those who believe in a largely invented glorious German prehistoric past dating all the way back to a supposed Aryan Atlantis called Thule. Those who will tell you that Christ was actually Krist, a Teutonic God-leader lost to recorded history.'

'You make it sound ridiculous.'

'It is. But not in the way you may imagine. There are real things here that they are playing with, some consciously, as I say, some not. Real forces. Tell me, has either of you ever drunk Bovril?'

Horace looked confused, whereas Harry just lost his patience.

'Bovril? Will you stop talking in riddles and kindly just get to the point?'

'I assure you I am.'

Grey smiled like a small child.

'There is, in all the world's traditions of which we will speak today, a force associated with creation, one found in varying degrees in human beings, in the earth, in the universe itself, and in the tiniest flecks of matter. It takes various names, but the Nazi occultists have taken to calling it *vril*. Typically, blinded as they are by hatred and ideology, they have misunderstood it, and will misuse it if given even half a chance.'

'*Vril*, you say?'

'Yes. The Celts called it *druis lanach*, or Druids' lightning. There are other names for it in other cultures. The East Anglian witches call it *spirament*. It is a kind of *prana*, a kind of *qi*, when stored in the earth it is called the *sleeping dragon*. It should only be accessed with great care, by those suitably prepared. I am one such. The Nazis have others. In Paris there were people . . .'

'Where does Bovril fit in?' Harry rumbled.

'In the late nineteenth century, an Englishman called Bulwer-Lytton published a very strange novel called *The Coming Race*, in which a people called the *vrilya* make use of a psychic force called *vril* to dominate other races, power their machines and build an extraordinary civilization.

Bulwer-Lytton is often said to have invented this term, perhaps as a contraction of *virile*, perhaps just made up out of whole cloth. The book was an enormous success, though barely read now.'

Harry felt another protest surge, but saw Horace was listening intently.

'Bulwer-Lytton was not making things up, though he was embroidering them in various ways. As an initiate in at least one branch of the Western mystery tradition, he was fully aware of what he was doing – hiding a secret in plain sight, as all initiates must when they achieve a certain level of mastery, so that others may come later and follow the path. The point is this: the term *vril* became hugely popular, whereas previously it had been restricted to small circles such as the Theosophists around Helena Blavatsky. Its popularity in Germany led to the formation of societies to study *vril*, some overt, some secret, and in England even convinced the makers of a new yeast-based hot drink to incorporate it, purely to help it sell, into the name of their product. Hence Bovril.'

It was too much for Harry. He stood up and walked around the library, fuming at the prodigious amounts of time they were wasting.

'Go on,' Horace said, smiling slightly at Harry's distress.

'The makers of Bovril are of course highly patriotic and decent people, and not in any way associated with Nazis or any of their ilk.'

'What do you understand by these powers?' Horace asked. 'These capacities?'

'They allow us, by focusing of the will, to direct and control energies far greater than ourselves: the creative and destructive forces of the world itself.'

'A bomb,' Harry shouted across the room. 'We are simply talking about the Nazi capacity to build a bigger bomb.'

'Far bigger,' Grey said. 'Bigger than you can imagine. We are talking about acquiring the powers of gods. And about those powers being turned against this country.'

~

After mid-morning tea and biscuits, Grey gave them a summary of the various mystics, seers, crackpots and magicians who had become associated in one way or another with the rise of the Nazi party. Some were deluded fantasists, others had acquired genuine insight and subsequently lost their minds, still others were extremely dangerous.

'We can start with the grand-daddy of them all, Guido von List, a nostalgist for a non-existent Wotanist German past. He posits rule by Aryan mystical priest-kings such as himself. The *von* is not really kosher; a lot of these people are self-appointed aristocrats. Prophet of an Aryan super-race called upon to rule the sub-humans, you get the idea. Dead in 1919 but his ideas live on, not least in his admirer Lanz von Liebenfels, a defrocked monk and scholar, also barking mad.'

Harry laughed softly. Horace didn't.

'Lanz is inclined to see hidden references to sexual bestiality everywhere in historical artefacts and scripture. He founded an Aryan New Templar Order and a magazine, *Ostara*, which Adolf Hitler read in Vienna before the war. Hitler even visited Lanz to ask for back numbers, I hear. Another self-appointed user of the *von*.'

Harry fidgeted in his seat.

'Next we have Karl Maria Wiligut, also known as Weisthor, a randy old man who claims to have ancestral memory of the Aryan people, and to be a descendant of Thor, no less. Heinrich Himmler gave Wiligut his own office as part of his personal staff. Retired in 1939 after his psychiatric records came to light. Otto Rahn, a gifted scholar and writer, worked for Wiligut. He was obsessed with the Holy Grail. Resigned suddenly from the SS, no one knows why, mysteriously found dead on a mountainside in 1937.'

'Was he done in?' Harry asked.

'Died of exposure, they say. Some kind of ritual suicide, I'd say. The SS wasn't for him. Now, an interesting one. Rudolf Glauer, who calls himself Baron von Sebottendorff, though he was born the son of a railwayman. Glauer had some genuine exposure to Sufism in Turkey but filtered it all through a Jew-hating, Bolshevik-baiting prism. He founded the Thule Society after the Great War as a kind of armed esoteric discussion group. Its symbol was a rounded swastika or sun-wheel. Rudolf Hess and Hans Frank, lately of the Nazi party, were members, and Rosenberg sometimes showed up. The Thule Society was in some ways a direct predecessor of the Nazi party, but Glauer's fallen out of favour now, the Thule is all washed up, and the last news I have indicates he's in Istanbul, doing some low-grade spying for the German *Abwehr*.'

Horace frowned. 'What more do you know about Hess?'

Grey smiled to himself, as though guarding secret knowledge.

'We know he is very interested in astrology. He chose the night of his flight to Scotland, for example, because it was marked by a very rare alignment of the planets.'

'Are there many more? I'm losing track of all the loonies,' Harry barked. 'Too many of them.'

'Just one or two more. Dietrich Eckart, a virulent anti-Semite, alcoholic, drug-addicted dramatist and propagandist who introduced Hitler to moneyed supporters and high social circles, also visited the Thule Society. Also an occultist. The second volume of *Mein Kampf* is dedicated to him. I think we can skip over Siegfried Adolf Kummer, who went in for mystical yodelling, and Friedrich Bernhard Marby, whose thing was Odinic yoga. Marby's in a concentration camp now, not psychotically pro-Aryan enough, I imagine.'

After a reflective pause, Horace spoke up.

'Who is the most dangerous?'

'The one who believes in them all, and wields actual power. The one who dreams of an elite corps of warrior-priests, each with his harem of wives, settling farmlands newly cleared of their sub-human former inhabitants, now re-categorized as slave labour. The one who authorizes torture and murder with punctilious initials on SS memoranda, but vomits at the sight of blood. The failed chicken-breeder, with a pigeon chest and spectacles like bottle-ends.'

'Himmler.'

'Quite.'

'Anyone else?'

'There is one other, about whom almost nothing is known, one who works directly with the chicken-farmer. He is from Alsace, the German-speaking part of France. He is called Isambard.'

~

As they were ending their session, Horace casually turned the conversation to Paris.

'Who is Fulcanelli?'

Grey frowned.

'Ah. The *anti-Isambard*, as the Parisian wags put it. The good twin, though I don't think they mean literally. Who is he? No one knows. None of my sources does, and I certainly don't.'

'Do you think he exists?'

'He did. Whether he still does is anyone's guess.'

After lunch, Harry asked Horace who exactly they had just spent the morning with.

Horace laughed.

'A monstrous egotist, styles himself the Beast, or used to. Very good self-publicist, very learned in the matters that interest us, mediocre practitioner, though not if you hear him tell it. Primarily fascinated with himself. Good source of information. Your British press like to call him *the wickedest man in the world*. Ring a bell, as you say?'

'Can't say as it does.'

'His name is Aleister Crowley. Living penniless in Hastings, I believe. He is not well.'

After some time on the shooting range, they were summoned at three o'clock for another briefing with Smith, the officer Harry had first met at the house in Primrose Hill.

'The main thing you need to know now is that your hunt for Fulcanelli will be opposed,' Smith said, chewing on his pipe between sentences. 'The Nazis are looking for him too, and we have learned they have Himmler operatives in Paris on his trail, identities unknown. As for you, you will be working with a member of the *résistance* who's been recommended to us. He's familiar with Parisian esoteric circles before the war, and has been assigned to Steeplejack. You'll call him Faucon.'

London

27 June 2007

Peter Hale-Devereaux, seventy-one years older, a little stiffer but sturdy and vigorous still, walked his route again along the streets of London for the first time since 1936, singing lightly to himself and remembering scenes from his long, tumultuous life.

Oranges and lemons . . .

From St Paul's Cathedral he headed down Ludgate Hill, then dipped south and west along Pilgrim Street, directly along the line of the sleeping dragon that was the city's hidden power, across the course of the old River Fleet to Bride Lane, and to the site of the holy well dedicated to St Bridget, and before her to other powers, perhaps the Celtic goddess Brighde, she of healing, childbirth and fire, in the shadow of the great Wren wedding-cake spire of St Bride's church.

It was his task now to revive the form he had walked into London all those years ago, to satisfy himself that the poison was still lying there dormant, and to revive it. And he would be seen to perform his task.

Peter sat on a bench in the churchyard, focusing his mind on the site of the old well, near the plane tree in the south-east corner of the church, and summoned back to memory the time, decades before, when Peter Hale-Devereaux, a young man looking but not seeing, his head lost in his own private hunt for meaning, had become Falke, loyal advance man for the Black Order, special operative of Heinrich Himmler's perverted creation, the inner core of the *Schutzstaffel*, a spiritual warrior on the wrong side of grace.

For several minutes, he wept.

He could not resist Isambard and his kind, even now, when they called upon his abilities. He bore fragments of Isambard within himself, in his very genes, in his very soul.

But with the approaching crack in time, there was a glimmer of hope that he, the cuckoo's egg, the eternal outsider, the renegade, might be able to pull off a final, breathtaking escape, and finally come home.

It was a woman who had offered him the chance of survival, or even of salvation. And she had done it by slapping his face. The scene was still vivid in his mind: her diminutive form, her clear, fearless blue eyes, her determination. Had he seen his mother's eyes in hers? He couldn't tell. But she had reawakened his mother's heritage in him, one day in October 1940.

He had been following a lead suggesting that Fulcanelli was the pseudonym of a certain Jewish Kabbalist, and they had cornered one of the man's associates on the Petit Pont in Paris. The young American woman's courage astonished him still: to attack him and his men, to risk her life, to leap into the Seine to try to save the suspect's child.

Peter, astonished, and still unworldly for all his travels and feats, had fallen in love with her at that instant. And in doing so, he had found a corner of his inner life where Isambard could not see. She had given him permission to feel love. She had opened the possibility of selflessness in his heart. For decades on end, that was what had kept Peter alive. And he had repaid her . . . poorly.

Eventually rising from his bench in the grounds of St Bride's, Peter walked on. Leaving the church precincts, he headed west along St Bride's Avenue, a short, covered alley, and to his surprise, as he emerged, found that an obelisk-shaped monument had been erected directly on the principal line of the city's hidden power. He was sure it had not been there in 1936, when Salisbury Square had housed much older buildings, destroyed subsequently, he imagined, by Nazi bombing, or perhaps by post-war developers.

The obelisk had been dedicated in 1833 to one Robert Waithman, a nineteenth-century Lord Mayor of London, he read at its base, and a more recent plaque said it had been moved here in 1989 from Ludgate Circus . . . The man had been a Mason, he suspected. Had they known they were marking the dragon line?

Peter paused to gauge his surroundings, to read the air around him. At the very fringes of consciousness, he felt a presence, and after a few seconds knew who it was: Horace Hencott. The man whose fate was so intimately linked with his own was following Peter's route across London. Good. This knowledge, too, he kept secret, in the space that Rose Arden had opened up for him.

Soon, it would be time to repay her, and to atone for his weakness.

A ghastly modern office block impeded any further direct progress, and to reach his next site Peter had to box south on Dorset Rise and head up Hutton Street, then dip into Ashentree Court and through Magpie Alley, where he was delighted to find an old view of the city, painted onto the white tiles of the narrow passage, that allowed one to trace the route he had walked, now and in 1936, once and always: picking up the line at St Helen's Bishopsgate after coming up from the south, then St Mary-le-Bow, St Paul's, St Bride's . . . Joining Temple Lane, he boxed south again to the barriered entry gate to the Temple precincts and then crossed the courtyard, used as a car park, before picking up the line again through a passageway in the north-western corner.

The passage led him directly to his target: the round church that had stood on this site since the twelfth century, stripped now of the conical, pepper-pot roof he had seen atop it in 1936, restored after virtual destruction by his erstwhile compatriots in World War Two, the church of the Knights Templar in London, the Temple Church. He went inside.

It was a dangerous decision. A small group of choristers were singing in the centre of the round, an impromptu performance in street clothes, their voices soaring and resonating, harmonies sustained for what seemed endless time in the echoing stone vault.

And suddenly, his heart resonating with the beauty of the music and the setting, Peter Hale-Devereaux found himself weeping again.

The fear and idiocy of the young man he had been.

He put up barriers, disguising his distress, shielding it from the looming presence in his mind that was Isambard, a force of raging hatred trapped between worlds, dead and yet not dead, clinging to earthly life through his son.

~

Leaving the Temple Church, Peter walked north along Inner Temple Lane to Fleet Street, emerging to see the clock of St Dunstan-in-the-West across the street, just as Isambard had taught him it would be. He crossed Fleet Street at the Temple Bar and walked west to Aldwych, heading toward the spire of St Clement Danes, and coming within a few minutes to the focal point of all that had happened and all that was to come in these days, the site of a holy well whose waters still lived.

The eastern arm of his route completed, Peter rested. He took tea at the Waldorf. Then, after a while, he made a decision.

Peter hailed a cab and directed it south across Waterloo Bridge to the Imperial War Museum, just past Waterloo train station. He was tempted to take one of the Eurostar trains there directly to Paris, to return to his childhood, to do things differently this time. But there was no going back.

In the cavernous lobby of the museum, amid the tanks and missiles and planes suspended on wires, under the V-1 flying bomb perpetually frozen in time on its final murderous dive into London, Peter tried one more time, for the last time, to contact his love, to tell her he was making good the damage he had caused her.

He walked into the permanent display on Britain's secret services, smiling sardonically at the James Bond music that greeted him as he entered, and headed straight to the exhibits on the long-defunct Special Operations Executive.

There, behind a glass case, he found his own special link to the past, and perhaps to redemption: a display of clandestine radio sets, and beside one of them a photograph of the woman who had used it, and whom he had given to the Nazis. Those unforgettable blue eyes, wide in wonder. Peter's head swam as he stood before her image, long-ago scenes playing themselves out again before him: a young woman hauling the heavy suitcase across Paris day after day, from one secret transmission point to another, constantly risking arrest and death; the same woman who had slapped his face on a bridge over the Seine in 1940; the same woman manacled and chained in a Nazi prison cell, desperately rapt in prayer; the gates of Dachau concentration camp. Urgent pulses of Morse code echoed in his memory.

'Rose,' he whispered. 'Forgive me.'

France

September 1943

Harry watched the red light glowing in the gloom of the Halifax fuselage, his legs dangling into the hole in the bottom of the plane as the air ripped by below, the hypnotic throbbing of the engines so intense that he no longer heard but only felt it deep in his entrails. They were dropping from 300 feet, there would be no time to think once the light turned green. With all his strength he focused on a single thing: not banging his nose on the other side of the hatch when he jumped forward and dropped.

Green light.

Harry fell like a stone, feeling the pops of the strings breaking as the static line pulled his parachute open above him, holding his bandaged ankles together, nothingness and a distant roar all around him. Then almost before he'd had time to be scared the shock hit him of the parachute breaking his fall and he was nearing the ground in the darkness, pulling down hard on his control strips, indistinct shapes and patterns surging up at him. He hit the ground with a bone-jarring bang and rolled to his left, legs straight out, his vertebrae cracking, his newly acquired French-style dental work loosened by the impact. He lay still for an instant, winded. Out of the corner of his eye he saw another parachute open then collapse. Harry twisted the buckle on his midriff and punched it to release himself from the straps, then rolled to his feet and hauled on the parachute cords. The silk had snagged on a bush. As he pulled at it he looked around for his two colleagues.

A whistle to his left identified Horace. He whistled back, managing with a vigorous pull to extract his parachute from the branches. Bundling it together, he scouted the flat landscape for Charlie, their radio operator. Nothing.

Harry undid his one-piece jumpsuit and unclipped his helmet. He hadn't seen their clothing and equipment land. He made his way over to Horace, who was already surveying the moonlit landscape with more care from within a slight hollow in the ground.

'Our kit is over there,' Horace whispered, pointing to a clump of bushes near the edge of the field. 'I don't know about Charlie.'

In the dead silence of the night, they scoured the fields for more information, the soft shadows thrown by the moon tricking their eyes with imagined silhouettes and distorted patterns. Time was altered, flowing both faster and more slowly as the adrenaline pumping through their bodies from the jump slowly dissipated. They had to get away from the drop zone, but first they had to reconnoitre their location. No sign of a reception committee.

A raging thirst gripped Harry. It was always the same after he jumped.

'I could murder a cup of tea,' he whispered to Horace.

Horace reached for a hipflask and took a swig.

'Quick shot of rum?' He offered Harry the metal bottle with a twinkle in his eye.

Before Harry could answer, they heard another whistle, from the tree-line off to their right. It was like birdsong, a short phrase, repeated once.

Horace nodded to Harry. He replied with a sonorous bird call of his own, repeated twice. For a few seconds, nothing happened, then they heard the bustle of men approaching close to the ground. A black silhouette appeared, a Sten gun on its arm. A voice came out of the blackness.

'*Bienvenue en France*, Steeplejack. Your colleague is dead, he fell into a tree and broke his neck. We have recovered your bags. Come with us. We will take care of your parachutes.'

Their radio was smashed, they learned as their reception committee briefed them in a barn. Everything else was in order.

'You have two hours to sleep, if you can. You are safe here, I have twenty men between us and the nearest Germans,' the leader of the group told them, a man with lively eyes and the weathered face of a hard-bitten farmer. He went through the satchels of supplies and messages the two men had brought with them. 'We'll bury your colleague and make sure the location is remembered. He will be honoured when there is more time, but today we just have to get him out of sight quickly.'

He pointed to a giant hay bale behind them in the barn. 'There are 20 tonnes of explosives and ammunition under there. It is quite comfortable on top. I suggest you rest until we are ready to move out. The overnight train for Paris leaves at five in the morning. We will leave here at three thirty.'

The platform was almost deserted. Horace and Harry were now deep into their cover identities, every single item on their persons chosen to fit their stories, down to the labels in their French-cut civilian clothes and the ticket stubs, matchbooks and loose coins that made up their 'pocket litter'. Harry, standing well apart from his colleague, carried a photograph of a woman he had never met and was not attracted to, so that if captured and taunted with never seeing her again, he could maintain a dimension of mental advantage, mocking his interrogators with the inner knowledge that he had fooled them and was laughing at them. It would be a slim edge, one he hoped never to have to deploy. But he had thrown away his L-pill, without telling anyone. Two gendarmes waited further along the platform, ignoring them as the wind whipped across the concrete and autumn rain began to fall.

When the train wheezed into the station, clattering and hissing amid great clouds of steam and smoke, Horace and Harry discovered it offered standing room only, all the way to Paris. Wedging themselves into two separate carriages, Horace stood next to some travelling German soldiers and Harry between a farmer's wife and an unhappy-looking priest, and the two men suffered and slowly froze on the unheated train all the way to the Gare d'Austerlitz in Paris.

Their first contact was a woman London had set them up with to provide an initial safe house. Harry telephoned her from a café a few blocks from the station.

'Madame Lacour? This is Maurice from Nantes. Your cousin asked me to telephone and tell you that all is well with his family.'

'My cousin Henri?'

'No, your cousin Jules.'

'Ah, Jules. Of course. Thank you so much.'

After the exchange of passwords, Madame Lacour invited them to visit her and drop off their suitcases, though she was clear that she was expecting guests the following night, and so could only put them up until the morning.

They already had her address, a spacious apartment on the Rue de la Faisanderie in the upscale 16th arrondissement.

The street's north-eastern end opened onto Avenue Foch, facing the three large houses that served as Gestapo headquarters, barely 200 yards away.

Claire Lacour was the widowed headmistress of a girls' school, a stylish woman in her early forties who had offered lodging and concealment services to those opposing the Occupation from the earliest days of the war.

Armed with discreet contacts by Claire, Harry set about establishing further accommodation for them both, while Horace took the initial steps to get them in touch with their Resistance counterpart, who had been told to expect three F Section officers led by Steeplejack (Horace), whose codename would also be that of their network.

Harry considered and dismissed the first safe house option put to him on grounds of security, before settling on a first-floor apartment with a good choice of exits on the Rue du Cygne, near the run-down, largely empty market stalls of Les Halles, for himself, and then a small flat on the other side of the river, above a shop on the narrow Rue St André-des-Arts near the St Michel fountain, with good access to nearby roofs if required, for Horace. But he only wanted these to last a day or two, while he set up further *cachettes* and boltholes known only to himself and his colleague. On a mission such as this, even more than on a regular F Section mission, they could trust no one.

Harry, whose memories of the inter-bellum city were those of a privileged childhood, was shocked at what had become of Paris and the Parisians. Beyond the obscenity of seeing the swastika flag flying outside the Hotel de Ville and the Opéra, of German *feldgrau* uniforms guarding major public buildings and black-clad SS goons lording it about in the cafés and on the streets, there was the sense of depression and want: a grey pallor in people's faces after three years of malnourishment, a grime on skin and on buildings that wouldn't wash off, a pinched, ground-down misery. He saw virtually no cars on the streets except those commandeered to serve the occupiers; a disproportionate number of old men and young boys, apart from the German troops; a thinned-out, desperate populace clinging on to its self-respect with a dash of colour or style here, a glare of defiance there, a sullen refusal to submit, even amid submission.

Harry knew little of what the Allies were doing in Paris. In addition to his own F Section's operations, he was aware there were SIS or MI6 circuits, and networks of RF agents – the Free French section of SOE, separate from his own – each cut off from the others, pursuing their own aims, though sometimes perhaps working, unbeknownst to each other, with the same core of fearless local resisters. For buried below the day-to-day resignation and drabness of occupation, there burned in some hearts the capacity for acts of incandescent courage.

It was a time of even greater danger than usual for those involved in such work. In late June, the Gestapo had cracked the sprawling Prosper network, a huge but leaky Resistance enterprise responsible for derailings, bombings and power-line sabotage in a broad swathe of territory centred on Paris, arresting its leader Francis Suttill and moving quickly in July to round up hundreds of *résistants*. Of all the group's sub-circuits, only one was known to have survived, a small team called Phono, whose wireless operator had, since the end of July, been F Section's only radio contact – their only eyes and ears – in occupied Paris. She was overworked, stretched impossibly thin, working for whoever needed her, constantly on the move between transmission points to avoid the radio detector vans of the Gestapo. Steeplejack had been instructed to contact her only *in extremis*. Now, with Charlie having broken his neck upon landing, they might have no choice. Her codename was Belle.

That evening, over dinner at Claire's apartment, Horace told Harry a message would be left for them the following day at a restaurant near the Place Vendôme called Chez Bosc, responding to Horace's request for a meeting with Faucon.

The next day, they learned from Faucon's reply that a rendezvous had been set for the afternoon, at the Place Clemenceau, just off the Champs Élysées. Horace was to meet him there alone. Harry was to await them at the Place des Invalides, across the Seine, on the far side of the carrot and potato plots into which the grand Esplanade des Invalides had now been divided.

At the appointed hour, Harry sat shivering on the windswept forecourt of the military veterans hospital which now housed Napoleon's tomb, one of the focal points of Hitler's visit to the captured French capital in 1940, when he had meditated in silence for several minutes before declaring the mausoleum unsatisfactory. Hitler, it was said, had found it lacking in sufficient grandeur and deemed it poorly designed, since it forced visitors to look down at the object of their veneration, rather than up.

Harry, all his senses on full alert, had been expecting to see them come across the Pont Alexandre III, but somehow Horace and Faucon contrived to come up behind him.

'*Bonjour*,' a voice whispered in his ear, and Harry nearly jumped out of his skin. Only his training kept him still and outwardly unmoved. Turning his head slowly, a studied expression of indifference on his face, Harry saw Horace, and standing next to him, the smiling face of Faucon, the man who was to lead them to Fulcanelli and the *geheime Feuer*. It was Harry's own brother, Peter Hale-Devereaux.

~

'The essential thing to know about my brother is that his mother was raped by a German soldier,' Harry told Horace several days later, as they walked randomly through the streets of the gritty 20th arrondissement, umbrellas raised against the drizzling rain. 'That's how he came into the world. Everything else is secondary. He hates Germans with a vengeance, however well he speaks the language. I know. He wrote to me when he came back from Berlin in 1936. You couldn't imagine anyone more disdainful of the whole Nazi charade. He'd seen it first hand.'

Harry, after overcoming his surprise and cursing the compartmentalized, 'need to know' rules that had failed to tell him he would be working with his own adoptive brother, got used to the idea of working with Peter pretty quickly. It was likely even London didn't know Faucon's real identity, he thought. Although Harry had betrayed no public trace of recognition on the windswept esplanade where they'd met, he'd been secretly thrilled to find that, after all Peter's travails and doubts about who he was and where he fit in, his brother had finally come down on the right side, and right in the thick of it too.

'Why did he go there in the first place?' Horace asked. 'Most people with any sense were going in the opposite direction. Those who could.'

'We all thought he'd gone to look for his real father, if he was still alive. I think he meant to hunt him down and horsewhip the man. There was an anger to him when he left. But when he came back, it was all burned out. He told me he'd found out his father had died, just as his mother had always told him. He'd been hunting a chimera, he said. He came to live in Paris then, before the war. I lost touch with him after the occupation. Then I got a letter he managed to send me via Lisbon. He said, in a coded way of course, that he was on active service against the Bosch, no other details.'

'And your judgement isn't clouded?'

'Blood is thicker than water, Horace.'

'He's not your blood.'

'He's family. I grew up with him. After father died and cut him out of the will, I found ways to support him. Trust me.'

Horace walked in silence for several minutes, leaning into the rain. Harry accompanied him quietly, unsure what else he could say. The mission was the main thing, the only thing. All other considerations had to be set aside.

Eventually, with an air of taking a heavy decision, Horace spoke again.

'So be it. Without trust, we are nothing. I trust you.'

Paris

October 1943

The three of them began systematically exploring the characters and locations of pre-war Parisian esoteric groups, their enquiries facilitated by Peter. Most of the circles had voluntarily closed down since the Occupation, or been shuttered by the Nazis. At the Petit Palais just off the Champs Élysées, the occupiers had opened an entire exhibition in October 1940 on the evils of freemasonry and its supposed secret alliance with international Jewry. Other groups with more active esoteric pursuits had taken the hint, even those with their own anti-Semitic leanings.

After weeks of slow, painstakingly discreet inquiries, Steeplejack began to focus on an address on Rue Jacob on the left bank, where the threads of several disparate stories seemed to converge.

The location – 20, Rue Jacob – was home to a legendary literary salon hosted by one of interwar Paris's most outrageous and outspoken figures, the lesbian writer and social lioness Nathalie Clifford Barney, who had left Paris for Italy at the outbreak of hostilities. Her salons had been conducted in a hidden wooded garden behind the building's bland facade, and centred around a small, mysterious, Grecian-style temple at the rear of the secret grove.

'Let's start again at the beginning. The key question is this,' Horace said as they sat at a bare wooden table, huddled in overcoats against the early October cold, in the latest of the safe houses Harry had arranged, this one in the drab working-class district beyond Porte St Martin. 'What became of the documents last seen by Peter in 1932 in the hands of Jean-Julien Champagne?'

They spoke urgently, unwilling to be all together in one place for longer than absolutely necessary. Each of them had had brushes with the Gestapo or local police in recent days. Harry had only barely managed to talk his way through a spot-check of identity papers in the Luxembourg Garden, after a French cop had taken against him for some imagined offence of disrespect.

'Who has seen them, has anyone copied them, could anyone be prepared to give them to the Germans?' Peter added rhetorically.

'Or have they done so already?' Harry threw in.

They were all moving around Paris on foot as often as possible, avoiding the Métro with its higher likelihood of security checks, walking themselves into the ground as they shifted constantly from one rendezvous to another with potential informants, any one of whom might find it personally easier to betray them than to let them live.

'To review what we know,' Horace said. 'Here in this city, in the period between the Great War and the 1930s, it seems likely that someone discovered part or all of the highly dangerous secrets of the Great Work. One of the indicators that the discovery was real is the lengths certain others appear to have gone to in their efforts to steal the knowledge, to punish those who would not share what they had found, or to extort it out of them. Exhibit one.'

Horace fished in his briefcase and took out a book, which he placed on the table. 'A strange novel, in the Dadaist style, fragmentary, syncopated, an unusual piece of writing, supposedly by a woman named Irène Hillel-Erlanger. *Voyages en Kaléidoscope*. Travels in a Kaleidoscope. It was published here in 1919, and virtually all copies were mysteriously bought up and taken off the market within days. It has been virtually impossible to find ever since. This is one of only three copies known to have survived.'

A shout went up from the street below, followed by the sound of running feet. Each of them tensed, senses straining. There were more shouts, barked orders in German, a cry of pain, a man's voice. The sound of wooden-soled shoes scraping on the pavement, as though for traction, as though in resistance. Harry reached for the .32 pistol nestled under his left armpit, meeting Horace's eyes. They heard a car engine, a shriek of tyres, more shouting and scrabbling and cursing. A woman was weeping now, lamenting in a language neither French nor German. They heard the slamming of car doors, the impacts of what might have been rifle butts on a human body. Then silence, except for the sobs of the woman on the street.

Harry relaxed his grip. The room smelled of fear and wet wool.

After a few moments, Horace went on.

'Within a year of her book's appearance – and disappearance – Irène Hillel-Erlanger was dead, having suffered a strange affliction of the throat for much of the period between the publication and her demise.'

'Punishment for refusing to talk?' Harry asked. 'Or for saying too much in her book?'

'Either explanation is possible,' Horace replied. 'It is traditional, they say, for those few who achieve the Work to leave behind a marker, a kind of testimony, in plain sight for those who come afterwards. It must be veiled, but open: impenetrable to those who are unworthy of the knowledge, but obvious to those who are on the right path.'

'A fine balance,' Peter observed.

'Hillel-Erlanger also wrote poetry, under the name Claude Lorrey, and wrote scripts for the cinema, in the days of silent film. But nothing she did really compares to this *Kaléidoscope* book. On the face of it, it's almost like a scrapbook, just a series of random scenes, extracts from letters, newspaper reports, all thrown together. Perhaps, read with different eyes, it hides extraordinary secrets.'

'It even has an illustration,' Peter said. 'A drawing of a thermometer, of all things. Was she giving different temperatures? Something required in a chemical process? Or an alchemical one?'

'Perhaps our code-breakers and chemistry boffins could work on this?' Harry asked hopefully, impatience getting the better of him. 'If this so-called Great Work leads to the Secret Fire weapon, we should have them ripping the book apart. Just what is it supposed to be, anyway, this Great Work? Something you do in a laboratory? Or something you do in your mind?'

'They say it can be either,' Horace said. 'There are two routes to the Great Work. They are known as the dry path, and the wet path. The wet path involves the use of chemicals, preparing minerals, spending long weeks heating and drying, powdering and calcinating them, imbuing them with one's own mental and spiritual force, eventually to produce substances of great power, such as the physical components of the Secret Fire weapon. These then harmonize and resonate with the powers of the earth, known as dragon lines, or leys.'

'Stuff and nonsense,' Harry spat.

'On the dry path, the only substances worked on are those of the practitioner, or pilgrim, himself. His or her body, mind and spirit, in harmony with the dragon lines and the force of the universe itself.'

Horace seemed to bite his tongue, and changed the subject slightly. 'For now, all I have been able to find is that Hillel-Erlanger uses the French word *vrille* several times. Not a word I knew.'

'A spiral, or a tendril,' Harry said.

Peter joined in. 'The verb *vriller* means to spiral, to twist, to bore into something.'

'Thank you. But forget the literal meaning, just look at the spelling. It's *VRIL*. Whatever the Nazis are working on, or whatever tradition they are twisting to their own ends, she knew about it too.'

'What else do we know about her?'

Peter spoke up again.

'Irène Hillel-Erlanger, like Natalie Clifford Barney, hosted a noted literary and political salon. It was one of just a handful also attended by members of the esoteric demi-monde. She probably attended Natalie's, too. Her work was mentioned by Fulcanelli himself – whoever he was – in his second book, *The Dwellings of the Philosophers*.'

Harry sighed.

'What other instances are there of this?' he asked. 'Of what happened to this poor woman?'

'There was a similar case in England in the nineteenth century,' Horace replied. 'Mary Anne South, after years of study, published a book in 1850 entitled A *Suggestive Enquiry into the Hermetic Mystery*. Within days of publication, without explanation, she and her father recalled all copies they could get their hands on, and burned them on the lawn of their house.'

'Why?'

'Friends claimed she suddenly felt she'd given too much away,' Horace replied.

'After all those years of work?' Peter sneered. 'Clearly someone got to her, threatened her.'

Horace now placed on the table a photograph of Marie Curie.

'Exhibit two. Radioactivity. The scientific approach to transmutation. The Curies, or at least Pierre Curie, moved in esoteric as well as conventional scientific circles, we hear. They are another part of the puzzle. Pierre Curie attended séances, declared himself persuaded that some occult phenomena were genuine, is said to have been a friend of Fulcanelli . . .'

'There is even one unconfirmed report, which I have second-hand from a single source,' Peter said, 'that Pierre Curie attended a secret transmutation, carried out by Fulcanelli himself, in Bourges.'

'When?' Horace asked. 'He died in 1906.'

'My source was vague on the date, I'm afraid. He was not there himself. But another source, separately, said this to me, in no uncertain terms: *Pierre Curie dealt with alchemy. He sought the philosopher's stone. His work on magnetism and the components of matter was not just physical in nature.*'

Harry whispered: 'Do we think Marie Curie and her husband were killed? And for the same reasons as Irène Hillel-Erlanger?'

'Marie Curie died a withering death, associated with the radioactive materials she worked with, not even ten years ago,' Horace replied. 'We cannot know. Her husband, though, slipped and fell under the wheels of a horse-drawn carriage in the street, eighteen years earlier. An unusual way to go. There's more room for doubt there. It has the hallmarks of an assassination. Perhaps a punishment. For revealing the discoveries he and his wife made, or for refusing to share other secrets they knew? Their daughter and son-in-law, the Joliot-Curies, are here in Paris.'

'I hear they are with us,' Peter said. 'Active with the Resistance. Communists.'

Horace stared curiously at Peter.

'I don't know. I have heard no such thing. Exhibit three. Jean-Julien Champagne.'

Horace placed a photograph of Champagne's gravestone on the table. 'This man died in atrocious circumstances, of gangrene poisoning, barely able to speak.'

'He refused to give up the secrets he had learned,' Peter said. 'When I met him he claimed to have recreated the reds and blues of the Chartres stained glass, an aspect of the Great Work. I have looked further into this. I've spoken with sources who say Fulcanelli himself recovered the glass fragments and the relevant papers and hid them, to keep them from the Nazis.'

'We have all heard of this . . . black creature called Isambard,' Horace said. 'I see a pattern here. He was in this city, moving in these circles, pursuing the Great Work. And, one by one, it seems clear to me he was seeking to torture or extort its secrets out of those who achieved things he could not.'

Peter was silent.

'Let's pray he failed,' Harry said. 'Now look, before the curfew traps us all here, there's something else we need to decide today.'

Part of the Steeplejack mission also entailed verifying intelligence reports of unusual Nazi activity in north-western France, in the countryside around Lille. The reports, from the network known as Farmer, focused on strange installations being built, some underground, some using dangerous chemicals and steam generators, in secluded, forested locations. The Steeplejack mission had specific, secret concerns about such sites.

'And what about Rue Jacob, meanwhile?' Peter asked.

'I believe,' said Horace, 'that Rue Jacob is where Peter and I must head next. And Harry, you are off to Lille to meet up with Farmer.'

'Good,' said Harry. 'Something solid I can get my teeth into at last.'

~

With Natalie Clifford Barney away, the house and grounds at 20, Rue Jacob were tended by Berthe, the housekeeper, and a gardener, her husband. The gardener, they learned upon discreet inquiry, bore unhappy memories of being taken prisoner by the Germans in the Great War, and worked with considerable industry, now that they were in his city, to make their lives as miserable as possible by smuggling, stockpiling and distributing as many weapons as he could for one of the larger Resistance groups in the capital.

He and Horace had been introduced in a café, over small hot drinks bearing no resemblance whatever to coffee, a few days earlier, and now it was the gardener who let Horace and Peter in.

The sense of space was immediate. Before them, a first-floor raised veranda jutted out from the house proper, its facade covered in strands of ivy. To its right was a garden, and as soon as Peter entered it, he realized it was also the place where many years earlier, when he was still called Pierre, he had been hoisted up from the grass at a glittering reception, aged no more than four, and been presented to a man with cold, haunted eyes, the man he now knew to be his father.

He stood and stared for a moment. The memory left him speechless.

'Peter?'

He felt Horace's steady gaze on him.

'Sorry. It reminded me of somewhere else.'

'We don't have much time. Stay alert.'

They walked deeper into the garden, led by Berthe's husband, and round the corner to the west, where they found, nestled between the brick garden walls at the far end, the famous early-nineteenth-century Doric temple, the words *À l'amitié* engraved in gold leaf into its tympanum. It had served as the focal point of the *Amazone*'s legendary Friday literary salons, and, as several informants had now told them, a sometime meeting place of the capital's esoteric underworld.

They walked to the far end of the garden and ascended the three steps to the tiny temple's narrow porch, which was carpeted in dry yellow and brown leaves. Peter saw that another set of steps led down to a lower level, and caught Horace's eye.

'*C'est fermé, là,*' the gardener said, following their gaze. It's closed. Neither Horace nor Peter believed him for a second.

'*Suivez-moi,*' Berthe's husband said, and led them inside, into the temple's domed chamber.

Near Morbecque

October 1943

Harry awoke with a start. He had been dreaming of the waters off Lizard Point, far away in time and place from the muddy hole where he lay, on the edge of a remote grassy field in northern France, chilled to the bone. Binoculars in hand and Sten gun by his side, he quickly gathered his thoughts, resisting the temptation to cough, angry with himself for sleeping.

He shifted his weight slightly and focused again on the woods at the far end of the field, and on the Luftwaffe troops standing just inside the tree-line.

Observe and report back, he had been told. No sabotage unless directly ordered. He shivered against the damp earth.

Harry and the members of the local Farmer resistance network had been watching the construction of the strange complex in the forest near Morbecque for weeks. Some work was being done by Luftwaffe engineers, some by local men for money, some by wretched-looking prisoners brought in from God only knew where. Spread over five acres, the installations included long, curved buildings like hangars, semi-buried bunkers, an arched, brick-built building fitted with leather hinges and wooden doors, and a 45-yard-long set of massive parallel walls that, from their compass bearing, pointed directly at central London across the English Channel.

What was it all for? They had caught a glimpse of one odd-looking machine brought in by truck, shaped like a bullet, about 25 feet long, with a tube like a stovepipe fixed atop it at the rear. That was all. They knew there were other similar sites being built nearby in the Nord and Pas de Calais areas, all within perhaps 150 miles of the British capital. As far as Harry understood from his briefings, they were launch sites for a new kind of robot bomb.

It was Farmer's job to blow up railway lines, derail trains and generally impede the German war effort as much as they could, and very good they were at it. But in the case of these strange construction sites they were tasked, to their frustration, simply with locating as many of them as possible and reporting their coordinates back to London.

And Harry was not of their network, however much he helped them and relied on them in turn for assistance. He was a member of a different team, one with a purpose so secret he'd had to lie to his own colleagues, the very ones who were risking their lives to help him.

It was Harry's job to look for a particular combination: a launch site, a weapon and a tall man with striking white hair. For that, even his communications were secret: in addition to the regular messages he sent and received via Farmer's radio operator, a bilingual Cockney he knew as Albert, Harry had his own link back to his SOE commanders in London, in the form of the homing pigeons regularly dropped to him by British planes. His most secret messages were sent back in a small leather pouch attached to the leg of the pigeons, which so far had unerringly made it home, even though the Germans were deploying hawks and falcons to kill them en route.

Though he yearned to take more direct action, Harry was glad to be out of Paris. He was in the place he wanted to be, doing the thing he desired to do.

Night was falling. Harry observed a group of slave labourers climbing into the back of a German military truck, one being carried by his fellow prisoners, the victim, he had no doubt, of a punishment beating. He recorded everything, his anger and disgust under tight control. If he could, he would make sure the guards responsible were identified. Justice would come.

When it was pitch black, Harry carefully withdrew from his hide and made his way over the fields to a barn on a farm outside the village of Morbecque. He was stiff, cold, dog-tired. The following day he'd move on to another observation post, and inspect a different construction site. He'd keep going until he dropped dead or was captured.

Cambridge

26/27 June 2007

After seeing Dr Romanek safely through the crowded court-yard of The Eagle after closing time and into a cab on Bene't Street, Robert tried to walk off the pain in his chest and kidneys, defying his confusion and worry and gathering fear. He felt watched, harried.

He walked the city, south and east, eventually looping back to the Eagle, then taking King's Parade north past King's College and the Senate House, dipping along the narrow alleyway of Senate House Passage towards his old college, Trinity Hall, then heading to the river along Garret Hostel Lane.

At the crest of the steep, curved bridge he paused, resting his hands on the metal rails, and stared along the Cam at the gorgeous weeping willows and carefully tended lawns of the Backs. He did not know a more restful, beautiful place.

It was twenty-six years since he had met Katherine, just a few hundred yards away in her rooms at King's, when she had dressed as a witch, and he as a warlock, for one of Adam's game-playing evenings. What if he hadn't accepted the invitation for a blind date that night? What if he'd never met either of them? Would the challenges he'd faced have come anyway? Would his gift have found its way out into the daylight, regardless? Or would he have lived an entirely different life, unaware of what he was, of what he could become?

Horace had been clear: *Even I am not as gifted as you are. For all my training and years of preparation, I could not do what you one day may be able to do. I could not withstand what you have already gone through. But one day, soon, you will have to go up against the Enemy alone. That is what your gift requires.*

Still he felt pursued, observed. Robert looked around. No one.

In the months after Manhattan, Robert had struggled to integrate his experiences into daily life. Returning to his job at GBN had held no attraction for him; and yet he and Katherine needed to live.

Money concerns had evaporated, though, when Horace unexpectedly told him in 2005 that he and Katherine had been made beneficiaries of a small fund previously used by Adam, a kind of permanent stipend set up by Horace's family many decades earlier to foster practical study and use of the Great Work, or the Path. And so Robert had left GBN, his long-time employers, and the news industry in its entirety, with barely a regret, his mind now entirely elsewhere.

He'd tried to keep things as simple as possible, while waiting for the next challenge: He'd tried to recover from the trauma of 2004, and from the roller-coaster ride Horace had put him through to prepare him for those events, though nothing could have prepared him for killing Adam, nor did he know how he could ever forgive himself. He'd tried to devote himself to Katherine, who needed him as badly as he needed her; and to develop the physical and psychic techniques – the fighting arts, the healing hands, the long hours of meditation and breathing exercises – that would help exploit his gift further. He'd tried to make himself useful to others, to people in pain, whether they were dying or recovering; to instruct himself as widely and deeply as he could about the witchcraft traditions of his native land; and reach out to his own people, to those who followed the living practice, who kept the family secrets. Only in the last had he failed.

The bandages on his chest stuck to the dry blood of his wound, pulling and itching, and below the superficial irritation he felt the deep ache, still wet and raw, of the cuts themselves.

He'd learned things from Romanek that were his birthright; hearing them for the first time, he'd been tempted to anger against his parents for bringing him up in such ignorance of the lore of his people, the rich traditions and native abilities of his own folk.

He knew they'd wanted to protect him, and he knew, too, that they'd had good reason – the *elder faith* was dangerous, it could lead to madness, to palsy and death, if mishandled, or misunderstood, or taken for granted. Remember Great Aunt Margaret, the whisper went, though he'd never heard his own parents speak of her in his presence.

And then there had been Hickey's accident, the event no one spoke of that had left his childhood friend an addled, strapping giant with the mind of a child, dear old boy. That event more than any other had frightened Robert's parents into keeping him in ignorance, because they thought he had been responsible, though Robert's cousin Jack Reckliss had got the blame.

Robert cast his mind back.

They would have been eight, maybe nine years old. Robert, Hickey and cousin Jack.

Hickey was the biggest and bravest of them, but also the cleverest. He'd built a radio all by himself, from parts in a catalogue, by the age of seven, and already would help take engines apart and fix broken machinery on the estate, where he spent all his free time. He was friendly, open, always looking out for Robert and Jack. His father ran an agricultural machinery business in the village, and Hickey was the only child. He'd nearly killed his mother during labour, they said, weighing nearly 10 pounds when he was born.

He was gentle, and slow to take offence, but not to be pushed into anger without damage being done. They said he didn't know his own strength.

They had been three boys, climbing a tree in the grounds. Each daring the other higher.

One, suddenly, his face blanching, couldn't go any higher. Vertigo seized him. Clinging onto his branch for dear life, the boy was unexpectedly afraid. He couldn't move. Tears formed in his eyes.

The boy was Jack.

The other two teased him. They were boys, they were cruel, they'd found Jack out, and the sensation was a novel one. For a few moments, they enjoyed the sense of power. He was scared and they were not.

But Jack shrieked in fear and hurt, bursting into tears, fearing he would lose his grip, and Hickey relented.

'Stop now, Robert,' Hickey said. 'Let's help him down.'

But Robert, less mature, didn't want to stop. He sang one more taunt, and Jack howled in distress.

'Stop, Robert!' Hickey boomed. 'Don't be an idiot!'

Hickey had climbed down, angered, to the branch where Jack was clinging. He reached out to give Jack his hand.

'Come on, Jack. You'll be all right.'

Robert climbed higher, deciding to ignore them both, stung by Hickey's insult. He looked down at them both. Jack wouldn't let go of his branch. Hickey was stretching towards him, confident in his strength, holding on to his own branch with one arm, reaching out his hand.

'I'm not an idiot,' Robert said. 'I'll stop, but I'm not an idiot, all right, Hickey?'

'Well, you were being one just now,' Hickey shouted. 'Help me with Jack, will you?'

Anger and hurt flared in Robert's mind.

'I'm NOT!' he shouted.

And Hickey's branch shattered, and suddenly Hickey was falling, a look of surprise on his face that would never leave him, and on the way down he was hitting his head on the branches below, and then with a thump he was on the ground, on his back, and Hickey wasn't talking, and blood and a kind of straw-coloured liquid were coming out of his ear.

Had Robert really done it? Jack was blamed, for being scared and making Hickey stretch to reach him. Robert had spoken up and said it wasn't Jack's fault, but then had stopped when all eyes had turned upon him in turn, seeking someone to blame.

What had Jack thought? What would he think now, all these years on? Robert could ask him directly, very soon. Robert had called him earlier in the evening, receiving at last an invitation to visit Jack the next day, to get to the bottom of the old stories, to follow this side of things to wherever it led.

The bells struck midnight.

Helter skelter.

The grating, chopping guitar riff roared back into his mind, and Robert suddenly felt eyes upon him. Someone was behind him, drawing closer. Instinctively, he shivered.

'Excuse me. I think you dropped this.'

He turned to see a tall, well-built old man holding something out to him in his hand. It was a gold ring. The man gave an impression of vigour, of barely concealed capability for violence. He reminded Robert very much of Horace.

The world around Robert fell away.

The man before him was the face he had seen in the darkness at Adam's apartment, looking like the men he had fought in New York, and yet different. Through all their slightly different features, a single face seemed to stare at him, and he knew, without any doubt, who it was. Working through this man in front of Robert, as he had worked through the others. *Isambard.*

The jagged electric guitar, shrieking, tore at his inner ear.

Now Robert understood the song. Cielo Drive, Benedict Canyon. Robert saw Charles Manson, the crazed leader of the murderous Family, with the tattooed swastika between his eyes. The slaughter of Sharon Tate, her unborn son and four other people. Helter Skelter written in blood on the walls. The song that Manson, in his insanity, thought predicted race war in America.

Robert saw that it was the Enemy's work. That it had somehow broken into Manson's twisted psyche, and fed on it, as now it was trying to feed on that of the man before him, who was speaking to him. They were alone on the bridge.

'I'm sure you dropped it. It looks very valuable.'

The man reached forward, holding the ring between his fingers.

It was Katherine's wedding band, the gold heirloom that Robert had inherited from his family – from Great Aunt Margaret herself, one whisper had been – and given to Katherine as his most precious possession.

Robert snarled and stepped forward, jaw jutting, ready to fight.

'Where's my wife?'

The older man closed his fist, hiding the ring, and with an almost languid movement seized Robert by the throat with his free hand. Then he pushed Robert back against the bridge's metal rail. He was astonishingly strong.

'There are some things that do not concern you,' Peter said, his face pressed against Robert's. 'You need to consider your actions very carefully, or someone you care about is going to get hurt.'

Robert wrapped both hands around the claw-like grip Peter had taken on his throat, but couldn't break it. Blackness began to cloud his vision. A man in his nineties with the strength of a forty-year-old. Robert was choking. All strength seemed to drain from his body under the gull-like stare of his attacker.

Peter held up a cellphone with a colour screen before his eyes, loosening his grip slightly. It began to show a video clip. Katherine!

Her curly black hair was dishevelled, half-covering her face. Her hands were bound. She wore a T-shirt, sweat pants. She was kneeling in the middle of a room without features, apparently unaware she was being filmed. Her shoulders were hunched and her head was lowered, as though fearing a blow, or as though the air itself around her were heavy, toxic.

'She is hearing very unpleasant sounds,' Peter hissed. 'They are very loud. The only break is when she is being questioned. She has not been physically harmed, as yet. But she will be.'

Robert tore his eyes away from the screen and met Peter's gaze.

'What do you want from me?'

Peter smiled, his lips a thin, flat line. He loosened his grip on Robert's throat slightly.

'You don't understand what's going on here. You haven't been able to protect her, just as you've always failed to protect others in your life. You survive, others suffer. Have you asked yourself why that is? Your actions have already caused this to happen to her, and even if you just stopped and went home now, we'd still hurt her, for what you've already done. This is your fault.'

'You want me to stop? Stop what?'

'You know what. Leave Horace to his doom. Let matters take their course. Go back to New York and forget about everything that happens on this side of the Atlantic. If you do those things, we'll return her to you alive. Damaged, but you'll be able to nurse her back to health, eventually. It'll be very touching, you can devote yourself to her.'

Robert made a sudden lunge for Peter's throat. Peter saw it coming, swayed backwards, then punched Robert on the jaw. Robert's knees buckled. For a moment, he almost blacked out.

'If you continue with this – if you go near your family, if you go back to London, if you interfere in any way with events that are about to unfold, your beloved Katherine will be sliced to pieces. The pieces will be sent to you, one at a time. You'll be sent images of each act of amputation. Do you hear me?'

Now Peter was tracing the swastika on Robert's chest, using the gold ring to dig into his wounds. The pain was excruciating.

'Why don't you just kill me, if I'm that much of a threat to you?' Robert shouted in defiance. 'Go on. Try it.'

Peter suddenly let go of him.

'Because for now you are of more use alive, fearful and grovelling to us for mercy,' Peter spat. 'You are of more use humiliated, suffering and aware of just how little you have managed to protect your girl. Just like Terri in Manhattan. Just like Adam.'

Suddenly, a punch exploded in Robert's solar plexus. He went down on the ground, gasping.

And then Peter was gone.

Morbecque

November 1943

Within a few weeks, Harry knew a lot more about the mysterious construction site in the woods, and about its cousins all along the inland band of northern France that aimed their concrete sights at London.

He knew the German forces were from the 155 Anti-Aircraft Regiment of the Luftwaffe. He knew there were more than fifty of the bases in his zone of operation and neighbouring zones, and he knew that the prisoners made to work on the construction came from a camp called Buchenwald. He knew the names of some of the Belgian and French men who had worked on the site here at Bois des Huit-Rues, halfway between Calais and Lille.

He had seen more of the weapons intended for the launch sites, and knew they were a terrifying new development in the war: soulless robot planes, loaded with high explosives.

All of this he and his Farmer colleagues had reported to London, and the increasing demands for accurate details of location of the sites, and over-flights by camera planes, made him sure that an effort was being planned to attack them all soon, before they could start raining their death on the British capital.

But now there was more.

Reviewing intelligence gathered by his Farmer colleagues some days earlier, Harry had come across a detail in an observation report that finally, seven weeks into his secret search, offered a glimmer of hope that he might be in reach of his quarry.

He had returned immediately here to Morbecque, to the Bois des Huit-Rues site, defying the danger of a German anti-resistance sweep going on at that very moment, to see for himself. For the report had said simply: 'Tall subject, SS uniform, close-cropped white hair.'

A long shot, but it was now paying off right in front of his eyes. Through his binoculars, from his cramped hide a field away, Harry could see at the edge of the woods the angular features of the man he had been tasked with finding. He was sure of it. The long white hair was gone, and the short leather jacket he was wearing now was more like a fighter pilot's garb than an SS officer's. But there were mannerisms that had been described to him – a certain way of standing, one leg forward of the other; a way of jutting out the chin and fixing his interlocutors with a stark, unblinking stare – that the figure was exhibiting.

And there was the unusual flying machine. Brought in amid great secrecy two nights ago, it was one of the robot bombs, but – from the glimpse Harry had had – its profile was different. Boxier, somehow.

He couldn't use Albert, even if he'd wanted to break security protocols and send a radio message through him about his discovery. Albert had been picked up by the Gestapo the day previously, in a raid on a house in Roubaix, and was surely undergoing the worst of what they had to offer now, in an effort to make him talk.

Albert had a strong cover story, and a fluency in the local *patois* that might, just, allow him to pass for a local caught up in a terrible misunderstanding. But they would work on him anyway, Harry didn't doubt it. Hiding in his hole in the earth, Harry prayed for Albert, and then said another prayer for him under his real name, 'whatever it may be, oh Lord, known only to thee.'

A few hours later, Harry tried to contact London. The pigeon thrilled and cooed in his hands as he took it from its basket. Mere possession of a homing pigeon was sufficient cause to be shot, because of their success rate as carriers of clandestine messages, and he had come out to a remote barn eight miles from Morbecque to release it. The pigeon was his last till the next re-supply flight at the full moon.

With a kiss to the back of its head, Harry flung the bird with its precious message for London into the air.

The pigeon circled for a few moments and then found its bearings, shooting off west into the early morning sky. Harry watched it as far as he could, and then at the outermost distance, where he could no longer be sure if he could see it or not, a blur of black shot down from the clear sky and collided with the remote, almost vanished dot.

A falcon.

Had the pigeon escaped? Harry couldn't be sure of it. He didn't think so. He couldn't assume so. He had no other communications options except one emergency back-up.

He had to go back to Paris.

Oldwick Fen

27 June 2007

They called Hickey half-sharp, though not often to his face, for he had shoulders like a bull and hands like hams, and didn't care to be mocked. He knew how to do most things on the estate, but new things threw him off, and here was a new thing, nestled in his cupped hands, a mass of blood and feathers with a tiny thrilling heart.

Hickey carried it all the way from the stable block where he'd found it, across the great lawn at the front of the House, to the tied cottage where Jack Reckliss lived, his boss and guide in things Hickey didn't understand. Jack would know what to do.

'Falcon nearly had him,' Jack said, examining the bleeding, exhausted pigeon cradled in Hickey's mighty fists. 'He's a lucky'un.'

'What's he got on his little leg, Jack?'

'Take a look, Hickey. Take it off and show it.'

Hickey fingered a small cylindrical pouch clipped to the pigeon's leg. Deftly, with infinite care for the suffering creature, he loosened and removed it, placing it on the plain wooden table between them in Jack's kitchen.

'Can we get him to the vet, Jack? He's all cut up. Where'd he come from?'

'Where'd you think he came from? From the sky.'

'Falcon nearly had him?'

'Look at the cuts. Razor could have made those. Falcon came at him from above. He must have dropped just in time. He'll need stitching up so much we should take him to Mrs Reckliss and her sewing machine, never mind the vet.'

Jack smiled kindly at Hickey, waiting for him to catch up and laugh.

'Sewing machine. Sewing machine,' Hickey repeated to himself, eyes sparkling. 'Not the vet.'

'There were pigeon lofts in the stable block during the war. All very secret, it was. Homing pigeons. My uncle told me.'

'What were they for, Jack?'

'They brought messages back from occupied France. When we were fighting the Nazis. Very hush-hush, it was, too. There were lots of secrets, back then. They dropped them to spies, and fly-boys carried them too, in the bombers, in case they were shot down. Better than radio, they said. Unless the hawks and falcons got 'em.'

'Is this one from the war? I bet it is.'

Jack looked at Hickey with indulgence.

'You daft a'peth. War was over sixty years ago.'

Hickey picked up the small pouch he had taken from the pigeon's leg and held it in the palm of his hand. Opening it carefully, he extracted three sheets of tightly folded, very thin paper.

Jack helped Hickey smooth them out on the kitchen table. Jack took a few seconds to register what he was looking at. Then his heart seemed to freeze. He stared at what they showed, disbelieving.

'What is it, Jack?'

No reply.

'Jack?'

Jack riffled through the sheets of paper, as though looking for evidence of a trick. He examined each one carefully. Then he put them down and sank deep into his own thoughts.

'Jack? Why you look so scared, Jack?'

'Some things you're better off not knowing about, Hickey. Did you do your special rounds this morning?'

Hickey looked confused for a moment. Then he seemed to remember. 'Yes, Jack, I did.'

His mouth dry, Jack struggled to speak.

'Look after that poor little pigeon. I'm going to check on old Aunt Margaret for a few minutes.'

'What's the picture of?'

Jack sighed.

'It's . . . a kind of rocket. A kind the Germans used in the war, Hickey. When our kind tried to stop them coming. You wouldn't understand.'

'I know the story of the three crowns,' Hickey said. 'They couldn't come to East Anglia 'cause of the three crowns that were buried to protect us from invasion in the old days, only one was lost when the sea washed Dunwich town away, and one was dug up at Rendlesham 300 years ago and melted down, but one's left buried and that's the one that saved us. That crown and our Aunty Margaret, bless her, that's what they say.'

'Is that what they say, Hickey?' Jack's face darkened, then he shouted. 'Get that pigeon to the vet, and put stupid ideas out of your stupid head! Get moving.'

Hickey jumped, unsure what he'd done wrong.

'What's the rocket called, Jack?'

'It's called a V-1. A doodlebug. Now get!'

Hickey carefully picked up the wounded pigeon and fled.

There were rules about the estate's secret military history, even today. If anything came up from the past, especially concerning the most secret episodes of that past, they had to call a special number in London.

Jack Reckliss had lived in the stone cottage in the grounds of Oldwick House since the death of his uncle, who was Robert's father. If his cousin Robert had wanted it, then the job on the estate, and the tied cottage that went with it, would strictly have been Robert's to take over, but Robert was one of the other Recklisses, the ones who held themselves apart, and had been raised for better things, they said, grammar school and college. As he lived in America, and wouldn't know one end of a billhook or an eel gleave from another, or want to, Robert had said no. So the work and the cottage had come to Jack's side of the family, first to his old dad and now to Jack. Oldwick Fen had seen them all born, and drew all of them back in its own good time. It even wanted Robert to come back now, Jack saw, and that could only be bad.

Jack looked again at the papers on the kitchen table. One was an official-looking message form, with a long series of characters that made no sense, and had to be in code. One was a sketch map of a section of terrain, with markings that might have meant military installations. The third was a sketch of a V-1 flying bomb and a long launching ramp. On the message form, a date appeared to have been written in clear. And it said 1943.

It was just as Old Margaret had said. The closer the day came, this year of reckonings, the worse things would get.

Jack reached for the telephone, then thought better of it. His hand was shaking. He should check on Old Aunt Margaret first and, he had no problem admitting, he was afraid to do so. Birds were messengers of death.

Paris

November 1943

Horace met Peter near the Lycée Montaigne at the southern end of the Jardin du Luxembourg, and they walked east along Rue de l'Abbé de l'Épée.

'What's going on?' Peter asked.

'Harry.'

'What about him?'

'All I know is, I got a message from our letterbox at the bookstore. We're to meet him at St Severin church, last row of seats on the left, in half an hour.'

It began to rain as they passed the Sorbonne's green-domed observatory tower. A Nazi staff car, followed by a grey-painted military truck, sped past them heading south.

They entered St Severin through the church's eastern entrance on Rue St Jacques, which ushered them into the semi-circular choir, behind the altar. There they found a German corporal, rapt in concentration, sketching the re-nowned twisting, spiralling column at its centre, surrounded by soaring Gothic arches.

They dipped their fingers in a stone bowl of holy water and crossed themselves. The church smelled of wet paper and cold stone. Peter walked to the west end while Horace lingered in the choir, as though they had entered together only by coincidence, each covertly looking for their anonymous contact among the rag-tag dozen or two people sitting in contemplation or sheltering from the grey, damp weather.

After a while Horace moved forward and sat down in the last row, nearest the western exit. He made to pray, following the Catholic gestures and mannerisms of his neighbours. There was no one nearby. After a few minutes, Peter sat down a few chairs to Horace's right. Still no sign of their contact.

Looking ahead, Peter saw that the twisting column stood directly behind the altar, marking the centre line of the nave. For a moment, sheer fatigue and the constant tension of clandestine life won out, making his eyes swim and his mind play tricks on him. He thought he saw the stone spirals turning, conjuring the arched, vaulted ceiling from its coils, resonating with light.

Who was he betraying? To what was he faithful?

He lost count of how long they sat, but eventually Horace moved again, heading for the exit behind them onto Rue des Prêtres St Severin. Peter took a couple of minutes and then left too. Dusk had fallen quickly. He saw Horace waiting for him at the corner, making a discreet signal to be cautious but to join him, then disappearing along the narrow alleyway as Peter started walking toward him. Only a limping widow of indeterminate age, muffled in layers of black clothing, followed Peter out, a headscarf obscuring her features. She walked away, softly humming a hymn to herself. What had happened to their man? Had he been compromised? Had they? Ordinarily there would be a fall-back meeting, at another location, in perhaps an hour or two. Was it safe to go?

Peter turned right onto the dark, slightly crooked street Horace had taken, noting its name. Rue de la Parcheminerie. Parchment-making. An image of flayed skins soaked in lime came into his mind, skins stretched and scraped to a fine translucence. He imagined skins written on with fine inks, scraped clean, written on again, and again. Palimpsests. Writing hidden under the surface of other writing. Stories under other stories. Identities under other identities. Who was to say which was real?

He blinked with surprise. Horace had vanished.

He walked down to the end, where the street ran into Rue de la Harpe. Nothing.

Ducking into the shadows, he looked casually back, and thought he saw a silhouette in a doorway halfway back along the narrow street. Horace. How on earth had Peter missed him?

Then the hairs stood up on the back of his neck. He saw Horace's stance, and realized he was waiting in ambush. Coming towards him along the Rue de la Parcheminerie, Peter saw the limping widow. Horace caught his eye and signalled: danger.

God, no.

Horace clearly thought the woman was following them.

Everything happened very quickly. As she reached the doorway where Horace stood, Peter walked rapidly towards the woman, shouting '*Madame!*' Distracted, she seemed not to notice Horace emerging from his hiding place, now behind her, pistol held close to his body. Peter closed in, convinced Horace was mistaken.

The woman turned on her heel, swinging her walking stick so fast Peter didn't see it. He felt the side of his head crack with pain and fell to one knee. He saw Horace double over, winded, from a blow to the solar plexus she must have delivered in the same violent movement.

The woman, now neither stooped nor limping nor particularly female, grabbed Horace's pistol from the ground and hid it in the folds of her clothing.

'Get up,' she hissed at their prostrate forms, in a surprisingly baritone bark. 'Bloody fools.'

'*Merde*,' said Horace, with feeling. 'Harry.'

'Damn right,' Harry said from beneath the layers of his disguise. 'Now get up. Hurry.'

~

'I wasn't expecting a woman,' Horace said sheepishly – the only time Peter ever saw him evince such a characteristic. 'I mean, I didn't realise you were one. I'm very sorry.'

Harry soaked up every last drop of the unidentifiable soup they had managed to prepare for him, tearing chunks off the loaf of scratchy grey bread.

'Rough place to be a woman, France,' he said. 'Can't smoke, no cigarette ration for women. Can't vote, only let men do that here. Don't let it rub off on you guys. Did I break your ribs?' Horace was rubbing his chest with a grimace as he spoke.

'Almost.'

'Shame. Sorry. I just wanted to be sure you weren't being tailed.'

They sat in the safe house on St André-des-Arts, planning to use it just the one night before moving on, three of them in a tiny kitchen.

'The good news is that the bombing is starting,' Harry said, resuming his summary of his piece of Steeplejack. 'The RAF are going to bomb as many launch sites as we were able to identify for them. And the *Farmer* network has found a lot. The bad news is that we surely haven't found them all, and the bombing won't destroy them all. But it's bound to slow them down. If we can cripple their launch capabilities . . .'

'I still don't understand exactly what they are,' Peter said. 'Are there different kinds of Secret Fire weapon? Are they all related to Steeplejack? Steeplejack is not about destroying launch-sites for wonder weapons, real or imaginary.'

'The one we know about – the one I've seen – is a pilot-less plane, with a ton of high explosive in the nose. There may be others. I've never seen one fly. The ones I've seen have no propellers, just a kind of long tube mounted on the back, with short stubby wings and fins. They must be able to guide them by compass bearing, somehow. There are buildings at each site that contain no metal. They must set the compasses there. The launch ramps have blast walls on either side, and the fuel they use is very dangerous. They keep its components separated for as long as possible, but they have accidents. We've seen them blow themselves up a few times. Saves us the job. Though it's mostly the slave labourers who get killed.'

'So a device like this,' Peter said, 'one of these pilot-less planes, could deliver one of these doomsday bombs we are trying to stop the Nazis getting, the *geheime Feuer* device, right into the West End of London, is that what we're saying?'

'Right. That's what we think.'

'Christ.'

'That's right. There's a particular site I've been watching. I saw the man I'm supposed to look out for there. I take it he is Isambard.'

Peter and Horace both stared in silence. Eventually, Horace answered. 'Yes.'

'What is so important about his being there? I know he's a bad hat, but . . .'

Horace took a breath.

'The *geheime Feuer* weapon requires several components. The device itself, a delivery mechanism, a suitable target and the operator. Only a special person will do.'

'Why?'

'There are two answers. The one you want to hear is that

it needs a skilled technician to make it work. The explosion is greater than anything mankind has ever seen. But it requires someone to guide it to the right target, and to trigger it in the correct sequence at just the right time. Someone riding aboard the delivery mechanism.'

Harry snorted in disbelief.

'I thought we were talking about pilot-less planes.'

'We are. The thing flies itself to the approximate vicinity – say, London. But to hit a specific target in London requires a navigator to trigger and control the final dive. Someone prepared to die in the explosion, naturally.'

'And what is the answer I don't want to hear?' Harry asked.

'The one you won't believe, and don't have to, is that this is not regular science, at least as you understand it. The operator must trigger the dive and guide the weapon to its target, yes. But more important is his mind.'

'How so?'

'The *geheime Feuer*, for Nazi purposes, needs an operator who has been engaged for many years in deliberately causing great suffering in other human beings. It is a weapon that reflects and feeds on the psyche of those using it. It is, in a very real sense, the Great Work perverted, turned to evil. A black sun, where there should be a white one.'

'What rot,' Harry declared. 'So much stuff and nonsense. I'll stick with the first answer. All I need to know is it's the biggest bomb the world has ever seen, and this man knows how to set it off. Let's kill him, and destroy all his toys. I need a radio operator. This is why I am here. My Farmer radio man Albert is taken. My pigeon was attacked by a falcon and is probably dead. I need that specific site bombed, as a priority.'

'You want immediate radio communication with London. Do you know what you're asking?'

'I do. We have to use Belle.'

'Impossible. Too dangerous.'

'There is no option. Getting a message out by Lysander would take too long. There's no full moon for two weeks.'

'We were told to use her only for matters of life and death.'

'That is what this is. For all of us.'

Horace stared out of the window, weighing his decision. After a few moments, he spoke.

'Very well. I agree.'

'Can you arrange it now?'

'Yes, immediately.'

Horace got up to leave.

'I'll try to reach someone who can contact her before curfew,' he said. 'It's dangerous, but I want both of you stay here tonight. I'll be in touch tomorrow.'

Cambridge

27 June 2007

Robert struggled back to his Cambridge hotel, limping, his shirt covered in fresh blood.

As soon as he was back in his room, he collapsed onto the bed.

He dreamed.

It began in a familiar place: the Fenland copse where, as a child, he had always gone to think through the problems that life threw at him. The birds sang endlessly there in his memory, in joyful, carefree harmonies. Dappled green light shaded him from a world of hostility and confusion, of unspoken secrets.

But something was different in the copse now as Robert dreamed himself there. It was bigger, darker. The peace he had always found was absent, and the birds were silent. In the spectral light of a waxing moon, tall shapes moved from shadow to shadow, and fear was in the air.

He could not see the faces of those present as they strode about the clearing in the centre of the copse, for they wore dark hooded apparel, and the shadows were deep. They moved with grim purpose about the circle, some holding implements he could not quite identify, others with their hands clasped, and Robert realized after a few moments that the fear he had felt in the air was not within this place, but all around it. It could not reach into the heart of the copse.

Robert saw a figure coming towards him, and suddenly a man's face was just inches from his own, gnarled and weathered, speaking directly to him. The sound coming from his mouth was muffled and distorted, as though he were speaking against the wind.

'When the time comes . . .' was all Robert could hear. 'Be ready when the time comes.'

He strained harder to hear. The face of the man looked familiar, but unlike anyone he knew.

'. . . can destroy us all. They mustn't pass . . . not these hellhounds . . .'

The man made to place a reassuring hand on Robert's shoulder, and then walked forward and stepped straight through Robert as though he were not there. Turning, Robert saw the man had been addressing a youngster directly behind him, and now Robert stood to the side and saw the older man take the child's head in his hands.

'Whatever you see . . . don't be afraid . . . play your part . . .'

The boy – he must have been ten or eleven – looked up, his face framed by the great rough hands, and blinked back tears, resolution vying with fear in his demeanour. Again the face was familiar, but unplaceably so.

Robert turned again to look at the rest of the figures as they moved about the copse. Among them now was a woman in her mid-twenties, wearing white when all the others wore black, her hood pulled back and her long red hair flowing onto her shoulders, standing apart in the middle of the circle. Staring straight at him, she held out her arms and beckoned, though Robert realized she could not see him, that he was a ghost to them.

Margaret.

The boy strode gravely across the clearing to her, holding out his hands to take hers as she knelt to whisper in his ear. And as the boy walked past Robert, Robert realized with a bolt of fear who he was, and why all the faces around the copse were oddly known to him, yet unnameable. In looking at the boy, he suddenly knew, he was looking at his own father.

Robert awoke with a jolt, gulping in a great lungful of air, not knowing where he was.

Then his cellphone rang.

Paris

November 1943

To reach Belle, Horace had been given a number for a sheet-music shop, which he was to call from a public telephone and ask if they had in stock a certain work by Messiaen.

Dropping a *jeton* into the slot in a phone booth on the Rue de Rivoli, outside the former W. H. Smith's that had now been converted into a German-language bookstore – a swastika flying outside, the familiar lettering replaced by a sign reading *Frontbuchhandlung* – he'd asked his question.

'Not currently, sir, but we can obtain it in a day or so, if that is convenient.'

'I'm keen to get hold of it as soon as possible, to prepare for an important recital.'

'I'll see what I can do, sir. Can you call back at three o'clock?'

At three he'd phoned from another public call box, this one just off the Champs Élysées.

Accès interdit aux Juifs, a card stuck on the upper pane of the booth proclaimed. Even the public phones were now forbidden to Jews.

'We have located a copy of the work you requested, sir. Since you need it so quickly, one of our suppliers would be glad to let you have it this evening, if you can meet him near his office?'

'I'd be glad to.'

'Very well. Seven o'clock, Café de la Source, Boulevard St Michel. You know it?'

'Yes. How will I recognize your supplier?'

'He always wears a yellow scarf. He'll be reading a copy of *La Gerbe*.'

Horace's contact at the café that evening, after some desultory conversation, had walked him a mile further south, away from the student haunts, and left him a block short of the address where he was to meet her, a drab four-storey apartment building near the Paris Observatory.

He knocked on the door of the second-floor flat.

'Who is there?'

He spoke the codename he'd been told to use only for dealing with Belle.

'My name is Philippe. I am looking for Marie-Jeanne.'

'One moment, please.'

He heard a chain being slid back, then the door opened. What shocked Horace was her beauty.

She had the widest, most luminous blue eyes he had ever seen, framed by stylish light brown hair that looked newly cut and tinted. She was tiny, perhaps five feet three inches, and couldn't weigh even a hundred pounds. She was darker in complexion than he had expected, though quite what he had expected he now didn't know – perhaps someone more robust-looking? Less vulnerable? A strapping blonde, better fitted for carrying a 33-pound clandestine radio set from one transmission site to another? For all her apparent fragility, though, her eyes spoke of iron determination as they fixed on his and coolly assessed him.

'You'd better come in.'

She wore a navy-blue skirt and an expensive grey wool polo-neck jumper. The room was bare, he saw: the location had been chosen only for this meeting. They spoke in French throughout, and he noted a slight foreignness in her pronunciation, though in other regards she spoke like a native.

'I cannot be here long, I have to meet someone in another part of the city,' she said. 'I imagine you are in a hurry too. Do you have a message you want me to send to London?'

Horace nodded.

'It's short, but very important.'

'I can transmit it tomorrow afternoon, not before. Do you expect a reply?'

'Yes, we hope very soon.'

'I'll do my best to listen every day for you. Some days it's just not possible. The Gestapo have almost caught me several times now. They know what I look like – at least, what I looked like until a few days ago. They're looking for a peroxide blonde, though.'

She flashed him a frightened smile that amplified his admiration for her grit and determination.

'If your message is short, I can try to memorize it,' she said.

'I was going to suggest the same thing.'

He gave it to her, a few lines from Harry to SOE headquarters. She repeated parts of it several times under her breath, asking him to repeat it just once, and then reeled it off back to him in a single stream of words, smiling like a conscientious schoolgirl. Only the sadness in her eyes spoiled the effect.

'That's it,' he said, smiling. It was the first time in days, perhaps weeks, that he had smiled.

'I won't forget it now,' she said. 'When I have a reply, I'll contact the music shop. You can call to check. Ask for something by Scarlatti.'

He hesitated at the door before leaving. She looked so young, though he calculated she was about his own age.

'Is there anything I can do for you?'

She stared at him, and for a moment he lost himself entirely in her gaze.

'Are you a praying man, Philippe?'

'After a fashion . . .'

'Oh, good,' she replied, a tinge of relief in her voice. 'I wanted to ask if you'd pray for my mother. She doesn't know I am here – she doesn't know where I am – but I feel sure she must be worried. It's so rare for me to be able to write to her, and even then the letters are posted in England.'

Still he lingered by the door, his hand on the knob, not opening it.

'How long have you been in France?'

'Three and a half months.'

The expected survival time for a radio operator in occupied France was six weeks. He hadn't realized until now how remarkably well she'd done.

'Are you . . .'

'Going back to London? Don't worry, I'll stay in Paris at least until you have your reply. I won't leave until they can replace me. It would be the next full moon at the earliest. And, you see, there's no one else. I have to be here. As long as I can remain one step ahead of the Gestapo.'

He opened the door and walked out, wanting more than anything else to stay and protect her.

New York

27 June 2007

The dreadful sounds suddenly cut off, and Katherine knew she was going to be questioned again.

They'd been ramping up the volume, then lowering it randomly, then pumping it up again. It was all to mess with her head: to make her anxious, to whiplash her emotions. She'd found herself worrying she was going deaf, then welcoming deafness if only it would end the nerve-shattering sounds, then falling into panic when the volume rose again beyond her ability to bear it.

It all was part of the trick, she told herself – to make her look forward to human contact, to the brief times with her inquisitor, to the silence punctuated only by his understated, probing voice.

Through it all, Katherine had withdrawn to her core, to a deep fortress within herself, and waited for an opportunity. Just one.

Be like Rose . . . be like Rose . . .

The sound loop they played was endless. A young woman confessing to betrayal, to war crimes, to cracking under interrogation, to giving other human beings up for torture to save her own skin . . . *My name is Rose Arden, known in the résistance as Belle . . . my name is Rose Arden . . . I have betrayed my friends . . . I have betrayed strangers . . . I do not deserve to live . . .*

They were tapes made, her inquisitor had told her, at Avenue Foch in Paris, after the Gestapo broke her.

As an adult, Katherine had imagined herself grown beyond the idealistic yearning to be like her grandmother, to be just like the idea she'd painted for herself of Rose. But now she was seeing, to her horror, just how much her sense of identity had been vested in this woman, this light of her childhood. At her lowest ebb, she'd found herself hallucinating, imagining conversations with Rose when she was a little girl, imagining seeing Rose at her mother's funeral, wishing Rose would hold her hand and make all the vulnerability and loss go away.

Rose had been an image of strength to her. A woman of integrity, unsullied by the world. Now they were tearing holes in that image and, in doing so, they were trying to tear down Katherine herself, her very idea of who Katherine Rota was.

Jumbled words came to her, from an imaginary London that made no sense. *Temple to St Martin in the Fields . . . St James . . . St Nicholas in the Fields . . .*

Katherine had felt *shame* at her mother's funeral. Amid all the emotions, the lonely twelve-year-old girl had felt *blame*. Why had she felt it was her fault? It was her dad, after all, her philandering, absentee Anglo-Argentine dad who had made her mother so miserable.

But if Katherine had been good, her mother would have stayed. That was how it had felt. And the imagined presence of Rose had helped her to stop blaming herself. Rose had been someone who got through adversity, no matter what, so Katherine would be too.

The tallest one, the interrogator, was not as professional as he imagined. His most amateurish slip, as he grew more comfortable with her and his sense of power over her, was unconsciously to step in front of the shotgun, between her and the weapon, for a second or two when leaving the room. That was all she needed.

The hatch opened, the gun appeared. The instruction came to step back against the wall. Then he came in, carrying his chair, while an unseen henchman kept the shotgun trained on her through the hatch.

Katherine looked into the sharp eyes of the leader. He'd be quick in a fight, Katherine felt. Vicious.

'We've been talking. Discussing what the best punishment would be for you, within our orders.'

'You can't kill me. That's evident. You're not allowed to.'

'Perhaps. But we can hurt you.'

'You can try.'

He reached for a short scabbard he wore on his belt and withdrew a dagger.

'Katherine, it's time to get down to business. The next stage.'

It was an SS-issue ceremonial dagger, a swastika moulded into the handgrip.

'What do you mean?'

'This is your husband's fault.'

'What do you think you are going to do?'

'He was warned to stop, and he didn't. There are consequences.'

'Robert . . .'

'Gave you up to us. He could have avoided this, but he chose not to.' He raised the dagger and pointed the tip towards her face. 'There is no nobility, Katherine. Everyone gives up others to save themselves. It's human nature.'

'Even you?'

'We're different. We learn to transcend human nature.'

'What are you, exactly?'

'We honour the Third Reich, and those who survived its eclipse. Its *temporary* eclipse.'

'Does it involve killing people?'

'Only sub-humans, street litter, vagrants. And never here. We travel for that. You, being white, are spared death. But you have to pay a price.'

'Where did you get that knife? It's German army, isn't it?'

Taken aback, he hesitated.

'Not army. It's SS.'

And if you lay a hand on me, I'm going to use it to kill you, you pig.

'You don't have to rape me. Do you realize that?'

'Actually, we do. In addition to everything else we have planned.'

She feigned fear, shrank from him, made out to be negotiating with herself, calculating her best interest. She looked behind him and saw that the shotgun was no longer pointing through the hatch. Whoever was out there was getting ready to come in.

'What if I let you? How many of you are there? Three? I'm going to take my sweatpants off, OK? So I can move? I need to free my hands first.'

'I'll take them off.'

They were his last words that day.

As he stepped toward Katherine, knife pointing at her in one hand, leaning down to tug at her sweatpants with the other, she swept her legs in a sudden, violent arc, knocking his feet out from under him. She was on him instantly. Winded and surprised, he barely had a chance to shout before she head-butted him as hard as she could. She grabbed the knife and whipped its handle against his head, then used its razor-sharp blade to cut through the duct tape on her wrists. He'd had a gun concealed in his waistband. Now it was in her right hand.

Katherine was on her feet in seconds, her sweatpants pulled up, pressed against the breeze-block wall by the hatch where they couldn't see her from outside.

The other two came running into the room without checking, one holding the shotgun, and turned to face her. They froze.

'Run or I'll kill you,' she shouted. 'Fucking Nazis!'

One of them raised the shotgun. Katherine pulled the trigger of her pistol. The boom was deafening in the enclosed space. It was as though she'd been kicked in the head. Dust and cordite filled the air before her eyes. But she held her position and discipline, and when she could see and hear again, the thug was lying still on the floor, eyes open, a ragged red hole in his forehead. His friend was staring, whey-faced, paralysed with fear, emitting a whining sound.

'Your friend is dead. Do you understand?'

He stood gaping, his legs trembling.

'Listen, master-race. Answer my questions, or you're next. Understand?'

She looked at his trousers. He was urinating himself. He had to be nineteen.

'Who is Isambard?'

She could barely hear her own voice, still deafened by the gunshot. He stammered, making no sense.

'Look at me. Who is Isambard?'

'Our leader,' the young man whined.

'What's his full name? What does he look like? Where is he?'

'I don't know. Never seen him. I don't know.'

'How does he communicate with you?'

'I don't know. I don't know. I just do what I'm told. Please don't hurt me.'

He fell to his knees, crying. Katherine gripped his hair in one hand and pulled him back up.

'Who's this?' She kicked the unconscious leader of the group. 'He's your boss, right?'

'We don't have names!' the kid shrieked. 'I'm number five! I'm number five! I'm number five!'

He started rocking on his knees, working himself into a frenzy. She let him go, and he fell face forward onto the ground, weeping.

'You just like the part where you get to go out and beat up vagrants, is that it?' she shouted at him, suddenly searingly angry. She kicked him hard in the midriff. 'Now shut up!'

Katherine looked at the unconscious man, then knelt down beside him. A search of his pockets produced nothing. She suddenly felt crushingly tired. She wanted nothing more than to get out of this place, away from these tawdry, messed-up boy-men.

'Where do you live?' she shouted to the kid.

He whined a response. 'Scranton.'

'Go there. Stay there. If I see you again, if you do anything to get in my way, or have anything to do with people like this again, I'll find you, and you'll get the same as your friend. Yes?'

She stepped forward, pointing the gun down at him.

'Go!'

He clambered to his feet and ran.

~

Katherine ransacked the space where her captors had set up their base, finding her red dress, her bra and shoes, her purse and cellphone, her engagement ring. There was no sign of her wedding band. She'd been held in an old warehouse, the breeze-block cell built in one corner of an abandoned office.

She ran out into the light, eyes aching. Where was she? Brooklyn, somewhere. She walked towards the sound of traffic. As she walked, she dialled Robert's number. The connection, when it came, was patchy, fading in and out. Her battery was low.

'Robert? Where are you? I'm out, I escaped.'

'Kat? Kat? Oh my God, my darling, thank God you're all right. Are you OK? Are you hurt? Are you OK?'

They babbled at each other in the desperate words of people in shock, talking past one another, shards of language that barely made sense.

'What's going on? Where are you? Are you home?'

'I'm in England. In Cambridge. Are you safe? You have to get away from them. Come to England, as soon as you can.'

'Where's Horace? Are you OK?'

'There's no time to explain. Get to England. Meet Horace at the Waldorf. I'll tell him you're coming.'

He retched with pain, trying to hide it from her. She was safe. Thank God. She was alive.

'Did they hurt you, Kat?'

'Not as badly as I hurt them. Nazis. Can you believe it? I'm OK. I'm fine. Are you hurt?'

'I'll be fine. Listen. Horace will explain to you. You need to move, to get here. They don't want you here, so come.'

'Is this it? Is this what we've been waiting for? Is it IWNW? Are they back?'

'Yes. We have two days, that's all. I'm seeing my old family people tomorrow. It's something to do with them. I don't understand.'

'How bad is it?'

'It's very bad. I don't know if we can stop them.'

'I love you, Robert. I love you.'

'I love you, Kat. Get to London. I'll see you there as soon as I can. I love you. Come tonight.'

Day Two

Paris

November 1943

Horace could not help himself. Three days after first meeting Rose Arden, alias Belle, he went to see her again, at a different secret location, with no message to deliver.

'You asked me to pray for your mother,' Horace said.

'Yes. Yes I did.'

'I did pray for her. But then I began praying for you. And I haven't stopped since.'

'You mustn't worry about me.'

'I can worry about little else.'

'You shouldn't have come back.'

He couldn't take his eyes off her. She felt the same way, he was sure of it.

'All I want to say is . . .'

'You have a mission. We both do. In wartime, none of us has a right to personal feelings. You know that.'

'I know. But the simple fact is . . .'

She stood and walked over to him. She placed a finger on his lips.

'Don't say it. Don't say a word.'

Horace looked into the wide blue pools of her eyes, and felt himself lost. Dissolved.

To the Russian dolls of identity within identity, and mission within mission, that defined his life, to the circles of secrets and deception in which he moved, Horace had now added another layer: love.

No one could know of it, just as no one could be told of his other calling, the one that had truly brought him on this mission.

Horace was to hunt down Fulcanelli, yes, and to deny the man's knowledge to the Nazis, as per his military orders.

But he was also to influence the Allied use of the *geheime Feuer*, and if possible to deny it to them too. The world was not ready for it. He was to recover the secrets, and hide them away.

Horace had been schooled in several parts of the world during an itinerant childhood, attending university in the United States and England, receiving private, specialized schooling in the Middle East too, all for one purpose: he was to serve the group known as the Perfect Light.

Born in Alexandria to an American adventurer, explorer and spy who also served the group, he had been initiated at an early age into its mission: to gather together and protect the shards and fragments of higher science, of divine knowledge, that humankind, through the millennia, had been able to discover.

The Perfect Light – a name given to them by others, since they referred to themselves only as *friends*, or *travellers*, or any number of other loose terms – did not believe that the knowledge had ever been assembled in a single place, nor that any past civilization had gained it all and lost it. The Perfect Light believed, though, that the knowledge, when assembled, would form an unfractured perspective, an enhanced way of seeing, that would allow humankind to survive and to evolve to a higher plane. Lacking it, or misusing it, humanity would in time bring about its own destruction.

This quest was known as the communal Great Work of

humankind, and each individual within it had to achieve his own Great Work as part of it. In Horace's case, his understanding had developed to the point where he hoped Fulcanelli himself could provide him with the final instruction he needed.

The *friends* were not a secret society, did not seek worldly power, and interfered in world events only when they felt they had to, and when they could achieve a useful aim. They were directed by men and women who had previously achieved their own Great Work, through whatever tradition they belonged to. They lived nowhere, had no secret cities, and died like other men and women, Yet they could be known, by others who attained the state of mind known as Heliopolis, the city of light, and would themselves contact those who were ready to learn.

Before each attempt at the individual Great Work, an ordeal had to be undergone, in isolation. For this reason, Horace's father had cut all ties with Horace after he'd joined the OSS, letting him know only that he would be expected to go up, alone, against Isambard, one of the greatest enemies of the Light.

He knew the ordeal was coming. And he knew exposing himself to love could exacerbate it. But he couldn't help himself.

Horace removed her finger slowly from his lips, staring still into the depths of her eyes.

Then he kissed her.

Oldwick Fen

28 June 2007

Margaret felt the shadow fall on her bed, and knew that something was wrong. With a weak, reedy voice, she called out for her carer, but no one replied.

'Hickey? Hickey?'

She was burning with fever, her bedclothes damp with sweat. The struggle to live had been intense, a no-holds-barred battle in her dreams with the Lantern Men and their creatures. Two more days was all she needed.

Blind and fearful, Margaret reached to her neck for the pendant that held her protective glass-stone. She felt the presence of a body near her: big, looming, male.

'Who are you?' she croaked.

Then, to her surprise, she felt a cold, damp cloth applied to her forehead. The body settled on to the bed, sitting to one side of her. He had an unfamiliar smell, and the touch of his hand, as he dabbed her cheeks with the refreshing cloth, was new.

'Is that a little better?'

The voice was deep and soft, yet somehow cold.

'Where's Hickey?'

'Hickey looks after you, doesn't he?'

She swallowed with difficulty, her throat burning.

'I'm sorry,' the stranger said. 'Would you like some water?'

She nodded into the darkness. He was a Lantern Man.

Margaret heard the clink of the ice in the jug, and then a glass of cool water was pressed into her hands. She sipped at it, gathering her thoughts.

'Hickey's soft, but he's a good boy,' she whispered. 'Don't hurt him. If you've hurt him . . .'

'Ssshhhh. Hickey is fine. But I have come instead. To ask you something.'

'How did you find me?'

'I was told by some . . . acquaintances . . . where to find you. You have been hidden away, well hidden, for a long time.'

'No one has found me in sixty-three years.'

'Your strength is waning. Your gift is about to expire, and with it, all your spells. That's how you were found. The candle is starting to gutter. Your power to hide is not what it once was.'

'What do you want to ask?'

Suddenly she felt him holding at bay a terrible evil. He was speaking to her as though within a cocoon, and only the two of them could hear.

'How may I lend you more strength?' he asked her. 'How can I help you?'

She felt the strain upon this Lantern Man, who no longer wanted to be one. But she saw that he could not hold out. The sense of protection was about to collapse.

'Forget me,' she whispered. 'Follow your own path. Try to escape, at the very end.'

Then the cocoon tore apart, and evil was in the room. She felt him slump, felt his shame and anger.

'Now I know you,' she hissed.

'We have never met, my dear.'

'No, but I know you. You are one of the ones I stopped. You have that . . . stench . . . about you.'

'I am not as simple a creature as you seem to think.'

'You want the crack in time to open. The window in time. In two days.'

'Yes.'

'Best left closed, or we'll all catch our deaths. No good will come from opening it. Too dangerous. Best kept sealed.'

'My acquaintances aren't interested in the good, my dear.'

'Hand me my stick.'

'No.'

'Hand . . . me . . . my . . . stick!'

She heard him shifting his weight, looking around the room.

'There is no stick here.'

Good boy, Hickey, she thought. He had done as she'd asked.

Now Margaret clutched the pendant to her chest, a small soft leather pouch. She invoked its protection.

'You've come to kill me. So I can't hand on the art to my successor when it dies in me. So we can't renew the spell, so we can't stop the window in time from cracking open.'

'Yes.'

'Try your best, Nazi.'

With the last drops of her strength, Margaret smashed the water glass hard against the iron bedstead, shattering it, then slashed in the direction of the shadow looming over her. She felt flesh tear, felt blood spurt. He roared in pain. Margaret shrieked the vilest curses she knew, her frail body rigid, her sinews like steel.

Then as she felt a shaking hand smother her nose and mouth, she took herself off to another place, while Falke, in furtherance of his father's hopes of resurrection, quickly and efficiently used his Fairbairn-Sykes dagger to kill her.

Paris

November 1943

The radio reply from London came three days later. The Bois des Huit-Rues site at Morbecque would be bombed as a matter of priority, Belle told Horace. Raids should be expected in the next week.

'I'll come to you tonight,' she said as they parted. 'I can't be alone any more.'

The pressure on them was unbearable. Each worked a crushing schedule of meetings, of transmissions, of delicate inquiries and time-consuming, security-conscious movement around the city. Counter-surveillance alone took hours out of each day: travelling on foot, taking circuitous routes, moving from one safe house to another. It was what kept them alive.

Yet somehow, each night, they were together for a few hours. It was time they both felt they were snatching from death.

'Do we have a right to love?' Rose asked him one night. 'Amid so much hatred? Does anyone have the right to seek happiness in such a world?'

'Love sought us out, we didn't seek it,' Horace whispered, kissing her damp forehead, losing himself in the warmth of her body against his, in her perfume, in her hair. 'I couldn't fault anyone for stealing a few moments of beauty, of perfection, in a world gone mad.'

'Is there a future for us? I don't see how there can be.'

'We have today. We have now. For the rest . . . I ardently wish it.'

'Don't mock my name,' she giggled.

He held her tight, squeezing the breath out of her.

'In the face of death, there is no option but to embrace life. All of it.'

He kissed her again.

'When you first came to see me,' Rose said, 'I was scared of you. Not because you looked fearsome, but because you looked kind.'

'Why do you say that?'

'Because I can resist a frightening man. I don't expect to live through this mission. I never have. I just swore to myself to do my best, and hope I was brave at the end. And it seemed a terrifying man of some kind, someone I could hate, would finish me off, and I'd have the strength to resist because he would make hatred easy for me.'

'These people make hating them easy, it's true.'

'But you weren't someone I could resist, however hard I tried. I knew I'd stay for you, stay longer than I should, maybe even miss my Lysander back to England. Once I'd seen you, I didn't belong back there any more.'

'Rose . . .'

'Horace, one thing. If I'm taken, do nothing for me. I won't be a hostage. I won't be traded. If a circumstance arises where you have to weigh my welfare against something the enemy wants, don't give it to them. Promise me.'

'Honey . . .'

She raised herself on one elbow and fixed him with her most serious gaze.

'Promise me.'

He stared back at her till he could see nothing but her eyes.

'That has to be a mutual promise. If I'm taken, the same rules apply. I won't be traded. Give them nothing.'

'I promise.'

'I do too.'

London

28 June 2007

Katherine caught the last of the morning rain as her taxi dropped her at the Waldorf. Exhausted by her kidnapping ordeal, she'd slept right through her storm-delayed flight from New York, having learned long ago to grab rest whenever she could get it. Now she was tightly focused on the task at hand. Alerted by Robert, Horace met her in the lobby and took her directly to breakfast.

'What's going on, Horace? Where's Robert?'

'He's gone back to his origins, looking for the strength we'll need if we are to survive these coming days. All of us. He is looking for a part of himself that lies in the past. Then he has to get back here. We must all be here, at Aldwych, at St Clement Danes church, in two days.'

He explained to her about the *geheime Feuer*, the V-1 flying bomb, the colossal evil its detonation would unleash.

'Imagine. On 30 June 1944, the D-Day invasion of Normandy was three and a half weeks old, and the Allies had barely got off the beaches. It had taken them a week even to link up their five landing forces into a single beachhead. They were hemmed in, one of their two floating ports had been destroyed in a storm, the British had failed to capture Caën in the east, a first-day objective, the Americans were mired in the *bocage* in the west – high hedgerows and narrow lanes separating thousands of fields, each one an ideal German defensive position. They were bottled up, unable to break out of the narrow sleeve of land they had taken. It could all still have failed.'

'And?'

'Imagine then the effect, at that time, of a Vengeance attack – *Vergeltungswaffe Eins*, a V-1 – of such power that it destroyed London. Churchill dead. The War Cabinet dead. The European centre of resistance to Hitler, perhaps the greatest city in the world at that time, wiped from the face of the map. An attack that rippled and propagated from its point of impact to the entire south-east of the country, to the coast, to Portsmouth. Eisenhower, Patton, Montgomery – all the Allied commanders – dead or dying, poisoned. A catastrophic blow.'

'What would have happened in the wider war?' Katherine asked.

'It would have been impossible to regroup to save Europe. America would have had to cut its losses and focus on the Pacific, on beating Japan. They didn't have the atom bomb yet, remember. Hitler would have been able to pull his forces from the west to help fight the Red Army in the east. He wouldn't have invaded England. He would have left it to rot. Perhaps sent just a small scavenger garrison to mop up in the north and west. Could he have driven the Soviets to a standstill, enforced a stalemate, however much he hated them? Threatened to use the same weapon on Moscow? Even on New York? A *pax germana*. Whichever way you cut it, Britain is dead, a smoking, poisoned ruin, its inhabitants, those who were unlucky enough to survive, feeding on each other, tearing each other apart.

'The situation is this: however it was achieved, and I believe both Robert's family and I had something to do with it, the anomaly in time, the incantation or spell, whatever you want to call it, is unravelling. It is doing so rapidly. As it weakens and falls apart, fragments of the past come to life again, and begin to intrude ever more forcefully into the present. The spell-caster could halt this process by passing on their fading powers to a suitable successor, renewing them. But I fear the Enemy will make sure, if they have not done so already, that no handover can take place.'

'You mean kill the maker of the spell?'

'Yes.'

'So the knot will come entirely undone, in two days.'

'Yes.'

'What happens then?'

'For a few vital minutes, past and present will fuse. Things that might have been, will have a chance to be again, for good or for ill. The past may be healed, or poisoned. And in the midst of this opening window, Isambard will try to drive the full fury of his hatred into the present. Live again, and in doing so ensure that everything he stands for lives again too. We have to fight it out with him, ensure the opening window is not used for evil. If we can, use it for good. And somehow close it again.'

'Live again how? What can we do? What can I do?'

'I still can't see the whole picture. But there's a riddle left by Adam that I want you to look at.' He showed it to her.

'Robert found a note from Adam that pointed out several locations that don't fit,' Horace said. 'I've begun to track the movements of someone who has come to London. Who has stepped out of the past. The London route is coherent, a straight line – St Bride's, Temple Church, St Clement Danes at Aldwych, St Anne's in Soho.'

'OK.'

'So here's what doesn't fit: St Martin in the Fields, to St Nicholas, to St James, to St Julian, to St James again . . .

'there's no line in London you can draw using those names.'

They were the locations Katherine had heard, believing she was hallucinating, while being held in the cell.

She suddenly saw a scene in her mind from when she was a little girl: a juxtaposition of stained glass and scientific instruments, precisely calibrated brass tools and soaring stone arches. She couldn't place where . . .

Horace kept on talking as she tried to tie down the image in her memory. Katherine's mind drifted. She was holding her mother's hand. There were old automobiles, a primitive airplane, a giant metal ball swinging on a steel wire from the soaring heights of a church dome . . .

'St Martin des Champs!' she shouted suddenly. 'Not St Martin in the Fields in London! St Martin des Champs in Paris! They're all in Paris!'

It was one of her earliest memories, from a time when her mother was still alive, and they had gone to visit Paris. Perhaps 1966? Her mother had taken them to the Conservatoire National des Arts et Métiers, which housed part of its museum displays in the former abbey church of St Martin des Champs . . . And she'd felt Rose very close, and even imagined she'd heard her words. *A very big secret was once stolen from here*, Rose had whispered to her. *Perhaps one day, if you are good, I'll tell you about it* . . .

'Yes,' Horace said. 'Yes. Paris. Of course! Wait here.'

He stood and left the breakfast room, returning a few minutes later with a piece of folded off-white paper.

'This may prove useful. You need to go to Paris.'

'When?'

'After you see your friends at Shadowbox. Go see them now, then report back to me.'

The paper was a hand-drawn sketch map, though with no street names, and some old French writing on it.

'What will you do now, Horace?'

'I have a man I need to see.'

~

Shadowbox dwelled at a secret location far from the main MI6 headquarters.

Katherine strode north from the Green Park Underground station into Mayfair, an area crammed with spookery, past and present. On Curzon Street east of Clarges Street, there was the former MI5 building, known for its massive underground bunker in which, until the 1990s, the organization's fabled registry of secret files had resided. It had always been said to connect via tunnels to shelters under Buckingham Palace. On nearby Grosvenor Street, at number 70, the American OSS had set up its wartime European headquarters, taking over a fistful of other houses in the area too. At the bottom of Down Street, glazed red-brown brickwork and arches announced the presence of a disused Piccadilly Line Underground station, an alternative secret site used by Winston Churchill's War Cabinet.

MI5, with which Katherine had never been involved, was now long departed to Millbank; and the SIS that she had joined at Century House in Lambeth, with her tough-girl training imparted at Fort Monckton on the south coast, was now ensconced in its Egyptian-Maya-Legoland wonderpalace at Vauxhall Cross. Shadowbox, a disreputable branch of the Firm even at the best of times, was not to be found there.

At a discreet house on the west side of Berkeley Square she found the premises she had been invited to. Katherine noted with some amusement that it was next to the legendary number 50, in Victorian times reputed to be the most haunted house in London, at one time home to the eighteenth-century occultist-fraudster Cagliostro, now the venerable chambers of Maggs Brothers, the book dealers.

'Hello, Katherine,' a rangy man in his fifties, with a red beard and thinning hair, greeted her as she crossed the threshold.

She smiled at him. 'Desmond.'

'Very glad you're here. I need to show you something.'

It had been fifteen years since they'd seen each other, though she'd spoken with Desmond on the phone only a few days previously, when he'd called to enlist her help with the mystery that was vexing him.

Back in her MI6 days, Katherine had taken part in a wholly deniable and highly secret series of experiments run by Desmond at Shadowbox's former premises in Bermondsey, aimed at exploring whether psychic or mental influence could be brought to bear on key players in the Troubles in Northern Ireland. She'd never been told the results of the experiments, which she'd found painful and exhausting. The leaders of the various armed groups involved had had minds she'd never care to visit again.

They climbed a spiral staircase that seemed to go on for ever, right up into the attic. At the top of the house, in a small room lit by a single skylight, Desmond showed her, with something approaching a fetishist's fervour, a World War Two era transmitter/receiver.

'It's a Type 3 Mark II suitcase radio, commonly known as the B2,' he said. 'Beautiful device, if it didn't weigh an absolute ton.'

'Whose was this?'

'This was one of Rose's.'

She placed a hand on it, softly. 'This was my grand-mother's . . .' For an instant she felt the simultaneous chill and heat of a fever: the comfort of a warm hand, the cold sweat of sickness, of danger.

'There's been another message, again in Morse,' Desmond said. 'We were wondering if it made any sense to you.'

She focused on Desmond's need for information, clearing her head. 'Tell me what it said.'

'It was very garbled and patchy. But the gist was: Bring the defector in before the next full moon, or a terrible catastrophe will happen.'

'That's it?'

'Yes. And here's the odd thing.'

'What?'

'June 30, 1944 was not a full-moon night. But 30 June 2007 is. That's the day after tomorrow.'

'I'm going to ask you something strange,' Katherine said.

'We're used to strange, here.'

'I need to take this radio set with me.'

Paris

November 1943

The betrayal was a simple thing. A young woman, jealous of Belle, contacted the Gestapo, offering to sell them a British agent. The sister of a *résistant* whom Belle had worked with from the very start of her mission, the woman had felt overshadowed by the radiant young radio operator. At least one dashing agent in their circle had stopped paying any attention to her whatsoever once Belle had arrived.

Peter, getting word of the offer of betrayal through Isambard, read the description of the radio operator and felt an immediate pang of recognition. Those eyes ... He carried out surveillance on the address given by the informant.

And he learned two things:

The young woman who pervaded his dreams had returned to Paris.

And she had taken Horace as a lover.

Whether it was his own jealousy, a desire to have Rose all to himself, or a wish at least to control the circumstances of her inevitable arrest, Peter was not sure. He told himself several different stories. But he undertook the operation himself.

Peter was waiting for her, hiding behind the door, when she entered the first-floor apartment at 98, Rue de la Faisanderie. He grabbed her wrists, expecting her to acquiesce immediately. She was just a slip of a girl, after all, and Peter was a strong young man who was more than capable of throwing his weight around. But he was wrong about Rose. The 100-pound woman sank her teeth into his wrist and bit down with all her strength.

Peter screamed and cursed as his skin shredded and blood began to pour from between her clenched teeth. He gripped her hands more tightly, wheeling about the room and smashing into furniture to try to shake her loose as Rose bit deeper, shrieking in fear and anger.

She loosed one wrist and shouted at the top of her lungs. '*Salaud! Sale boche!*' Then she sank her teeth into his other wrist, drawing even more blood. He let her go, pushing her hard back onto a couch on the far side of the room. He reached into a pocket for his handcuffs as she sprang back from the sofa, and tried to grab her long enough to snap them onto one of her wrists. But she wriggled and squirmed, kicking and clawing at his face, throwing at him everything she had learned about unarmed combat at Wanborough Manor and Beaulieu, everything that her raw animal instinct to survive now told her. Teeth are weapons. Nails are weapons. Eyes. Groin. Throat.

Peter threw her across the room again and stepped back, giving himself time to draw his pistol. Sweating, bleeding and angry at the embarrassment she had caused him, he aimed directly at her heart.

'Sit down or I will shoot you.'

Rose stared at the dark barrel of the Luger pointing at her, and then looked up at the confusion in his eyes. Slowly, her eyes focusing again on the gun, she sat down.

Peter picked up the telephone receiver and held it to his ear. With his free hand he dialled Gestapo headquarters.

'This is Falke. I have Belle in my personal custody. Send a car.' He looked at her in amazement. Now her gaze rose to meet his, contempt and defiance rippling from her. She raised a hand and made a tiger's claw, then tore at the air between them with it, cursing him in French and English.

In her anger, she didn't recognize him, he realized. She only saw a Gestapo thug.

'I am going to protect you,' he whispered to himself. 'I am going to help you.'

Within minutes, three more Gestapo men arrived. Rose unleashed a new wave of insults at them as they entered, glaring in disgust.

'I was almost free!' she shouted. '*Sales boches*, I was almost back in England! Another few days!'

Peter, still bleeding profusely, face pale and shirt wet with sweat, told them to handcuff her.

They took her away to Gestapo headquarters, a few hundred yards away at 84, Avenue Foch. Peter didn't let her out of his sight.

Her betrayer had sold Rose to the Gestapo for 100,000 francs. They would happily have paid ten times as much.

～

A few hours later, before the news of the arrest had broken, Horace met Peter at Les Halles, and they walked south, towards the river.

'Meeting in person is a greater risk than I would like to take,' Horace said. 'Things are getting more dangerous. The Gestapo have raided Claire Lacour's apartment. But I needed to speak to you.'

Claire, a fearless, selfless woman, had been detained for providing an apartment for the leader of an espionage circle in Paris codenamed Parsifal. The Gestapo had arrested him, and in short order had rolled up virtually the whole operation, which was run not by F Section of SOE, but by the rival house, MI6. Nazi agents, knowing that Claire's little dog had a habit of barking at strangers and nuzzling up to her friends, had been seen parading the creature along the streets near her home in the hope of identifying possible *résistance* contacts of hers.

'I know,' Peter said. 'You are aware, are you not, that I have certain contacts at Avenue Foch. I am even able sometimes to enter the building, to have a certain level of contact with the authorities there. You should have been briefed on this. Claire is important, but I have learned more urgent things than this.'

'I know about your game with the Gestapo. I can't say I like it, but I accept it. What have you learned from those animals?'

Peter tried to read Horace, to see if he really knew the extent of his skein of deceptions. He couldn't tell. He didn't think so.

'Who is virtuous? Who is not? I am able to play a double game. You benefit greatly from it. Steeplejack depends on it. Without me, you will never get the Secret Fire. That is the urgent thing I have learned at Avenue Foch.'

'What?'

Peter looked into the distance, unsure, troubled.

'We may have a chance to steal the Nazi half of the document.'

Horace blinked in amazement.

'What? When?'

'It is being brought here. Next week. To see if the atomic scientists, the Joliot-Curies and their friends, can make anything of it. It will be a great risk, but we can, perhaps, get someone near it for a few minutes. We can steal it.'

London

28 June 2007

Walking away from Aldwych along Drury Lane, then turning west on Russell Street, Peter continued to revive the shape he had first walked into London in 1936, tracing the London ley line. He came to the Scottish Crown Court Church, almost invisible next to the Fortune Theatre, its narrow frontage on Russell Street surmounted, chiselled in stone, by the word *Holy*.

Pausing in meditation for a few moments, Peter felt deep down with his senses into the London marshland that had once stood in this area, criss-crossed by rivulets and streams making their way down to the Thames, a fen like the other fen he had recently come to know.

He spoke the secret phrase. *Lucem in tenebris occulto* . . .

Unlike the work he had done in Paris, his London dosings of psychic poison had never been fully activated, and had never had the chance to seep into the minds and souls of the city's inhabitants as they had in the French capital during the Nazi occupation.

Now, though, they could be activated at last, for a new purpose. A different one.

Peter walked on, crossing Covent Garden and eventually coming to St Martin's Theatre at the east end of Litchfield Street, where he connected again with the trace of the dragon.

Litchfield Street led directly to the octagonal keep of the now-deconsecrated Welsh Presbyterian Chapel on Charing Cross Road – directly on the line of power.

From the former chapel he walked to Romilly Street, where he looked west and saw above the roofs the strange clock tower of the next point on the line: St Anne's of Soho. Only the tower, topped by its spherical clock, remained now of the church he had known in 1936, the rest destroyed by German bombing. Yet still the beacon persisted. The line would always be marked, one way or another.

At St Anne's he entered the churchyard from Wardour Street and found a quiet corner to reflect for a few minutes. It was around lunchtime, and someone in the street was listening to the radio news. He heard reports of new prime minister Gordon Brown's cabinet appointments.

The voice that suddenly spoke was instantly familiar, decades after Peter had last heard it.

'This church was the site, I believe, of Lucie Manette's marriage in *A Tale of Two Cities*.'

Horace.

Peter turned to see the man he hated, and needed, most in the world. Hated, for throwing him to the wolves in 1944. Needed, because now, at last, Horace could bring him back.

'*Manetta*, actually, is also the name of a restaurant in Mayfair that SOE occasionally used for discreet chats with agents before they began their missions,' Horace continued. 'It was on Clarges Street, part of the Fleming Hotel. Vera Atkins was in charge of the officers going in. She took Rose there just before she flew into France. Never saw her again, of course.'

'You'll never forgive me for that.'

'How could I?'

'She is alive to me, still, after all these years.'

'Your father had her killed.'

'My father . . .'

'He's coming back, isn't he? Trying to. And you must know that as the possibility of his doing so gets closer and closer, you'll find it harder and harder to throw off his influence.' Horace's voice was hard, resigned, tipping over almost into hate for this creature who had taken Horace's beloved Rose from him. 'He is coming for you, Peter. As he always said he would.'

'What do you know of me?'

'All I need to. And I must tell you this: I will not allow him to return. He will not succeed. You don't know what I am saying when I say that to you. But one day soon you will.'

'Get out of my way, old man.'

More than anything, Peter wanted to cross to Horace, slough off the vile skins he had accumulated, layer upon layer, in the service of those to whom Horace had condemned him. But already he could feel the mounting, looming presence of Isambard, within and around him, wherever he looked, wherever he went. Peter had to hide, till the last possible moment, when the power would be greatest, and his only real chance would come.

'Come across now, Peter. Defect before it's too late.'

'It's already too late!' Peter shouted, his voice thick with anger. He lunged at Horace, going for his eyes with both thumbs. Horace stepped back and grabbed Peter's wrist, turning sideways and twisting downwards, trying to force his man to the ground. But Peter turned faster and drove the heel of his shoe hard onto his opponent's instep, then slammed his elbow into Horace's midriff.

Horace went down on one knee, gasping. For a moment, Peter had a clear shot at the back of Horace's head. But then he turned and ran, as onlookers began to shout and converge on the novel scene of a fight between two tough-looking, white-haired old men, neither of them in the least bit frail.

Peter pushed his way past a gaggle of tourists and marched quickly on towards his next point, west from St Anne's, the wound in his gut reopened and bleeding, hiding his emotions deep in his past. He plunged into memories of his own shame, to blot out any more thoughts of the present.

After the war, it was the Americans who saved Peter. Horace was not among them, though.

A top secret mission called ALSOS drove into Paris, directly behind the first liberating Allied troops, in late August 1944. ALSOS was ancient Greek for *grove*, which went an oddly long way towards giving away its purpose: one of its primary sponsors was Major General Leslie Groves, head of the US atom bomb project.

ALSOS was all about tracking down German atomic secrets – how close the Nazis had come to being able to build a bomb themselves, where their materials and scientists were, and whom to take into custody.

In Paris, ALSOS made a beeline for the laboratory of Frédéric Joliot-Curie, where they placed him as gently as possible under protective custody and took charge of his remaining collection of Molotov cocktails. Joliot-Curie had turned his workplace into a factory for making improvised weapons against the Nazis during the uprising.

Peter, by then on the run from everyone, his double and triple games unravelling, observed ALSOS from afar until he was able to contact a certain major, part of a hidden programme within the mission, unknown to most of its members, whose remit was somewhat more unusual. The major was associated with an undertaking called Operation Paperclip, which sought to acquire for the United States –

and deny to the Soviets – Nazi know-how in such matters as rocketry, jet engines and other more unusual scientific endeavours of military use. Eventually its activities spread into anti-Soviet intelligence, freeing many Gestapo men and setting them against the soon-to-be Cold War enemy.

A special 'deep black' section within it also sought occult know-how.

Via Paperclip, years before anyone had heard of US psychic spying programmes such as Stargate or Sun Streak, or their equivalents in the Soviet Union, Peter Hale-Devereaux, a fake death certificate issued in his name, soon found himself with a new identity, a new home and a new job at a remote, run-down army base in Maryland.

Peter became a clandestine psychic spy, and sometime warrior, for the United States of America.

It was always the same room, the same drill. Only the mission changed. Usually, it was to snoop remotely on distant locations, and to draw what he saw there. Occasionally, it was bloodier.

He would lie comfortably on his back on a couch, a pencil in his right hand poised over a standard military-issue pad of paper. He would be in shirtsleeves, his belt loosened, his shoes off. There would be one person with him in the room, who at the appointed hour, when all was ready, would give him some random numbers to focus on.

They had begun with real grid measurements, latitude and longitude, but after a while they had found that any series of numbers, once associated with a target, would do the job.

The initial sensation was always the same, too: he would feel his mind detach from his body, lying there on the half-busted army couch in the nondescript office. For a moment, he would lie in a state of semi-consciousness, feeling himself equally present, superimposed, in two places at once. Then his mind would soar into the sky.

These were some of the skills he had learned from Isambard. For just as he had been part of the secret, closed-off SS state-within-a-state that Himmler had constructed in Nazi Germany, running its own secret programmes unknown to the rest of the government, so now he was part of a 'deep black' US programme that had taken over many of those activities, transplanting them and hiding them away so deeply they could never be found. For some of them worked, but only at too great a cost in human suffering. Peter worked at the barely acceptable end of such programmes. Sometimes, when ordered, he crossed the line.

At the very beginning, his main handler had been a British Navy petty officer from Birmingham, who had helped share some knowledge of this darker corner of British intelligence activities during the war, and stayed on for a few months afterwards to kick things off in the States. But he hadn't lasted long before home-grown talent took over.

In the 50s, the focus of Peter's work was the Soviet H-bomb project, the Korean war, the mental state of Chinese leaders. In the 60s, it was the Space Race, captured US troops in Vietnam, the location of Soviet submarines.

He would range at dizzying speeds over the surface of the earth, or hurtle upwards into the stratosphere and watch the world turn beneath him. He would hold the coordinate numbers in his mind, having no idea where they would lead him, till it felt right to head to the location. Peter would hold himself apart, neither wanting nor fearing any particular destination, indifferent to what he would find there, clearing his mind of any desired outcome.

And then he would be there, floating over unfamiliar structures, sketching them on the pad as images came to him, speaking his impressions at the same time. Heat or cold. Wet or dry. Confidence or fear.

With technical training, he came to recognize some of the structures he saw. Others he never understood. He had heard once, in later years, of a gifted psychic who had been asked to remotely view a nuclear reactor. Not knowing what a nuclear reactor was like, she had drawn something she described as a boiling teapot of unusual design. She had been right in her impressions, but she hadn't known what she was seeing. Sometimes he felt like he, too, was drawing teapots. He never received feedback on whether any particular viewing had been accurate or not, useful or not to the country's broader intelligence aims.

Yet sometimes he knew. When looking for lost airmen, or captured troops, he knew that he had made contact with them, at some level, and knew that they had felt his spectral presence. At times, he tried to give comfort, though often he found he only caused them greater fear and anxiety.

Then there were the other, dirtier jobs. His first, very early on, was to cause an air crash. It was the late 1940s.

The session began in the usual way, his monitor sitting by him on a chair to keep track of his physical reactions while viewing, to do such mundane things as picking up Peter's pens and paper if he swiped them to the floor, and to provide basic mission instructions.

It was important, they had found with experience, to make sure the monitor had no knowledge of the target being viewed in any given session, so that he couldn't unconsciously colour the viewer's experience with his own knowledge or desires for a particular outcome.

Peter's monitor was his regular man at that time, an army captain from Minnesota with the manner, though not the dog collar, of a military chaplain. In the usual way, he read Peter a string of numbers in his rasping voice, which were written on a sealed envelope placed on his lap. Inside it was a photograph of Peter's target, never seen by either of them. The only departure from standard protocol was that he had a second envelope with him, contents unknown.

Peter closed his eyes.

He felt heat, humidity. There was a blazing sun. He felt lush richness below, a stew of ferment and decay, teeming life. A strobing, thrumming vibration seemed to fill the air. Peter smelled sweat, hot oil and cordite.

He was sitting – his target was sitting – in a military helicopter, flying over a vast expanse of jungle, calm in his professional knowledge, knowing how to fly the aircraft blindfolded, but tense, alert, afraid.

Peter drew symbols, unsure what they were, eyes still closed. Pips. Rank. They were to do with rank. He was transporting someone important, a general, more than that, a national leader . . . a hunted man? A man fleeing danger? The flight was clandestine, he felt sure. The images in his mind rippled and flickered. He struggled to hold focus.

His monitor whispered into the darkness, and Peter felt his voice as an intrusion into the scene he was witnessing. Why was his target the pilot and not the passenger, he found himself wondering, and almost lost the images and sensations entirely.

'Peter, I have additional orders. They read as follows: *seek to induce terminal mental state in target.*'

Now Peter, to his surprise, was able to stay coldly on the mission.

Fill the pilot with such fear and anxiety that he crashes, killing everyone on board. That was what they wanted.

He felt a thrill, one he wanted to deny but couldn't. His

own power was beginning to astonish him, even delight him.

He saw his mother's face.

I'm sorry, maman, he wanted to say.

Peter eased his way towards the pilot's anxiety, his fear of discovery and attack, and began to ... *empathize*. He felt the man's courage, his commitment to his duty and loyalty to his eminent passenger. Peter snuck past his trained technical mind's defences, past his sense of competence, to a place where he was weak. The man, like all men, wanted to live. Not for anyone else, but for himself. He was young, smart, able. He would do well in the world, but he was afraid to die, and especially afraid of dying ...

How was he afraid of dying? Peter sought the image. And he saw it. By fire. Flames licking at flesh. The pilot had seen someone die that way ... a training accident. A fellow pilot burned alive in his cockpit, the agony of his efforts to free himself evident in the posture of the body when they'd found him. Peter entered that fear, and began to resonate with it, as though pouring on gasoline.

He felt the helicopter lurch. He felt the pilot's heart racing, his breathing accelerating out of control, the sweat of panic. Peter heard shouts of alarm, a fist punching his shoulder. He poured it on. He felt the pilot's own mind-numbing fear take control of his body, force the stick down, veer left and right in an insane series of manoeuvres to avoid attackers who were not there, fists or missiles or imagined rocks.

Peter instilled the primal fear of attack in his target, triggering the fight or flight response, then watched.

The helicopter flipped and plummeted like a stone, hundreds of feet down, into the maw of the jungle. He extracted himself just before the explosion.

*

'Accomplished,' he said. 'Request a break.'

And slowly, over five or ten minutes, he returned his own breathing to normal, and his mind to its regular moorings, and eventually left the viewing room with his monitor for a cola drink and a detailed, rigorous debriefing.

At home, that night, he expected to weep, but he didn't.

Then over the decades, he did it perhaps thirty times more, till the moment came to hand over to younger men.

Retirement in his case meant semi-house-arrest in a series of obscure towns in New Mexico, Kansas, Ohio and finally Nevada. Peter was never meant to see the light of day again.

He had his own thoughts about that. For years he had been planning his escape, and now, his powers returning as the mysterious window in time began to open, he had a chance.

And Rose was going to help him.

For the most important experience Peter had had in several decades of remote viewing had not been a spying or military operation. It had not even been on the books. No session report had recorded it, because he had shielded it from his masters for years, because it had terrified him.

Rose, the woman he had lost, had somehow tracked him down, in whatever forlorn psychic space it was that he entered on his missions. Reached out to him. Offered him a bridge. *Forgiven him.* And she had wanted Peter to defect. Rose had offered him her help to cross over, and in his own way, that is what he was planning to do.

Peter's love and loss of Rose were, he now knew, the defining moments of his life – because they had allowed her to give him a chance of salvation.

Paris

November 1943

'Now, soon, I'll have you to myself,' Peter whispered to Rose. 'We'll be together, and we can talk.'

She sat on a wooden chair in a converted maid's room, now a cell, at the top of the Gestapo offices at 84, Avenue Foch. She was close to hyperventilating, her breath coming in short, shallow spurts that she was trying desperately to control.

At Peter's shoulder stood Isambard, who was setting out on a low table, within Rose's eyeshot, an array of slender steel instruments, like a dentist.

'I've been looking forward to this day for a long time,' Peter said. 'Since you slapped my face on the Petit Pont, to be precise.'

For a moment, it seemed to him she remembered. Then she closed her eyes, dismissively.

'I have nothing to say,' she sighed. 'I won't help you.'

'You're not expected to help us,' Isambard interjected. 'We know everything we need to know about Steeplejack, about F Section, about the Special Operations Executive. None of that matters. You're here to suffer, not to talk.'

'Father, since I made the arrest, I'd like to make a special request,' Peter said. 'Please let me handle this one myself. Let me have her for my own while you're in Berlin.'

Isambard eyed Peter with surprise.

'You're ready?'

'Yes.'

Isambard ran his hand over the metal instruments.

'So be it. Use her suffering to raise your own power.' His eyes fell on Rose, who stared unflinchingly at him. 'You've deserved it.'

~

As soon as they were alone, Peter went to work.

'I am going to arrange your rescue,' he whispered, while pretending to check her handcuffs. 'I arrested you myself to make sure you were not mistreated, to keep control of the situation. Do you remember me?'

Rose spat at him, then sat in silence, glowering.

'You won't understand this, but I've chosen love,' Peter said. 'The idea of helping you is the only thing that keeps me alive. I'm going to file fake reports of this interrogation. I'll make sure no one else comes near you. But I need you to scream now, very loud, as though I were truly hurting you.'

Still she said nothing, fearing a trick, fearing he was simply the good cop, to be followed by the terrifying bad cop who had just left. *Father*, this one had called him.

'Here's what I want. I want to free you. I will arrange your freedom, with the help of Horace, with the help of Harry. I am the third member of Steeplejack. You are the fourth, brought in because our original radio operator was killed in the jump. Charlie. His parachute didn't open. Trust me, please.'

She blinked but gave nothing away. He knew she was working through the information he had given her, trying to assimilate it.

'There is a thing called the Great Work, a state of power unlike any other, which will allow me to free myself of my father,' he whispered. 'I seek to achieve it in order to free myself. A key component of it is understanding, or acquiring, the Secret Fire. This is what you are looking for. That is what I am looking for too. We are going to steal it, and I am going to use it to find freedom, after I have freed you. Then we will both be happy, perhaps even together.'

She seemed to soften towards him, though he found it impossible to tell. Perhaps she just thought he was insane.

'Now, I really do need you to scream.'

Paris

Mid-November 1943

Horace convened an emergency meeting of Steeplejack in the basement room of the Temple de l'Amitié in the grounds of 20, Rue Jacob.

Candles lit the chamber, in the centre of which a stone column supported the circular floor of the room above. He sat, waiting for the others, praying for Rose.

Word of her arrest had reached him at a meeting with local *résistants* at a café in Clichy. A British radio operator, a woman, they'd said. They weren't to know she was from California. He'd made further urgent enquiries. Yes, 98 Rue de la Faisanderie. It could only be Belle.

It was as though his soul had shrivelled away.

He couldn't stop imagining the treatment she was undergoing. He knew that she, like he, had thrown away her L-pill. Now he wished, despite himself, that she'd kept it. It was easier to imagine her already dead than still suffering.

Horace tried, again, using every skill he had learned in his initial years of study, to reach her mentally, feel out to her with his heart, somehow convey to her some comfort, some hope.

Wait for me, darling. I'm coming. I'm coming to get you.

He knew what she'd say, what she'd said. That he shouldn't risk anyone's life for hers. To consider her dead, as she already did.

But the taste of her was still on his lips, the smell of her in his flesh, the love of her in his blood.

Against that, there was the crushing imperative of the mission. Finding Fulcanelli was more important. Denying the Nazis the *geheime Feuer* was more important. It had to be. Yet it couldn't be.

After a while, three ringing blows of metal on stone echoed in the closed chamber where he sat. The sound came from below.

Leaping up, Horace pushed a particular flagstone in the floor and watched it pivot smoothly away. A square hole opened up in the floor, through which, after a moment or two, there appeared the head of Harry Hale-Devereaux.

'Good evening,' he said, using a ladder to climb up into the Temple basement. He was followed, moments later, by Peter.

Berthe's husband, who used the secret entrance to the catacombs for hiding and moving weapons for the *résistance*, brought them hot water to make herbal tea, then left them.

They got immediately down to business.

'The Nazi half of the Newton document – the one they stole in London in 1936 – will be here in Paris next week,' Horace said. 'The organizer of the German drive to build the Secret Fire device is bringing it personally from Berlin, in conditions of maximum secrecy, to see whether Joliot-Curie and his wife, and a few other Frenchmen of suitable knowledge and background, can be convinced to try and extract its secrets, or otherwise work with it, without access to the other half.'

'Who is this organizer?' Harry asked, fearing the answer he would get.

'It is Isambard,' Peter said, and Harry's heart sank, though he allowed no trace of emotion to show on his face. If

Isambard was coming from Berlin next week, then their efforts to kill him by bombing the launch site had failed. Harry had hoped he would have stayed to work on the project *in situ*. Clearly not.

Horace continued. 'We are going to steal it.'

'How? Where are they bringing it? Avenue Foch?'

'No, the Conservatoire National des Arts et Métiers, Rue St Martin,' Peter said. 'A special room is being set aside there. We'll need a diversion at the right moment. Something to distract attention.'

'You'll have your diversion,' Horace said. 'Harry, I'm asking you to do this.'

'We can arrange to get you in to the meeting,' Peter said.

'What's the escape route? There is the entrance to the sewers, there, just across the street.'

'They are too well guarded.'

'And so?'

'In the other direction, slightly to the east, where the Templar City used to stand, there are unmapped underground chambers,' Peter said. 'They're reached by a disused water pipe from the old St Martin's abbey church. That is how you can vanish. Joliot-Curie is prepared to help you reach them.'

'I'll need to get away quickly.'

'On the contrary, you'll need to hide right there, right under their feet, until the heat dies down,' Peter said. 'Maybe 24 hours, maybe longer. Until they assume you couldn't possibly be still so close to the scene of the crime. In the meantime, you won't be able to go anywhere. The entire German army and virtually every policeman in Paris will be looking for you.'

'Harry? What do you think?'

Harry took a few seconds to respond, his eyes never leaving his brother's face as he considered his answer.

'I think Peter's right. It's a good plan.'

'Very well. We'll go over details in a few minutes. Now, about the diversion.'

Horace took a deep breath.

'Belle has been captured. We are going to rescue her.'

Harry and Peter looked at him in horror.

'What? Are you mad?' Harry hissed. 'When? What happened?'

'I have never been more serious in my life. It happened yesterday. I don't know how yet, but we can't let it stand.'

Harry lapsed into speechlessness as he considered the threat to the mission, the ramifications of losing their only radio link to London.

'Horace, I agree we have to try to rescue her,' Peter said. 'But these two things on the same day?'

'Better together than separately. If we mount a rescue for Belle before the document is brought here, they'll almost certainly change their minds about bringing it, for security reasons. If we steal the document before we try to rescue her, there'll be such a Gestapo crackdown it'll be ten times harder to get to her.'

'If Harry is stealing the document . . .'

'I'll need you to help free her, yes. I need you on the inside,' Horace said. 'Use your Gestapo contacts. Be in the prison van with Belle to let her out. I'll take care of the escort car.'

'Think of the reprisals!' Harry said. 'They'll shoot dozens! Hundreds, even.'

Horace gave them both a long, agonized stare.

'She is worth it to the operation.' He hesitated. 'To us.'

'Your judgement is clouded,' Harry said. 'I know she's a pretty young woman, but you're putting Belle before scores of innocent people. You're not God. You can't make this decision.'

'I have to. We are going after them both. Belle. And the *geheime Feuer*. On my head be it.'

Oldwick Fen

28 June 2007

'Cousin Robert.' Jack Reckliss wasn't smiling. He leaned against the front door jamb of the cottage where Robert had grown up, filling the entrance – blocking it – with his dark and burly form. Robert thought he looked fearful. 'The boy from the big city. Looking a bit rough, if you don't mind me saying so.'

Seeing Jack so aggressive in his possession of the cottage would have made Robert angry a few years previously. Now he had no time. No one had any time.

'How are you, Jack?'

'Surprised to get your phone call. You've probably forgotten, but the likes of us don't much care for folk inviting themselves. There are good times and bad times.'

'I take it this is a bad time. Even for family.'

To Robert's surprise, Jack leaned forward to extend his hand. Robert put down his carry-on bag and shook his cousin's strong, calloused mitt, looking sharply into his eyes. The movement sharpened the pain in his chest from a dull throb to a new, piercing pitch. He felt his scalp prickle. He started to sweat.

'I got your letters. I said I'd see you. When the right time came round.'

Jack held Robert's hand, after he'd stopped shaking it, trying to unsettle him, to assert dominance. 'But that's the city boy for you. Always a rush. Writing a book, are we?'

'Nothing so grand.'

Jack directed Robert into the cottage's narrow hallway and through into the kitchen. 'Not much room here. You can stay the night if you need.'

Robert thanked him.

'The wife's away, and Hickey's off somewhere. So you'll have to make your own bed and all.'

Hickey. Dear God.

'How is he?'

'Mensa turned him down again.' Jack smiled shiftily. 'He behaves if you're firm with him. Always had a black side, that old boy.'

'Hickey? A dark side?'

'Once in a full moon. On account of all the poppy tea his mother gave him, they say. Though it was the accident that did it. The one they all blamed me for.'

Robert made conversation for as long as he could bear, noting Jack's efforts to slow things down to a pace he was comfortable with, or to a pace that Robert was uncomfortable with. Eventually, after a pot of tea and a sandwich, they came to it.

'Family history,' Jack said.

'Family history. I was kept in the dark about a lot of it, you know that.'

'Your mum and dad didn't hold with us. Kept themselves apart like we had the ague, like we had webbed fingers and toes. Right stuck-up, they were. Came across that way, at least.'

'So I grew up without aunts and uncles, without family except for them. They meant well. Dad . . .'

'He knew more than he let on, your old dad,' Jack said. 'That's why he wanted you kept from it. 'Cause he knew, not 'cause he didn't.'

'There were stories . . .'

'Lots of stories out this way. It's always made for stories, and not happy ones at that. All the flat waters, just the odd island. Then all the flat lands, after the drainage. Flat lands and that low looming sky. Lantern Men. Poppy tea. Wise women and toadsmen. Witch bottles. The horseman's word. It's not surprising.'

'Were you brought up in it? To believe, I mean?'

Jack's eyes danced.

'I heard the stories. Who knows what's true and what's not, hereabouts?'

'One thing I heard about, in World War Two . . . something dreadful that happened. A relative of ours who got hurt . . .'

Jack stood up suddenly, grabbing the teapot from the kitchen table and holding it so that, for a moment, Robert thought he would hit him with it.

'I've got work to do. Ask your questions at dinner time.'

The core of Oldwick House dated from English Civil War times, though only the grand hall and some sections in the rear had survived untouched. Extensively remodelled in the Georgian manner and extended in the nineteenth century with Victorian vigour, the house brooded atop a low rise, looking across a sweeping formal lawn to the spire of the abbey church that once had served it.

The great house, a fixture in Robert's imagination for as long as he could remember, loomed darkly as he walked through the grounds to the stable block, looking for Hickey to say hello. Jack had said he didn't know where he was, that he'd taken the day off. But Robert knew Hickey rarely left the grounds. Failing to find him in the old octagonal tack room where he sometimes dwelled – a strange Victorian folly, said to be haunted, which had served as a pigeon loft during the war – Robert walked on to the copse a few hundred yards further along the path.

Now it was smaller than he remembered. A wooden picnic table and benches had been added, over freshly dug earth in the centre. He stood and listened to the birds for a few minutes, casting his mind back in search of the ease he had found there as a child.

He found none. The magic was gone, whether from the place or from himself he couldn't tell.

Robert strode from the copse along the gravel path to the grounds' East Drive, and from there out of the estate itself into the village, to the churchyard.

Built and rebuilt on the ruins of one of the early Fenland Abbeys, comparable in wealth and influence in its time to Thorney and Crowland, Ramsey and Peterborough, the abbey church at Oldwick Fen had served for almost three hundred years, since the Reformation, as the semi-private chapel of the aristocratic family who owned the estate, providing in addition a place of Christian worship to villagers and estate workers. The grandfather of the present incumbent had sold off part of the estate and handed the church over to the Ecclesiastical Commissioners in the early twentieth century. Although it was no longer within the grounds, stories had always been told of a secret tunnel running from somewhere in the estate into the crypt of the abbey church – from Oldwick House itself, from one of the cottages, from the stable block. His father had told him it was nonsense.

Now the bright blue sky of the morning had turned, and Robert reached the churchyard as the first drops of rain began to fall. Moving among the gravestones and cowslips under a black umbrella, he came to his parents' resting place after a few minutes and stood before their headstones in silence, recollecting.

They had wanted him to be free of the darkness that could cling to these haunted flatlands, to be something other than they had been, see other things than they had seen. He couldn't blame them. He couldn't thank them for it either, though he could thank them for their good and loving hearts, for the warm home they had made, for the safe and unworried childhood he had been granted.

It was after long minutes deep in thought that he looked up and saw the black dog. It was barely 20 yards away, staring at him across the graveyard, its great ugly head set with eyes shining like hot coals. Then it was gone.

He blinked, looked again, dismissing it as a figment of jet lag, of his fear and overwrought senses. The pain in his chest was mounting, driving into his teeth, the backs of his eyes. For a moment he was alone again in the churchyard. Then he saw it again. His vision closed in a tunnel about the malformed snout, half-open and drooling, the matted black hair of the body, the eyes now flickering with green. It was the size of a calf. His heart began to hammer, his ears to buzz. See it and die within the week, some said. Not you but a loved one, others said. Dead within the day. Black Shuck. Odin's Hound. The Galley Trot. Hellhound.

Barely breathing, covered suddenly in clammy sweat, Robert stood still and focused with every ounce of his being on the apparition. Churchyard, headstones and abbey melted away. In a world between worlds, he saw for an instant a vision of hell: the great black dog savaging a young woman, ripping at her throat with bloody jaws, tearing at her white shift with claws like a wolf's . . .

When he came to, he was drenched in the pouring rain

of the afternoon shower, his umbrella lying beside him at the gravestones of his parents.

~

Robert told Jack nothing of his experience in the graveyard. Yet, that evening, he felt Jack knew, that he could read it on Robert's skin, in his eyes.

'Tell me about Old Dolly Redcap,' Robert asked. 'Kids said she'd gone mad, or was walled up in the big house, or sent away to a mental hospital. The gorier ones said she was raped. Sacrificed. Torn apart by Black Shuck.'

'Stop,' Jack said, angered. 'Enough.'

'Tell me what happened,' Robert insisted. 'Please.'

'It has no name. Not when practised by us, not when practised by them. It doesn't often sway or decide things. People usually do that, with the tools everyone knows about. Armies and politics, guns and parties and organizations. Money. But the nameless art can influence things. Tip the balance. Help steer things one way or another. Sometimes more. And some of the Nazis used it. Being who they were, they used methods the rest of us wouldn't touch. Slavery. Torture.'

'And what happened?'

'They were after some kind of weapon, something to waken the dragon, people said. Waken it and turn it against us. And it wasn't the first time the elder faith was roused to defend these islands.'

'Was our family involved?'

'Always.'

'1944? 30 June 1944?'

'Well there's the thing. The Fenland Workings looked into time in a different way. Linked things together in a way clocks and calendars can't measure. Past and future. Different cycles.'

'Jack, what happened?'

'Eight hundred moons, a witch's power lasts. And a spell can't last longer than the powers of the witch that cast it. Eight hundred moons.'

'Eight hundred full moons?'

'That's right.'

Robert tried to do a calculation quickly in his head, knowing already what the answer would be.

'Old Dolly Redcap became a witch in 1942, the night of the full moon of the Battle of El Alamein. That's . . . that's . . .'

Jack looked at him coolly.

'You've been doing your homework. Don't fry your brain. It's now. The eight hundredth moon is almost here. It's the day after tomorrow, Saturday. June 30. Now I'll say no more. I'm going to bed.'

'Wait!'

'Time enough in the morning, cousin Robert. I've said enough. Talked too much for one evening.'

'What about Old Dolly? Was she Great Aunt Margaret? Is that right?'

Jack's eyes moistened, and for a moment he seemed unable to speak.

'Aunt Margaret,' Jack said. 'That night in 1942 was the night she became a full witch for the first time. She took it over from her grandmother, after that. Called her own workings. Then there was a special one she called on 30 June 1944. Very short notice, just before dawn. It was a waxing moon, but not full. She had a fit. Possession, some said. Beautiful girl she was. Red hair like a flame, skin white as snow, eyes golden like the sun. They destroyed her, that night. Half blew out her mind.'

'Did she die?'

Jack looked away, anger stitched on his face.

'She suffered the witch's palsy for the last sixty-five-odd years, Robert. Bless her, Aunt Margaret, sick and tormented and maddened old maid that she was, lived till just . . . a few days ago. She took the full brunt of their attack onto herself that night, locked it away inside herself, to protect the rest of us. You should say her name with reverence, cousin.'

'Did she pass on her powers? Did she initiate a successor?'

Jack glared at Robert now in raw hostility.

'She died before she could do it. For the spell to be renewed after her death, the bell will have to be rung again.'

'Which bell?'

'The Sanctus Bell. The bell at Aldwych, at St Clement Danes. The only one that survived the Blitz.'

'I know about that. The iron magic.'

'And there's more. The curse she took on will have to pass to someone living. And someone will have to die.'

'Did she at least name a successor? Did she say who she wanted to pass her powers on to?'

'Go to bed, city boy. I'll speak no more tonight. Whatever you need it for, it'll have to wait till morning. If that ain't good enough for you, you can get back to America.'

Paris

Mid-November 1943

'My mother lectured here once,' Frédéric Joliot-Curie said, gesturing from the stage where the four of them stood – himself, Isambard, Harry and Isambard's SS adjutant – at the raked seats of the amphitheatre above them.

Outside the lecture hall, they were protected by three concentric rings of security, made up of Isambard's personal inner SS detail just outside the doors, a detachment of SS Death's Head men around the building, and regular German army troops in a four-block area around the Conservatoire National des Arts et Métiers.

The attaché case was chained to the adjutant's wrist, Harry noted.

'A sentimental choice of location?' Isambard asked, fixing the Frenchman with a cold, appraising gaze. He wore his full *Schutzstaffel* black uniform, Joliot-Curie a crumpled but formal suit.

'Not at all. I thought a small office would be appropriate, but the building administrators, you know, given your eminence, the special trip you have made from Berlin . . . they preferred to offer you a commensurate venue . . .'

A wooden table and chairs had been set out for them on the stage. Pencils, paper, water.

'Quite so.'

'My colleague,' Joliot-Curie said, indicating Harry and pronouncing a false put plausible French name, 'joins us as a guest of honour, as the man who worked most closely with my wife and myself in our studies of artificial radioactivity. He has performed great services for science and will be my closest advisor in this matter.'

Isambard fixed Harry with an icy stare.

'Your area of expertise?' he asked, in flawless French. Disdain and suspicion flared coldly from him.

Harry saw Joliot-Curie's face drain of blood. Harry's French was good, but not native. He took a risk, and replied in atrociously pronounced German, heavy on the French, and lending Isambard the highest SS rank he could think of.

'*Die Radiumstrahlen, Herr Obergruppenführer.*' Radium rays, general.

He saw Joliot-Curie and Isambard's adjutant both wince. Then he did something Horace had taught him: he made a mirror of his mind, and imagined he was simply already dead. He met Isambard's gaze, and felt he was being stripped naked. Then a warmth surrounded him, and Harry felt a presence protecting him. He could have sworn Horace was interposing himself between Isambard and his fear.

After what seemed an age, Isambard nodded perfunctorily.

'Very well, if you need him. Sit.'

They did as Isambard commanded. The adjutant laid the attaché case flat on the table, eyes straight ahead, awaiting word to open it. Harry tried to assess him and found a blank wall. It was as though he were dead.

Below the stage was a cellar. Below the cellar, unmarked on the plans of the Conservatoire, were the remains of a medieval cistern the monks of the Abbey of St Martin had built to store fresh water they had piped, in a joint project with the Knights Templar, from the hills of Belleville east of Paris. The underground terracotta aqueduct still existed, and it was just big enough to take a man.

Across town, Peter sat in the narrow aisle of the prison truck, between twin rows of metal cells in which dangerous prisoners were transported between Gestapo facilities. An armed guard sat next to him. Only Rose was in the van, handcuffed and shut inside one of the cells.

Their plan was to attack the van as it transported Rose from the Gestapo prison at Rue des Saussaies to the Avenue Foch offices. Neither building could be assaulted directly with any hope of success.

For the *coup de main*, Horace had brought in a supporter of the *résistance* who had friends in the Parisian underworld and could arrange an armed attack at an hour's notice, day or night, anywhere in the city.

They had called it Operation Picasso, after choosing the intersection of Rue la Boétie and Rue de Miromesnil for the assault on the prison van, just past the artist's pre-war studio and home, now shuttered, at number 23.

Horace waited in the back of a large Citroën, Sten gun by his side, five armed men waiting for his signal.

Slightly further ahead, another vehicle waited for the right moment to create an impromptu roadblock in front of the van.

~

Isambard took a key from his pocket and handed it to his adjutant. 'Open it.'

Upon doing so, the SS man swivelled the attaché case on the tabletop so that it was facing his master. He retained the key, Harry noted in case he needed it.

Soon. It would be soon. He avoided Joliot-Curie's eyes. In his jacket pocket, Harry had a substitute document. Not good enough to withstand scrutiny for more than a few minutes if one had seen the original, it might nevertheless serve to buy him precious time when the moment came.

'Professor Joliot-Curie,' Isambard said, 'this paper is one half of a document of incalculable value written by Sir Isaac Newton. I wish to encourage you to study it, and to engage any colleagues you may have who can help in the clarification of its contents. It details certain materials that may be of use in . . .'

The explosion was far louder than Harry had expected. Auditorium seats flew into the air as the blast hit the stage, wooden splinters and orange flame spitting towards the ceiling. Harry overturned the table onto the adjutant as Joliot-Curie launched himself onto Isambard, ostensibly to protect him.

Gunfire started outside. Shouted orders, running boots, responding fire.

Isambard's bodyguards burst into the amphitheatre, marching through clouds of black smoke towards the stage. Harry, the attaché case briefly in his grasp, reached inside it and switched the papers. He hid the real one in his jacket pocket, falling on the case and the adjutant as he did so, as though protecting them with his life.

Isambard leapt to his feet, hurling Joliot-Curie's bulk to one side, barking orders, pistol in one hand.

Harry rolled over, groaning. The adjutant was unconscious, the attaché case on his chest. Isambard went through the man's pockets, finding a key ring and unfastening the handcuff that bound the case's chain to his wrist. He took the case and turned to Joliot-Curie, who was kneeling up, looking stunned. SS troops leapt onto the stage and formed a protective ring around them, weapons pointed outwards. More shooting could be heard outside, a local *résistance* diversion in full swing. Further away to the south-west, Harry hoped, Horace and his men would also be going into action to free Belle.

'The cellars!' Joliot-Curie shouted, shaking his head as though to clear it, still on one knee. 'It's safer.' He pointed. 'This way.'

Isambard nodded.

Harry went first, and as soon as he had reached the bottom of the staircase, Joliot-Curie pretended to trip, delaying the others behind him. Harry made his move. The pile of old rags, innocent-looking but laced with a smoke-producing chemical, were exactly where they had pre-positioned them. He lit them, and shouted.

'There's fire down here!'

Joliot-Curie stopped and turned round at the foot of the stairs, blocking the SS guards who were shielding Isambard in front and behind. Black smoke began to billow in the cellars. In the mayhem, Harry found the hidden trapdoor to the cistern, and dropped down, closing it behind him.

~

The van appeared at the corner of Rue la Boétie, turning left from Rue Cambacères, a yellow smudge of chalk on its rear driver's side tyre confirming that Peter and Rose were aboard. A spotter signalled to Horace's team.

'*Allons-y*,' Horace said. 'Go.'

As a slow-moving truck lurched into the intersection ahead of the prison van, Horace's driver gunned the engine and brought them up behind the follow-car, which was crammed with armed Gestapo guards.

The prison van, horn blaring, screeched to a halt, unable to get around the truck. The Gestapo guards' car behind slewed to a stop, its doors opening instantly. With practised ease, the Citroën drew up behind it, and Horace's men tumbled out.

Gunfire exploded like thunder. Bullets sprayed over Horace's head, zipping and buzzing, as he ran to his right, rolled to the ground, and returned fire from a prone position behind the base of a lamppost, the Sten gun kicking into his shoulder. One of the leather-coated thugs fell, clutching his stomach.

One of Horace's men went down as he ran towards the Gestapo car, and the security guard who shot him, firing bursts from his sub-machinegun, riddled the Citroën with holes. Horace's head buzzed, adrenaline pumping through his veins, heart hammering, He ran forward to the van, half-deafened by the booming of the guns all around him, firing to his left. Another Nazi went down, blood pouring from his shattered skull, and then Horace was at the van.

He climbed onto the rear bumper and pressed his face against the grille.

~

The water pipe, cleared of debris early in the war by men from Joliot-Curie's *résistance* group, was still so narrow that Harry could barely drag himself forward. A crumbling conduit of terracotta that cracked under his knees and elbows, it led under Rue des Fontaines du Temple, which took its name from the aqueduct that had led to the old Templar complex.

Harry struggled along it, fighting claustrophobia, his heart hammering, pushing himself forward inch by inch. Eventually, the pipe opened out into the underground remains of a Templar cistern on the same medieval water supply system.

Harry rested for a moment in the darkness, straining to hear if he was being followed. He could hear nothing. Joliot-Curie, he knew, would provide as much distraction as possible, gulling the SS and trying to mislead even the terrifying creature Isambard, before making good his own escape. Harry marvelled at the Frenchman's nerve, and the sangfroid with which Joliot-Curie had told him: 'Isambard and his kind cannot see past selflessness. They are blind to love. And I love France more than I fear him.'

From the cistern, a low tunnel had been knocked through in more recent times that led to an adjacent stone chamber under Rue Dupetit-Thouars, located beneath what had once been the grounds of the Temple Church. Harry lit a stub of candle and found the entrance, then pushed himself in. He prayed there would be no rats. The tunnel was stone, now, cold and clammy to the touch. Harry crawled forward, bracing his elbows and knees in rhythm, losing all sense of time.

He came in the end to a circular chamber, surmounted by a dome pierced by a now-closed oculus at its summit, perhaps twelve feet high at its highest point, nine or ten feet across. To Harry's mind, it reverberated with intense emotion, of a kind he couldn't calibrate. It had not been used for mundane purposes, he felt. Had it been an initiation chamber of some kind? A punishment cell?

It was well-appointed for his vigil. There was food, water, a wooden stool, a gun and two hand grenades, a bucket for his physical necessities. And there he would hide.

Breathing hard, Harry composed himself.

He had the document.

Closing his eyes, he permitted himself a prayer for Horace

and Rose. For some reason, he found he couldn't pray for his brother.

~

Blue eyes appeared at the grille at the back of the van. But they were not Rose's, they were the eyes of her Gestapo guard, bulging in panic. Peter had a cord around his neck and was strangling him.

'Peter!' Horace shouted. 'Open the door.'

Bullets banged into the back of the van just by Horace's shoulder, and he jumped back down onto the street and rolled.

The gunfight was resolving quickly. There were two men left on each side, apart from Horace, and each was manoeuvring rapidly for cover and advantage. Horace fired a covering burst and leapt back up to the grille.

'Peter!'

Now he saw Peter had released Rose from her metal cubicle inside the van. She ran to the rear of the van and pressed her face against the grille. For an instant, their lips touched.

'I love you,' she whispered to Horace.

Then the van started to move. The driver, wounded, had to be still alive. Peter and Rose were still inside. Horace couldn't see Peter.

Horace leapt down as one of the Gestapo guards broke cover and ran towards the van, which was lurching up onto the pavement and almost had its nose past the *résistance* truck that had blocked the road. Horace opened fire with the last of his clip, emptying the Sten gun into the man's back. Then Horace leapt for the ground and rolled into the gutter as the last security man fired back at him, swivelled and shot down Horace's last surviving man in a hail of bullets.

'Peter!' Horace shouted.

Inside the van, Isambard's presence came to Peter, furious, raging, demanding total obeisance. It was crushing, paralysing. Peter fell to his knees, crippled with pain, unable to move. Rose knelt down beside him as the van careened from side to side, the driver trying desperately to escape the ambush.

'What's the matter? What's happening to you?' she shouted.

The key to open the rear doors of the van was in Peter's hand, taken from the dead guard. Peter tried to hand it to her, but his fingers were involuntarily locked in a bone-crushing fist. Isambard was in every pore of his body, threatening the most savage punishments he could devise.

Peter realized it was blind anger. The *geheime Feuer* document had been stolen. Harry had succeeded. Isambard was raging against the world, lashing out at everyone in his reach, yet he still could not see into the secret corners of Peter's heart. His rage was devastating.

For as long as he could, Peter desperately hid his location from his father, believing with all his heart that he was nowhere, non-existent, merely an incorporeal shadow. He hid his love, he hid his desire to escape, he did all he could to unlock his hand and give the key to Rose that would allow her to get away. Isambard's wrath poured into him, and into the world, like black burning rain.

Then Peter lost consciousness, Rose still trying to pry apart his fingers. The van began to accelerate.

Horace ran desperately towards the front of the van, trying to reach the driver, drawing his pistol. Bullets tore past

Horace's head from the last Gestapo guard. Horace turned and fired back, saw the guard dodging and weaving towards him. Horace fired again, hitting the man in the shoulder, and leapt at the driver's door of the van. He grabbed the handle and pulled it open as the vehicle bumped down off the pavement. The driver, bleeding, met Horace's eyes for a moment and then punched him in the face as Horace tried to climb in. Horace fell, and his pistol jolted out of his hand. He banged into a lamppost as the van pulled away.

'Rose!' he shouted. 'Rose!'

The van accelerated.

He had lost her.

~

The deportation orders issued by the SS that afternoon were clear. The SOE radio operator known as Belle was to be placed immediately under the classification *Nacht und Nebel* – Night and Fog – and sent to Germany for further processing. She was removed from Peter's authority and placed on a train to Germany that night. *Nacht und Nebel* meant simply that she was to disappear, and no information about her fate was ever to be released. Her file was marked *Rückkehr unerwünscht* – return undesired.

Oldwick Fen/London

28 June 2007

Robert called Katherine, who dialled Horace into the same call. It was almost midnight.

'What have you learned, Robert?' he asked. 'Quickly, we have very little time.'

'Kat, are you OK?'

'I'm fine, honey. I love you. I'm fine. You need to concentrate. Did you see Jack?'

'Yes. Here's the key thing. Margaret's dead. Old Dolly, as she was known. The witch whose spell helped hold the Nazis at bay, who stopped the Secret Fire attack in 1944. Jack says she died before initiating a successor.'

'It's what I feared. How did she die?' Horace asked.

'He didn't say. Wouldn't.'

'Find out.'

'Tomorrow. Jack's very afraid of something. Angry. And I'm being tracked. Stalked. One of them attacked me, an old man, strong as an ox. They want me to go back to New York, to stay out of this. They threatened Kat.'

'They want to mess with our heads,' Katherine said. 'They want us fearful and confused, unable to think straight, minds full of noise. They want us to suffer.'

'Why?'

'So we can't see what the Enemy is doing,' Horace said. 'So we can't focus our minds against it, against Isambard and his cronies. And because the greater our pain and confusion, the stronger Isambard becomes.'

'I have my grandmother's radio,' Katherine said. 'The

people at Shadowbox say another message came in. There's a defector trying to cross, and it has to happen before the full moon.'

'The man who attacked you, Robert,' Horace said. 'I need to bring him across.'

Robert shuddered.

'He's . . . malevolent. Beyond evil.'

'Trust me. He must be redeemed, or we all fail. What else did you learn?'

The jagged shards of guitar music sounded again in Robert's exhausted mind. *Stealing it back . . .* He told them about the Sanctus Bell, the iron magic. The need for a successor to ring the bell, the need for someone to take on the curse, for someone to die.

'Romanek told me about the fylfot, about its power before the Nazis took it over. This is about stealing it back, isn't it, Horace? Taking back the swastika?'

'It is about redemption in many senses,' Horace replied. 'If we succeed. And we may not. We need to focus on Paris, now.'

'Adam's riddle was about Paris,' Katherine explained. 'The churches that didn't make sense. Not St Martin in the fields. *St Martin des Champs.*'

Robert tried to visualize the other churches Adam had listed.

'The word Temple is key to this,' Horace said. 'Temple in London is directly on the line I've been tracking Peter along. It's nonsense to say it doesn't fit, as Adam's note suggests. But there is a Temple in Paris too. It's a neighbourhood, a square, even a Métro station.'

'How does it relate to a line in Paris? I can't envisage it,' Robert said. 'What shape does that give?'

'It's a north–south axis,' Katherine said. 'Rue St Martin

on the right bank, crossing the Île de la Cité, then Rue St Jacques on the left bank. At the top, Temple to St Martin des Champs is east to west. It gives a kind of inverted L.'

'And the Abbot's Word?'

'Oh my God. It's not Abbot's Word. It's Abbot Sword. Rue de l'Abbé de l'Épée. It runs east to west at the bottom of the line, from Rue St Jacques to the Luxembourg Garden. All together, it makes a flat S. It makes half of a swastika.'

'With the other half in London,' Horace said. 'That's the shape Peter has been walking. From the Tower of London north along Minories to the ley line, then from east to west, the Gherkin and St Helen's through Aldwych as far as Grosvenor Square, then north again to Marylebone Parish church. Combine the two routes and you get a single swastika. They are routes he walked in the war, in Paris. And before the war, in London. They combine two places in one. Just as we are about to experience two times becoming one.'

'What do we do, Horace?'

'Katherine, you have to go to Paris as soon as possible. Robert, how soon can you get to London?'

'Say 11:30. I absolutely have to talk to Jack again in the morning. Beat more out of him, if I have to.'

'Katherine, take a noon train.'

She checked online, calling up the timetables.

'There's one at 12:09.'

'Get yourself a ticket. Here's what you need to do. On the paper I gave you the other day is written a phrase in Latin. In following Peter in London, I have been able to detect the phrase he has used to sink his poison into the dragon line, to poison the energy of the sites he visits. It is

Lucem in tenebris occulto. I hide the light in darkness. This is the phrase you will hear at the key sites in Paris too. What I have written on the paper is a counter-phrase you can use. To fight his poison. A kind of antidote. *Libero in tenebris occulta.* I free the things hidden in darkness. You must go as soon as Robert gets to London to help me. But be very careful. Once you start, you will awaken opposition. And the powers you will be dealing with are great.'

~

After they had spoken, Robert stared at the ceiling, lying on the bed in his childhood room in the cottage, now a guest room. It was impossible to sleep. He was afraid even to close his eyes, for fear of what he might see.

It was all connected. To find his own history, to decipher Adam's notes, to avert the attack – it was all one thing. And they all had to do, he could see, with bringing in the defector by Saturday, by the eight-hundredth moon.

He'd have to leave by nine in the morning to have any chance of getting to London in time. He looked at his watch. 2 a.m., Friday 29 June.

It was no use trying to sleep. His unconscious was warning him of something terrible in the vicinity, but he couldn't see what. He knew he had to face it, whatever it was, if he was to be of use to Katherine and Horace, and to the world. The answer lay beyond his own fears, on the dark side of his own consciousness. Something was here that had called him, that needed him. The powers he needed were on the far side of this. Black Shuck stared at him, eyes ablaze, whenever he closed his eyes.

Childhood stories, childhood fears.

He had to take action. Wishing he had a torch, Robert sneaked out of his room and down the stairs. He stepped out into the night.

Robert made his way by moonlight toward the copse, intending to seek there, as he'd always done as a child, the answers to the questions that exercised him.

On his way, though, something caught his eye in the octagonal tack room as he passed. Was it a guttering light, or a figment of his imagination?

Robert, his heart hammering, senses at full stretch, crept towards the door. The Lantern Men. They lived in the remote Fens, they said, and lured the unwary to their deaths with their flickering lights in the night. Sometimes, the estate people said, they came onto the grounds, and visited the tack room. Robert had seen lights here, or imagined he had, as an adolescent, when he would sneak out with dear slow Hickey and explore. The Lantern Men were the Enemy, Adam had said. IWNW by another name.

The door was unlocked, though that had often been the case when he was young, when few doors were fastened on the estate.

He crept inside. All was dark and quiet.

A spiral staircase led upstairs to the airy wooden room they called the pigeon loft. Once, he and Hickey had imagined they saw a face at the window up there, an old woman's face . . . now he understood. It had to have been Great Aunt Margaret.

He stepped forward, towards the stairs. No light came from the upper room, now. He stood still, listening, remembering.

Whispers. Echoing on the stone floor, on the brick walls,

around the octagonal chamber, at the very edge of perception. Then a shout. Distant, brittle, but clear, an affirmative, throaty shout: *Ka!*

It was behind and below him, somehow. Robert turned on his heel and walked forward a pace, two paces. Then the ground opened beneath his feet.

Paris

Mid-November 1943

The day after the failed rescue attempt, Horace waited in the chamber beneath the Temple de l'Amitié on Rue Jacob, distraught, self-doubting, forcing himself to focus on the Steeplejack mission to the exclusion of all else.

The reprisals had already begun. The very same day of the action, posters had appeared all around Paris announcing the imminent execution of fifty hostages in retaliation for 'failed acts of rebellion, terrorism and banditry in the Paris area', with more to come if 'certain documents and materials, stolen from the Conservatoire Nationale des Arts et Métiers' were not returned.

The following day, at Mont Valérien to the north-west of Paris, all fifty had been tied to stakes and shot, five at a time. A threat had since been issued to shoot fifty more hostages, and deport a further 500, if the documents were not returned within two days.

Horace felt the crushing burden of the consequences of his decisions. He could not be swayed by the reprisals. Yet his actions had caused them, and he would have to live with that fact, now and for ever. He felt his mind tearing apart.

'Rose,' he whispered to himself. 'I've failed you. I've failed everyone.'

Peter, after telling his raging father that he had helped thwart the rescue attempt on Rose, fearful of losing his own humanity now that Rose was taken from him, had focused, like Horace, purely and solely on the mission. He had gone to extract Harry from his hiding place near Arts et Métiers and escort him and the *geheime Feuer* paper to Horace.

'Do we even have the damned document?' Horace asked himself, pacing in the underground chamber as the hours ticked slowly by, the strain unbearable.

Eventually they arrived. Harry was sweating, his face flushed with excitement.

'We have it,' Harry whispered, with an air of vindication, as he climbed up through the floor, followed by Peter.

Horace was not in a mood for celebration.

'We have no time to waste. Show me the document.'

'In a moment. The rescue . . . what about Belle?'

'No. Now.'

Horace drew a pistol and held it to Harry's head. Harry stared into Horace's eyes. Peter leapt forward in protest. 'Horace!'

Horace swung his pistol to point it at Peter.

'Too much is at stake,' Horace shouted. 'Give it to me.'

Coolly, Harry reached into his coat pocket and withdrew a leather wallet.

'Here it is,' he said, his eyes never leaving Horace's.

Horace, strain creasing his face, his eyes haunted and lonely, took the wallet, then lowered his gun.

'Thank you.'

He holstered his pistol under his left armpit and opened the wallet, carefully removing the document. Harry sat down, exhausted and indignant, but saying nothing.

'Well done, Harry,' Peter said.

'Yes,' Horace whispered, distractedly. 'Yes. Well done. This is it.'

After a while, Harry spoke.

'Horace, there's still a chance . . . with Belle . . . Perhaps another plan.'

Horace raised his eyes and stared at them both.

'No. I've already pushed the limit. It is not operationally acceptable to try to rescue her again.'

'But . . .'

'We have to accept that she is lost. The mission must come first. We have to find Fulcanelli. We have to find the location of the Paris half of the document.'

Horace turned away from them, until his face was hidden from view.

'We have to let her go.'

Day One

London

29 June 2007

Evil attracts evil. Blood will have blood.

On Haymarket in the early hours of Friday 29 June when London's West End revelry was at its hedonistic height, Horace stood guard.

He saw that the gathering force of the *geheime Feuer*, like a magnet for hatred, was infiltrating the world, staining the fabric of reality around it. Like wind whipping up before a rainstorm, Isambard's coming attack was drawing minds and actions together, towards the same place and time, towards itself, in ways that were inexplicable in rational terms.

And so, now, two men unassociated with Isambard, following their own lights, lost in their own sense of wounded righteousness and anger, were planning to detonate bombs in central London.

One was a medical doctor, a healer perverting his craft, Horace saw. The other was a technician of some kind, a scientist or engineer.

Horace positioned himself halfway along Haymarket, trying to track what was happening.

He was less than a mile from Aldwych.

There were two cars.

They had been driven down to London from the north in the previous hours, and Horace had seen them as they approached the capital, perceiving their threat. Now they were drawing near.

He felt anger in the men. Raw, pulsing anger, barely under

control, and within it a burning disdain for the life of the city, for the life of London.

Horace saw a pattern, briefly, a flash of intention, an image . . . he saw a bomb at either end of Haymarket.

There was a nightclub at the northern end, which he had passed earlier. Tiger Tiger. It would be crammed with people partying. What could nightclubs hold? A thousand, two thousand people?

He saw the intention to cause at least two simultaneous explosions . . . or perhaps one slightly later, catching people fleeing from the first, or rushing to respond . . .

Again he tried to reach toward the minds of the men planning this. The healer and the engineer. He felt determination in them, a deep-seated belief, a conviction of rectitude. Burning rage.

Horace saw cars loaded with gasoline, with shrapnel, with gas cylinders. They were getting closer . . .

Paris

March 1944

The net was tightening.

Harry, Peter and Horace moved around constantly, never spending more than one night in the same apartment. They never met as a group, seeing each other when necessary only in twos to compare notes, working through cut-outs and dead letter boxes whenever possible. Harry moved back and forth between Paris and the Nord region.

For four months, through the bitter winter, they tried every route they could think of to locate Fulcanelli, and through him the Paris half of the Newton document. Repeatedly, constantly, they failed. Only Horace knew the exact location of the other half, the part they had stolen from Isambard.

Then disaster struck for the Paris anti-Nazi underground. On 21 March 1944 the Gestapo, acting on an informer's tip, arrested the legendary British agent known as Shelley, on the steps of Passy Métro station.

He had been heading to meet Harry at the top of the stairs to pick up messages for London.

Brandishing pistols to force the crowds back, the arresting officers, their glee uncontained, shouted to all who could hear: *Wir haben Shelley! Wir haben Shelley!* before bundling a well-built man in a business suit, handcuffed, into a waiting black car.

An ebullient, fearless, charming businessman and bantam-weight boxer, Shelley, working with his friend and *résistance* leader Pierre Brossolette, was famed as a driving force in getting the *résistance* properly supplied and coordinated – personally bending Churchill's ear in London, banging heads together among Communist and anti-Communist resisters in France.

He was also the man Rose had inveigled into giving her a job as a seamstress at the Molyneux fashion house before the war. Forest Yeo-Thomas had taken the huge risk of coming to Paris for his third clandestine mission in barely a year to mount a rescue of Brossolette, captured by the Nazis some weeks earlier.

Too far away to help, outgunned and outmanned, Harry could only watch in horror as the blows began raining down on Shelley's head and face before the Gestapo vehicle pulled away.

London

29 June 2007

Isambard was growing stronger.

Horace felt it when he looked at the car bomb plot, and saw he was going to have to fight Peter over the outcome.

Fight Peter and, in him, Isambard.

The cars were fearsome devices, potential fireballs laden with nails and propane gas cylinders, freighted with anger, vehicles of hate. The intention had been slaughter. Young people, dancing and drinking. Young women, especially.

Fear, too, had driven the intending bombers, Horace felt: an unacknowledged fear, masked as disdain and right-eousness, of women free of male tutelage, free to dance and mess up, drink and kiss, dress crazy and flirt with any man they chose. *Slags*, was the hate-laden word in their minds.

There was more, much more, to their anger; and some of it Horace could even understand, without ever justifying their intent: thousands of civilian dead in Iraq. Guantánamo. Torture at Abu Ghraib and Baghram. Other parts of their rage, he could never commune with.

But Isambard could. And he could bend it to his purpose.

Horace had seen the doctor and the engineer park the car bombs, one at each end of Haymarket. He had been able to track each one of them as they distanced themselves from the vehicles.

And now he could see them calling the numbers of the cellphones attached to each of the bombs.

Closing his eyes, blocking out the noises of the London

night, Horace placed his life on the line, even though he knew the importance of surviving until the next day, even though he knew how much depended on him. He could not stand by and let the attacks proceed. He projected himself towards the impending explosion, towards the cellphone signals travelling at the speed of light towards the bombs.

And he met Peter there, in a space beyond time, in a microcosm of the place where they would all meet tomorrow, a fore-echo of the great time-slip to come.

Peter's eyes were green. His father was working through him, desiring the carnage, wanting the suffering to help him grow more quickly back towards life.

They fought.

Redoubling his energy, Horace protected the cars, visualizing the cellphone signals as waves of light of impossible colours, propagating through time and space to repeater towers, and thence to their targets. He placed himself in their way, splitting himself, shielding each of the cars, making himself a mirror to reflect the signals away. And Peter and Isambard came for him, grabbing him by the shoulders, kicking and punching him, trying to wrench Horace away from the cars. Horace held firm, sinking his weight into the earth, hunching his shoulders and absorbing their attacks. Two of them attacking him at each location.

They came again. And again.

Horace began to fight back, trading punches and kicks. After soaking up their initial onslaughts, he grew stronger, more confident in his ability to hold them off. Isambard was still struggling to break through, though growing stronger by the hour.

The cellphone signals kept coming, wave after wave, and Horace reflected them, blocking the murderous intent behind them as the cars slowly filled with gasoline fumes and Peter and Isambard exhausted themselves trying to shift him.

Horace stepped into a punch from Peter, ducking and responding with a haymaker that lifted Peter off his feet. When Isambard aimed a kick at his head, Horace knelt and swept Isambard's other leg from under him.

Both men were down.

It ended.

The calls stopped.

Horace drew back into himself, lungs fit to burst, drenched in sweat.

He had seen them fail, but he realized that the true attack, the true catastrophe, was yet to come.

He had to rest.

For the next few hours, Horace kept a watching brief, doing his best, as he prepared for the coming ordeal, to watch over police defusing the Tiger Tiger bomb, over the tow-truck operators taking the Cockspur Street car bomb to a garage on Park Lane, oblivious to its contents.

He lost track of the intending bombers as they fled London for the north.

He searched for Katherine and Robert, exhausted by his vigilance, knowing that Peter Hale-Devereaux was still somewhere nearby, and with him Isambard, readying for their ultimate encounter.

Horace prepared himself, knowing he was entering the final stages of his own Great Work.

London/Paris

29 June 2007

Katherine awoke to the radio news in her hotel room on Aldwych, shattering a dream in which Rose had been trying to reach her with an urgent warning.

An unexploded car bomb has been discovered outside a London nightclub on Haymarket, packed with nails, gas cylinders and petrol, the BBC announcer said. *Police have . . .*

It was just over half a mile from her location. A crushing sense of personal danger gripped her, eating into her will, her ability to think. Whatever it was, it was coming, as though the growing full moon were drawing all hatred towards London, towards Aldwych.

She called Horace but got no reply. She dialled Robert. No answer. She tried reaching them mentally, and failed.

The boom of the gunshot in her breezeblock cell still echoed unceasingly in her head. Katherine told herself, over and over: *You did nothing wrong. You did nothing wrong.*

She forced herself to focus. What needed to be done? How was she going to carry the radio? She weighed it on the bathroom scales. Nearly 33 pounds, almost a quarter of her bodyweight.

'Fuck,' she hissed. Did she need to take it?

She had to have it with her, she decided, in case it lit up again. But carrying it in one hand as a suitcase . . . She knew clandestine operatives had done it during the war, even rehearsing in the streets around Marylebone Station, they said, to get used to looking natural with it. But Katherine couldn't. She was strong, but it would eventually break her arm.

Katherine went out into the rain to buy a rucksack so she could carry the radio on her back. The kit she'd brought with her from New York – some basic tools, a change of clothes – could fit in it too. She could connect the earphones and wear them on the back of her neck.

The weather was unsettled, changing every hour. By eleven it was sunny and dry as she paced up and down on Aldwych, trying once again to raise Robert. Nothing.

She had to go to Paris. It was time. She looked up at the blue sky, sick with worry for her husband, then down the facade of India House. Two sculpted swastikas, right there on the facade, stared down at her. She felt a pattern forming around her, around the curving streetscape of Aldwych.

Blood will have blood.

It was irrational, she told herself. The facade of India House was festooned with peacocks, elephants and other symbols drawn, like the swastikas, from its own timeless traditions, nothing to do with the Nazis.

But . . . Fear gnawing at her stomach, she hailed a cab for Waterloo train station. On the way, she checked the BBC website on her handheld. The car at Haymarket had been removed. Police spoke of 'carnage' if it had gone off outside the night club.

~

Rain streaked the train windows as the Eurostar pulled away from London shortly after noon.

Katherine caught a glimpse of Big Ben, her back to Paris, her face towards London, then a big Christie's depot, Battersea power station, a glimpse of the Millennium Eye, then the space-age obelisk that she'd learned to call the

GPO Tower when she was a kid, and never stopped calling it that.

The rain got heavier. They were accelerating through bands of weather, cellphone service coming in and out, trees and green fields, distant white houses and electricity pylons speeding by. A quarter of an hour later it was sunny again, blue skies and white clouds.

They entered the Channel Tunnel for the 20-minute crossing and emerged 80 minutes later to a perspective of flat fields and watery tones, grey overcast skies, shades of green, brown fallow fields, pylons of different design.

She ate again, loading up on fuel, avoiding alchohol, grabbing a half-hour of extra sleep to conserve energy before they got to Paris. The train arrived shortly after four in the afternoon.

Katherine hauled the rucksack onto her back and made her way along the platform to the great front concourse of Gare du Nord, then down the stairs to the Métro.

She took the 4 line towards Porte d'Orléans. The familiar smell hit her immediately, a unique bouquet of wet cardboard, garlic and ionized air. The cars were the old ones, lime green and cream livery, with the self-operated metal hooks on the doors. She was always surprised by the speed between stations compared to London: there were eight stops to Cité, and she was there by 4:30 p.m.

Katherine got off and walked to the exit at the front end of the train, a great riveted, grey-painted metal drum housing an elevator and a spiral staircase. She took the former with a dozen other people, trying not to bang them with her rucksack.

A breeze of cold air struck her as she walked up the steps to the street, dodging a wave of descending children, chattering and screaming, as she rose. She emerged under the sinuous green arms and pod-like burgundy eyes of one of the city's art nouveau Métro entrances, Place Louis Lepine, at the flower and plant market.

The first thing she noticed was a white plaque of the kind found all around Paris, memorializing the legendary De Gaulle radio speech from London of 1940 in which he had proclaimed undying French resistance to Nazi occupation.

She imagined her grandmother living here, choosing to stay when she could have left, her long fight against the monsters who had defiled her adopted city, her fate at their hands . . .

Let me live up to you . . . let me make you proud . . .

Katherine had booked a hotel room on Quai St Michel, in case she needed a base of operations. It lay south, past the forecourt of Notre Dame and across the river to the Left Bank.

But before she could take more than a few steps towards the cathedral, the radio burst into life. She grabbed the headphones and felt a wave of humidity envelop her as the Morse signal, insistent high-pitched dots and dashes, filled her head with chatter from God only knew where.

Her grandmother. Rose. Katherine fought tears, no longer knowing what made sense and what didn't, focusing on the radio message. The Morse was a repeating cycle, two words over and over with just a minimal pause, in the 'fist' – the unique personal keying style – of a woman dead for nearly sixty-three years.

. -.-- --- - / ..-. -.-- .-.. ..-. --- -

Eyot. Fylfot. Eyot. Fylfot. Eyot. Fylfot.

What language was it? She didn't know either word. French? English? Something medieval?

The signal vanished as suddenly as it had come, and Katherine was left with an ineffable sense of dread, dripping sweat as she stood in the street, wondering if she was losing her mind.

She stepped out of the way of other pedestrians, leaning against a wall, and took a notepad from a pocket of the rucksack. She double checked the message, broke the letters up differently, tried them as an anagram, a palindrome, an acrostic, anything that might make more sense.

She looked at her watch, and to her amazement nearly 90 minutes had passed, in what she would have said were no more than ten since the radio had lit up.

Disoriented, she again tried reaching out mentally to Robert, then Horace. Then Rose. She got only static. Static and dread.

She had to keep the radio with her, though it was an inert brick that would weigh her down. She couldn't risk not hearing it start up again.

Eyot. Fylfot.

She tried to look the words up online with her handheld, but couldn't get a strong enough signal for Internet access.

Katherine caught her reflection, unexpectedly, in a window. She looked dreadful, pale with worry, her black hair falling about her face in wet strands like rat-tails. Katherine felt as though she were separated from past and future by just an atom's width, as though her every thought and choice were propagating both backwards and forwards in time. It was as though she were holding everything together; as though she were, somehow, a lynchpin between different eras.

She shivered.

It was colder now, just after six-thirty. There was a breeze, and the sky was white, flecked with grey clouds.

She had to take action. She had to move. Find the line.

Katherine walked to the western rim of the great empty parvis of Notre Dame cathedral, brass insets in its stone marking the outlines of demolished churches from earlier ages.

She checked her handheld again. Still nothing from Robert. But there was a new news alert, one that left her cold with fear. It was now coming to light that a second car bomb had been left on Cockspur Street overnight, like the first one just over half a mile west of Aldwych. It had been ticketed for illegal parking and towed, unexploded, to a garage in Mayfair. Police had closed off Fleet Street, just east of Aldwych, to investigate a third vehicle. It was a constellation around Aldwych, a ring of hatred closing in around a single location. The image came to her of Gestapo radio detector vans, closing in with ever-tightening triangulation on clandestine radio operators. Operators like Rose.

She looked towards the cathedral facade, lost in the image. Then she listened for the words Horace had told her she would hear. She reached out mentally, searching for the voice of a man whispering secrets, nearly seventy years previously.

She heard nothing.

Listen.

Then she heard it. A man's voice, deep and urgent.

Lucem in tenebris occulto.

She responded, without thinking, whispering under her breath: *Libero in tenebris occulta.*

She heard her own voice, treble over bass, talking over the damning words of the Enemy, in counterpoint and contradiction.

The very pronouncement of the words seemed to stir a breeze around her, a cleansing turbulence in the air. She stood still for a moment, feeling the sense of healing, as though water blocked for decades were flowing again at the site.

It was one point. Horace had said there would be five. Now that she'd drawn attention to herself, it would be a race against time. She had awoken the Enemy.

Suddenly she felt a brush of warm air around her, as though the radio had burst into life again, but the headphones at her neck were silent. Time seemed to stop, to swirl and eddy about her. Then she heard the voice, as though on the wind, a soft woman's voice. It was in the radio headphones.

'North. North. Move quickly. He'll come for you.'

'Rose? Grandma?'

Silence.

It was the voice that had come to her at the Arts et Métiers museum, at her mother's funeral, in her breezeblock cell, the voice that had come to her throughout her life. Her grandmother. Katherine trusted it.

Marching back towards the Cité Métro station, along Rue de la Cité, heading north past the plant and flower market stalls, she emerged onto Quai de la Corse on the north side of the island.

Eyot? Fylfot? She racked her brains.

Crossing Pont Notre Dame, she looked up and saw the summit of the riotously Gothic St Jacques Tower poking above the roof of a nondescript riverside police building. It was surmounted by a standing figure, gazing off to the south.

'St James,' she whispered to herself. 'Help me.'

Resettling the heavy backpack on her shoulders, she advanced along Rue St Martin towards the tower, seeing as she approached that most of it was shrouded in scaffolding and white canvas, only its top set of windows uncovered.

The voice returned.

'My dear, you are meddling in very powerful things, and they may end up hurting you. You must be careful. This is a very powerful spiritual route, trodden for centuries by pilgrims making their way south to Santiago de Compostela. That's why its southern leg, south of the river, is called Rue St Jacques.'

'St James. Santiago. St Jacques. They're all the same guy. Rose?'

'Listen, my dear. Don't question. Pilgrims from everywhere would gather here, at this spot, before heading south. Do you understand your pilgrimage today, Katherine?'

'I don't understand.'

'Then listen. Sshhh. This tower is all that remains of a church called St Jacques de la Boucherie. One of its biggest benefactors was the reputed alchemist Flamel, who arranged to be buried beneath it. It's said he learned the secret of transmutation while travelling the Way of St James in Spain. Your pilgrimage, like all pilgrimages, is about transmutation.'

'Of what?'

'Of a man. Several hundred years ago, there was a sanctuary room in this tower, on a fourth storey, long vanished now, where criminals could seek asylum from the law . . . In a sense, that is your role, now. To help a man find sanctuary.'

'The defector.'

'Yes.'

'How?'

'By countering the poison at these sites. If you don't, he cannot cross. Walk north.'

She crossed Rue Rivoli and continued on Rue St Martin, entering a pedestrian zone. Gusts whipped her hair, wanting to bring rain.

'Faster. It's dangerous.'

Katherine redoubled her pace, straining under the weight of the rucksack. She came to St Merry church.

Netting covered its grey stone facade, as though holding it together and restraining its stone sculptures in place. Intensive renovation was going on. She looked through, along the nave, to the church's stained-glass windows behind the altar.

Here? She listened. There were no words.

Then the radio crackled into life, briefly, insistently, and the voice came again.

'Further north. North.'

Swearing to herself, Katherine kept marching, the weight of the radio keeping her from breaking into a trot. Two minutes after St Merry she crossed Rue Aubry le Boucher, and then she was at Beaubourg. The forecourt of the Pompidou Centre was milling with people, portrait artists vying to draw her picture, Chinese artists offering the same coloured ideograms as they did on Times Square, school groups congregating about the great white ship-deck ventilation funnels, tourists picking through the racks at the postcard shops opposite the brightly coloured, tubing-festooned box.

She marched on, crossing Rue Rambuteau, where St Martin broadened out into a block of more Bohemian atmosphere. There was a Maison de la Poésie, a window display at the Librairie Scaramouche showing gorgeous stage masks, then a theatre.

'Hello?' she said into the air.

Nothing.

After Rue aux Ours, the atmosphere morphed into something more rag-trade and run-down: shuttered clothes-store frontages, municipal green garbage bins filled to brimming. Then the tone changed again, as she crossed Rue Turbigo and came to the striking Gothic arch and ironwork at the corner of St Nicholas des Champs church. St Nicholas in the Fields.

Barely a minute later, she was at the imposing site of the deconsecrated abbey church of St Martin des Champs, nestled within the walls of the Conservatoire National des Arts et Métiers, at the corner of Rue St Martin and Rue Réaumur.

For an instant she was five years old again, holding her mother's hand, marvelling at the great machines and scientific instruments on display under the soaring arches and stained glass of the church-turned-museum.

The radio fired up again, and she heard the voice in the earphones.

'Here. Here.'

Heavy traffic poured along Réaumur. The breeze had died down, and the weather was close and humid again, sweaty under grey skies. It didn't feel like it wanted to rain any more.

She listened.

She heard it.

Lucem in tenebris occulto.

She responded, speaking out loud this time, with conviction. *Libero in tenebris occulta.*

Treble over bass. A woman talking over a man, the sounds intertwining, echoing one another, cancelling each other out.

Then suddenly she felt dizzy, nauseous. Her knees were shaking.

'What's . . . what's happening?'

'It's the effect of the power of the route, my dear. It's resisting you. Its protectors are coming.'

A wave of black pain flooded through her body. Dry heaves convulsed her stomach.

'You are sensitive to it. Resist.'

The pain receded, though she felt intensely vulnerable: it was at the fringes of her consciousness, ready to return at any moment.

'On this spot, legend has it, St Martin kissed a leper and cured him in the fourth century, as he was entering Paris. That's why the abbey was established here.'

'Someone wants a kiss, is that it?'

Silence.

Then she felt the cold metal nose of a pistol digging into her ribs from the side.

'Don't move.'

It was a man's voice, at her shoulder. The accent was American, from the north-east. She recognized it immediately: the leader of her kidnappers.

'You followed me all the way here? What do you want?'

The pistol jabbed into her ribs.

'Shut up. Walk east. I don't want to make a big public scene, but if you try to escape, I'll blow a hole in you as big as my fist. You won't survive, but it won't be quick, either.'

Katherine took a deep breath, beating back her fears.

'I said what do you want?'

'A little personal pay-back. We have some unfinished business. And the people I work for want you fucked-up and incapable, not messing with their plans. Does that work for you?'

She sensed a throbbing engine sound, deep and throaty, that matched the pulsing promise of pain at the edge of her mind. She turned her head for an instant and caught, out of the corner of her eye, an image of a large black car, Nazi markings on its hood and doors, crawling along the kerb behind them.

Time was rubbing through, one era to the next. As they

walked east along Rue Réaumur, she saw how the former abbey church had been remodelled and remade over the years: blind arches, filled-in doorways, different courses of brick. All times in one time. The past in the present.

The gun barrel jammed into her side, hidden from onlookers by the rucksack.

'Walk.'

They took a couple of pedestrian crossings to get past Rue Turbigo, then found Réaumur widening out into a street of wholesale jewellers and import–export companies. At the end of the street, she could see a flare of greenery. As they got closer, it resolved into a leafy railed-off park around to the left. The car tailing them stopped at the end of Réaumur.

Katherine and her captor entered via an iron gate.

An oval path of beaten earth surrounded a lawn with leafy trees. Mainly young people sat, resting and reading, on the grass and on benches.

Beyond the north-east corner, a gorgeous blue metal cast-iron structure rose like a nineteenth-century railway station, the Marché du Carreau du Temple.

He forced her to sit on a bench.

'My master wants you to feel the power of this site,' he said. 'It is a significant point of power in the city. The treasures of kings, and kings themselves, were held here. It was part of a city within a city, the great Knights Templar fortress, a law unto itself, walled off, closed to any authority but its own, hermetically sealed, we might say . . . but the King of France, in the fourteenth century, tore up their privileges, had them all arrested, thrown into their own dungeons and tortured, forced to confess all manner of blasphemies . . . and the leaders burned alive.'

'And?'

'This beautiful, restful park, and the couple of blocks north to the Temple Métro station, were all part of the Templar enclave. They say it's all gone, but that's not quite true. There are still underground chambers. Paris is full of them, here and elsewhere. I'm going to show you one, a little further south. My master wants you to suffer there, to make him stronger.'

The blackness surged again around her, and Katherine heard the words.

Lucem in tenebris occulto.

They brought with them a burning flood of vileness, of darkness and fear, and Katherine suddenly felt she was drowning in hatred. Her skull began to split apart.

Oldwick Fen

29 June 2007

Jack tied Robert's hands and feet and dragged his cousin's unconscious form through the old tunnel that led from beneath the tack room all the way to his hiding place, a vaulted space under the abbey church, where so many generations of Oldwick holy people – some monks, some not – had kept their secrets.

It had all gone wrong for Jack, and now he didn't know if he could make anything right. He'd been seduced by the idea of Margaret's power, of succeeding her – but he'd never wanted the burdens that came with it. He hadn't wanted the curse, only the gift.

Sweating, back bent in the low passage, Jack hauled Robert yard by yard, berating him under his breath.

Jack had always expected that Margaret, after his decades of service, after all the years of caring for her and that lump Hickey, would pass on her gift to Jack at the last. He'd made a plan, prepared for years for the glorious day: he would accept the initiation from her dying hand, and then use the kind of bitter, dark magic she shunned, just once, to slough the curse off himself, and onto poor, witless Hickey. There were ways to do such things. Jack had studied them, hidden from Margaret's gaze, consumed with the imagined power of what he saw as his birthright.

Jack straightened his back as they reached the small stone chamber beneath the abbey church. Hickey was slumped there where Jack had left him, bound to the chair, moaning.

'Shut up, Hickey,' Jack whispered. 'Be quiet, now. Let me think.'

First there had been the bird, all cut up, a messenger of death and of the coming together of different times. Then Jack had found poor dear Margaret, herself frail and tiny like a bird, stabbed to death in her bed. Dead before she could hand over the power.

Jack, his initiation lost, had tipped over into darkness. Decades of resentment and anger had burned through him like consuming fire, and Jack had taken it out on Hickey. Fearful of the old boy's strength, Jack had drugged Hickey and brought him, subdued and rambling, to the secret vault. And here, Jack had lost his mind. Who else but Hickey could have killed her? Who else could have torn Jack's birthright from him?

Something elemental had entered Jack, a raw yearning to cause pain, and he'd heated wall irons kept in the vault, and hurt Hickey. Jack didn't know what he'd been trying to do. Had he been trying to make Hickey confess? Trying to reclaim Margaret's power from beyond death, using Hickey's suffering to try to unlock the grave? He didn't know. He'd learned only one thing in doing it, and it had driven Jack further into darkness. He'd learned that in the delirium of her final days, Margaret had babbled about her successor to Hickey, and she'd said it was not going to be Jack. It was going to be cousin Robert.

How could she? The city boy. Jack had cursed Margaret's name. She hadn't breathed a word of her intentions to Jack. Had Hickey told Margaret about Jack's dark studies, about his intentions? Jack, beside himself with rage, had made Hickey pay the price.

Now Robert, sticking his nose in where it wasn't wanted, asking too many questions, had come to bring retribution,

Jack was sure of it. Somehow, Robert knew. Somehow, he was Margaret's messenger. What could Jack do to make things right?

There was only one path: to take himself and Robert to see Margaret, and let her decide.

Paris

29 June 2007

Doubled over on the park bench at Square du Temple, Katherine moaned, trying to hide her thoughts from her captor and those working through him, feeling their power to look into her, and yet perceiving too their terrible blindness. She strained to form the counter words, syllable by syllable.

Libero . . . in . . . tenebris . . . occulta.

The words struck her captor like an electric shock.

Then she drove her elbow down into his crotch and ran. He screamed, his body momentarily out of his control, the pistol falling to the ground.

Sprinting along Rue Réaumur from the Square du Temple as fast as she could, the radio banging against her back, its weight crushing her spine and legs, Katherine heard the black car, its driver taken by surprise by her sudden dash, rumbling along the street behind her, slowly picking up speed after turning awkwardly on Réaumur. Pain rose behind her eyes, in her bones and under her nails, as it drew closer, its engine throbbing, roaring in anger.

Katherine turned and stepped into the road to face it, screaming defiance. For a moment there were no other vehicles, no modern traffic. She saw the car ripple, as though seen through water, through a dream. She saw a pair of stark eyes staring at her through the window, green hating eyes. Then the car vanished, like a soap bubble bursting.

She saw the man she had hit, her neo-Nazi captor, sprinting to catch up with her. Car horns sounded, and she jumped back onto the pavement as a bright yellow Renault sped past her, its driver cursing, the world around her flickering between times.

Katherine turned and kept running. When she again came to Rue St Martin, by the great abbey church, she turned south. She saw some trees ahead, the ones at Beaubourg. Pain broke over her in waves. Her knees buckled, and she fell just outside the church of St Nicholas.

She felt detached from quotidian reality, as though she were floating above herself. She fought off dry heaves again in her stomach, pulled herself to her feet, forced herself to keep walking, dizzy, her vision rimmed with dark circles.

Just past Rue aux Ours she came again to Scaramouche bookshop, with its beautiful theatrical masks. A small group of college students were inspecting them through the glass of the shop window, and Katherine, one eye on the street behind her, hid herself among them to rest for a moment. There was a grinning old man mask with wrinkled eyes, mouth lasciviously open; a strange, unsettling beaked bird face; a white-painted half-mask fit for a costume ball; and a highly naturalistic mask of a woman struck by ineffable sadness.

She felt her grandmother, somewhere close. She felt Rose. But the radio was silent.

She moved on. As she reached Rue de Rivoli, the Tour St Jacques came into view, framed at the end of St Martin. Looking south, she could see a green dome up ahead, on the far side of the river, marking the line of the pilgrimage of St James. What was it? She looked around for a cab, hoping against hope, knowing how hard it was to flag one down in the city. Nothing. No rank nearby.

She crossed Avenue Victoria, a block from the Seine, and

caught a glimpse of the twin towers of Notre Dame cathedral up ahead, past the massive rounded towers of the Conciergerie.

Crossing the Pont Notre Dame, she felt another wave of fatigue, and stood for a few moments in one of its bellied-out observation points, resting her rucksack. Had she lost her pursuer? She couldn't see him, couldn't tell. She was exhausted.

The pain was just at the edge of her consciousness again, lurking. She breathed deeply, deliberately. She undid her hair band, shook her hair out, tied it again. Set herself to carry on.

When she had recovered her energy, Katherine walked past the flower market and the Cité Métro station again, checking her watch – it was just after 8 p.m. – and came again to the forecourt of Notre Dame Cathedral.

Now she was able to get a signal and call up a search engine on her handheld. She found a dictionary.

Eyot – In British English, a riverine island. Pronounced like the number eight. Alternative spelling *ait*.

Fylfot – in heraldry, the gammadion or swastika, often with slightly truncated hooks.

She realized she was standing on an eyot, the Île de la Cité. And then she thought of Aldwych, and its island church of St Clement Danes. Another eyot, an island in traffic rather than water, but still . . . it was as Horace had said. She heard a voice on the breeze. A woman's. Rose.

'Isis. Dark Lady. Go closer.'

Katherine had once read that there had been shrines to Isis in the city. Some even suggested the name Paris might reflect the worship of her by the Parisi, as the early inhabitants were known.

She walked across the parvis to the cathedral and stood before the middle of the three great entrance arches.

'Between the two doors . . . look.'

Katherine saw a sculpture of a long-haired woman holding a sceptre, an open book in the other hand, a closed book semi-hidden behind it, with a ladder rising from the earth at her feet up to the top of her heart. Above her head, the sky was rippling with lightning.

'Lady Alchemy . . . lady of wisdom-lovers . . . Dark Lady . . . *dark* means *wise*. Remember this.'

Rose. She felt Rose was near. So close.

The radio crackled again. Then the voice.

'South. South.'

Katherine crossed the Petit Pont, coming to a small park right opposite the hotel where she'd booked a room. She wanted desperately to dump the radio. The flesh on her shoulders was chafing raw, her back and thighs were screaming at her. But she didn't dare to do so.

She looked north, back towards Notre Dame.

The scene shimmered and rippled like water. Katherine saw the bridge as though through a heat haze.

On the Petit Pont, three men were attacking an older man and a child, jostling him, forcing him against the bridge's balustrade. A young woman was walking towards them, peering in Katherine's direction, then looking again at the attackers.

Rose?

Katherine started moving towards her, waving.

The young woman walked up to the tallest man in the group of attackers and remonstrated with him. The men, two shorter thugs and the tall one, wore Nazi armbands.

Katherine crossed the street.

The young woman looked at Katherine again, as though in puzzlement. Then she slapped the tall man's face.

'Run,' Katherine heard the young woman tell the man and his boy. 'Run!'

Before Katherine could reach them, the figures rippled more intensely, tearing in the air. Then they vanished.

Paris

Late May 1944

The man was waiting for Horace, sitting in an armchair facing the door, when he got to the safe house on Rue du Faubourg St Martin, an apartment Horace used only once every week, for security reasons, and on randomly chosen days.

No one could have known Horace would be there. He himself had only chosen to go to this particular apartment an hour earlier. The electricity was off, and Horace didn't see the man or catch any hint of his presence until he'd struck a match to light a candle.

Within a second his training drill kicked in, even before he'd fully absorbed what he'd seen, and Horace was pointing his .32 pistol at the man's heart.

'*Qui êtes-vous?*' Horace barked.

The man, who looked to be in his mid-forties, raised his hands, palms towards Horace, in a gesture of surrender. He seemed oddly confident that he was not about to die, and respectful, even admiring, of Horace's reaction.

'I believe you have been looking for me, Mr Steeplejack.'

Horace peered along his gun barrel at the unexpected guest. His first impression was of an athletic man, cleanshaven, his black hair worn short, a smile of amusement on his lips. Fatigue battled vitality in his demeanour.

'Have I?'

'Word has reached me to that effect.'

'Who?'

'As I believe you say in English, *a little bird told me?*'

'Not good enough.' Horace raised the gun to point between the man's eyes. 'What do you want?'

'Please. Let us be civilized. I mean you no harm, and have come to help you. You seek Fulcanelli. Seek, and ye shall find. I have made a decision.'

His eyes bored into Horace's, and slowly the American began to feel it was safe to lower his weapon, however much the paranoid, security-conscious side of his nature screamed at him to get out of the apartment as soon as possible.

'They say that Fulcanelli is dead,' Horace said. 'That he never existed.'

'Yet you seek him.'

'Perhaps.'

Horace sat down, his pistol back in its holster but within easy reach.

'But I know you. You are . . .'

'Frédéric Joliot-Curie, yes. At your orders. A reluctant emissary, we might say. The Nazis must be denied the knowledge I hold. I had thought the Allies must be denied it too. But I have come to believe there is greater danger in not giving it to you.'

'You speak of atomic secrets.'

'No. I speak of something more powerful still. The Secret Fire. In addition to his work in conventional fields, my father-in-law Pierre Curie was an alchemist. This is a great secret of the family, of the French state, even. For myself, I don't care for the things he meddled in, and which cost him his life. He was killed, you know, for refusing to share what he had learned with a certain rival, a dog named Isambard. But his family inherited from him certain responsibilities, certain documents, as well as certain knowledge that may only be imparted orally. He made his daughter memorize some phrases when she was very young. She has passed them on to me.'

'Pierre Curie. Your father-in-law.'

'Fulcanelli. Yes.'

'He was Fulcanelli.'

'Let us not play games,' Joliot-Curie said. 'The name Fulcanelli is a convenience, and, what's more, does not refer to a single man. It is a plural. Little Vulcans, or blacksmiths. It is an identity assumed by different people at different times, in a chain of succession. So, strictly, I am a Fulcanello. A Vulcan, one who works with metals in the forge, seeking to transmute them.'

'And the Fulcanelli books? *The Mystery of the Cathedrals*, *The Dwellings of the Philosophers*?'

'The manuscripts were among my father-in-law's papers. There could be no question of publishing them under his real name. I had Jean-Julien Champagne take them to a publisher, and illustrate them as he could do so beautifully, twenty years after Pierre Curie's death.'

'Do you have the Newton paper? The Paris half, the one discovered by Jean-Julien Champagne, taken from him by . . . you? By Fulcanelli?'

'By me, yes. And no, I do not have it.'

'Do you know where it is?'

'That is, in part, why I am here. With the arrest of the man called Shelley, things accelerated. Gestapo scrutiny has increased drastically. The situation has worsened, yet the Allied landings cannot be far away. I have chosen to reveal myself to you now in case I, too, fall into their hands. I am heavily involved in preparations to rise up against the invaders.'

'Does it contain everything we have been led to believe? The knowledge that will allow its holder to make this new kind of bomb?'

'Combined with the other half, the paper we recovered from the hands of Nazi Germany, yes. Not just an atomic bomb. More, far more. I am here to tell you the location. To give you permission to go there and take it. And to place myself at your disposal, when you are ready to get it.'

'What are you? A scientist, I understand. A Communist, also. But an alchemist?'

'As I said, I am a reluctant emissary. I believe the physical sciences alone are now showing us the route to transmutation of metals. But I honour my father-in-law.'

Joliot-Curie reached into his pocket and handed Horace an item wrapped in black silk and a slip of paper.

'You may need these.'

The paper contained a sketch map and some lines of writing. It read:

> *Cherchez Nostre Dame aux Ténèbres*
> *Si Dieu le veult*
> *Vous la trouverez*

'It's older French, perhaps sixteenth-century,' Horace said. 'Seek Our Lady in the Shadows. If God wishes it, you will find her.'

'So it is. It is a very old map, useless without knowing what it refers to. But it shows the location of the paper you seek. It also gives useful advice. And there is something else.'

'What is that?'

'I am here to tell you I intend to pass on the burden. You are to be next in the line of Fulcanelli.'

Horace blinked, astounded.

'I am not remotely prepared. I am not in the least ready.'

342

'Your sacrifice has made you so. The loss of your love.'

Horace stammered. 'How did you know? No one knows.'

'For those with eyes to see, it is clear.'

Horace's voice thickened. 'Are you saying she is dead? Have you heard . . . ?'

'No. Her fate is unknown.'

'I cannot . . .'

'You have proven yourself worthy. When the pupil is ready . . .'

'The teacher appears. Yes.'

'I am the man you have been seeking, in all regards. I am to help you perform your Great Work. In doing so I am to help you, perhaps, to find a way through the darkness you must endure, now and in the future. And then, if I survive the war, I will leave these things, and return to my own vocation, to the rational sciences I prefer.'

'I am . . . honoured. Undeserving.'

'Listen,' Joliot-Curie said. 'Have you heard, young man, of the Château Vauvert, and of the tales Parisians used to tell of it? Of the goings-on along the Rue d'Enfer, which now lies in part beneath the Boulevard St Michel?'

'*The road to hell*. Are you pulling my leg?'

'Please do not interrupt. This is an initiatory story. At what is now the southern end of the Luxembourg Garden, there was once a magnificent residence, built in the tenth century, which fell into ruins, called the Hôtel Vauvert. In the Middle Ages it was a fearful place, said by Parisians to be the lair of the Devil. Gangs of criminals moved in there, and into the old quarries below it, as the towers and walls fell down. They lit their fires there, and lived a life of violent, drunken debauchery. The smoke, the smells, the echoing cries from the underground quarries, all combined to give it a Satanic air in the popular mind. A phrase even entered the French language: to send someone *au diable Vauvert*, to the ends of the Earth.'

'Go on.'

'Inspired by this, confidence tricksters would take the gullible and foolhardy on tours to see the Devil, who would naturally be a colleague in some frightful horns or goatskin . . . In the thirteenth century the Carthusian monks were given the land, on condition they expel the Devil and his creatures from the location, which they managed to do, history does not record quite how, though the stories speak of three days and nights of thunder and lightning, and explosions and cries, and terrible stenches. The ruins of Vauvert château were demolished, the brothers cut more stone from the quarries and built a monastery, where in the fullness of time they received a mysterious gift from one François Hannibal d'Estrees, King Henri IV's marshal of artillery.'

'What gift?'

'At the beginning of the seventeenth century he brought them a manuscript, already very old, alchemical in nature, containing instructions for making a herb- and plant-based Elixir of Long Life. He didn't understand it, and for many years neither could they, but they began trying to make the elixir, right there in the underground chambers beneath the monastery. It took them 130 years before they finally understood the whole manuscript. They were long gone from Vauvert by then, but they've been making the elixir ever since, along with a milder version, not intended as a medicine but for enjoyment, a liqueur called Chartreuse. You may have heard of it.'

'I look forward to a glass of it with you, when the war is over,' Horace said, impatience tingeing his voice.

'If we are both so lucky as to survive. Even today, they say only two monks at any given time know the secret of how to make it. Each knows half the secret. Here ends the story.'

'I don't understand.'

'The Great Work is achieved by uniting two fragments of ourselves split asunder, the dark and the light, two kinds of time. It is about healing, of ourselves and others. These are among the phrases passed along by my father-in-law. You will see. And I also tell you this story,' he said with a smile of great amusement, 'because it contains the location of the paper you seek.'

'Where?'

'The cellars and caverns under the Vauvert monastery are still there.'

'And?'

'The Nazi occupying forces have taken over a large part of them, under the Lycée Montaigne and the Pharmacy Faculty, as air-raid bunkers. They have cut new tunnels, walled up old ones, and created underground corridors that allow their people to get all the way from Odéon to the Lycée Montaigne without ever seeing daylight. Oddly enough, given such mole-like behaviour, they are from the Luftwaffe.'

'Don't tell me the other half of the document is hidden where the Nazis are.'

'Almost.'

'Good Christ.'

'Not all is lost. The Nazis don't know. And the place where it is hidden is not actually part of the Nazi bunker. It is, however, right next to it. There is a chamber in the former monastery cellars, a forgotten crypt, carefully kept hidden by certain of us for many centuries now. It has contained very precious items. It seemed the ideal place to conceal the Newton paper.'

'When can you take me?'

'Tomorrow evening. But before we go . . .'

'Yes?'

'There is something you must know about a young man working with you.'

'Peter?'

'Yes. You must decide what to do about him. His fate is, in a sense, that of all of us. He is the son of Isambard.'

Horace stared at him, thunderstruck.

'There is more. He is in play, so to speak. He seeks to throw off the influence of his father, and yet is not strong enough to do so. He seeks to cross over to you, and yet needs your strength, your assistance, to do so. The benefits of his crossing would be immense. You should bring him across. And yet it is he who arrested Rose and took her to the Gestapo. There are consequences for such actions that perhaps outweigh his usefulness. You must decide what to do about him. That is part of your own Great Work.'

~

Later that night, Horace ordered the immediate arrest of Peter by *résistance* forces.

~

Underneath Paris a network of disused quarries, tunnels, abandoned crypts, forgotten hiding places, bunkers and catacombs stretched for hundreds of miles. People had become lost, gone mad, died of starvation in the endless dark passages below the City of Light. In some sections, the bones of millions of Parisians from disused cemeteries had been relocated in official areas of rest, skulls and femurs arranged in patterned rows and artistic groupings, open to the public on guided tours – though not during wartime. Into other sections, officially closed to all but specialist subterranean police patrols and city workers, only the daring, the fool-hardy and those with something to hide ventured to penetrate.

Since the Nazi occupation, the Germans had organized bunkers and military passageways for themselves, while *résistance* workers had begun using the catacombs immediately to move people and weapons about the city. Black marketeers and smugglers were not unknown. Enemies never saw each other. The underground city was too vast.

There were unmapped stretches of the underground world, crawlspaces into the bellies of cavernous hollows that, in some cases, had been walled off and disguised hundreds of years before.

Guided by the man who did not want to be Fulcanelli, Horace and Harry descended into the catacombs. After more than three hours of twists and turns through the dark passages, they came to a wall of very old brick, a couple of columns on either side of it shoring up the roof of a dead-end tunnel.

'This is it?' Harry asked in frustration. 'It doesn't look like anything to me.'

Joliot-Curie placed his foot in a cavity in the column and stretched up, finding a handhold and then reaching into the wall at the very top to pull out a brick. A narrow gap opened in the wall, just wide enough for them to squeeze through one by one.

347

Inside, initially, they could see nothing. Then, as their eyes became accustomed to the dark, they breathed a sigh of awe.

In the centre of a natural domed cavern, its round walls augmented and supported by criss-crossing Gothic arches and ribbed columns, stood a statue in black stone of a woman, her form draped in fine white and blue fabrics, her head tilted very slightly and elegantly to one side, one hand raised as though in blessing.

When the entrance was sealed again, Harry stared about him wild-eyed, speechless.

'Good God,' he said. 'Good God.'

'Or Goddess, more appropriately,' Horace said.

Joliot-Curie gestured all around, spinning on a heel and pointing up at the domed roof of the shrine. Light seemed to emanate faintly from the walls themselves.

'Where are we?' Harry asked.

'We are under the southern end of the Luxembourg Garden,' Joliot-Curie whispered. 'That way' – he pointed south – 'is the Nazi bunker, under the Lycée Montaigne.'

Harry stared in amazement.

'The other half of the document is kept in this place,' Joliot-Curie said. 'It's rigged in such a way, like the entrance itself, that if someone tries to force it or tries to open the hiding place in any but a single prescribed way, the whole thing will blow. Collapse. Tiny explosives, a knowledge of arches and weight distribution, a few pulleys and . . . *pouf.*' He gave a very Gallic shrug.

Still Horace stood still, his eyes now closed, speaking very softly. 'If they match . . .'

'Then we have won the war,' Harry said. 'Please get it now.'

'Horace, please give me the item I handed you yesterday.'

Horace reached under his shirt and removed it. It was an innocuous-looking pendant which Joliot-Curie twisted to reveal a slotted stone, a kind of key, hidden inside. He stooped at the foot of the black statue, then slid aside a stone slab and inserted the key into a slot behind it, at the same time as he held her outstretched hand. A small drawer clicked open in the base. Joliot-Curie felt inside.

'I have it.'

Joliot-Curie withdrew a piece of paper. Horace took another from his pocket. With Harry holding a flashlight on them, the two men joined the pieces. The tear matched perfectly.

Paris

29 June 2007

Her head spinning, Katherine stared in amazement at the bridge. The people she had been walking towards had simply vanished, melting into the air, like the car before them. Who had that young woman been, remonstrating with Gestapo thugs? Katherine had felt so drawn to her. Could it really have been . . . She was losing her mind. She was failing.

Then the voice came again. Rose.

'South. South. Quickly. They are looking for you.'

She looked along the Rue St Jacques toward the mysterious green dome. It was not yet a quarter past eight.

She forced herself to march into the *quartier latin*. She passed tourist souvenir shops, hip bars. It started to spit with rain as she came to the church of St Severin, its stained-glass windows faintly aglow with light inside. The rucksack weighed a ton. She could barely move. She needed some answers, some time to think.

She went in and walked to the rear, taking off the rucksack with relief and sitting down in a location where, looking along the nave towards the altar, she could see the stone-traced palm grove of the choir and its glorious, spiralling central column.

Staring at it, Katherine thought, for an instant, that she saw her grandmother. She blinked, and the impression was gone.

Katherine fixed her eyes on the ghostly twisting column. Then she was seeing something entirely other. It lasted only a few seconds. It was unbearable. She caught glimpses of what otherwise her brain couldn't absorb: hundreds of square miles of scorched earth, shattered, blackened buildings, skeletal survivors, scavengers with staring dead eyes, hunting one another like dogs in the ruins. Hiroshima. Dachau. Slivers of horror. It was England.

Needles of black pain pierced her again. She wept.

'That didn't happen,' Katherine hissed. 'That didn't happen.'

Eventually the voice returned.

'It still could. You need to keep moving. To stop this happening, you need to move. Head south.'

'I can't move. The radio is so heavy.'

'Leave it. I've found you now. We don't need it. Leave it for now. Come back for it later.'

'I can? Thank you.'

Katherine stood, every muscle in her back and legs aching, and took the rucksack over to a side chapel, where she concealed it behind a column.

But when she came out of the church, back onto Rue St Jacques, the black car was waiting.

'Get in,' her kidnapper said from the rear compartment, the pistol pointing between her eyes. A driver stared straight ahead, paying her no attention.

She climbed into the back seat. There was no sign now of the man with green eyes she had seen in the car earlier.

'Someone is waiting for you up ahead,' her captor said. 'We are going to see him.'

They drove. She could see that they were heading uphill now, towards the site of the Sorbonne, then the Panthéon. She remained silent, trying to preserve her strength, listening to him prattle. He no longer sounded American, nor even like himself. His voice had taken on a colourless British accent.

She shivered. Horace had described this voice. Isambard was talking though her captor.

'This has always been a route of power. It is a privilege to travel it with one as gifted as you,' he said. 'The Romans called the Rue St Jacques the Cardo Maximus, the main artery of their city. It was on the left bank, primarily. They lived on the island, and south of it.'

Katherine said nothing, her flesh creeping. She could see the man fully now. He was still bruised from their encounter two days earlier. Good. And they were still tracing the Nazi line, the form of the swastika. Why? To revive it for their purposes, as she was trying to turn it to hers, to Horace's?

'Up ahead is the highest point of the old city, Mont St Geneviève as it was known, though in Roman times it was the Forum. There was also a Temple to Mercury. To Hermes.'

They crossed the Boulevard St Germain.

'A few blocks to your right, there was a temple to Isis, on the site where the church of St Germain des Prés now stands. Paris, as a whole, is a centre of female energy, as London is of male.'

Katherine said nothing, deep in thought, wrestling to understand.

They came to the site of the green dome she had glimpsed, like a beacon, from the St Jacques tower.

'The Sorbonne,' her captor said. 'The old observatory dome, directly above us. There is another one, the Paris Observatory, directly south along our line.'

Katherine looked south to the next towers along their route, one looming above the Oceanographic Institute at the corner of Gay Lussac, the next the steeple of another church.

'St Jacques du Haut Pas,' her captor said. 'The name

comes from an Italian order of the Alto Passo, or the High Pass, who protected pilgrims on routes such as this.'

They drove towards it. The rain began to fall more heavily.

Her captor opened the car door when they reached the church. 'Head west,' he said. 'I'm right behind you, and I'm aiming my gun at your spine.'

It was an escape opportunity. But as soon as she was out of the car, she heard the words.

Lucem in tenebris occulto.

She responded before the effect of the site could hit her.

Libero in tenebris occulta.

Again she felt the breeze rise, the cleansing. The moment to try to escape was gone, but she'd had to respond. And deep within herself, she suspected she was going to have to face this man's master in order to complete her own mission.

Katherine turned, and the car was gone. His pistol was pointing right at her.

'My master wants to see you. Keep going.'

Paris

Late May 1944

Horace took the conjoined parts of the Newton document and placed them in a leather wallet, which he hid under his clothing. Joliot-Curie again opened the hidden door and led them out into the labyrinthine tunnels of underground Paris.

They walked in almost complete darkness in single file, the Frenchman taking the lead, then Harry, then Horace, fingers over their flashlights letting out just the faintest red glow.

Horace heard the danger first, behind him.

A German security patrol, protecting the Luftwaffe bunker under the Lycée Montaigne, was coming straight for them.

Using their pre-arranged danger signal, Horace tapped Harry on the shoulders twice, and pressed himself against the cold stone wall. They all doused their flashlights. But they were sitting ducks.

The first soldier, an officer, walked straight past Horace without seeing him, but spotted Harry just ahead in the beam of his torchlight. The other two riflemen were level with Horace when the officer suddenly reached for his Luger, starting to shout *Achtung!* but never finishing the word, because Harry had punched him in the throat.

Horace leapt on one of the guards who was bringing up his Schmeisser to fire, grabbing the Nazi's neck in a stranglehold. The sub-machinegun fired off a burst into the ceiling, deafening them all, as Horace broke the man's neck.

They were at a crossroads of underground corridors. A

fallen German torch cast grotesque shadows as they grappled in the darkness. Harry grabbed the pistol from the officer and turned it against him, pulling the trigger. Horace, deafened and disoriented by the sub-machine-gun blast, saw the man jerk once, then crumple. Harry dived to the ground as the remaining guard swept the tunnel with a burst of gunfire, narrowly missing Joliot-Curie. Then Harry raised the Luger to the guard's head. The guard body-checked him, unable to get his Schmeisser around in time to shoot him.

The gun fell from Harry's hand into a crack in the stone.

Joliot-Curie flung himself at the guard's knees, bringing him down, and Horace punched him in the face as he hit the ground. Harry finished the job, rolling onto the man's chest and stabbing him twice in the heart with his fighting dagger.

They all lay on the ground for a second or two, breathing hard, adrenaline pumping. Then Joliot-Curie spoke.

'Go. Now. This way.'

They put as much distance between themselves and the dead patrol as they could, following the Frenchman's lead, retracing the tortuous route they had followed to reach the vault of the Dark Lady.

After three hours, they emerged into the chamber below the Temple de l'Amitié at 20, Rue Jacob, drenched in sweat, exhausted.

They, and the Allies, had won control of the Secret Fire.

That night, they went to the securest safe house they knew. They made plans to extract the document, as soon as possible, and convey it to London. It was two weeks to the next full moon and a potential Lysander or Hudson rendezvous that would allow them to hand-carry it back.

The following day they dispersed, for greater security,

each to a separate safe house, Harry guarding the Nazi half of the Secret Fire document, Horace the newly recovered French half. Horace went to the house where Peter was being held under 24-hour armed guard.

Paris

29 June 2007

Katherine and her captor took Rue de l'Abbé de l'Épée alongside a long, medieval-looking stone wall punctuated by bricked-up arches, a heavy drizzle blowing almost horizontally into her face, whipped up by the wind, like foam from the sea.

Not Abbot's Word. Abbot Sword. L'Abbé de l'Épée.

As they crossed Boulevard St Michel onto Rue Auguste Comte, Katherine's captor started talking again.

'Beneath our feet, just slightly further west, is something that may resonate for you. A gatekeeper at the great military hospital at Val de Grâce, behind us back to the east, decided in 1793 to enter the subterranean tunnels under all this area to seek out the cellars of the Carthusian monks, which lie just up ahead, under the southern end of the Luxembourg Garden, and help himself to the legendary elixir or liqueur they were distilling there. He got lost, hopelessly lost, and died in the tunnels, right under our feet. His rat-gnawed body was found eleven years later, and he was buried on the spot. His name was Philibert d'Aspairt, and to this day, lit candles are often found at his tomb, left by other *cataphiles*.'

'I can't imagine a worse way to go.'

'Can't you? Maybe that's what we're going to do to you.'

The rain fell more heavily again as they came to the wrought-iron railings marking the southern limit of the Luxembourg Garden. There was not another soul on the streets. Looking south, Katherine saw what at first she took to be the moon, low in the sky, gleaming white.

'The Paris Observatory,' her captor said. 'Directly on the Paris north–south line, if we continued it further south.'

He steered her to an address on Rue de Notre Dame des Champs, on the south side of the Lycée Montaigne and the Pharmacy Faculty. It was a nondescript residential building, closed up for the night.

The rain started again. She felt tears coming, whether from frustration, anger or exhaustion she couldn't tell.

He took her to the entrance to an underground garage.

'Open it. You know how.'

There was a padlock on it. That was all. Breaking and entering was something she had been well schooled in, back in the day. Silent entry. Part of an array of skills. Silent movement. Silent killing. She might be rusty, but some things never entirely left you.

She had it off in 30 seconds.

Inside, he led her to a metal door at the rear, in the corner, behind a Peugeot that had seen better days. She checked it. Two more padlocks and an old-fashioned security lock. With the tools she'd brought with her from New York, she was through them in five minutes.

The door led to a long, gradually sloping concrete passageway. They advanced 50 yards, perhaps more, flashlight in his hand, before coming to another steel door. Double padlocked again. She picked them. Then Katherine descended a rickety metal spiral staircase into the darkness, down a shaft cut into the stone of the city's underbelly.

She saw a light guttering at the bottom of the stairs. Winding round and round as she went lower, she saw it vanish and grow, vanish and grow, like a secret message in Morse, summoning her into the mystery.

The man behind her had gone. A chance to escape?

'Are you there?' she called out. No reply.

She reached the bottom. In the red glow of a flashlight filtered through fingers over the lens, she saw a face appear, where there had been none a moment earlier. White hair. Green eyes. Black uniform. A knife in one hand.

Instinct kicked in immediately. She twisted and dropped like a stone, firing off a blow with her right foot at the figure's groin. He stepped sideways, eluding her. She punched but hit only a wall. She jumped to her feet, breathing hard, head buzzing, ready to kill if she had to.

Then something hard and metallic slammed into the back of her head, and she fell.

Katherine came to curled in a ball, her head splitting with pain, her right fist aching. Her shoulders were raw from the rucksack straps. She checked her body. Nothing else. No pain anywhere else. Her boots were off, but she was clothed.

She looked up, and saw German writing.

Notausgang.

Hinterhof.

Ruhe.

Rauchen Verboten.

Black, red and blue painted arrows on whitewashed backgrounds pointed to exits in streets above: S. Michel and N. Dame-Bonaparte.

She was in the World War Two Nazi bunker under Paris.

Her attacker was reclining in a hammock slung between two concrete pillars set into the rock, observing her dispassionately. She couldn't gauge his age. He wore a Gestapo uniform. A rusted metal door behind him bore a red cross, and the words, in faded white paint: *Krankenrevier. Entgiftung.* An infirmary of some kind? A baleful twilight filled the chamber.

He followed her gaze.

'*Entgiftung*. It means decontamination. Unpoisoning, to be precise. This is a very well-equipped air-raid shelter. They are – were, from your point of view – prepared for all kinds of attack, even poison gas.'

'Who are you?'

'My name is Isambard.'

'Why am I here?'

'To ensure that tomorrow, I can live again.'

'I don't understand.'

'In just over seventeen hours, the anniversary will take place of my death, my semi-death, in 1944, at Aldwych in London, in the explosion of the V-1 that I piloted into the ground there.'

'I know about that. You failed.'

'Only barely. It's not over. Tomorrow, these things can be revisited. It took a unique combination of events to stop me, one almost impossible to reproduce. All it will take for me to win is for you – or your husband, or Horace – not to be at Aldwych tomorrow. You are all needed to stop me. And even then, you may not be able to.'

She remembered her neo-Nazi captors, and the prohibition they had seemed to be under.

'So kill me.'

'I can do better than that.'

'Why can't you kill me?'

Isambard stared at her with cold venom, his green eyes glassy. He was weak still, she saw.

'You are kept alive in return for a far greater prize for the power I serve. But that doesn't mean you can't be made to suffer. It doesn't mean you can't even be brought to join me.'

'You can't beat Horace,' Katherine said.

Isambard took a monogrammed black handkerchief

from a pocket of his uniform and slowly dabbed sweat from his temples.

'Can't I?'

'How will you live again?'

'Not only me. Elements of the Third Reich. The SS. A new world, under undying rulers. Himmler. Me. People like us. Like you and me.'

'How?'

The green eyes probed her, reaching into her essence, searching for weakness, for purchase.

'In exploring the nature of the Great Work – the joining of our personal *vril* or power with that of the world about us, to alter reality – there are certain highly secret and forbidden practices. Forbidden to some. I can teach you them all. Those who follow only the way of the light, upon achieving the fabled state of consciousness that is the goal of the Work, may learn a technique to project their consciousness, at the moment of death, into the world itself, into a realm beyond time and death. In the book often mistakenly called the Tibetan Book of the Dead, it is called *phowa*.

'But there is an allied technique, a very great secret, forbidden to those who follow only the light, known as forcible projection – *drong-juk* – in which the consciousness may be projected into another body. It may be a corpse, but I chose to make and prepare my own vessel, a kind of homunculus who would receive my consciousness on 30 July 1944, at the moment of my physical death in the explosion of the *geheime Feuer*, which was the culmination of my own Work.'

'You're insane. Who?'

'My son. Peter. That was his purpose. That is still his purpose. It is why I created him. To receive my consciousness, in its entirety. To allow me to live on, in your time and in 1944. And then to allow me to teach others to live on. Himmler, next. The most loyal SS men.'

'Not Hitler?'

'No. Just the true believers. The armed occultists, not the politicians. The true SS, those of the *Schwarze Sonne*.'

'But that didn't happen. The Nazis were defeated.'

'It almost happened. It half-happened. It can happen again.'

Katherine felt utter dread.

'At the key moment, in 1944, some people you know got in the way,' Isambard said. 'Horace Hencott, making his first attempt at his own Great Work in Paris, somehow connected, unexpectedly, unforeseeably, with the actions of a group of Britons, led by a witch of enormous power, in the Fens of East Anglia. These two, in their turn, connected with the dying prayers of a woman being beaten to death in Dachau, on my orders. Your grandmother.'

Rose. He'd taken delight in telling her, she could feel it.

'No, shut up,' Katherine said. She had never known what happened to Rose in Dachau. And now, from the mouth of this creature, from the mouth of the man who'd ordered Rose's death, Katherine didn't want to know.

'The Fenland witch had the greater part of it, and the cost to her was enormous. The combination of these factors, at just the key moment, threw my Work, the explosion of the *geheime Feuer*, my projection of consciousness into Peter, into complete disarray. I virtually died. The explosion was kicked into a different state of space and time, trapped for six long decades, until the spell dies. The same happened to me. I held on by my fingernails, projecting myself into Peter, but it didn't take properly. It was a botched job. He could never escape me, but I could never wholly rule him. Only now, as the spell dies and the time approaches, am I growing stronger again.'

Katherine tried to absorb what he was saying. That Rose had helped stop him. That without Rose's dying prayers, he would have succeeded.

The flashing, piercing eyes stabbed her again. He could reach right through her.

'Now. What would you do to save your grandmother? What would you do to save the legendary Rose Arden?'

At that moment, Katherine heard the words, and realized she was at the last of the five points, the fifth point that completed the swastika shape.

Lucem in tenebris occulto.

Isambard was chanting them, projecting them into her head. She heard them shouted, chanted, in unison, an army of distorted male voices barking the words into her body and mind, a deafening tide of hatred. She tried to raise her hands to cover her ears. Tried to speak, to utter the counter-phrase. Couldn't move her lips. She was paralysed, pain ripping through every cell in her body.

Entgiftung. Unpoisoning.

She saw Rose.

Rose at Dachau. Thick army boots kicking her, over and over, crouched on the ground. Punches raining down on her beautiful face. A pistol being raised, then brought down on her bones, breaking them. Hour upon hour. Beating after beating.

'Make it stop,' she screamed in her mind. 'Make it stop.'

'Join me,' Isambard shouted. 'Join me and tomorrow I will alter this. I ordered this to happen to her. I'll wipe it away. I'll annul my order. I'll let her live. Live to know you. Live to raise you when your mother died. Live to love you.'

He spat the words at her. 'Join me! I'll teach you everything I know.'

'Make it me! Make it me!' Katherine shrieked in her mind. 'I take it all on me! Leave her alone!'

Isambard couldn't hear her. He was deaf to such words.

And in that space of deafness, where only Katherine could hear her, Rose came.

Her voice was quiet, calm.

'It's over for me, Katherine. It was all over a long time ago. I'm not suffering any more. Don't cry. I'm here to help you. Seek the dark lady. Say the words with me, then seek the dark lady.'

Katherine felt Rose's warmth, right by her, whispering in her ear. She felt her lips unfreeze, felt she could begin to enunciate the words. Rose said them with her, one by one.

Katherine fixed Isambard with a steady gaze, staring straight into the haunted, boiling green of his eyes.

Libero . . .

In . . .

Tenebris . . .

Occulta . . .

She saw Isambard's mouth open. He screamed.

As the last syllable left her mouth, a thunderclap, deafening, shattering, exploded in the enclosed vault. Katherine flew through the air, landing on her back, winded, weeping.

Isambard was gone.

Katherine traced her steps back to the spiral stairs, a flickering, damaged torch she'd found in the bunker in one hand, focused purely on escape. She gave herself no time to think as she climbed. When she got to the top, she pushed . . . and found the door locked. She banged on the door, hollering. Nothing. She tried again, for five minutes. No answer. It was a good 50 yards back to the door in the parking garage, she remembered. No one would hear her. She tried to force the door, pounding against it, driving her shoulder into it. All the locks she'd picked had been put back on.

She put her head in her hands. She started to shake, then to cry. All her fear, her adrenalin, her anger, flowed out of her in shuddering sobs. She let it all go.

She'd survived. She'd completed her mission. She was alive. But she was trapped in the Paris catacombs, with no idea of how to get out.

Oldwick Fen

29 June 2007

When he came to, the first thing Robert saw was a stone wall covered with swastikas.

The biggest, painted in black on a grey background, scorched by fire and pocked with what looked like bullet holes, was the size of a dinner plate. Next to it was an array of iron wall anchors, some straight-armed like the Nazi symbol, some backwards, like a mirror image, others with rounded arms. Then there were urns and fragments of pottery, each with the fylfot design, backwards and forwards, some displayed on the wall, others on the ground, as though smashed. Finally there were delicate brooches of what looked like gold, or polished bronze, also in the swastika form.

And his wrists and ankles were bound.

He was underground, but a light was burning. Looking up, he couldn't see where he had fallen through. He could pick out a rounded arch, just, in the flickering light. It had to be an old oil lamp, or a kerosene lantern.

He twisted violently, grunting and shouting with anger, trying to loosen his bonds, kicking with his feet. They only got tighter. Stopping, suddenly soaked in sweat, he breathed hard, fighting a black wave of fear.

'The big one's from a downed German plane in the war,' a voice said from behind him. Robert screamed in surprise, starting away from whoever had spoken.

'Jack?'

'Then you have Thor fylfot wall anchors. The urns are

very old. Anglo-Saxon cremation urns. Maybe a thousand years old. The brooches too. They're all prosperity charms. Apart from the Nazi one. They were all used in the Fenland Workings. This is where they're kept.'

'What's going on, Jack? Untie me, for Christ's sake!'

'I lied to you, cousin Robert.'

'About what? Why?'

'Old Aunt Margaret. She didn't die of the curse she took on. She was murdered.'

'I said untie me! Have you gone mad?'

'She was killed. It was my fault. I was supposed to protect her. Two days ago. It's all happening as she said.'

'Who killed her?'

'She said, babbling as she would, that I'd know she was dead because a bird would come out of time to tell me. And one did.'

'Talk sense, Jack. And untie me!'

'It's all happening, now the time is coming round.'

'Who killed her? What happened?'

Robert lost patience, and twisted and kicked again, trying to propel himself back to hit Jack, do him harm somehow. 'What the fuck, Jack!' He made contact with nothing, falling on his side. Then he felt an iron bar on his neck. Jack was resting it at the base of Robert's skull.

'Steady now, Robert. One thing at a time. I'll untie you soon enough.'

Robert lay panting, afraid now of Jack, the heavy metal's weight underlining how fragile his skull's thin walls of bone were, how easily he could die. Just at the edge of his field of vision, he could see someone else was in the vaulted space, sitting in a chair. Breathing heavily, not moving. Hickey?

'Whoever killed her, she cut 'em up nicely, though.

367

Smashed a drinking glass and stabbed 'em good and proper. I saw the blood on the floor.'

Robert calmed himself, controlling his breathing. Jack had to be talked down, somehow, from the state he'd got himself into.

'Where was she?'

'After the wartime workings, she couldn't be in the sunlight. Her skin would erupt and bleed, her eyes would burn. She had to be in darkness in the day. She could only come out in the moonlight.'

'The old tack room. She lived there?'

'Under it. There's a chamber beneath it, and a tunnel that leads here.'

'Here? Where are we?'

'Under the abbey church. Here, let me sit you up.'

Jack hauled Robert by the shoulders till he was leaning against a stone column.

'The crypt?'

'The crypt is behind the wall you're looking at. This is more of a hiding place. They used to keep a lot of holy relics here. Monks all over England would even ride out and steal them from each other's abbeys. So and so's skull, so and so's thigh bone. So this would have been a secret treasury. A hidden strong room. It's cut down into the old holy mound, of course, which is why there was an abbey here in the first place. The high ground. Not many places hereabouts could have a cellar, with the water table being so high. But all the old estate's on higher ground.'

'What else did Margaret say, Jack? Whatever's going to happen, it's barely a day away. In London. It's something terrible. I have to stop it.'

'I know, cousin. I know. I've got to make amends. I've done bad things. I've hurt Hickey.'

'Is that who's behind me there in the chair? What did you do to him?'

'Never you mind, now.'

There was a note of panic in Jack's voice.

'The best way to make amends is to let me go. What did Margaret say?'

'She said difficult things, Robert. She told Hickey you'd be her successor, not me. Never told me that. She told me if she died before the 800th moon, and the great galster working died with her, someone'd come as a stranger, asking questions.'

'I'm not a stranger. I'm your bloody cousin.'

'Stranger to me, Robert. You've always been a stranger to me. A stranger'd come to settle accounts, she said. To see punishment and reward where they were due. And I can't be having that, not after what I've done.'

'What are you talking about? It wasn't your fault! She was murdered!'

'It was my job to look after her, cousin. I didn't do it right. And then . . . I took it out on Hickey.'

Hickey – Tom Hickathrift, by his full name – was as strong as an ox, for all his gentle nature. Robert found it hard to imagine Jack or anyone else overpowering him, or causing him harm.

'I blamed him, you see. He was supposed to guard her, in these special days, if I wasn't there. Tried to make him tell me everything he knew. Thought he'd killed her. He didn't know anything, of course. He's a harmless child, for all his years and size. I lost my temper with him. You know how Hickey is. He cried.'

'Is that all?'

Jack hesitated.

'That's all.'

Robert knew he was lying. He could feel Jack's desperation, and something more. Beyond Jack's fear of retribution, there was shame. There were things Jack could not bring himself to admit to Robert, or even perhaps to himself. Robert felt a great thirst, a great longing. Jack wanted forgiveness.

Robert had to get out, and he had to get Hickey out too. His cousin had lost his mind.

'So what are we doing here, Jack? What were those shouts I heard before I fell down the trap door? I'm guessing that's what happened.'

'I'd left it open, yes. You didn't know it was there, didn't see it in the dark and fell right down. It was convenient. I was going to get you later, at the cottage.'

'What were those shouts? *Ka!* I heard.'

'Margaret told me years ago how to try to renew the spell, if she died. To take one of these fylfots, and make it a talisman, as she and her forebears did in the war. Dedicate it to a specific task. *Ka* is the affirmation we use around here at the end of a galster, or a working. It means *let be it so*. Other traditions say: *so mote it be*. We start with *Karinder*, which means hearken, pay attention. End with *Ka*.'

'And then?'

'A descendant of Margaret's line needs to take it to Aldwych, to the holy well on the dragon line in London, and ring the Sanctus Bell while the moon is waxing. Before whatever is to happen, happens.'

'Who?'

'That's what we're going to find out. You, or me. We're the only living grown descendants. One goes to London. The other . . .'

'What?'

'It's a desperate situation, Robert. That's why I had to tie you up. With Margaret dead, and the hell that's coming, making amends and renewing the seal requires a great sacrifice. A willing death. You, or me. One of us has to die, to empower the working, and the other has to succeed Margaret, and take the curse onto himself.'

'I'm not going to die here!'

Robert twisted and bucked again, driving himself violently against where he thought Jack was sitting. He fell, again, into thin air.

'Getting yourself all worked up will help, actually,' Jack said, taking some leaves from a pouch and placing them in a bowl. Now Robert, panting on the stone floor, could see where the light was coming from. It was a modern camping stove, back in an alcove. Jack was boiling something in water.

'Like the old dances. The cunning men and wise women used to come back at dawn, sweating and exhausted from the moonlit ceremonies, they say. Trance dancing. It's one of the ways to contact the other world.'

Robert shouted at him, sarcasm in every syllable. 'You're going to make some poppy tea? Is that your solution?'

'Wise people don't ever use that,' Jack said. 'They know what damage it does. Makes the mind feeble, and the spirit, they say. The nameless art uses wormwood – I'll burn these leaves in a moment – sometimes together with a tea, or a witch broth, as they call it hereabouts. *By yarrow and rue, and my red cap too!* they say.'

'What?'

'We're going to consult the other world, Robert. To see which of us lives.'

Pforzheim, Germany

Late May 1944

Six months into her solitary confinement at Pforzheim prison in Germany, chained hand and foot, unable to feed or wash herself, Rose sat on the iron bed in her cell and fought tears.

Her baby was going to come early. She could feel it. Her belly before her was huge, her breasts swollen, the kicks were coming more vigorously. The life inside her was fighting to survive.

She was a *Nacht und Nebel* prisoner. Anything could be done to her. But what would they do to her child?

For months, with rare exceptions, her cell door had been opened only to admit the chief warden, bearing water and food – watery potato-peel soup, perhaps a little cabbage – or a female guard to change her clothes and dress her once a week.

In messages to fellow female inmates, scratched into mess tins, she had given her name as Belle Arden, describing herself as very unhappy, asking them if they could report news of her survival, if they got out alive, as she would of them. She had tried to raise their spirits, and when allowed out for a rare few minutes of exercise, would smile at them as they watched her through the bars of their cells.

On more than one occasion, she had heard her fellow prisoners beaten. The prison governor, an old man who took it upon himself to talk with her, even sometimes to share his food with her, had spared her such treatment because of her condition, and had ordered her chains loosened, until reprimanded by the local Gestapo. The terms of her detention were inflexible, he was told, pregnant or not.

He had promised her he would do his best for the baby.

She thought of her mother, her only consolation being that she knew SOE back in London would keep sending her postcards saying Rose was fine, as she'd requested, until they definitely knew she was dead. Her family had no idea where she was, only that she was serving with the British.

She thought of Horace. He would fight on, she knew, and to the bitter end. He had almost rescued her, he had tried and almost died trying.

She prayed to him to release her, to let her go.

Before departing on her mission, just over a year previously, Rose had been taken to a Mayfair restaurant by Vera Atkins, the formidable intelligence officer of F Section, who prepared agents before they went into the field.

She had given Rose the chance to withdraw from her upcoming mission if she wanted, with no blemish on her record. Rose had declined the offer, and even now, despite the pain and loss, she didn't regret her decision. She had been of service. She had fought tyranny. She had not killed.

Except . . . the Nazis had captured her radio. Could they use it? Might it be used to lure other agents to their deaths?

Despair was so close, yet she had found love. She would think of Horace, and her family, and be comforted.

If something could be imagined, her mother had told her once, when she was small, then she could be sure it existed, at some level, somewhere in the universe.

And so she imagined Horace with her, keeping her and her baby safe.

And then she imagined there was a world in which those who had handed her over to the Gestapo could be forgiven.

She prayed for her unknown betrayer. She prayed for the strange man who had arrested her, and soon, rapt in her imagination, she found him.

He was terribly afraid, a lost man, in a timeless place that could as well be 1944 as 1974 or 2004. His name was Peter. She tried to reach for him.

And in that same placeless time, she found her radio, and saw it was back in good hands.

The hands of a granddaughter . . .

Then her child would live, even if she didn't.

As she gave a smile of gratitude into the world, she felt her innards twist. Then her waters broke.

'Help me!' she screamed. 'Help me!'

~

The aged prison governor sat with Rose, holding her hand, in the prison infirmary, a look of torment on his face. She had been unconscious.

Panic suddenly tore through her.

'My baby?'

He held her hand, tightly.

'Your baby was premature, a tiny thing. But she is alive, and well.'

'Where is she? I want to see her!'

The governor looked up at the armed guards posted at the end of her bed. She saw the look in his eye.

'No! What . . . ?'

'I am sorry,' the old man said. 'I have done everything I can. But the child will be taken from you. Gestapo orders.'

'No!'

'I have argued with them. Pleaded to let my wife and me look after her until . . . until the war is over. We will keep her for you. They had wanted to give her to an SS family, but I was able to persuade them.'

She tried to sit upright, to stand and find her baby.

'No! No!'

She didn't have the strength even to move her legs.

'No!'

'I am so sorry. We will treat her as our own child until you return.'

Rose's insides pulsed with the violation, the ripping away, the theft of the child who was her own flesh, her own body. She tried to sit up again. Forced herself. Tears of rage and helplessness burst from her eyes. She couldn't move. She could only scream.

'No! No! No!'

~

Two days later, on Gestapo orders, Rose Arden was taken by train to the Nazi concentration camp at Dachau. The baby remained in Pforzheim.

London

29 June 2007

Walking his London route west from St Anne's, exhausted by the increasingly strong presence of Isambard twisting and raging in his mind, Peter ignored the sex shops and clip joints of Soho and turned into the comforting dullness of Lexington Street.

His gut was bleeding. It was the wound Horace had dealt him in 1944, reopened by Margaret's vicious attack with a broken glass. Activating the route again was killing him.

To die clean, was all he asked. To make amends. He'd have to mask his true intentions, he told himself, right to the end. He'd have to put up all the defences he could muster, feigning obedience to Isambard's wishes, hoping – praying – that at the very end, he'd be granted a chance to die well. A chance to make Rose proud, to be the kind of man she could have loved.

He came to the former site of St Thomas's Church, the next point on the great London line. The church itself was long gone.

He had to go on. There was no stopping now. It was almost midnight.

Rose was with him. He could feel her presence, calling him towards her, calling him towards the light, towards an almost impossible redemption, one he was entirely unfitted to accept.

Peter saw Horace in his mind's eye, lost in meditation, seeking him, matching his poison with counter-poison, preparing for their inevitable encounter. He saw Robert Reckliss and Katherine Rota, each in their own darkness, trying to gather from it the strength they would need if transmutation was to be achieved. His own transmutation.

The starting point for the Great Work, the sages said, the raw material with which one begins, was everywhere despised. Everyone can see it, yet almost no man values it. It was said to be vile, despicable, hateful. Yet it could be transmuted. Vile mud could be turned to gold.

It was himself. The vile raw material was himself, Peter Hale.

The pain from his wound was almost unbearable, yet still he walked. Over and over in his mind, he considered ending it, walking to the Thames and just drowning himself.

Yet he knew, at the level of belief that was simply certainty, that even death would be no escape. Not for him. His mother had taught him, very clearly, that there was no escaping the consequences of his actions. Dying now would only return him to unending torment at the hands of the discarnate Enemy, the IWNW, the force that worked through Isambard, that fed on human suffering in this world and the next. He'd been created to be fodder for it.

But the following day, he'd complete the defection. He'd pull off, if he could, a miraculous escape. His death would serve for something, as his life had not. This was the secret story he told himself.

And he would serve as a source of new life for his father. He would serve Isambard at Aldwych, as commanded. He believed both things. He had to, to shield his true intentions.

The rest of the route lay before him, the London component of the swastika. It ran right through Sotheby's. There was a new rear door on St George's Street, an entrance that hadn't been there in 1936 when he'd attended the Newton auction, when he'd left via the front door on New

Bond Street, tailing the man from Francis Edwards who'd had so little time left to live.

At the rear entrance of Sotheby's, Peter saw Horace standing in the doorway. Waiting for him.

'I'm here to bring you in, Pierre.'

'Not quite as simple as that.'

He couldn't be seen to offer any hope to Horace. Isambard would know immediately.

'You still can come in. Walk away from it before it's too late.'

'*I . . . tried!*' Peter roared with anger now. 'I tried to escape. And you threw me back to serve the Enemy. You could have brought me across, made me whole . . . and you condemned me to this . . . *half-life* . . . for another sixty-three years!'

Horace stepped forward out of the doorway and grabbed Peter, almost gently, by the lapels of his coat.

'I didn't make you evil, you did that to yourself, you and your father,' Horace whispered. 'I wasn't strong enough to bring you over, then. All I could do was keep the spark alive. I condemned you to a lifetime of desiring the light, of not wanting to serve your masters. It was deserved punishment.'

'I have never been free of Isambard since you threw me back,' Peter screamed, anguish cracking his voice, twisting from Horace's grip. 'He has always come to me, all the time. Sometimes alone, sometimes with his henchmen. Sometimes I see him in the street, then I look again, and it's no one, just a regular person. He is in my dreams. He owns my soul. He has never let me go. He never will.'

Horace looked at the well-dressed old man, blood seeping through his cotton shirt. He saw a twisted, suffering version of himself.

'There's a chance now.'

'Listen. I have done the dirty work for three governments, I have lied and killed, tortured and corrupted, in defence of dictatorship, then in defence of democracy. In defence of slavery, then in defence of freedom. I have corrupted myself to the last hair on my head, till I lost my strength and finally got put out to grass. It's too late for me, Hencott. I'm my father's creature. For ever.'

This was almost Peter's last chance to transmute the vile, corrosive thing he had become into . . . something else. Yet he couldn't breathe a word of his desire.

'If you won't come quietly, I'm going to have to take you.'

'Good luck trying.'

'Tomorrow.'

And Horace walked away into the night.

Peter leaned against a lamppost, in agony.

Sotheby's was closed, so instead of walking through the auction house, he limped round the block. From Sotheby's he made his way to Grosvenor Street and walked all the way to Grosvenor Square, then headed north, past church steeples left and right, to the white and gold beacon of St Marylebone Parish Church, its domed, cylindrical steeple always in view, its gilded angels calling to him.

Lucem in tenebris occulto . . .

There, he projected the line further northwest, along York Gate into Regent's Park, and off into Primrose Hill.

He paused, meditated, connected with the spiritual force, for good or ill, he had deposited at this place, as at all others, then turned and retraced his steps, all the way back down to Grosvenor Street, and so off again, west to east, walking all night, past the Gherkin to Aldgate and south, along Minories to the Tower of London, the holy white hill of

Celtic Britain, *Bryn Gwyn*, the other end of his London swastika route, where many years earlier, babbling nonsense that concealed unheard grains of truth about the *geheime Feuer*, the mentally fragile Rudolf Hess had been held, as the Tower of London's very last prisoner.

Portsmouth

June 1944

In the last hours of a waxing moon, early on 6 June 1944 – the moon would reach fullness that evening, at 18:58 GMT – thousands of seafaring vessels of every kind set out from bases all along southern England, in the greatest seaborne invasion in history, a military operation that Winston Churchill called 'the most complicated and most difficult that has ever taken place'.

As the vanguard of an invasion army of 3.5 million men, some 160,000 troops were to cross the Channel that day, aiming for five Normandy beaches between Le Havre and Cherbourg.

Airborne troops were to go in first, some dropping behind enemy lines from 1,000 transport planes, others landing in flimsy gliders. Then the bombers were to go. A total of 12,000 aircraft were to take part in the invasion, dropping 10,000 tons of bombs on the German defences.

Massed in England for the invasion were almost 140,000 jeeps, trucks and half-tracks, some 4,000 tanks and tracked vehicles, 3,500 artillery pieces ... At dawn off Normandy, the ships would fill the horizon – the biggest fleet ever assembled. There would be nine battleships, twenty-three cruisers and 104 destroyers protecting landing craft and troop transports, mine sweepers and merchant vessels – some 5,000 ships in all.

The day before, sitting alone for a few minutes after briefing journalists on the upcoming operation, General Dwight D Eisenhower had taken a pencil and scribbled a short note on a pad of paper. It was a draft communiqué, to be issued only in the event of catastrophe.

The full text said: *Our landings in the Cherbourg–Havre area have failed to gain a satisfactory foothold and I have withdrawn the troops. My decision to attack at this time and place was based upon the best information available. The troops, the air and the Navy did all that bravery and devotion to duty could do. If any blame or fault attaches to the attempt it is mine alone.*

In what was perhaps a sign of the immense mental strain he was under, just hours after giving the final order for the D-Day landings to go ahead – 24 hours later than planned, because of dreadful weather in the English Channel – Eisenhower dated the note, in error, *July 5.*

When he had finished, he put the scrap of paper away in his wallet.

The invasion of Normandy would prove itself to be the only successful opposed crossing of the English Channel in nine centuries. But it was a close-run thing, and a huge gamble.

When Eisenhower made his decision to go ahead with the invasion, unforeseen freezing rain was pouring down outside his headquarters at Southwick House, near Portsmouth. Gale force winds were threatening to blow in the windows. Fine weather had deteriorated rapidly in early June, and now strong south-westerly winds were blowing through the English Channel, churning up violently stormy seas. Cloud conditions made bombing impossible. But as Eisenhower listened to Group Captain James Stagg of the RAF and the Met Office – a softly spoken Scot, the coordinator of British and US forecasters – on the evening of Sunday 4 June, Stagg was able to give him tentatively good news.

A British Navy ship off the south coast of Iceland, stationed there for the specific purpose of monitoring the weather in an area that greatly influenced the meteorological conditions around the British Isles, had reported something new: sustained, rising pressure.

Stagg told Eisenhower that this suggested a ridge of high pressure might follow the cold front now roiling the Channel, opening a window of fair weather for just long enough to allow the invasion to go ahead in the early hours of 6 June. Other forecasters disagreed, but Stagg stuck to his guns.

On the wall was a huge map of the French coastline, made especially for the D-Day operation by the English toy manufacturer Chad Valley. The workmen who'd installed the key panels showing the invasion beaches were being held under tight security, their knowledge too valuable to allow them to leave.

It was a momentous decision. Eisenhower polled his commanders one by one. Then, rain and gale-force winds still battering the window panes, he made up his mind. Eisenhower reaffirmed his decision in the early hours of the following morning, 5 June: 'OK. We'll go.'

The weather was everything. Had they not sailed on 6 June, the next ostensibly favourable tides would have been almost two weeks later, under a dark sky, on 17 June – and they would have run into the worst weather to hit the English Channel in twenty years.

~

Some 150 miles north of Portsmouth, in the Fenland community of Oldwick, a group of thirteen local people, led by a woman called Margaret, were meeting in the light of the waxing moon, encouraged by certain secret sections of the

British government, which took the view that no aspect of the national talents should be left untapped in the effort to defeat Nazism. In their dance and in their galster-work, the Fenland witches focused their minds, too, on the weather off Iceland and in the English Channel, as they had done in 1940, and as their forebears had done in bygone centuries to thwart Napoleon and the Spanish Armada.

Paris

June 1944

Isambard came to Horace and Peter in their dreams, infiltrating their safe house, looking to bargain. Steeplejack now possessed the full secret of the *geheime Feuer*, and Isambard wanted it. The Enemy needed it.

Peter was under arrest, his status yet undetermined. Horace and Harry had been unable to leave Paris, barely able to communicate with London by radio except to say, via an agreed password, that Fulcanelli had been identified and both parts of the Secret Fire documents won for the Allies. The contents of the documents themselves were far too secret to be broadcast by radio, even if heavily encrypted.

But the full-moon slot they had been counting on for their Lysander back to England was not available, and they both guessed why: it had been reserved for the long-awaited Allied landings in France. Now it was upon them. While open rebellion had not yet broken out in Paris, it could only be a matter of time, if the Allies could break out of their beachheads. Harry and Horace were helping the *résistance* to prepare, Joliot-Curie among their principal contacts.

The London half of the Newton paper, stolen by Peter in 1936, was more than familiar to Isambard. He had studied it for eight years. It described the materials required for the manufacture of the Secret Fire. It contained some phrases in Latin, in Arabic. It spoke of vitreous metals, or metallic glass, of certain kinds of gold ore, of the need for certain arrays of focusing lenses. It spoke of the need for certain states of mind in the maker of the fire, and of certain astronomical requirements. But it didn't say what to do with the materials, how to prepare and assemble them. Those key details were contained in the other half, the Paris half. That was what he wanted.

The SS division of the Nazi war machine, Isambard's own Section Four, had stockpiled the materials. The assembly was said to be a matter only of days. Now that the Allied invasion had begun, it was the only way to reverse the tide of the war.

Isambard came simultaneously to them both.

For Horace, it was in the form of a dreamed face-to-face meeting, on the windswept parvis of Notre Dame cathedral.

'Speak,' Horace said.

'You have a secret, Mr Hencott.'

'Many, no doubt. Too many, perhaps.'

'You did not trust even your own colleagues with it. You could not.'

'You are not without secrets yourself.'

The two men stared with hostility into each other's eyes, standing at the zero marker on the cathedral forecourt. It was the centre of the world.

'You have a son,' Horace said. 'He wishes to be free of you. I have been observing him. You are losing him.'

Isambard replied: 'You have a lover.'

'Your son, despite everything, is precious to you.'

'Necessary. He is necessary. Whereas your lover is dispensable.'

'No. I want her back.'

'More than anything?'

Horace was silent for a moment. Eventually he said: 'I have your son.'

Isambard sneered.

'A trade? You would be getting too much for too little.'

'How so? Do you not need him?'

'I own him. I already have him. He will return to my side when I wish it badly enough.'

'You can't be sure.'

'Your position is weak, Hencott. Your lover was pregnant. She has given birth to a daughter.'

'You are lying.'

Yet Horace, deep in his dream, deep in his soul, knew that it was true. Every day, all day, he had tried to reach Rose, to send her hope, to give her protection. And he had felt a new life within her, so far away, beyond his capacity to shield. For months, now, he had barely slept, unable to bear the nightmares.

'You know I am not lying,' Isambard said. 'And so we negotiate.'

I won't be traded. I'll never be a hostage. Promise me . . .

'What is there to negotiate?'

'You can choose who lives. Rose, or the little girl. Or I can have them both killed. You decide.'

'If either of them comes to harm, I will make it my life's work to hunt you down and kill you.'

'If they both die, what life will you have worth dedicating to anything?'

'What do you want? I can offer your son. I can free him.'

'No. You get Rose only in return for the Paris document. The Secret Fire paper that Fulcanelli held. I know you have it.'

'Rose, in return for the Secret Fire?' Horace stared into the dead green eyes. With every strand of his being, he wanted to accept. He looked up at the stars in the crystal-clear night,

387

unobscured by city lights because of the blackout. But it was impossible. He would never be able to forgive himself. Rose had forbidden it. But their daughter? What rights did she have? He looked deep within himself, sought strength. He had to refuse. The weapon was too powerful. It took every last jot of his willpower to speak.

'No.'

Isambard smiled.

'You are cold. How cold it is, to have a conscience.'

'I have nothing to offer but your son and myself. I propose something different. My daughter lives, in exchange for me. To do with me as you choose, I imagine execution. Your son returns to you, in exchange for Rose.'

'You are offering yourself?' For a moment, Isambard looked disconcerted. Then he spat his disdain. 'Anyone who makes such an offer does not deserve to live,' he sneered. 'If you don't offer me the *geheime Feuer*, Hencott, I will find it another way. You have lost your woman. Rose is not negotiable. I have her. I keep her.'

'You will kill her anyway. She was already lost.'

Yet Horace's father had told him that, in certain circumstances, even the Enemy, even IWNW could be held to a bargain. The devil kept his word.

'I will honour a pact made with sincerity,' Isambard said.

Now the words rushed out of Horace's mouth before he could allow himself time to think about them, about the renunciation, about the deal with the devil, that they contained.

'Myself for my daughter. But I cross at a time of my choosing.'

Isambard smiled.

'Let's see. The sooner you hand yourself over, the quicker

388

you die. Wait a year, take a year to die. Wait a day, die in a day. A decade . . .'

'My choice.'

'I find this . . . appealing.'

'But I would add one condition.'

'What?'

Horace raised his head. He sought Rose, seeking her forgiveness, even though she had prohibited him from negotiating with her life.

'I want not only my daughter, but her descent, if she have any.'

'Your daughter to live, and her children to live too. In return for you.'

'I cross at a time of my choosing. And finally, the Gestapo cease all reprisal executions in Paris. Free the hostages.'

'You prize yourself highly.'

'I know my worth.'

Isambard looked at Horace with renewed disdain. He paused, weighing the deal. Weighing his prizes.

'You are a sentimentalist. But you have value. And I think you are unlikely to cross soon. The longer you delay, the greater your suffering. The deal is struck. None to speak of this.'

'None to speak of it. It's done.'

Isambard came to Peter at the same time, in the same way, meeting with him in a dream set in a cell at Dachau. He showed Peter the savage beating of Rose that was to come. For Peter, it was a present experience, before his eyes, unending. Boots kicking. Fists and truncheons pounding.

'Stop it!' Peter screamed.

'I will. If you trade. Her torment will end, in return for the *geheime Feuer*.'

'Just stop!'

'Trade.'

'I don't have access to the Secret Fire,' Peter whispered, distraught. 'They are holding me under arrest. They know I'm your son.'

'You have offered to defect to them. You desire to do so.'

'No.'

Isambard poured on the images, the sounds and physical impact of the beating of Rose. Peter cracked.

'Stop it, please! Don't let them hurt her any more!'

'Trade.'

'How can I get it?'

Isambard relented.

'Rose will always be alive to you,' he said. 'That I promise. Now where is the *geheime Feuer* document I need? Why can't I even see it when I look for it? I can't even see where you are.'

'It never leaves Hencott's side. He carries it with him everywhere, in a leather wallet. He exerts great power around himself, I can't see past it either. That's why you can't see where I am. Even I don't know where I am. I was brought here blindfolded, after being driven around the city for three hours hidden in the back of a delivery truck.'

'Then I simply need you to touch the paper. I can do everything from there, as long as you cooperate. Touch it, and get yourself thrown out of that safe house. Get yourself taken to another location, away from Hencott.'

The following day, Peter asked for a meeting with Horace, who came down to the converted cellar where Peter was being held. They sat on either side of a plain wooden table, two armed guards outside the door.

'What do you want, Peter?'

'I want to know what you intend to do with me.'

'To keep you on ice.'

'For how long?'

'Until I can decide what to do with you. What you are. Or perhaps, until *you* decide what you are.'

Peter tried hard not to appear to be looking at how Horace was dressed. Yet he noticed the leather wallet under his jacket and shirt, held by a thong around his neck. Could he make a dive for it? At what cost?

'I got you the first half of the document. I told you it was coming to Paris. I made the arrangements for Harry to join Joliot-Curie's team so he could steal it. You owe me.'

'You arrested Rose.'

'To protect her.'

'You took her to the Gestapo. You could have freed her.'

'I needed to protect her.'

'By taking her to Avenue Foch? Witness the result. You failed to rescue her.'

'So did you.'

'You didn't let her out of the van.'

'I tried my best. You didn't kill the driver.'

'You bear your father's infection. You can never be clean, never free of him.'

'Not true. I want to cross. I want to defect.'

'That is what I am considering. Whether your value to us, to the Light, given your gifts, is worth the risk and effort of trying to bring you across. I doubt I have the strength, I doubt anyone does, to rid you of your father's influence. And your arrest of Rose doesn't entitle you to any help. On the contrary, it entitles you only to punishment.'

Yet Horace had come to understand, deep within, that

finding a way to save Peter – to transmute him – was his own Great Work. This was his task, now and for the rest of his life. To find a way, and a time.

'You gave up on her too easily,' Peter said. 'Who exactly deserves punishment, Horace?'

Suddenly Peter launched himself over the table, fists flying. Taken by surprise, Horace fell to the floor, rolling from his chair, as the guards burst in. Peter leapt on top of him, ripping at his shirt, grabbing the wallet containing the Secret Fire paper.

Rifle butts slammed into Peter's ribs, and he flew across the room, howling. Yet he had touched it, he had managed to touch the paper: for a few precious seconds while punching Horace with one hand, he had managed with the other to touch the paper containing the secret of the *geheime Feuer*, and he could say to Rose, and to his father, that he had tried his best to ease her torment, or even to save her life.

Isambard concentrated, deep into meditation, focusing all his attention onto his son, his creature, who would soon deliver him the world.

He felt the boy moving, appearing somewhere in eastern Paris as he emerged from the mental barriers erected by Horace. He felt Peter's distress, and saw him bound and gagged, ribs broken, as they transported him to another safe house.

Isambard brought his attention to a burning point of focus, like light through a magnifying glass, and scoured his son's sense memory, the sensations he'd received upon touching the document.

And slowly, gently, he began to see the words on the document, under the moving pen of their author, as they were written nearly 300 years earlier. Isambard connected to the psychic content of the document itself, to the echoes and harmonies trapped within it, and painstakingly, letter by letter, he read the secret of the *geheime Feuer*.

Morbecque

25 June 1944

Harry scanned the launch site with his binoculars. Despite all the Allied bombing, despite all his efforts and those of his *résistance* colleagues, the Huit-Bois site was still operational, and now heavily defended.

The Germans had barely used it, and it made no sense to Harry, unless it was being preserved for a special mission of some kind.

All along the Nord and the Pas de Calais, the *Flakregiment* 155 of *Luftwaffe Oberst* Max Wachtel, the man in charge of launching the robot bombs at London, had been setting up new, more easily disguised launch sites, using mobile components, taking over farm buildings, reducing the permanent fixtures to a minimum.

Luftwaffe men at the site had been informed with great pride, Farmer's spies had told them, that Berlin was calling the weapon *Vergeltungswaffe Eins* – Vengeance Weapon One, or V-1 – and that, alongside other secret weapons soon to be deployed, it was going to win the war for the Nazis, regardless of the Normandy landings.

Suddenly Harry's traversing scan of the site froze.

Then a feeling of utter dread filled his stomach.

A convoy of vehicles had arrived at the site a few minutes earlier. Disguised as regular lorries, they had sparked a flurry of activity around the camouflaged hangar where newly delivered bombs were received.

And then he had seen him. Isambard.

He was there, in plain clothes. Harry had no doubt it was

him. It had been only a glimpse, but the angle of the head, the shock of white hair, the demeanour . . .

Isambard, within miles of the Allied advance, at a robot bomb launch site clearly being held back for a special purpose.

Surely not . . .

Later that night, a spy was able to report to Harry what he had seen inside the hangar.

It was a regular flying bomb, except for one modification: it had a cockpit for a pilot. And rumours on the site had spread like wildfire: a special weapon was going to be placed on board this flying bomb. The pilot had brought it himself.

There'd been a leak.

Harry knew it, with utter clarity.

Isambard had obtained the Secret Fire.

Which meant it had been stolen from them in Paris.

Which meant there was a traitor in their midst.

And Harry knew who it had to be. Since he'd learned that Peter was Isambard's son, he'd feared the worst. Now he knew.

He had no radio contact with London. He had one remaining homing pigeon. Harry sent it with an urgent message to his superiors in England, pleading for blanket bombing of the site.

Then he went to see his local *résistance* contact, cold with anger.

'I have to get to Paris. Immediately.'

'It's too dangerous. The roads are impassable. In God's name, *cher ami*! We've blown up half the railways ourselves!'

'Forget all of that. Find me a way.'

Day Zero

Oldwick Fen

Robert lost all sense of time. The smoke from the worm-wood filled the air in the secret room beneath the church with a living mist, and he began to see shapes moving behind it, as though in a shadow play. The mist was imbued with geometric forms, zigzags and triangles and kaleidoscopic shapes folding into one another in a rhythm that seemed to match the flow of his blood, the race of his pulse.

Jack sat beside him, bowls of tea empty between them, breathing deeply.

Then the mist cleared, and Robert was back in the copse.

A young woman, flame-haired, golden-eyed, stood in the centre, surrounded by a circle of twelve people in dark, simple robes, their heads uncovered, each standing stock-still. In one hand she held a stick, forked at the top, as high as her shoulder. She wore a dazzling white shift, and at her waist a knotted cord, wrapped several times about her.

All of Robert's perceptions were piercingly acute. The smell of the grass, of the dry earth, made his head spin. The pre-dawn silence lay on his skin like dew. He looked at the young woman, recognizing her as Margaret. He knew with intense certainty that she was naked beneath her robe.

Robert and Jack were kneeling on the grass inside the circle, to Margaret's left. Behind her several items stood on a low table: water jugs, bowls, a thick yellow candle. The stone wall Robert had been leaning on – the whole cellar beneath the church – was gone. His hands were no longer bound, yet he was not free to move. The best he could do was move his head to look around at the circled figures, six men and six women, and up at the fading stars. It was almost daylight. A fat crescent moon hung in the sky, bathing the copse and all those in it in a diffuse twilight.

The young woman, intensity illuminating her face, looked directly up at the heavens. Then she raised her horned stick and rammed it with all her might into the ground. Stepping back from it, keeping just her fingertips in contact with the shaft, she confirmed that it would stand by itself. Then she leaned forward and placed her forehead against the fork at the top, closing her eyes.

For a minute, perhaps two, no one moved. All was silence. Then Margaret opened her eyes. Unwinding the cord from her waist, her lips whispering quietly to herself, she tied one end of it to the standing rod at chest height. Then she settled her eyes on one of the older men in the circle, took six or seven paces towards him and, her eyes never leaving his, handed him the end of the cord. He lowered his head in respect, and she stepped back one pace.

'*Karinder!*' she shouted, raising her hands above her head. 'Let the compass be marked deosil for this working. *Ka!*'

At her word, the twelve figures began to walk a clockwise circle, *deosil* as Margaret had called it, pausing after each step, guided by the man holding Margaret's cord. They walked with solemnity and grace, each with a hand on the shoulder of the person in front, intensely focused on each step. Three times they circled, and as the cord approached Margaret's position, she curtseyed elegantly beneath it each time, letting it pass over her head. As they turned, she sang, in a chant taken up by the walkers:

From the Watchtowers, four in all
As the compass edge is paced
Are the ancient powers now called
Are the wardings strongly placed
Round about and bound around
Spirits of the elements four
Powers I call from hill and mound
From rock and forest, beach and moor
Guard this compass as we tread
Make the serpent power race
Sisters as you spin your thread
Hallow all within this place

When the third turn was completed, each taken slightly faster than the previous one, the man handed the cord back to Margaret. She walked to the forked stick in the centre of the circle, gathering her cord as she went, and after untying it from the staff, wrapped it in several turns again about her waist.

Then Margaret uprooted the stick and carried it to the place where she had been standing during the marking of the compass. She drove it firmly again into the ground, shouting *Ka!,* her hair flying with the effort.

Taking a pace back from the stave, she gathered herself, and spoke.

'In the name of the sky father, and the earth mother, the darkness and the brightness, power and wisdom of the all holy . . .'

Then she took what appeared to be a small stone from a hidden pocket in her gown, kneeled and placed it the foot of the stave.

'North,' she said. 'White spirits arise! Ye powers of the rich earth be with us.'

Now three other members of the circle stepped forward, each walking to the centre of the circle to retrieve an item from the low table. Then each walked back, facing outwards and kneeling at the remaining cardinal points. One placed a wooden bowl of water on the ground, saying: 'West. Green spirits arise! Ye powers of the misty waters, be with us.' One placed a lit candle, saying: 'South. Red spirits arise! Ye powers of burning fire, be with us.' The last set fire to a fistful of herbs on the ground, saying: 'East. Black spirits arise! Ye powers of the midnight winds, be with us.'

When they had finished and rejoined the circle, Margaret returned to the centre and poured water into a bowl, then walked about the sacred space, flicking drops onto the ground with her fingers, singing words that Robert could barely catch ... *this banishing song*, she sang. *This cleansing galster* ... When all the water was gone, she returned once again to the centre, and set fire to some sticks of herbal incense.

'May this place be hallowed,' she shouted. 'Welcomed be, who wish us well, banished be, who do not. *Ka!*'

The air was thick, crackling with energy. Robert could feel the hairs on the back of his neck stand up, as though he were caught in a powerful magnetic field.

Now Margaret spoke to the members of the ring around them.

'I have seen a great danger in the coming hours,' he heard her say, her voice fading in and out as though he were hearing her words borne on the wind from a far more distant place. 'So we meet unexpectedly, out of our regular time, at my call. Such a working as we'll make tonight is permitted only in times of great danger. The moon is still six days from full, and we are working with the night almost gone. We will work into the day.'

From the table she took a short wooden staff, perhaps the length of her forearm, and marked a shape into the grass beneath her bare feet. Robert saw a straight line, a curve atop it, a small eye at one end.

'*Karinder!* Oldwick be Aldwych. London be Fen. Time and place elide. As we enhazel this field, so we enhazel our old settlement at the sacred well in London, we enharden and protect each place, the one for the other. We protect it in this time and in no time, for as long as the art flows through me. We call on the power of the Sanctus Bell, buried in sand in the bombed ruins of St Clement Danes. For an evil one comes to despoil our land, who would render it gast, barren, polluted. I, Dolly Redcap, will sing this galster, I, Margaret, will affirm this. We all shall say, as one: he shall fail. *Ka!*'

She looked up, and her gaze fell on the two kneeling men, Robert and Jack. For a minute, she was silent, her golden eyes holding them both in her hypnotic regard.

'We'll settle this matter before proceeding,' she whispered.

She walked over to them. As she did so, she seemed to become almost transparent to Robert's eyes, hovering between different forms. At one moment, he saw her as a luminous bird of great beauty. Yet she was still a woman, standing before him, her shining eyes transfixing him, then shifting to Jack, who jerked under her gaze as though stabbed through the heart.

'We do not kill, in the nameless art,' she said. 'But we do sacrifice ourselves, by which we mean we do *make ourselves sacred*, when the greater good requires it, as it does now. The fate of the land, perhaps of the world, hangs in the balance. This hatred will fall from the sky, and it cannot be stopped. But its pollution may be contained, its spread halted . . . at a cost.'

Robert felt his heart pound, the wounds on his chest swelling and tearing.

'One of you must ring the Sanctus Bell at Aldwych,' she said. 'The other must lay down his life, willingly, to allow this working to live.'

Sadness filled her shining eyes as she stepped forward and placed a hand on each of their heads.

'Between us, we will defeat the Lantern Men, and drive them back into the darkness for three generations.' She lowered her hands. 'Jack, are you worthy to ring the bell?'

Jack tried to meet her eyes, but couldn't. He threw himself at her feet.

'Forgive me, Margaret. Forgive me! I was afraid,' he shrieked. 'I wanted your power, but I would have cheated you. I would have cheated everyone.'

She knelt and rubbed his hair with sadness.

'You protected me for years, and Hickey too. Then you sought to betray me. What else have you done, Jack?'

'I hurt Hickey. I hurt poor Hickey. I can't ring the bell. Let me die for you! I'm so sorry!'

'We reap as we sow, Jack Reckliss.'

Margaret turned to Robert.

'And you, Robert? My question is, for whom would you die?'

Robert saw, again, the ceremony he had first seen in his nightmare, the one that he knew was now about to begin. He saw the great black dog savaging Margaret, the red-haired beauty before him. Black Shuck, the hellhound, tearing her apart. An ocean of vileness spreading across the world, until she stopped it. He saw that she was asking nothing she was not prepared to do herself.

'For you,' he whispered. 'For you, Margaret.'

She stood up and reared before them both, her eyes closed, head raised towards the sky.

Then Margaret spoke, her face radiant.

'The Sanctus Bell, since its casting over three centuries ago, has been known as Robertus,' she said. 'Robert, you must ring it. You are my successor.'

'I accept,' he whispered. '*Ka!*'

Margaret nodded once.

'Jack, the world will visit upon you what you have sown. There, you may fight it, but here, between worlds, you have accepted to die for this working, and I forgive you.'

The scene before Robert's eyes rippled and tore, and he found himself back in the hidden chamber under the church, his head swimming.

Hickey and Jack were fighting, slamming each other from wall to wall, knocking fylfot artefacts to the floor and careering into the furniture just feet away from him.

Jack tried to scream, his hands flailing, his arms reaching out to Robert. Yet he couldn't speak. Robert saw a multi-coloured cord around his throat, and saw that Hickey was slowly strangling him.

'You were bad to Great Aunt Margaret,' Hickey shouted. 'You were going to betray her. And you hurt me, Jack. You blamed me and you hurt me.'

Jack's eyes bulged, his face turning purple, his tongue protruding from his mouth. Robert couldn't move, still bound, still transfixed by the vision of Margaret.

'He hurt me, cousin Robert,' Hickey shouted. 'He tried to make me say I killed Old Aunt Margaret.'

Jack gave a long, drawn-out rattle, his eyes misting over, legs dancing, as Hickey drew the cord even tighter with his massive forearms. Then Jack stopped moving, and Hickey let him drop to the ground.

He turned about, looking for something. Then Hickey grabbed a thick wooden staff and raised it over his head.

'Hickey! That's enough!' Robert shouted.

But Hickey brought the staff down violently on Jack's head. His skull cracked audibly. Hickey brought it down again, and this time the sound was just mush.

Hickey stomped over to Robert and rolled up the sleeve of his shirt. 'Jack heated up the wall irons, see?' There were burn marks, brand marks, on Hickey's arm. In the form of a fylfot. 'He thought I'd killed Aunt Margaret! Tried to make me say I'd done it.'

'It's OK, Hickey.'

'I wouldn't do that. I looked after her. Poor sad old Aunt Margaret, who was soft in the head, after the war.'

'You did well, Hickey.'

'Man came and killed her. Do you know who he is, cousin Robert?'

'I do, Hickey. I'm going to take care of him now.'

'Before he came, she told me to hide her stick. I think she knew he was coming.'

'Did you keep it somewhere safe, Hickey?'

'It's this one,' Hickey said. 'The one I just beat Jack's head in with. It's special. Look.'

Hickey unscrewed the heavy, bulbous top of the staff. It was glistening with blood and brain matter. Inside was nestled a fragment of the dark Saxon funeral pottery strewn around them in the secret room. It was a reverse swastika.

Robert saw what he had to do. Margaret was dead, and the 800th moon was upon them. But he could stop it still.

'Let me have this, Hickey,' he said, closing his fist on the fragment of pottery. 'I need to take it to London.'

Paris

30 June 1944

It took Harry five days to reach Paris, handed off from one *maquis* group to another. He had a radio operator attached to one of the networks send a repeat of his bombing request to London on the second day of his journey.

It felt like he'd walked the whole way. As soon as he reached the capital, he called an urgent meeting with Horace. They met again below the Temple at 20, Rue Jacob, surrounded by a discreet but heavily armed *résistance* security detail.

He did not beat around the bush.

'Isambard has the Secret Fire. He is at Morbecque, getting ready to fly it into London. The Allied land forces may not get to the launch site in time. They should have bombed it by now, but there's no guarantee they'll get him.'

'Can Farmer attack the site?'

'It's very heavily guarded now. Isambard and the weapon, even more so. I did ask Farmer to attack it, but it would take a hundred men to make the least impression. They'll try with what they have, but they don't have enough forces. I don't know what else to do to stop the launch. But I do know what to do about how he got the Secret Fire. It must have come from us. There's a leak in this group. A traitor in Steeplejack.'

'Get Peter,' Horace said to the guards. And after a moment he added: 'And please bring Professor Joliot-Curie.'

Morbecque

30 June 1944

The cockpit looked ridiculously small, but somehow the tall, gaunt figure was going to try to fold himself into it. He strode about the base of the launch ramp, patient yet demanding, with a tight focus about his movements, a centred discipline. He wore an aviator's leather jacket, goggles, a Luftwaffe flying suit.

Albert, Farmer's English radio operator, knew the figure was the man they had been told to watch out for by Harry months earlier. The man's demeanour made Albert, for no reason he could fathom, think of a contemplative monk. The contrast with the preparations for mechanized death Albert saw before him almost made him laugh.

Technicians scurried around the base of the mobile launch ramp, loading the highly explosive fuel that drove the steam catapult, connecting cables, checking connections.

Albert knew the launch procedures well. Since his release from weeks of Gestapo interrogation a few days earlier – his cover intact, and with apologies for mistaking him for an English parachutist, no less – he had worked with the local resistors of the French Interior Forces to sabotage the German war effort in any way they could. A week after the Normandy landings, the Germans had started launching their robot bombs at London, and Albert's men had thrown everything they had into thwarting them – sneaking into V-1 sites to twist flaps out of shape, pollute the fuel tanks with sand, pour acid onto delicate connections.

For this latest launch, the technicians had already attached the wooden wings and checked that the bomb's fuel tank was full. Another crew had made sure the frame of the 150-foot mobile launching ramp was correctly assembled, pointing directly at London.

The device's gyrocompass had been set, though in this case – Albert shook his head at the insanity of it – the man intending to pilot the flying bomb would presumably use the cockpit controls to aim it more precisely once he was over the target, or even override the autopilot completely. Albert had never seen a cockpit on such a device before. How could he possibly hope to survive? Even if the pilot tried to bail out, it looked like he'd be sucked into the engine directly behind him.

Luftwaffe men were grouping around the command trailer, ready to enter when the signal to prepare to launch was given. Among them, unusually, were men wearing the black uniform of the SS.

There had been another departure from standard procedure: the pilot himself had taken great care, amid a display of extraordinary security, to install something in a compartment just behind the nose of the device, where the high-explosive warhead was usually housed. Only SS men had been allowed near him as he had done so.

Now, using a ladder, the pilot climbed up to the flying bomb on its launch ramp and crammed himself into the tiny cockpit.

Below him, ground crew attached the launch ramp's steam piston to the underside of the fuselage. The pilot gave a signal and a technician lowered the hinged canopy to enclose him in the cockpit.

The launch detail entered the command trailer. Somewhere inside, at a command from the firing officer, a lever was pulled, and a blast of flame issued from the stovepipe mounted above and behind the pilot: the engine ignited, triggering its unholy guttural roar.

After a few seconds, at a second command from the firing officer, the steam piston was released, propelling the flying bomb forward along the metal ramp at 200 miles per hour. Then it took to the skies, climbing to 2,000 feet along a straight line that would carry it all the way to its target, just twenty-five minutes away.

Paris

30 June 1944

Harry led them deep into the catacombs, followed by Peter, with Horace pressing a gun to his back, then Joliot-Curie, heading towards the former hiding place of the Secret Fire document. Along the way were side galleries, deep and remote, with shafts where a body could lie for decades and not be found.

When they were nearing the site of the Dark Lady vault, Horace called a halt.

Peter stood before them, his face white.

'Whatever you say, Horace, think about this,' Peter whispered. 'I can say I acted out of love. Do you know what that means?'

Harry, ice in his eyes, grabbed Peter's face by the chin before Horace could respond.

'How did you get the details to Isambard? How?'

'Does it matter how?'

Harry stared at his brother, shaking with rage. Then he pushed Peter away. 'Horace, he deserves summary execution. I vote we shoot him, right now. Dump him somewhere he won't be found. For treason.'

Horace looked at each of them, weighing the situation.

'I would say, Peter, that I acted out of love, too,' he said. 'Frédéric? Your view of what to do with him?'

'I say no to shooting him now. He should face a proper tribunal, at the right time. This city has seen too many summary executions.'

Horace holstered his pistol.

'I have the deciding vote, in the name of the Steeplejack team,' Horace said. 'I vote . . .'

Suddenly Peter jerked bolt upright. 'The launch,' he said. He closed his eyes. 'The *geheime Feuer* weapon. He's on his way. It's happening.'

'What nonsense is this?' Harry shoved his brother roughly against the tunnel wall.

Horace held up a hand.

'Wait.'

He met Peter's eyes, then placed his hands roughly on Peter's head and concentrated. Horace reached as intensely as he could towards Isambard, towards Morbecque, towards the English Channel. He saw it.

'Peter's right. The Secret Fire weapon has just been launched. It's heading towards London. We've very little time.'

Peter gave a sad laugh.

'And now you're going to kill me.'

'No,' Horace said. 'You can be put to good use yet.'

Harry barked in frustration. 'Shoot him! Or I'll do it myself.' He reached for his pistol, and Peter flinched.

Horace put his hand on Harry's arm to stop him, then turned his eyes to Joliot-Curie, who said quietly: 'Horace, this is your Great Work. To bring Peter across. To win him back from the forces that have driven him. He has remarkable gifts.'

Peter looked from one man's face to another.

'Am I fit to cross? Can I be forgiven? Even for the things I have done?' Peter's voice cracked. 'Can I?'

'Stand there,' Horace ordered. 'Don't move. Harry, stand guard. Watch our backs. I wanted to work in the Dark Lady crypt, but there's no time.'

To Joliot-Curie, he turned and said, 'I need your help, Master Fulcanelli.'

'Very well,' Joliot-Curie said. 'The role I have inherited, once you've drawn close to the requisite state, is to provide you with certain words that you must repeat, at the due moment, in the correct frame of mind. Also, to give you this, which will serve to magnify everything you do.'

He handed Horace a fragment of stained glass, the same piece he had taken from the dead hand of Julien Champagne in 1932. Horace took it in his right hand and turned towards the traitor.

'Peter, let me guide you,' Horace said. 'Look into my eyes.'

Peter nodded.

'How does Isambard expect to survive?'

'I don't know. He has never told me.'

'This is your only chance. Will you defect?'

'Yes. Yes.'

'Your father is a few minutes away from detonating the most monstrous weapon ever built. I don't know if we can stop him. If we fail, the war is over. The world is over. We need your help. Do you accept?'

'Yes.'

Horace raised his arms and placed his left hand on top of Peter's head, holding the stained glass in his right.

'Kneel,' he said, forcing Peter down. Horace concentrated, stilling his mind, drawing from deep within himself the awareness of other forms of perception, of other ways of being.

'The technique of the Great Work is to detach yourself from your own perspective on the world, to be aware of how little of the true world you see from within your own head, and to see through another's eyes,' Joliot-Curie said.

Horace nodded and breathed deeply, staring through Peter into his entire life.

'Although the perspectives of others are equally limited, the sensation of difference is liberating. Performed many times, or performed very well, you will develop a deeper perception of the unfiltered, unfractured world ... and the forces that flow there.'

Horace stepped outside himself.

He saw Peter as a shape in time, all in a single snapshot, like a star growing from seed to blazing sun to lightless husk in a single instant, seething with potential, his nature unresolved ...

He saw Peter's raging anger at the world, his burning need for acceptance, to belong, his conversion over many years of light into dark, of love into fear, his deliberate decisions to hurt, to poison, to seek power over others ... to seek the thrill of killing, wrapped in self-serving stories of having no choice, of following orders, of protecting those he damaged ... Horace saw Isambard twisting his strands of control over Peter tighter and tighter ... He saw his hope of love ... He saw Rose through Peter's eyes ...

Joliot-Curie drew close to Horace and whispered the necessary words to him, the words Horace was to repeat to bring Peter across, to perform his Great Work of transmutation.

Horace spoke.

Libero in tenebris occulta ...

Two hundred miles away, the bomb hit in London, causing Peter to burst from Horace's grip, eyes wide in horror, every

414

muscle taut with pain. Horace recoiled as though hit by a thunderbolt, his last mental image a flash of cold green eyes as Isambard attempted to complete his own, perverted Great Work, projecting his entire consciousness, at the moment of death, into his son, the creature he had created for this sole purpose.

'Peter!' Horace shouted, staggering backwards. His mind soared and roamed, a wild horse unleashed, reeling with shock across time and place.

Horace saw Rose at Dachau, her torment at last nearing an end. Kicked and punched almost to death on direct orders from Isambard, her beautiful eyes swollen shut, she was a bloody mess. Stripped and chained, she had not uttered a sound, had never given her tormentors the satisfaction of hearing her cry out.

Her executioner pulled her up from the floor for the last time and forced her to kneel. He placed his pistol against the back of her head, and she uttered just one phrase as he pulled the trigger.

She said: 'I forgive.'

Horace saw Margaret at Oldwick Fen, standing silently under the afternoon sun, motionless as she had been since dawn, surrounded by her devoted ring. When the V-1 ploughed into the street on Aldwych, she sang out a single, beautiful, endless note that seemed to split the very sky.

Then she collapsed. Writhing in pain, she screamed aloud, foam at her lips, her eyes turned upwards till only the whites showed. Still her song echoed.

Horace saw England blackened and burning, its own people scavenging in the rubble, tearing at each other's throats with teeth and nails, bludgeoning and burning, its cities in flames, its survivors slaughtering one another.

Misshapen, hating creatures roamed the land, jackals and hyenas with human faces and black uniforms. Hideous birds squawked and shrieked in panic, and an ocean of foulness poured down from the sky, rising and flooding the land in all directions, a predatory wave of hatred, tearing through towns and villages, overwhelming an entire nation.

Then he saw Margaret draw the full vileness of the attack onto herself.

She drew the great black dog onto her, and it savaged her, drooling from its snout, its fangs tearing at her throat.

He saw an old woman, toothless, racked with torment, *Old Dolly*, shrieking to herself in the darkness, her eyes begging for release from nightmare creatures dwelling in her half-destroyed mind.

He saw the nation as a woman, and the woman was red-headed Margaret, and the red-head was the toothless crone, locked in torment and agony for sixty years and longer.

Peter, shards of green ice flashing in his eyes, swiped at the back of Horace's knees, knocking him to the floor. He lunged at Harry, grabbing a knife from the scabbard at Harry's belt before he or Joliot-Curie could react, then leaped on Horace, slashing at his throat.

Horace grabbed Peter's knife hand and they wrestled, falling to the ground.

'*Libero in tenebris occulta!*' Horace shouted again. Peter cried out, a stab wound in his gut, blood starting to flow. Horace shouted the final word given to him by Fulcanelli, the final word of transmutation.

'*Absolvatur! Absolvatur!*'

May he be absolved.

Peter groaned and lay still, his eyes closed.

'Put pressure on that wound!' Horace ordered Harry.

Horace tried to see what had happened.

The red-headed witch, bloodied at the throat, her mind half-destroyed.

Rose killed at Dachau.

The V-1 in London.

His own attempt at bringing Peter across . . . they had all connected in the timeless place where the Great Work took place . . . he saw burning wreckage on Aldwych, bodies strewn in the street, shattered glass falling, cries of distress . . . but London was still standing, casualties were limited. He sought Isambard and found just a tenuous shadow . . .

Isambard's attack had failed. The *geheime Feuer* weapon had been defeated. But then Horace saw further. Not defeated. Frozen. Locked in a different time, locked in the spasms of a red-headed mage who had taken its force into herself, deflected by a mighty spell, a great song of magic that had drawn Rose and Horace and his own Work into its force . . .

He detected Isambard in Peter, still. More deeply moored within his son, though weak, almost spent.

A botched job. The Secret Fire attack on London, botched. Isambard's projection into his son, botched. Horace's Great Work, botched, as a price of defying Isambard.

'Peter?' Horace said to the unconscious form. He looked quizzically at Harry and Joliot-Curie, who were working on Peter's wound.

'He'll live,' Harry said. 'It's nasty but he'll get through it.' He added in a whisper: 'If we want him to.'

Horace knelt and placed a hand on Peter's head. He needed to vent his shattering loss. Rose, his love, so vilely killed. Horace's hands began to shake, his face to contort with grief, with the burning need to weep.

But first he had to make a different kind of peace.

'I failed you,' he said to Peter. 'I wasn't strong enough to free you. Isambard still has his claws in. You lent me your strength, and I've left you in hell.'

Horace saw that nothing was resolved, merely postponed. That all they had done today would need to be done again.

He stood and consulted with Joliot-Curie, a few whispered words. He confirmed what level of sacrifice it would take, in the end, to allow Peter to throw off his father, to deny Isambard his resurrection, as would ultimately be required.

He whispered again to the supine form.

'I'll bring you over, you have my word. It won't be soon, it may seem I've thrown you to the wolves, but when the hour comes round again when these things can be resolved, I'll bring you in. I already know I must cross one day, in return for my daughter's life. When I cross, I'll open the way for you, in the other direction. It's the only way to be sure. One day, before we both die, if you can meet me halfway, I'll help you to a good death, and that's how we'll defeat Isambard.'

Horace looked up at Harry. He and Fulcanelli had stepped back a few yards, had heard nothing.

'Get him to a hospital,' Horace said. 'Place him under guard. When he recovers, heaven help him, he'll be put on trial. I'll speak against the death penalty.'

Paris

30 June 2007

Katherine stared into the darkness of the Paris catacombs. The flashlight had died on her, and her eyes were playing tricks. She thought she saw shadows moving against the blackness, forms in the void surging towards her, making the face of the man she had killed in New York, then the face of Isambard, then melting away to nothing.

And from deep within the shadows, she heard whispers. *Trust the dark. Trust the blackness.* Beneath and above them, as though in harmony, Katherine slowly began to tease out a repeating cycle, a single phrase:

Rue d'enfer. Suivez la dame noire. Rue d'enfer. Suivez la dame noire. The road to hell. Follow the dark lady.

Heat filled the air. Katherine began to sweat in the sudden humidity.

The figure of Lady Alchemy at Notre Dame, the ladder leading from the earth to her abdomen to her throat, came back to her. The sky crackling with life above her head.

Rose. *Rue d'enfer.*

'I'm already in hell, grandma,' she whispered.

La dame noire. It echoed the words on the paper Horace had given her, back in London.

> *Cherchez Nostre Dame aux Ténèbres*
> *Si Dieu le veult*
> *Vous la trouverez*

Find Our Lady in the Darkness.

If God wishes it, you will find her.

Katherine dug into a pocket and took out the paper, unfolding it and smoothing it against her knee. She tried to turn on the damaged torch again, and got a flicker of light. She traced it over the diagram, seeing what looked like streets and intersections, though none with names. It was impossible to see what it referred to.

Katherine looked at her watch. Six in the morning. The torch brightened and then failed for the last time.

Sitting with her back to the locked metal door, exhausted, she tried to gather her last reserves of strength.

She saw a dark glimmer, like blackness moving against blackness. Katherine stared into the gloom. She saw it again. The darkness was almost shining, with a vague inner light, showing a hard edge, like a corner . . . and against it a softer form. Sinuous, curving, like draped cloth.

Katherine hauled herself to her feet and took a step towards it. It moved, slightly, away from her. A dark glimmer, a shadow in the black. She took another step forward.

Katherine made up her mind. She followed the shadow.

'Grandma?' she whispered into the black. 'Rose?'

The darkness shifted again, always at the next corner, picking out turns, corners. Katherine walked, blindly, trusting. All sense of time deserted her. She walked for what seemed hours, though it may have been only minutes.

'Grandma?'

It was a female form, she knew with great conviction. A dark lady.

Then as she walked, she suddenly heard the voice she had loved more than any other, whispering gently into her ear. She smelled perfume, the kind she'd been given as a little girl, the kind she was told had been her grandmother's favourite.

'Here,' the voice said. 'Through here.'

A crack seemed to open in a sheer wall facing Katherine. She was just able to squeeze through.

Katherine felt a deep sense of sanctity. It was a natural dome, a vaulted space criss-crossed with Gothic arches. The chamber seemed to glow with its own faint light. In the middle of the space stood a black statue of a woman, one hand uplifted in a gesture of wordless grace.

'Your grandfather came here in the war,' the voice said. 'Horace Hencott.'

Katherine felt her knees weaken. She shouted out in disbelief, recognizing as she did so, deep within, that this was also something she had always known.

'My God.'

'No one could know,' the voice said. 'We came together at a time when our lives were in each other's hands, when we didn't know if we would survive the night. The constant threat of betrayal. We both just needed . . . a human touch. Some warmth. Some trust.'

'You loved him.'

'Yes. Always.'

'Why could no one know?'

'Because of you. Because one day there would be you. To protect you. I trusted him.'

'You would have married . . .'

'If we could have. Yes. Surely. Your mother was rescued by an American soldier after the Liberation. The governor of the prison at Pforzheim told him she was the daughter of an SOE agent who'd been taken to Dachau. The man you knew in childhood as Grandpa, yes. He was a good man. He arranged to take your mother back to California, to my family, and then asked permission to raise her as his own. He did as well as he could.'

Katherine felt warmth all about her. The voice gently filled the vaulted space, disembodied but achingly familiar.

'Now look,' Rose said. 'The map you're holding was given to Horace by Fulcanelli himself.'

'Who was Fulcanelli?'

'Maybe one day you'll know. The intersection it shows is this vault. It shows you the way out. Follow the dark lady's hand.'

Katherine crossed the vault in the direction indicated by the statue's upraised arm. A crack appeared, again, in the masonry.

'These are the secret doors,' Rose said. 'Hurry now.'

Katherine forced her way through the gap. Then she scanned the walls where a luminous blackness seemed to settle. There were words chiselled into the stone, and she felt them with her fingers. RUE D'ENFER.

'The road to hell is the longest line on the map,' Rose said. 'Follow it away from here. Most of the underground passages under Paris are forbidden, but there is a part of the catacombs that is open to the public,' Katherine heard. 'It'll take you there.'

'Come with me,' Katherine pleaded.

'I can't. The Rue d'Enfer becomes the Rue Denfert-Rochereau, above ground. Head that way. You'll find daylight. You'll find the way out.'

'I want to stay with you.'

'You have work to do. My dear, I've waited so long to see you. Your grandfather is so proud of you. I miss him so. But now you must go.'

And the darkness lost its glow.

*

Katherine couldn't gauge how far she walked. But after timeless lonely pacing in the dark, she came to a staircase, and just as she was about to mount it, a door opened at the top, and a man in coveralls and a hardhat began to descend, leading a group of perhaps 20 people. As they came down the stairs, she went up, politely excusing herself, ignoring the protests of the guide, and at the top of the stairs walked out into a vestibule, and then out into the light.

Her eyes and lungs flooded. She stood and breathed heavily, eyes shut against the dazzle, until she thought she would faint.

Thank you, grandma.

Her head was splitting, her shoulders worn raw, her legs barely able to hold her up. Katherine checked her watch. She had almost no time. She needed to shower, to change her clothes. There was nothing to be done about that now. She started to walk in the direction of the Gare du Nord. There were a few taxis, but none stopped. She took the RER train one stop, walked to the church of St Severin to recover her rucksack and Rose's radio, then boarded the train again for the Eurostar terminal.

Peterborough

Robert ran into the Peterborough railway station. There was an 11:50 GNER express to King's Cross leaving in less than five minutes. It would take under an hour to London. He bought a ticket and ran onto the platform, jumping on the train just before it pulled out. He calculated the times. He'd get to King's Cross at 12:40, Aldwych maybe by 1 p.m. What time did the bomb hit? 2:07. What time was the moon full? He didn't know.

Robert closed his eyes, sweating, dirty, driven by a purpose that lifted him far beyond exhaustion.

He was Margaret's heir.

He was to ring the Sanctus Bell as the crack in time opened up, as the *geheime Feuer* weapon exploded.

Dear God.

Margaret.

He saw her in a timeless place. He saw the golden-eyed girl connect with a lonely, hideous death in Dachau, with men fighting in a hidden tunnel in wartime Paris, with the occult forces surrounding the monster who piloted the V-1 towards London.

He saw Margaret take onto herself the full violence of the Aldwych explosion of the Secret Fire, rendering herself the plaything of its violence and hatred, resisting for as long as her mighty heart could take, for as long as her art could sustain the spell, lasting almost all the way to the 800th and final moon of her extraordinary, selfless power.

He focused on her courage, her self-sacrifice, drawing strength from her even as he prepared to face her polar opposite: a creature who drew power only from the suffering of others. Isambard.

The fylfot wounds on his chest began to burn again, more intensely within him, deep beneath the physical scars.

'Margaret,' he whispered. 'Teach me what to do.'

He closed his eyes, mutely imploring her. This time, let him protect those in his charge. Let him protect them all. If he had to take on himself the burden borne by Margaret . . . so be it.

'I had your wife.'

The whisper in his ear took Robert completely by surprise.

The man looked like a businessman heading to London for meetings. Formal suit and tie, light raincoat. His face, though, looked like he'd recently been in a serious fight. He sat down in a seat facing Robert's, a table between them.

'In fact, we all had her. I think she liked it. She certainly made enough noise.'

Robert made to lunge across the table.

'Stop. Now before you get any smart ideas . . .' He had an American accent. Robert recognized something about the voice, the body language . . .

'You don't want all these people to get hurt, do you?'

There was something in the man's right fist. Drab green, round.

It was a hand grenade.

In a closed space like the train carriage, its effect would be devastating. There were children in the seats behind Robert, a young family. Perhaps two dozen people within close range.

'Your lovely Katherine is in the hands of Isambard. I

delivered her to him myself yesterday. He's taking his turn on her as we speak. She's not going to make it to Aldwych.'

He pulled out the pin.

'And neither are you. Stand up and walk to the back of the car, or I set this off.'

Paris

Sitting in the Eurostar departure lounge at Gare du Nord amid so many signals of normality – the homely variety of English and French accents, the mix of nervous and seasoned travellers – Katherine brought into play every instinct she had developed to blend into the crowd, and take on its calm and inconsequential air.

Acutely aware of how bedraggled she must look, she took herself to the ladies' toilets and did her best to convert her demeanour to something nonchalant and faintly rustic, the air of a happily unkempt backpacker. Katherine's phone was dead. She decided to try to call Robert once the train was moving. She opted to stay in the toilets until the last minute, giving herself just enough time to latch on to the end of the queue and take the raked moving walkway down to the platform before the train pulled away.

Coach nine. She walked forward to her car as calmly as she could, trying to maintain an air of control. Ushered politely aboard by the attendant in her close-fitting grey suit, Katherine made her way along the aisle and stowed the rucksack in the rack above her head, every nerve in her body at full stretch.

She sat in a single forward-facing seat. A table of four across the aisle was occupied by a happy young Arabic-speaking family, and the single seat facing her was empty.

She breathed a long sigh and let herself close her eyes momentarily.

*

After what seemed only a second or two, the train jolted, and she felt safer: they were moving.

Then her eyes shot wide open in alarm.

There were three of them. She saw them in her mind's eye. Older men with bloodless faces, close-cropped white hair. They were moving through the train towards her, one from the front, two from the rear, making their way systematically through the cars, closing in on Katherine.

There was something else strange about them . . .

They were wearing the black uniforms of the SS.

Aboard the GNER train to London

They were in one of the last carriages. Robert walked along the aisle, weighing his options, mind racing. The man was directly behind him. Robert's chest wounds were filling up with new pain now, of a sharper intensity, that cut though his ribs and deep into his vital organs.

This was the thug who'd done it to him.

Time for pay-back.

Whatever happened, Robert couldn't stop the train, or he wouldn't get to Aldwych in time. Even if he managed to grab the grenade, open violence in the cars would lead someone to pull the emergency cord, he was sure of it.

They reached the vestibule between the coaches. No one was there.

. . . steal it back . . .

Robert braced himself for action.

He implored Margaret to help him.

. . . steal it back . . . steal it back . . .

It was time.

'Now you're going to jump from the train,' the man whispered in his ear. 'Nice and quickly, and no one gets hurt but you.'

Robert made his decision. Took a deep breath.

Go.

He turned and grabbed the man's fist, closing his own hand over it and the grenade, squeezing with every ounce of his strength. At the same time, with his free hand, Robert hit the handle to open the sliding door of the toilet. He head-butted the man and turned with him like a dance partner, spinning them both into the cramped lavatory space. He slid the door violently shut.

Recovering from his shock, Robert's enemy lashed upwards with his knee, raging like a trapped animal. Robert turned his thighs, trying to protect his groin, clamping his hand tighter and tighter over the grenade. He raised his left hand to cover his face as fingers clawed for his eyes, his throat.

There was nowhere for either of them to fall or even double over. Robert forced his hand under the man's chin, forcing his head back, then drove his thumb deep into the cleft at the base of his throat, going for his windpipe.

Robert was drenched in sweat, his wounds raw with fresh agony. He began to lose his grip over the grenade, his hand slipping on the damp skin of the man's hand.

Robert twisted them round again, banging the man's head on the mirror, smashing the glass.

Then his hand slipped.

The grenade fell to the floor and bobbled between their feet.

Aboard the Eurostar

'Your papers,' the stark-eyed SS officer said. He wore a Nazi armband and carried a Luger 9mm pistol, the swastika embossed on its handle grips. It was pointing at her chest.

Katherine looked around at her fellow passengers. The family across the aisle was chatting merrily together, oblivious to what was happening. *They couldn't see the men.*

'Come with me.'

As he spoke, his two colleagues converged on Katherine from the other direction. One of them held a photograph of her.

'I'm not going anywhere.'

'You are under arrest. Stand up.'

The scene in the rest of the carriage shimmered and rippled. The conversations of her fellow passengers ebbed and flowed as though heard from another room. No one could see what was happening to her.

'Where are you taking me?'

'Come this way.'

He raised the pistol and aimed it between her eyes.

They led her towards the middle of the train, to a small, modern-fitted room that doubled as a base of operations for transport police and as a holding cell. A metal bar screwed into the walls ran alongside a narrow bench.

They made her sit on the bench, pistol to her head, and handcuffed one of her wrists to the bar.

'*Kathérine,*' one of the men said, pronouncing her name in the French manner. '*Je suis très heureux de faire votre connaissance.*'

431

'Who are you?'

'We serve Isambard, and the power that he himself serves.'

'What do you want with me?'

'We are removing you as an impediment. We are going to help strengthen Isambard's power.'

'How?'

'By hurting you.'

Aboard the GNER train to London

They had seconds to live.

Robert banged the man's head again into the broken glass and let him slump down onto the toilet seat.

Robert squatted and grabbed the grenade, reaching up at the same time with his other hand to slide the door open.

It didn't move.

He pulled on the handle again, the grenade in his fist.

The bathroom door slid half open and stopped, knocked off its runners in their fight, one of the man's feet jammed up against it. Robert kicked the foot out of the way and forced his way through the narrow gap, ripping his shirt and the wounds on his chest.

He ran to the train door and slammed the window down.

Open fields.

He threw the grenade as hard as he could. It sailed through the window, sucked backwards by the rushing wind.

He cried out to Margaret for strength, holding the grenade in his mind, shielding it from time, freezing its flow for just a few precious seconds . . .

The effort exhausted him. Blackness poured in from all sides. He fell to his knees, leaning against the door.

He heard the explosion, faint, way back behind the train.

Then he forced himself back onto his feet, nausea rippling through his body, and walked back to the toilet.

He stepped back inside, wrenching the door closed and locking it. With great effort, wounds screaming and seeping blood again, he hauled the unconscious man to his feet and turned him round so he could reach to bind his wrists. He relieved him of the pistol he carried in a shoulder holster.

Then Robert let him slide back down again, and leaned against the door, almost passing out, waiting for the train to reach London.

Aboard the Eurostar

The three of them crowded before her in the cramped cell space, its door locked shut.

Whatever she did, she couldn't risk stopping the train in the tunnel. She had to go defiant, egg them on, then go weak, then go strong. From the depths of her fatigue, Katherine dredged up the strength to play these men.

'Why don't you just kill me? You're not allowed to, are you?' she taunted them. 'You just have to try to mess with my head, drive me insane, bring me over to your side somehow, or leave me fucked up and incapable.'

The leader slapped her hard across the face.

'Shut up. Do you know how much of a coward your grandmother was? She squealed like a stuck pig under interrogation. Gave up the names of everyone she had worked with in Paris, all the networks, all the contacts, not just Steeplejack but all the others she served too, just to save her own skin.'

'Bullshit!'

'Isambard had Rose killed. But he agreed a long time ago that her daughter wouldn't be harmed, that any children she had would be protected too. Do you know what Isambard got in return? Do you know what's the only thing keeping you alive? It's your grandfather! Isambard gets your beloved Horace! He gave himself up for you sixty-three years ago, and he's about to keep his word!'

Katherine simply ignored him. That couldn't be true. That couldn't be how it would end. No, no. Hell no.

'You're going to let someone else take the fall for you,' the SS man shouted. 'Just like you've always done. Just like Rose did.'

Katherine saw sources she'd lost in her days in intelligence work. Spies who never came back, contacts she'd exploited without a second thought, who one day went silent, who fell off the radar screen, the faces and code names and betrayals and lies that ultimately had driven her out of the profession, her sanity under threat, her self-esteem shot to pieces. She saw the nightmares, the horror that ensued when the damage people like Katherine had done came back to haunt them.

'You're a parasite!' the leader shouted in her face. 'A bloodsucker! Worthless!'

'No!' she shouted. 'I made it right! I got out! I made up for my mistakes!'

She tried to reach out to Robert, but then stopped. She didn't need him. She suddenly felt Rose with her. She could take these animals on her own.

'Your little American neo-Nazis boys couldn't do the job, so they brought in the old men to get me, is that it?' She stoked her rage, feeling a deep power building within her, one she was drawing from the core of herself, from the depths of her anger. 'Hitler died! He killed himself! You lost! Now lay another hand on me and you're . . .'

She punched out with her free hand, deliberately weakly, trying to draw one of them in.

Another of the men leaned forward and grabbed it. With his other hand he seized her cheeks like a vice, forcing her jaws open. She felt blood flowing as the lining of her mouth tore against her teeth, salt taste filling her mouth.

'Horace is going to die, and it'll be your fault.'

She had them.

The man was twisting her arm. Suddenly she grabbed it and pulled him towards her with explosive force, his head falling against her shoulder, his hand releasing her jaw in surprise.

She sank her teeth into his neck, biting deep into the carotid artery, then kicked him into the man behind him, blood spurting from his wound. She sprang up, still handcuffed by one wrist to the metal bar, and kicked straight into the groin of the leader, who was raising his gun to club her on the head. He went down with a shriek of pain.

She grabbed the leader's gun and whipped it across the face of the one man left standing as he lunged at her. He hit his head on the door as he fell. Then she kicked the leader in the head as he tried to rise, breaking his jaw and knocking him unconscious.

The bleeding man, losing huge quantities of blood, tried to get up, whimpering for help, and fainted.

They were all immobilized.

Katherine strained for the keys on the fallen body of the leader with her fingers. On the third attempt, she snagged the key ring and pulled it towards her.

She freed herself from the handcuffs.

Then she lurched to a small stainless steel sink in the corner of the room, and spat blood. Katherine ran the water and washed her mouth out, over and over again. Anything to get the taste of the filthy Nazi flesh out of her mouth.

London

Horace walked rapidly along Fleet Street, heading west towards Aldwych from St Bride's, where he had spent a few final moments of meditation, preparing for what was to come.

Now, at last, he would have a final chance at the Great Work, to complete that which had begun all those years ago.

The cost was enormous, but at least it would fall fully, and entirely, upon him.

The shame of his failures, of the negotiation with Isambard, were his own Secret Fire, and it had consumed him for sixty-three years. But now he would make things right.

～

Peter strode along the Strand, heading east towards Aldwych. The wound in his gut was seeping blood. He covered it with his raincoat. Pain racked his body, every step agony.

The blast was coming. Death was coming. Time was unfreezing, and the full force of the V-1 explosion, fuelled by the *geheime Feuer*, was about to hit London. Time and place would melt.

He reached to his waistband, to the leather pouch there, and touched the hilt of his Fairbairn-Sykes fighting knife for comfort. He felt the weight of a pistol in his pocket.

His father's presence had revived in him, occupying every pore, boiling in his blood, directing Peter towards fulfilment of his only destiny, which he now understood: to be the means of Isambard's resurrection, the completion of the Secret Fire plot. He was to kill whoever got in the way.

Peter would do it, then he would die, destroyed within his own body, by his own father.

Then Isambard would seek fresh victims, younger bodies to colonize.

Peter knew what was required to halt it. And in his secret heart, where he hoped only Rose could see, he prayed he would still have the strength.

London

Katherine ran.

Out of Waterloo Station, towards the river. No time to try to get a cab. The rucksack, bound tightly against her back, dug deep into her raw shoulders and crushed her spine with its weight. But still she ran.

Past the IMAX cinema. Past St John the Evangelist church and the old Waterloo Hospital for Children and Women. Down the subway steps to the bridge. Onto the bridge.

She saw a landscape of desolation, black and abandoned. Nothing moved in the charred, dust-strewn streets. She felt a spiritual dread. Nothing was alive.

Then her eyes swam, and she was in modern-day London, mid-2007 – cars and buses streaming towards Waterloo Bridge, the Thames a living river, the great sweep of the city skyline, from the Gherkin to St Paul's to the Houses of Parliament, rising ahead of her.

She slowed to a walk, her legs screaming, her lungs close to spasm, her heart hammering. Then she started running again.

The bridge collapsed to a single blackened beam crossing the river beneath her feet.

She halted, dizzied, suddenly terrified of falling. She fell to her knees, hands clawing at the spar, grappling for something to hold on to.

A sound like angry bees flew past her ear. A split second later, Katherine heard the boom of rifle shots ahead of her.

In the haze above blackened ruins where the Temple had once stood, a Nazi scavenger patrol had spotted her, and was shooting.

The world melted, wrenching from frame to frame of time.

The bridge came back.

She ran, eyes ahead.

She reached the north bank of the Thames, drenched, and ran east to the narrow old side streets that would take her most quickly to St Clement Danes.

~

Robert ran to the taxi rank at King's Cross station, grabbing the first driver in line, shouting about an emergency. The man at the head of the queue, a businessman in a black suit, remonstrated loudly, and Robert pushed him hard out of the way.

'Aldwych,' Robert barked at the driver, forcing his way into the luggage space at the front of the cab, next to the driver. 'Police emergency. Go fast. Break the law.'

'You're not a fucking copper,' the driver shouted. 'Get out my fucking cab!'

Robert showed him the gun he'd taken from the thug on the train. Blood was soaking through his shirt.

'I'm whatever I say I am. Just get me to Aldwych. Go!'

London

It was an intermittent sound, at first barely perceptible: a low buzz in the air, a roiling in the clouds as the sky began gradually to darken.

People stood still in the street and looked to the sky. Older people first, then the young, for whom the sound could easily have been a propeller plane flying overhead. The tense faces of their elders, staring at the darkening clouds, gave them pause.

The sound came in and out, as though borne on the wind. It was a low, guttural roar, fading and strengthening. Only those people in their late sixties or older – those old enough to have heard it the first time around – recognized it for what it was, and felt the pangs of fear revive that had lain buried for so long in their childhood memories.

Australia House, India House, the Waldorf Hotel: all stood virtually unchanged, witnesses to the flows and eddies of time.

Double-decker buses still plied the Aldwych loop, drawing up outside Bush House as they had sixty-three years earlier. The wartime uniforms of British and foreign servicemen were long gone, but tourists from dozens of countries teemed in the streets, coach-loads of visitors milling outside the theatres. Road traffic was a flood compared to a wartime trickle. St Clement Danes, restored in the 1950s, was no longer the burned-out, Blitz-torn shell that had reverberated to the mechanical howl of the V-1 in 1944.

Then the other howl began. On the wind, mingled with the deep growl of the death machine heading their way from deep in the past, there came the sound of sirens. They were the air-raid sirens of sixty-three years past.

A thunderbolt tore across the sky, the light almost blinding, rattling the windows and half-deafening all who stood in the street, staring upwards.

The mechanical howl grew louder, the sirens screaming.

The clouds began to boil. The first drops of rain fell, and they were black, and stank of decay. Within seconds, they grew to a deluge.

The sun stood still in the sky, blazing with a sickly pale light as storm clouds tore across its face. People sank to their knees in fear in the streets of London, pointing at the heavens or clasping their hands in prayer as the guttural howl filled the air and the sirens roared their warnings of doom. Traffic halted in the streets, cars colliding, drivers oblivious of each other.

The sun turned black.

The mechanical roar filled the very air, and people shrieked in terror, bones and teeth and muscle alive with its metallic growl, buzzing and clawing in their core, buildings shaking and resonating to its pulse, the engine of the V-1 drowning out the sirens, drowning out the world.

The sky cracked open.

The machine tore out of the sun like a bullet, aiming at the heart of London, a black silhouette against the greater blackness of the sky, illuminated by red and orange lightning flashes as it burst from the mouth of hell, a machine made of human hatred, delivering damnation.

Then –

Silence.

The cut-out of the engine.

The stillness that brought the greatest terror of all.

The beginning of the death glide to earth.

Emerald-green eyes stared out of the boiling black sky, demanding to live.

~

The doors of St Clement Danes church boomed open. Horace did not turn to see who it was. He knew who had to come. Only three others could enter.

He felt a frantic, loving presence, drawing near, hectic and fearful. His granddaughter.

Katherine ran towards him, drenched in stinking black rain. She unstrapped her rucksack as she came, sliding it the last step, trying not to drop it. Then she wrapped her arms around him, her hair in his face, and held him in an urgent, shaking embrace.

'Grandfather. You're my grandfather. Oh God, Horace, I'm your granddaughter, and you've never told me, you could never tell me, you could never tell me, could you?'

'Gently, my dear. Gently now.'

The fruit of the intense, fleeting love Rose and he had shared in their desperate final days together. His to confess to at last.

'I could never say. Never tell. To protect you . . . Because of what you will do today.'

Katherine held his face, all anger gone, wanting to hold for ever the man who had made her flawed, beautiful, self-destroying mother. Who had loved her dear, courageous grandmother.

'I saw the Lady . . .'

'I . . .'

Before Horace could complete his answer, a gunshot sounded behind them, booming in the great vaulted space. Katherine raised her head and stiffened.

444

Peter walked into the main aisle from the area of the sacristy.

'Lock the door,' Peter shouted. 'Here are the keys.' He threw them towards Katherine. 'I'd ask the chaplain, but he's out cold. Do it now.'

Horace nodded to her.

'Do what he says, then stay by the door. Don't try to attack him, whatever you do.'

Katherine picked the keys up from the floor and trod slowly towards the door, her eyes never leaving Peter.

Peter marched down the aisle towards Horace, pistol raised. He was bleeding heavily from a wound in his gut. 'Hencott! Don't move!'

Horace raised his own pistol, unmoved by Peter's threats, and pointed it at him.

They faced one another, standing in the church's central aisle, perhaps 20 yards apart.

'I'm here to bring you in, Peter. To bring you across the bridge. To complete my Great Work, which is also yours: to free you from Isambard for ever. To allow you to live in love, not fear. For the first time in your life.'

'I'm not coming across!' Peter boomed. 'I serve Isambard, and the power that works through him. He's going to live again, through me! I will be Isambard! Listen to that thunder! That's him!'

Outside, the sky howled. Foul, stinking rain fell against the church windows, staining them black. Screams of panic echoed in the streets. Thunderclaps shook the church's very fabric.

The V-1 was falling. Time was melting around them like reflections on water, tearing their reality, reforming it.

The final fall, the death-dive of the killing machine, lasted fifteen seconds. They were within it, inside it, beyond clock-time. In the time of the *geheime Feuer*, the time of strangeness and transmutation.

Peter groaned with pain, looking for a moment as though he would faint. His skin was deathly white, his lips almost colourless. He leaned against one of the dark wooden pews, opening his coat, gesturing to his bleeding wound.

'This is your doing, you remember? 30 June 1944. It has never fully healed, in all this time. And that fetid old witch opened it up again. It's bleeding as though you'd stabbed me just yesterday.'

Peter lurched forward and pointed his pistol, a war-issue German Luger, at Horace's forehead. Their eyes connected. Horace saw the good in Peter. He was hanging on for grim life, covertly, deep below the obeisance he was offering Isambard. Hanging on till the last possible moment.

Horace was afraid, but looking within, he found now that he was indifferent to all fear, even his own.

The crack in time was upon them. The window was opening, a sacred circle of possibilities, where worlds and times could touch, to settle things for good or ill.

'The elements of the Work are coming together again, to end all of this, once and for all,' Horace said. 'Rose, in the form of her granddaughter. Margaret, in the form of her great-nephew. You, and me.'

'But how will it end?' Peter asked.

'Like this.'

Horace turned his gun around, slowly, until the butt was facing Peter, and handed it to him. Then he knelt at Peter's feet. Katherine screamed.

'No! Horace!'

Her grandfather looked up at Peter.

'I ask your forgiveness.'

Horace bared his head to the pistols in Peter's hands.

And then a new image burst into Peter's mind: the beautiful face of his mother, in the moment of perfection before he broke the golden chain of her necklace. Her eyes were those of Rose, urging love.

Defect, she said.

Peter fell to his knees, howling like a wounded animal, weeping with anger.

'Ah . . . Ah . . . I'm not . . . a complete . . . human *being*,' he shrieked. 'I never have been. I'm a cuckoo's egg. An aberration! I can't de*fect*! I'm a *de*fect!'

'But you loved Rose,' Horace said urgently.

'She can't save me! No one can!'

Peter stood again, raging, striding along the aisle, brandishing his guns at Horace.

'I love my father too! Father! I'm here! Come to me! I'm ready! I'm ready!'

Jamming one gun into his waistband, Peter fumbled at his finger, then raised his hand to show Horace the ring he had worn since the 1930s, the one given to him by his father.

'This ring bears a shape. It was given to me to remind me of what I had become, of whom I served.'

He knelt and, dipping a finger into the blood from his belly wound, marked it on the church's stone-flagged floor.

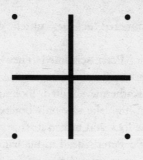

'Innocent in itself. But it can be made into a swastika very easily. Just join the dots in a certain way. I was once like this shape, undefined, pure potential, but Isambard joined the dots for me. He stamped the Nazi swastika on me, and *now it can never be removed!*'

Peter wet his fingers in blood again, and painted the shape of hatred on the stone.

'He's coming!' Peter shouted, warning and resignation battling pride in his voice. 'And you can't stop him!'

Orange and red lightning flared outside. Black rain pelted the windows. Demented, squawking birds crushed themselves, wave after wave, against the windows. The glass bowed and cracked under the strain. Thick black blood began to seep up through the stone flags, slowly erasing Peter's image.

Someone hammered at the church door. Metal on wood.

'Don't open it,' Peter screamed. Then Horace leapt at him, knocking him to the floor.

'It's Robert,' Katherine shouted, looking out through a spy-hole. Beyond him, she saw only boiling blackness. She put the key in the lock and turned it.

Horace grabbed Peter's head in his hands, shouting the

words of transmutation, pouring all his years of preparation into a final bid to bring Peter in, to allow him to defect.

'*Libero in tenebris occulta!*'

They were on a bridge over a dark river, on a freezing night, Peter walking from one direction, Horace from the other.

They approached the middle of the bridge. Behind Peter, at the far end, Horace could see the waiting figures of his future executioners, shrouded in darkness, led by Isambard. He saw those who would make it their business to torment him, to extract every last drop of suffering from him, to build the strength of Isambard and the Enemy, to empower their pestiliential new Reich, built on human pain.

Peter had been sent across the bridge by Isambard to welcome Horace at the halfway point, to bring him back, to have the honour of delivering the great prize to the Enemy.

It was the sacrifice Horace had agreed to make. To cross, at a time of his own choosing, in return for the life of his daughter.

He chose to cross now, and to bring Peter across in return.

He saw Isambard staring at him, realizing something was wrong.

Horace and Peter met in the middle of the bridge.

'Go,' Horace shouted. 'Now! Run!'

Horace kept moving towards Isambard, towards the Enemy, fearful, accepting his fate. He heard Peter running to freedom, towards the Light, behind him. He didn't look back.

The bomb hit.

A hellish orange light filled the interior of the church, and Isambard projected the full force of his wrath, his raging hatred, his burning desire to live, into the son he had created, for the sole purpose of crushing his soul, and stealing his body.

Peter threw Horace off, screaming.

Robert burst in, drenched in black rain, a dark and jagged shard of pottery in one hand, a pistol in the other, his shirt covered in blood.

Peter stood and raised both his guns, one pointing towards the door at Katherine and Robert, one towards Horace at his feet.

Robert stopped in his tracks and aimed his own gun at Peter. Horace met Robert's eyes with an intense stare.

Trust, it said.

Robert put his arm around Katherine and kissed the top of her head, pulling her into him. Then he winced, the wound in his chest igniting with dizzying pain.

'My God,' she said. 'Look at you . . .'

Peter, still aiming his gun at them, and looming over Horace, stood trembling in anger.

'No redemption!'

A storm of angry static suddenly burst from the radio near Horace's feet, where Katherine had left it. Horace pulled it from the rucksack and flipped the case open.

The static surged and then resolved into a ear-splitting, piercing shriek, a single tone.

Katherine began to run towards it and collapsed. It was Rose. It was the hour of Rose's death.

Peter strode up to Katherine, his eyes flaring glassy green, fully filled with Isambard, and grabbed her by the scruff of the neck. He was phenomenally strong. She couldn't stop him.

'This is how we killed Rose,' he shouted, and threw Katherine to the ground. He kicked her. Once. Twice. He made to raise his gun to strike her face.

'I forgive!'

The voice came at once from the radio and from Katherine, filling the soaring vaults of the church, time and place melding in one, in the time of the Secret Fire.

Horace shouted to Robert: 'You know what you have to do? Go! Now!'

Robert sprinted to a spiral staircase by the entrance and ran up towards the belfry, two steps at a time, stowing his gun in a coat pocket.

Peter turned away from Katherine, who lay retching on the ground.

'No!' he shouted, running after Robert. 'Stop!'

In his hands Robert now held the swastikas he had brought from Oldwick, the Saxon fragment of black pottery and the iron fylfot, both left-handed, male, to counter the female symbol so vilely abused by the Nazis.

Peter was close on his heels.

Robert reached the top of the stairs, three storeys up, and stepped out among the bells, careful to avoid the hole in the centre of the wooden floor, covered only by a thin layer of plywood and plaster, through which the bells were hoisted up. There were a dozen of them in the wooden coop, all of different sizes.

He skirted around the hole, looking for Robertus, the Sanctus Bell. The holy bell.

He found it.

It stood alone, the size of a man's torso, mounted on its own wooden frame. More than 400 years old. Tarnished, blackened by fire. The bell rung at the Alde Wych working. The bell that had vanquished the Armada, glowing with its own internal power.

It was his destiny.

Robert drew back his arms, a fylfot held tight in each hand, and prepared to strike. He closed his eyes.

'For you, Margaret. I take this violence, this pestilence into me. For you, and for all.'

Before he could strike, Peter burst into the belfry

and threw himself at Robert, his fighting knife in one hand.

'Stop! Let it happen!' Peter shouted. 'Let it explode!'

They wrestled on the floor, rolling over and over. Robert gripped the swastikas in his fists, stabbing Peter in the arms, in the back, with the sharp end of the fylfot wall iron.

Peter screamed and dropped his knife. He pushed Robert's head towards the thin wood and plaster covering the hole in the floor, a stranglehold on his throat, tightening his grip. Robert dropped the iron swastika. He pounded on Peter's head with the sharp fragment of pottery. The wounds in Robert's chest ignited with black, searing pain.

Peter grabbed the wall iron and drove it towards Robert's face. Robert seized his wrist and tried to force it back. The sharpened metal spike was over Robert's eye. Peter pushed down, harder, and Robert's arm began to shake, unable to resist. His field of vision blacked over as the spike drove towards his eye.

With a final, desperate surge of strength, Robert twisted out from under Peter. He punched him squarely on the jaw and grabbed the metal spike, the fylfot wall iron, from Peter's hand.

Robert lunged towards the bell.

'*Ka!*' he shouted.

And he sounded the Sanctus Bell.

Robert hammered at Robertus with the fylfots, one in each hand, pounding repeatedly, the millennial stone Saxon shard and the wall iron. The bell's peal sang through the fabric of the church, echoing and resonating, filling Robert's mind, filling the air, its overtones spreading over the city, along the dragon lines of London.

Robert took on the burden. He took the attack into himself. His chest wounds filled with blazing light.

He saw Margaret's torment passing to another, and the

other was Robert, and Robert saw himself under the dog's teeth, and he was an entire nation, perhaps an entire world, reduced to the state of Old Dolly. A devastated wasteland, in psyche and city, himself and London.

He absorbed it.

Then Peter leaped upon him, and they fell together through the hole in the wooden floor, each with his arms locked around the other, Peter shouting 'Horace! Now!'

Robert struggled to free himself from Peter's grip as they plummeted.

Horace, nursing Katherine, afraid to leave her, heard the bell ring. Then he heard them falling, heard Peter's cry, and took his decision. Time warped and surged around them.

'Rose's last words were *I forgive*,' Horace shouted. He raised his arms into the air, a fragment of stained glass in his right hand. 'And my last word is the last word of the Great Work. *Absolvatur*. May he be absolved! *Absolvantur omnes*. May they all be absolved!'

Peter smashed into the stone floor at the foot of the bell-tower. A second later, Robert landed on top of him.

The screeching, piercing tone from Rose's radio resolved into a pure and beautiful musical note.

Horace screamed, fulfilling his promise at last, bringing Peter across the bridge as he gave himself over to the enemy, taking the curse from Robert, taking Isambard from Peter, and pouring them all into himself.

～

Silence.

Agony boiled inside Horace. Unendurable hatred. He contained it. Forced it deep away within himself.

453

No time.

Horace helped Katherine to her feet. As soon as she could stand, he leaned on her arm and limped with her towards the fallen forms of Peter and Robert, who was stirring, his fall broken by the older man. The chaplain lay unconscious in the sacristy.

Slowly, Horace knelt by Peter's broken body as Katherine, her own ribs cracked by Peter's boot, helped Robert up. Horace placed a hand under Peter's head.

'A good death,' he whispered.

Peter coughed bright red blood. 'I can see Rose,' he whispered. Then, after a long moment: 'Thank you, Horace.'

His eyes rolled back, and Peter lay still, a last sigh of breath issuing from his throat.

Horace stood up. He asked for Katherine's arm and walked towards the door, out into the sunlight. Robert followed them, stunned. Margaret's curse had torn through him, one minute fully and willingly absorbed, the next vanished, leaving him breathless, gasping, half mindless.

The bomb was gone. There was silence, and nothing was falling but the rain. Clean, pure rain. A normal, everyday street scene surrounded them, the explosion of the *geheime Feuer* thwarted. Sunlight was restored. The black sun had been banished.

The world was safe again.

Horace collapsed on the cobbled forecourt of the church. Pain twisted his face.

'Where I go, you cannot follow,' he said. 'Help me up. I have to go now.'

'What's happening?' Katherine shrieked. Robert knelt beside Horace, who clutched his hand. Katherine grabbed him, holding on with all her strength.

'No! No! No!'

But Horace stood again, leaning on both Robert and Katherine now, and walked from the forecourt of St Clement Danes across the Strand, to where Milford Lane led down towards the river.

'It had to be an exchange,' Horace said. 'Peter wasn't strong enough to cross over on his own.'

'No!' Katherine shouted, hitting Horace with her forearm. 'No! He wasn't worth it! He wasn't!'

Horace sighed, closing his eyes.

'We are all worth it,' he said. 'Without him, Isambard can't live again. And I had to make amends for my own actions.' Horace winced in pain and almost fell. 'I failed Rose.'

Robert and Katherine steadied him. Following Horace's directions, they twisted along the narrow lanes leading down to the water.

'You were the defector,' Robert said. 'It was you.'

Horace smiled, but said nothing. At the end of Essex Street, they took the steps down to the embankment by the Thames.

'Each of us had to cross,' Horace whispered. 'Now Isambard is in me. Now it's all in me. Peter had to repudiate his father, to deny Isambard the chance to live again. I have taken on Margaret's curse, the violence of the *geheime Feuer* attack. I have taken Isambard and all his evil into myself instead of Peter. It's all one.'

Horace grimaced.

'Help me across the street.'

Once they had crossed, Horace struggled, trying to throw them off. Katherine would not let him go. He peeled her arms from him, handing her to Robert, firmly but gently.

'It's better like this,' Horace said. 'There is no other way.'

He fixed them both with a piercing, burning stare, ice-green and racked with pain, and suddenly neither of them could move.

Then Horace walked down the stone steps of the embankment into the river, and let himself fall forward. The water took him.

Epilogue

No body was ever pulled from the river. Horace simply vanished.

Two months later, giving up hope of there being any remains to bury, Katherine and Robert carried out a private leave-taking ceremony. At Robert's request, they went to the copse in the grounds at Oldwick Fen.

Holding hands over the unmarked grave of Robert's great-aunt Margaret, Robert and Katherine each spoke words of gratitude and sorrow, addressing Horace directly.

At the end, Robert looked up at the sky and recited words he had learned from Margaret's handwritten books, which Hickey had shown him, hidden by Jack in the relic chamber under the abbey.

'White spirits, ye powers of the rich earth, all hail! Green spirits, ye powers of the misty waters, all hail! Red spirits, ye powers of the burning fire, all hail! Black spirits, ye powers of the midnight winds, all hail!'

They were the words that safely closed the magical compass Robert had seen Margaret open on 30 June 1944. Turning his hand slowly three times counter-clockwise – widdershins, as she would have said – he spoke the words she had never been able to intone.

> This compass now we sweep aside
> With grateful thoughts we end this rite.
> All who have been on our side

Fade now from our inner sight.
The powers returned from whence they came
We waken now to earthly life.
Until we all shall meet again
Be peace upon us, not fear nor strife.
The compass done, away and gone
Spirits take flight from now.
All's returned from whence they come
For we have worked enow.

Robert inserted the shard of Saxon pottery and the iron fylfot he had used to sound the Sanctus Bell into the earth where Margaret lay buried.

'Thank you for your life,' he said. 'Thank you for Katherine.'

Katherine knelt, running her fingers through the grass.

'I love you,' she said.

A Note on Sources

I was especially privileged, in the course of researching *The Secret Fire*, to meet and interview four remarkable people: M. R. D. Foot, the distinguished military historian, who flew into occupied France as an SAS intelligence officer; Pearl Cornioley (née Witherington), SOE courier and later legendary head of the Wrestler network; Arthur Staggs, SOE radio operator for the Farmer network, who makes a cameo appearance in my story; and Jean Overton Fuller, the biographer of her close friend Noor Inayat Khan.

Noor, known to the French Resistance as Madeleine, was the SOE radio operator on whom I partly based the character of Rose Arden, and whose arrest in Paris and brutal killing at Dachau Rose so tragically shares. In entirely different ways, Rose was also inspired by my grandmother-in-law Betty Ozanich, née Wright, whose husband Joe went to war while she raised two daughters in Bakersfield, CA. Joe, happily, came back. I've also taken the liberty of distributing some of Pearl Witherington's highly acute recollections equally among the characters of Rose, Harry and Horace.

The supernatural elements of the story are of course my own addition.

I have drawn on several works by authors versed in the *elder faith* in writing *The Secret Fire*, combining aspects of ritual and wording in a way that, I believe, reflects no single authority, while broadly reflecting the world of the nameless art in East Anglia. If in doing so I have inadvertently caused offence, I apologize and declare my respect and good faith.

I drew especially on published works by Nigel Pennick and Nigel Aldcroft Jackson, while the compass chants used in the Fenland Working and at the end of the book are lightly adapted from those recorded by Nigel G. Pearson in his work *Treading The Mill*.

In describing the well-documented occult beliefs of some prominent Nazis, I have tried to restrict myself to the facts established by such serious academic researchers as Nicholas Goodrick-Clarke, leaving the outer extremes of the Nazi mystery genre to other writers. I have imagined that the Nazi occultists, like the Paris alchemists and the Fenland witches, were tapping into a single force that is mysterious, powerful and real.

The description of the 30 June 1944 V-1 explosion on Aldwych is based on almost a dozen eye-witness accounts, as well as on contemporary reports and photographs kept at the National Archives and the Imperial War Museum. I have drawn on accounts published by Derrick Grady, Daphne Claire Ibbott (née Herring) and Alan Haylock in the BBC online project *WW2 People's War*, as well as on those of Betty Young at *www.wartimememories.co.uk* and Alan Clark, 3 Squadron RAAF Association. Accounts of the explosion also appear in *The Doodlebugs* by Norman Longmate, *London at War* by Philip Ziegler, *Walking the London Blitz* by Clive Harris, *1945: The Dawn Came Up Like Thunder* by Tom Pocock, and *London 1945: Life in the Debris of War* by Maureen Waller, as well as on Stephen Henden's website *www.flyingbombsandrockets.com*. Manned V-1 flying bombs, known as Reichenbergs, were built towards the end of the war, though they were air- rather than land-launched, and were never used operationally.

The facts of Noor Inayat Khan's life have been reported by several people in addition to her friend and first biographer, Jean Overton Fuller. I have used works by Shrabani Basu, Sarah Helm and Leo Marks and the BBC Timewatch documentary *The Princess Spy*, and have also perused her SOE file at the National Archives.

For atmosphere and visual detail about the Nazi occupation of Paris, I drew especially on *Paris in the Third Reich* by author David Pryce-Jones and picture editor Michael Rand.

Gerald Gardner, Dion Fortune, Michael Howard and Katherine Kurtz have all written, in different ways, about a psychic Battle of Britain that may have paralleled the physical one.

My account of the 29 June 2007 attempted car-bombings in London is based on news reports at the time.

The Secret Fire is woven around published facts in the lives of Jean-Julien Champagne, Natalie Clifford Barney, Irène Hillel-Erlanger, the Curies and F. F. E. Yeo-Thomas (Shelley). The true identity of Fulcanelli, however, remains a mystery.

New York, September 2008

Acknowledgements

First and foremost, I am deeply grateful to Mari Evans at Michael Joseph for her insight, patience and wise counsel, and to Michael Sissons at PFD, who first gave me a chance, and who brought me to Mari's attention.

I'd like to thank the following people for their help, support and generosity: M. R. D. Foot; Nicki Kennedy, Sam Edenborough, Mary Esdaile and all at ILA; Gordon Easton; David Schlesinger, Bernd Debusmann, Tom Kim, Betty Wong and Charles Jennings at Thomson Reuters; Kate Burke at Michael Joseph; George Lucas at Inkwell; Claiborne Hancock and Jessica Case at Pegasus; Kate Nowlan and all at CIC; Sophie Jay and Rhiannon Griffiths at the *Thame Gazette*; Steve Duncan of *www.undercity.org* and Moses Gates; the staff of the Imperial War Museum and the National Archives at Kew; Reverend Group Captain Richard Lee and Head Verger Marcus Smith at St Clement Danes; Matt Caldecutt; Nichelle Stephens; Kevin Walsh; Kathy Lord; Jeremy Woan; Allison Collins; Bettie Jo and Denman Collins; staff at the Waldorf Hotel on Aldwych; Baptiste Essevaz-Roulet of *www.ruevisconti.com*; Alan Hughes of the Whitechapel Bell Foundry; staff at the Cambridge University Museum of Archaeology and Anthropology; Richard Reynolds at Heffers; Anna Elmore; Alex Gordon; Jonny Muir; and my son Christopher, for musical and other inspiration.

Finally, of course, I am indebted beyond words to my wife, Amy, and to my family.

Martin Langfield

THE MALICE BOX

DARE YOU OPEN THE MALICE BOX?

A plot is afoot. A device of extraordinary power is hidden somewhere in Manhattan. The cruel alchemy that made it belonged to the ancient Egyptians yet it goes by many names: Ma'rifat', Gnosis, the Soul Engine. The Ma'rifat' is armed and will detonate in seven days, killing millions.

Only one man – a journalist by the name of Reckliss – has the ability to uncover seven keys and disarm the device. Yet there are others, history's hidden shadows, who seek to stop him at every turn.

Does Reckliss have the courage to face his greatest fears and halt the devastation of the Malice Box?

'A race against time and an ancient secret' *Observer*

CHRIS KUZNESKI

THE LOST THRONE

Hewn into the towering cliffs of central Greece, the Metéora monasteries are all but inaccessible. The Holy Trinity is the most isolated, its sacred brotherhood the guardians of a long-forgotten secret.

In the dead of night, the sanctity of the holy retreat is shattered by an elite group of warriors, carrying ancient weapons. One by one, they hurl the silent monks from the cliff-top – the holy men taking their secret to their rocky graves.

Halfway across Europe, a terrified academic fears for his life. Richard Byrd has nearly uncovered the location of one of the Seven Ancient Wonders – the statue of Zeus and his mighty throne. But Byrd's search has also uncovered a forbidden conspiracy, and there are those who would do anything to conceal its dark agenda . . .

'Kuzneski's writing has raw power' James Patterson

'Excellent! High stakes, fast action, vibrant characters . . . Not to be missed!' Lee Child

NICCI FRENCH

LOSING YOU

Nina Landry has given up city life for the isolated community of Sandling Island, lying off the bleak east coast of England. At night the wind howls. Sometimes they are cut off by the incoming tide. For Nina though it is home. It is safe.

But when Nina's teenage daughter Charlie fails to return from a sleepover on the day they're due to go on holiday, the island becomes a different place altogether. A place of secrets and suspicions. Where no one – friends, neighbours or the police – believes Nina's instinctive fear that her daughter is in terrible danger. Alone, she undergoes a frantic search for Charlie. And as day turns to night, she begins to doubt not just whether they'll leave the island for their holiday – but whether they will ever leave it again.

'A shocking tale, dripping with both menace and love' *Daily Mirror*

'The heart pounds from the very first page' *Observer*

KAREN MAITLAND

COMPANY OF LIARS

1348. Plague has come to England.
And the lies you tell will be the death of you.

A scarred trader in holy relics
A conjuror
A musician and his apprentice
A one-armed storyteller
A young couple on the run
A midwife
And a rune-reading girl

A group of misfits bands together to escape the plague.
But in their midst lurks a curse darker and more malign than the
pestilence they flee . . .

'Irresistible' *Sunday Telegraph*

'A richly evocative page-turner' *Daily Express*

CHRIS MOONEY

THE SECRET FRIEND

Two dead girls in the river
Two tiny statues of the Virgin Mary concealed in their clothing
One CSI on the hunt for their killer

When Judith Chen is found floating in Boston's harbour, links are made with the murder of Emma Hale, a student who vanished without trace, only for her body to wash up months later.

CSI Darby McCormick is assigned to the case and uncovers a piece of overlooked evidence from the Hale investigation – which brings her into contact with Malcolm Fletcher, a former FBI agent now on the Most Wanted list after a string of bloody murders. And when a third student goes missing, Darby is led into a dangerous game of cat-and-mouse with deadly links to the past – and a man who speaks to the Blessed Virgin. A man who wants to be a secret friend to the girls he abducts …

'Masterful … dark and disturbing' Linda Fairstein

'Chris Mooney is a wonderful writer' Michael Connelly

MICHAEL MORLEY

SPIDER

> *'For a second she thinks she is dead,*
> *then she opens her eyes and wishes she was.'*

The press call him the Black River Killer and his stats are shocking: 16 murders; not captured in 20 years; the FBI's best profiler – Jack King – burned out and beaten, his career shattered.

Jack and his wife now run a hotel in Tuscany. And though he still gets nightmares, rural Italy is a whole world away from BRK's brutal crime scenes in South Carolina. Or so Jack thought …

As Italian cops discover the body of a young woman – her remains mutilated like BRK's victims – a gruesome package arrives at the FBI, twin events that conspire to lure the profiler back into the hunt.

But this time, who is the spider and who is the fly?

'A terrifying read that will keep you hooked' Simon Kernick

'*Spider* chillingly captures the harsh realities of a deteriorated mind' Lynda La Plante

'A chillingly vivid thriller. Don't read it alone in the middle of the night' Steven Bochco

CARO RAMSAY

ABSOLUTION

The Crucifixion Killer is stalking Glasgow, leaving victims' mutilated bodies in a Christ-like pose. DCI Alan McAlpine – a renowned and successful police officer – is drafted in to lead the hunt, supported by local officers DI Anderson and DS Costello.

But the past holds horrific memories for McAlpine. He last worked this beat some twenty years earlier, when he was assigned to guard a woman – nameless and faceless after a sadistic acid attack – at a Glasgow hospital. An obsession was born in that hospital room that has never quite left McAlpine and now it seems to be resurfacing. For a reason.

As the chase to halt the gruesome murders intensifies, so Anderson and Costello find chilling cause for concern uncomfortably close to home …

'The dialogue crackles…A most auspicious debut' *Observer*

'A cracker…many shivers in store' *The Times*

He just wanted a decent book to read ...

Not too much to ask, is it? It was in 1935 when Allen Lane, Managing Director of Bodley Head Publishers, stood on a platform at Exeter railway station looking for something good to read on his journey back to London. His choice was limited to popular magazines and poor-quality paperbacks – the same choice faced every day by the vast majority of readers, few of whom could afford hardbacks. Lane's disappointment and subsequent anger at the range of books generally available led him to found a company – and change the world.

'We believed in the existence in this country of a vast reading public for intelligent books at a low price, and staked everything on it'
Sir Allen Lane, 1902–1970, founder of Penguin Books

The quality paperback had arrived – and not just in bookshops. Lane was adamant that his Penguins should appear in chain stores and tobacconists, and should cost no more than a packet of cigarettes.

Reading habits (and cigarette prices) have changed since 1935, but Penguin still believes in publishing the best books for everybody to enjoy. We still believe that good design costs no more than bad design, and we still believe that quality books published passionately and responsibly make the world a better place.

So wherever you see the little bird – whether it's on a piece of prize-winning literary fiction or a celebrity autobiography, political tour de force or historical masterpiece, a serial-killer thriller, reference book, world classic or a piece of pure escapism – you can bet that it represents the very best that the genre has to offer.

Whatever you like to read – trust Penguin.